Contents

VV FX00 085689 9338

Leabharlanna Fhine Gall
BALDOYLE LIBRARY
Inv/07 : 07/557F Price €10.26
Title: Moby Dick
Class: F

WITHDRAWN FROM FINGAL
COUNTY LIBRARY STOCK

Moby-Dick

Herman Melville

Moby-Dick

◁ COMPACT EDITIONS ▷

PHOENIX

A PHOENIX PAPERBACK
COMPACT EDITIONS

This paperback edition, a condensed version of the original,
first published in Great Britain in 2007
by Phoenix,
an imprint of Orion Books Ltd,
Orion House, 5 Upper St Martin's Lane,
London WC2H 9EA

1 3 5 7 9 10 8 6 4 2

Copyright © Orion Books Ltd 2007

All rights reserved. No part of this publication may be
reproduced, stored in a retrieval system, or transmitted,
in any form or by any means, electronic, mechanical,
photocopying, recording or otherwise, without the
prior permission of the copyright owner.

A CIP catalogue record for this book
is available from the British Library.

ISBN 978-0-7538-2273-9

Typeset by Deltatype Ltd,
Birkenhead, Merseyside

Printed and bound in Great Britain by
Clays Ltd, St Ives plc

The Orion Publishing Group's policy is to use papers
that are natural, renewable and recyclable products and
made from wood grown in sustainable forests. The logging
and manufacturing processes are expected to conform to
the environmental regulations of the country of origin.

www.orionbooks.co.uk

About the Author

Herman Melville was born Herman Melvill (the 'e' was added in the 1830s) on 1 August, 1819, in New York City to a wealthy importer.

The Melvilles moved to Albany after Herman's father was bankrupted. His father died soon after and the young Herman worked variously as a farmer, bookkeeper, teacher and bank clerk. At the age of twenty he signed on as a deck hand of a trading ship, the *St. Lawrence*, sailing to Liverpool and back. Soon after his return he set sail for the South Pacific aboard the whaling ship *Acusnet*. In the Marquesas, Melville jumped ship and spent a month in the Taipi valley on the island of Nuku Hiva. Brought to Tahiti by an Australian whaler, Melville was taken ashore as a mutineer but escaped. He enlisted in the US Navy in Honolulu and sailed to Boston, where he was discharged in 1844.

Back in the USA, he began to write, turning his experiences in the Pacific into several fictionalized travel books. *Typee* in 1846 was extremely successful.

In 1847 Melville married Elizabeth Shaw, the daughter of the Massachusetts Chief Justice. After a few years they and their family moved to Arrowhead, a farm in Pittsfield, where Melville started ed *Moby-Dick*. During this time he met Nathaniel Hawthorne, who inspired him greatly.

Upon publication, *Moby-Dick* received mixed reviews. His next novel, *Pierre*, fared worse. Seeking a steady income, Melville turned to magazine writing. In the late 1850s he embarked on a tour of the Holy Land, financed by his father-in-law. The trip inspired much of his future writing. Upon his return to the USA Melville lectured extensively and began to write poetry almost exclusively. He failed to find a publisher for his poems and took a post as a deputy inspector of customs at New York port, a job he held for almost twenty years.

His relationship with his wife deteriorated so much in 1867 that they nearly separated. Later that year their son Malcolm died from a self-inflicted gunshot wound.

After his retirement Melville published two small volumes of poetry, dealing with the sea, art politics and sexuality. At his death on September 28, 1891, Melville left several uncompleted projects, including the novella *Billy Budd*, which remained unpublished until 1924.

Chronology of Melville's Life

Year	Age	Life
1819		Born New York City, 1 August
1825	6	New York Male High School
1832	13	Death of father, Allan Melvill
1838	19	Correspondence in the Albany Microscope Student of surveying and engineering, Lansingburgh Academy
1839	20	'Fragments from a Writing Desk' the *Democratic Press & Lansingburgh Advertiser* Deckhand, *New York to Liverpool and back, aboard the packet ship, St Lawrence*
1841	22	Whalerman aboard the Acushnet. Rounds the Horn Cruises the Galápagos
1847	28	Marriage to Elizabeth Shaw, daughter of Chief Justice of Massachusetts
1849	30	Birth of first son, Malcolm *Mardi* published. *Redburn* published. Visits to England and the Continent
1850	31	Purchase of farm in Massachusetts, which Meville calls Arrowhead *White-Jacket*
1851	32	*The Whale* published in London, *Moby-Dick* in New York Birth of second son, Stanwix
1853	34	Melville family seeks consular appointment for Herman Publishes first short stories in *Putnam's* and *Harper's* Birth of daughter, Elizabeth
1855	36	*Israel Potter* published in book form. Birth of daughter, Frances
1861	42	At outbreak of Civil War unsuccessfully seeks naval appointment

Chronology of his Times

Year	Literary Context	Historical Events
1819	Walt Whitman b.	Purchase of Florida
1825	Paulding, *John Bull in America*	Erie Canal opened
1832	Irving, *Legends of the Alhambra*	President Andrew Jackson re-elected
1838	Cooper, *The American Democrat* Poe, *Narrative of Arthur Gordon Pym*	First Atlantic steamships Underground railroad established
1839	Cooper, *The History of the Navy of the United States*	
1841	Emerson, *Essays, First Series*	John Tyler elected President
1847	Thackeray, *Vanity Fair* Brontë, E., *Wuthering Heights*	Mormons settle in Utah Irish Potato famine British repeal Corn Laws
1849	Thoreau, *A Week on The Concord and Merrimack Rivers*	California Gold Rush Zachary Taylor elected President Fugitive Slave Law
1850	Hawthorne, *The Scarlet Letter* Tennyson, *In Memoriam*	Death of President Taylor US population reaches 23 million
1851	Hawthorne, *The House of the Seven Gables*	Horace Greeley: 'Go West Young Man'
1853		Franklin Pierce elected President Railway from New York to Chicago
1855	Whitman, *Leaves of Grass* Longfellow, *The Song of Hiawatha*	Birth of Andrew Mellon
1861	Holmes, *Elsie Venner*	Abraham Lincoln elected President Formation of Confederacy American Civil War begins

Year	Age	Life
1863	44	Sale of Arrowhead to brother Allan Returns to New York City and takes oath as Inspector of Customs at Port of New York. Emancipation Proclamation
1867	48	Son, Malcolm, found dead of self-inflicted gunshot wound
1876	57	*Clarel* (verse narrative based on his visit to the Holy Land)
1886	67	Stanwix dies in Fever Hospital in San Francisco
1891	72	*Billy Budd* left in manuscript Death on 28 September and burial at Woodlawn Cemetery, the Bronx, New York

Year	Literary Context	Historical Events
1863	Hawthorne, *Our Old Home*	Battle of Gettysburg
1867		National Klu Klux Klan Reconstruction Act. Purchase of Alaska
1876	Alcott, Louisa May, *Rose in Bloom* Twain, *Tom Sawyer*	Bell's speaking telephone Battle of Little Big Horn
1886	James, *The Bostonians*	
1891	Dickinson, *Poems* Hardy, *Tess of the D'Urbervilles*	Populist Party formed

CHAPTER 1

Loomings

Call me Ishmael. Some years ago – never mind how long precisely – having little or no money in my purse, and nothing particular to interest me on shore, I thought I would sail about a little and see the watery part of the world. It is a way I have of driving off the spleen, and regulating the circulation. Whenever I find myself growing grim about the mouth; whenever it is a damp, drizzly November in my soul; whenever I find myself involuntarily pausing before coffin warehouses, and bringing up the rear of every funeral I meet; and especially whenever my hypos get such an upper hand of me, that it requires a strong moral principle to prevent me from deliberately stepping into the street, and knocking people's hats off – then, I account it high time to get to sea as soon as I can. This is my substitute for pistol and ball.

Now, when I say that I am in the habit of going to sea whenever I begin to grow hazy about the eyes, and begin to be over conscious of my lungs, I do not mean to have it inferred that I ever go to sea as a passenger. For to go as a passenger you must needs have a purse, and a purse is but a rag unless you have something in it. Besides, passengers get sea-sick – grow quarrelsome – don't sleep of nights – do not enjoy themselves much, as a general thing; no, I never go as a passenger; nor, though I am something of a salt, do I ever go to sea as a Commodore, or a Captain, or a Cook. I abandon the glory and distinction of such offices to those who like them. It is quite as much as I can do to take care of myself, without taking care of ships, barques, brigs, schooners, and what not. And as for going as cook – though I confess there is considerable glory in that, a cook being a sort of officer on ship-board – yet, somehow, I never fancied broiling fowls – though once broiled, judiciously buttered, and judgematically salted and peppered, there is no one who will speak more respectfully of a broiled fowl than I will.

No, when I go to sea, I go as a simple sailor, right before the mast, plumb down into the forecastle, aloft there to the royal mast-head. True, they rather order me about some, and make me jump from spar to spar, like a grasshopper in a May meadow. And at first, this sort of thing is unpleasant enough. It touches one's sense of honour, particularly if you come of an old established family in the land, the Van Rensselaers, or Randolphs, or Hardicanutes. And more than all, if just previous to putting your hand into the tar-pot, you have been lording it as a country schoolmaster, making the tallest boys stand in awe of you. The transition is a keen one, I assure you, from a schoolmaster to a sailor, and requires a strong decoction of Seneca and the Stoics to enable you to grin and bear it. But even this wears off in time.

What of it, if some old hunks of a sea-captain orders me to get a broom and sweep the decks? What does that indignity amount to, weighed, I mean, in the scales of the New Testament? Do you think the archangel Gabriel thinks anything less of me, because I promptly obey that old hunks in that particular instance? Who aint a slave? Tell me that. Well, then, however the old sea-captains may order me about – however they may thump me about, I have the satisfaction of knowing that everybody else is served in much the same way – either in a physical or metaphysical point of view, that is; and so the universal thump is passed round, and all hands should rub each other's shoulder-blades, and be content.

Again, I always go to sea as a sailor, because they make a point of paying me for my trouble, whereas they never pay passengers a single penny. On the contrary, passengers themselves must pay. And there is all the difference in the world between paying and being paid. Being paid – what will compare with it? The urbane activity with which a man receives money is really marvellous, considering that we so earnestly believe money to be the root of all earthly ills, and that on no account can a monied man enter heaven. Ah! how cheerfully we consign ourselves to perdition!

Finally, I always go to sea as a sailor, because of the wholesome exercise and pure air of the forecastle deck. For as in this world, head winds are far more prevalent than winds from astern, so for the most part the Commodore on the quarter-deck gets his atmosphere at second hand from the sailors on the forecastle. In much the same way do the commonalty lead their leaders in many other things, at the same time that the leaders little suspect it. But wherefore it was that after having repeatedly smelt the sea as a merchant sailor, I should now take it into my head to go on a whaling voyage; this the invisible police officer of the Fates, who secretly dogs me, and influences me in some unaccountable way – he can better answer than anyone else. And, doubtless, my going on this whaling voyage, formed part of the grand programme of Providence that was drawn up a long time ago. It came in as a sort of brief interlude and solo between more extensive performances. I take it that this part of the bill must have run something like this:

'GRAND CONTESTED ELECTION FOR THE PRESIDENCY OF THE UNITED STATES

'WHALING VOYAGE BY ONE ISHMAEL

'BLOODY BATTLE IN AFGHANISTAN'

Though I cannot tell why it was exactly that those stage managers, the Fates, put me down for this shabby part of a whaling voyage, when others were set down for magnificent parts in high tragedies, and short and easy parts in genteel comedies, and jolly parts in farces – though I cannot tell why this was exactly; yet, now that I recall all the circumstances, I think I can see a little into the springs and motives which being cunningly presented to me under various disguises, induced me to set about performing the part I did, besides cajoling me into the delusion that it was a choice resulting from my own unbiased freewill and discriminating judgement.

Chief among these motives was the overwhelming idea of the great whale himself. Such a portentous and mysterious monster roused all my curiosity. Then the wild and distant seas where he rolled his island bulk; the undeliverable, nameless perils of the whale; these, with all the attending marvels of a thousand Patagonian sights and sounds, helped to sway me to my wish.

CHAPTER 2

The Carpet-Bag

I stuffed a shirt or two into my old carpet-bag, tucked it under my arm, and started for Cape Horn and the Pacific. Quitting the good city of old Manhatto, I duly arrived in New Bedford. It was on a Saturday night in December. Much was I disappointed upon learning that the little packet for Nantucket had already sailed, and that no way of reaching that place would offer, till the following Monday.

As most young candidates for the pains and penalties of whaling stop at this same New Bedford, thence to embark on their voyage, it may as well be related that I, for one, had no idea of so doing. For my mind was made up to sail in no other than a Nantucket craft, because there was a fine, boisterous something about everything connected with that famous old island, which amazingly pleased me. Besides, though New Bedford has of late been gradually monopolizing the business of whaling, and though in this matter poor old Nantucket is now much behind her, yet Nantucket was her great original – the Tyre of this Carthage – the place where the first dead American whale was stranded. Where else but from Nantucket did those aboriginal whalemen, the Red-Men, first sally out in canoes to give chase to the Leviathan? And where but from Nantucket, too, did that first adventurous little sloop put forth, partly laden with imported cobblestones – so goes the story – to throw at the whales, in order to discover when they were nigh enough to risk a harpoon from the bowsprit?

Now having a night, a day, and still another night following before me in New Bedford, ere I could embark, it became a matter of concernment where I was to eat and sleep meanwhile. It was a very dark and dismal night, bitingly cold and cheerless. I knew no one in the place. With anxious grapnels I had sounded my pocket, and only brought up a few pieces of silver – So, wherever you go, Ishmael, said I to myself, as I stood in the middle of a dreary street, comparing the gloom towards the north with the darkness towards the south – wherever in your wisdom you may conclude to lodge for the night, my dear Ishmael, don't be too particular.

With halting steps I paced the streets, and passed the sign of 'The Crossed Harpoons' – but it looked too expensive and jolly there. Further on, from the bright red windows of the 'Sword-Fish Inn', there came such fervent rays, that it seemed to have melted the packed snow and ice from before the house, for everywhere else the congealed frost lay ten inches thick in a hard, asphaltic pavement. Too expensive and jolly, again thought I, pausing one moment to watch the broad glare in the street, and hear the sounds of the tinkling glasses within. But go on, Ishmael, said I at last; get away from before the door; your patched boots are stopping the way. So on I went. I now followed the streets that took me waterward, for there, doubtless, were the cheapest, if not the cheeriest inns.

Such dreary streets! blocks of blackness, not houses, on either hand, and here and there a candle. At this hour of the night, of the last day of the week, that quarter of the town proved all but deserted. But presently I came to a smoky light proceeding from a low, wide building, the door of which stood invitingly open. It had a careless look, as if it were meant for the uses of the public; so, entering, the first thing I did was to stumble over an ash-box in the porch. Ha! thought I, ha, as the flying particles almost choked me, are these ashes from that destroyed city, Gomorrah? But 'The Crossed Harpoons', and 'The Sword-Fish?' – this, then, must needs be the sign of 'The Trap'. However, I picked myself up and hearing a loud voice within, pushed on and opened a second, interior door.

It seemed the great Black Parliament sitting in Tophet. A hundred black faces turned round in their rows to peer; and beyond, a black Angel of Doom was beating a book in a pulpit. It was a negro church; and the preacher's text was about the blackness of darkness, and the weeping and wailing and teeth-gnashing there. Ha, Ishmael, muttered I, backing out, Wretched entertainment at the sign of 'The Trap'!

Moving on, I at last came to a dim sort of light, and heard a forlorn creaking in the air; and looking up, saw a swinging sign over the door with a white painting upon it, faintly representing a tall straight jet of misty spray, and these words underneath – 'The Spouter-Inn: – Peter Coffin'.

Coffin? – Spouter? – Rather ominous in that particular connexion, thought I. But it is a common name in Nantucket, they say, and I suppose this Peter here is an emigrant from there. As the light looked so dim, and the place, for the time, looked quiet enough, and the dilapidated little wooden house itself looked as if it might have been carted here from the ruins of some burnt district, and as the swinging sign had a poverty-stricken sort of creak to it, I thought that here was the very spot for cheap lodgings, and the best of pea coffee.

It was a queer sort of place – a gable-ended old house, one side palsied as it were, and leaning over sadly. It stood on a sharp bleak corner, where that tempestuous wind Euroclydon kept up a worse howling than ever it did about poor Paul's tossed craft. Euroclydon, nevertheless, is a mighty pleasant zephyr to anyone indoors, with his feet on the hob quietly toasting for bed.

Let us scrape the ice from our frosted feet, and see what sort of a place this 'Spouter' may be.

CHAPTER 3

The Spouter-Inn

Entering that gable-ended Spouter-Inn, you found yourself in a wide, low, straggling entry with old-fashioned wainscots, reminding one of the bulwarks of some condemned old craft. On one side hung a very large oil-painting so thoroughly besmoked and defaced, that it was only by diligent study that you could any way arrive at an understanding of its purpose. A boggy, soggy, squitchy picture truly, enough to drive a nervous man distracted. Yet was there a sort of indefinite, unimaginable sublimity about it that fairly froze you to it, till you involuntarily took an oath with yourself to find out what that marvellous painting meant. Ever and anon a bright, but, alas, deceptive idea would dart you through. – It's the Black Sea in a midnight gale. – It's the unnatural combat of the four primal elements. But stop; does it not bear a faint resemblance to a gigantic fish? even the great Leviathan himself?

The picture represents a Cape-Horner in a great hurricane; the half-foundered ship weltering there with its three dismantled masts alone visible; and an exasperated whale, purposing to spring clean over the craft, is in the enormous act of impaling himself upon the three mast-heads.

The opposite wall of this entry was hung all over with a heathenish array of monstrous clubs and spears. Some were thickly set with glittering teeth resembling ivory saws; others were tufted with knots of human hair; and one was sickle-shaped, with a vast handle sweeping round like the segment made in the new-mown grass by a long-armed mower. You shuddered as you gazed, and wondered what monstrous cannibal and savage could ever have gone a death-harvesting with such a hacking, horrifying implement. Mixed with these were rusty old whaling lances and harpoons all broken and deformed. Some were storied weapons. With this once long lance, now wildly elbowed, fifty years ago did Nathan Swain kill fifteen whales between a sunrise and a sunset. And that harpoon – so like a corkscrew now – was flung in Javan seas, and run away with by a whale, years afterwards slain off the Cape of Blanco. The iron entered nigh the tail, and, like a restless needle sojourning in the body of a man, travelled full forty feet, and at last was found imbedded in the hump.

Crossing this dusky entry, and on through yon low-arched way – cut through what in old times must have been a great central chimney with fire-places all round – you enter the public room. A still duskier place is this, with such low ponderous beams above, and such old wrinkled planks beneath, that you would almost fancy you trod some old craft's cockpits, especially of such a howling night. On one side stood a long, low, shelf-like table covered with cracked glass cases, filled with dusty rarities gathered from this wide world's remotest nooks. Projecting from the further angle of the room stands a dark-looking den – the bar – a rude attempt at a right whale's head. Be that how it may, there stands the vast arched bone of the whale's jaw, so wide, a coach might almost drive beneath it. Within are shabby shelves, ranged round with old decanters, bottles, flasks; and in those jaws of swift destruction, like another cursed Jonah (by which name they called him), bustles a little withered old man, who, for their money, dearly sells the sailors deliriums and death.

Abominable are the tumblers into which he pours his poison. Though true cylinders without – within, the villanous green goggling glasses deceitfully tapered downwards to a cheating bottom. Parallel meridians rudely pecked into the glass, surround these footpads' goblets. Fill to *this* mark, and your charge is but a penny; to *this* a penny more; and so on to the full glass – the Cape Horn measure, which you may gulph down for a shilling.

Upon entering the place I found a number of young seamen gathered about a table, examining by a dim light divers specimens of *skrimshander*. I sought the landlord, and telling him I desired to be accommodated with a room, received for answer that his house was full. 'But avast,' he added, tapping his forehead, 'you haint no objections to sharing a harpooneer's blanket, have ye? I s'pose you are goin' a whalin', so you'd better get used to that sort of thing.'

I told him that it would depend upon who the harpooneer might be, and that if he (the landlord) really had no other place for me, and the harpooneer was not decidedly objectionable, why rather than wander further on so bitter a night, I would put up with the half of any decent man's blanket.

'I thought so. All right; take a seat. Supper? – you want supper? Supper'll be ready directly.'

I sat down on an old wooden settle, carved all over. At one end a ruminating tar was still further adorning it with his jack-knife, stooping over and diligently working away at the space between his legs. He was trying his hand at a ship under full sail, but he didn't make much headway, I thought.

At last some four or five of us were summoned to our meal in an adjoining room. It was cold as Iceland – no fire at all – the landlord said he couldn't afford it. We were fain to button up our monkey jackets, and hold to our lips cups of scalding tea with our half frozen fingers. But the fare was of the most substantial kind – not only meat and potatoes, but dumplings; good heavens! dumplings for supper! One young fellow in a green box coat, addressed himself to these dumplings in a most direful manner.

'My boy,' said the landlord, 'you'll have the nightmare to a dead sartainty.'

'Landlord,' I whispered, 'that aint the harpooneer, is it?'

'Oh, no,' said he, looking a sort of diabolically funny, 'the harpooner is a dark complexioned chap. He never eats dumplings – he eats nothing but steaks, and likes 'em rare.'

'The devil he does,' says I. 'Where is that harpooneer?'

'He'll be here afore long,' was the answer.

I could not help it, but I began to feel suspicious of this 'dark complexioned' harpooneer. At any rate, I made up my mind that if it so turned out that we should sleep together, he must undress and get into bed before I did.

Supper over, the company went back to the bar-room.

Presently a rioting noise was heard without. Starting up, the landlord cried, 'That's the Grampus's crew. I seed her reported in the offing this morning; a three years' voyage, and a full ship. Hurrah, boys; now we'll have the latest news from the Feegees.'

The door was flung open, and in rolled a wild set of mariners. Enveloped in their shaggy watch coats, and with their heads muffled in woollen comforters, all bedarned and ragged, and their beards stiff with icicles, they seemed an eruption of bears from Labrador. They had just landed from their boat, and this was the first house they entered. No wonder, then, that they made a straight wake for the whale's mouth – the bar – when the wrinkled little old Jonah soon poured them out brimmers all round. One complained of a bad cold in his head, upon which Jonah mixed him a pitch-like potion of gin and molasses, which he swore was a sovereign cure for all colds and catarrhs, whether caught off the coast of Labrador, or on the weather side of an ice-island.

The liquor soon mounted into their heads, as it generally does even with the arrantest topers newly landed from sea, and they began capering about most obstreperously.

I observed, however, that one of them refrained from making as much noise as the rest, while in the deep shadows of his eyes floated some reminiscences that did not seem to give him much joy. When the revelry of his companions had mounted to its height, this man slipped away unobserved. In a few minutes, however, his shipmates raised a cry of 'Bulkington! where's Bulkington?' and darted out of the house in pursuit of him.

It was now about nine o'clock, and the room seeming almost supernaturally quiet after these orgies, I began to congratulate myself upon a little plan that had occurred to me just previous to the entrance of the seamen. No man prefers to sleep two in a bed. In fact, you would a good deal rather not sleep with your own brother. I don't know how it is, but people like to be private when they are sleeping. And when it comes to sleeping with an unknown stranger, in a strange inn, in a strange town, and that stranger a harpooneer, then your objections indefinitely multiply.

The more I pondered over this harpooneer, the more I abominated the thought of sleeping with him. Besides, my decent harpooneer ought to be home and going bedwards. Suppose now, he should tumble in upon me at midnight – how could I tell from what vile hole he had been coming?

'Landlord! I've changed my mind about that harpooneer. I shan't sleep with him. I'll try the bench here.'

'Just as you please; I'm sorry I cant spare ye a tablecloth for a mattress.' So saying, he went about his business.

I now took the measure of the bench, and found that it was a foot too short; but that could be mended with a chair. But it was a foot too narrow, and the other bench in the room was about four inches higher – so there was no yoking them.

I then placed the first bench lengthwise along the only clear space against the wall, leaving a little interval between, for my back to settle down in. But I soon found that there came such a draught of cold air over me from under the sill of the window, that this plan would never do at all. The devil fetch that harpooneer, thought I.

Still, looking round me again, and seeing no possible chance of spending a sufferable night unless in some other person's bed, I began to think that after all I might be cherishing unwarrantable prejudices against this unknown harpooneer. Thinks I, I'll wait awhile; he must be dropping in before long. But though the other boarders kept coming in, and going to bed, yet no sign of my harpooneer.

'Landlord!' said I, 'what sort of a chap is he – does he always keep such late hours?' It was now hard upon twelve o'clock.

The landlord chuckled and seemed to be mightily tickled at something beyond my comprehension. 'No,' he answered, 'generally he's an early bird – airley to bed and airley to rise – yes, he's the bird what catches the worm. But tonight he went out a peddling, you see, and I don't see what on airth keeps him so late, unless, may be, he can't sell his head.'

'Can't sell his head? Do you pretend to say, landlord, that this harpooneer is actually engaged this blessed Saturday night, or rather Sunday morning, in peddling his head around this town?'

'That's precisely it,' said the landlord, 'and I told him he couldn't sell it here, the market's overstocked.'

'With what?' shouted I.

'With heads to be sure; ain't there too many heads in the world?'

'I tell you what it is, landlord,' said I, quite calmly, 'you'd better stop spinning that yarn to me – I'm not green.'

'May be not,' taking out a stick and whittling a toothpick, 'but I rayther guess you'll be done *brown* if that ere harpooneer hears you a slanderin' his head.'

'I'll break it for him,' said I, now flying into a passion at this unaccountable farrago of the landlord's.

'It's broke a'ready,' said he. 'And that's the very reason he can't sell it, I guess.'

'Landlord,' said I, going up to him as cool as Mt Hecla in a snow storm, 'landlord, stop whittling. You and I must understand one another, and that too without delay. I now demand of you to speak out and tell me who and what this harpooneer is, and whether I shall be in all respects safe to spend the night with him. And in the first place, you will be so good as to unsay that story about selling his head, which if true I take to be good evidence that this harpooneer is stark mad, and I've no idea of sleeping with a madman; and you, sir, by trying to induce me to do so knowingly, would thereby render yourself liable to a criminal prosecution.'

'Wall,' said the landlord, fetching a long breath, 'that's a purty long sarmon for a chap that rips a little now and then. But be easy, be easy, this here harpooneer I have been tellin' you of has just arrived from the South Seas, where he bought up a lot of 'balmed New Zealand heads (great curios, you know), and he's sold all on 'em but one, and that one he's trying to sell tonight, cause tomorrow's Sunday, and it would not do to be sellin' human heads about the streets when folks is goin' to churches.'

This account cleared up the otherwise unaccountable mystery, and showed that the landlord, after all, had had no idea of fooling me – but at the same time what could I think of a harpooneer who stayed out of a Saturday night clean into the holy Sabbath, engaged in such a cannibal business as selling the heads of dead idolators?

'Depend upon it, landlord, that harpooneer is a dangerous man.'

'He pays reg'lar,' was the rejoinder. 'But come, it's getting dreadful late, you had better be turning flukes – it's a nice bed: Sal and me slept in that ere bed the night we were spliced. There's plenty of room for two to kick about in that bed; it's an almighty big bed that. Come along here, I'll give ye a glim in a jiffy'; and so saying he lighted a candle and held it towards me, offering to lead the way. But I stood irresolute; when looking at a clock in the corner, he exclaimed, 'I vum it's Sunday – you won't see that harpooneer tonight; he's come to anchor somewhere – come along then; *do* come; *won't* ye come?'

I considered the matter a moment, and then upstairs we went, and I was ushered into a small room, cold as a clam, and furnished, sure enough, with a prodigious bed, almost big enough indeed for any four harpooneers to sleep abreast.

'There,' said the landlord, placing the candle on a crazy old sea chest that did duty as a wash-stand and centre table; 'there, make yourself comfortable now, and good night to ye.' I turned round from eyeing the bed, but he had disappeared.

Folding back the counterpane I stooped over the bed. Though none of the most elegant, it yet stood the scrutiny tolerably well. I then glanced round the room; and besides the bedstead and centre table, could see no other furniture belonging to the place, but a rude shelf, the four walls, and a papered fire-board representing a man striking a whale. Of things not properly belonging to the room, there was a hammock lashed up, and thrown upon the floor in one corner; also a large seaman's bag, containing the harpooneer's wardrobe, no doubt in lieu of a land trunk. Likewise, there was a parcel of outlandish bone fish hooks on the shelf over the fire-place, and a tall harpoon standing at the head of the bed.

But what is this on the chest? I took it up, and held it close to the light, and felt it, and smelt it, and tried every way possible to arrive at some satisfactory conclusion concerning it. I can compare it to nothing but a large door mat, ornamented at the edges with little tinkling tags something like the stained porcupine quills round an Indian moccasin. There was a hole or slit in the middle of this mat, as you see the same in South American ponchos. But could it be possible that any sober harpooneer would get into a door mat, and parade the streets of any Christian town in that sort of guise? I put it on, to try it, and it weighed me down like a hamper, being uncommonly shaggy and thick, and I thought a little damp. I went up in it to a bit of glass stuck against the wall, and I never saw such a sight in my life. I tore myself out of it in such a hurry that I gave myself a kink in the neck.

I sat down on the side of the bed, and commenced thinking about this head-peddling harpooneer, and his door mat. After thinking some time, I got up and took off my monkey jacket, and then stood in the middle of the room thinking. I then took off my coat, and thought a little more in my shirt sleeves. But beginning to feel very cold now, I jumped out of my pantaloons and boots, and blowing out the light tumbled into bed, and commended myself to the care of heaven.

Whether that mattress was stuffed with corn-cobs or broken crockery, there is no telling, but I rolled about a good deal, and could not sleep for a long time. At last I slid off into a doze, when I heard a heavy footfall in the passage, and saw a glimmer of light come into the room from under the door.

Lord save me, thinks I, that must be the harpooneer, the infernal head-peddler. But I lay perfectly still, and resolved not to say a word till spoken to. Holding a light in one hand, and that identical New Zealand head in the other, the stranger entered the room, and without looking towards the bed, placed his candle a good way off from me on the floor in one corner, and then began working away at the knotted cords of the large bag I before spoke of as being in the room. I was all eagerness to see his face, but he kept it averted while unlacing the bag's mouth. This accomplished, he turned round – when, good heavens! what a sight! Such a face! It was of a dark, purplish, yellow colour, here and there stuck over with large, blackish looking squares. At first I knew not what to make of this; but soon I remembered a story of a white man – a whaleman – who, falling among the cannibals, had been tattooed by them. I concluded that this harpooneer must have met with a similar adventure. And what is it, thought I, after all! It's only his outside; a man can be honest in any sort of skin. But then, what to make of his unearthly complexion? I never heard of a hot sun's tanning a white man into a purplish yellow one. However, I had never been in the South Seas; and perhaps the sun there produced these extraordinary effects upon the skin.

Now, while these ideas were passing through me like lightning, this harpooneer never noticed me at all. But, having opened his bag, he presently pulled out a sort of tomahawk, and a seal-skin wallet with the hair on. Placing these on the old chest, he then took the New Zealand head – a ghastly thing – and crammed it down into the bag. He now took off his hat – a new beaver hat – when I came nigh singing out with fresh surprise. There was no hair on his head – nothing but a small scalpknot twisted up on his forehead. His bald purplish head now looked for all the world like a mildewed skull. Had not the stranger stood between me and the door, I would have bolted out of it quicker than ever I bolted a dinner.

I am no coward, but what to make of this head-peddling purple rascal altogether passed my comprehension. Ignorance is the parent of fear; I confess I was now as much afraid of him as if it was the devil himself who had thus broken into my room at the dead of night.

Meanwhile, he continued the business of undressing, and at last showed his chest and arms. As I live, these covered parts of him were chequered with the same squares as his face; his back, too, was all over the same dark squares. Still more, his very legs were marked, as if a parcel of dark green frogs were running up the trunks of young palms. It was now quite plain that he must be some abominable savage shipped aboard of a whaleman in the South Seas, and so landed in this Christian country. I quaked to think of it. A peddler of heads too. He might take a fancy to mine – heavens! look at that tomahawk!

But there was no time for shuddering, for now the savage went about something that convinced me that he must indeed be a heathen. Going to his heavy grego, or wrapall, or dreadnaught, which he had hung on a chair, he fumbled in the pockets, and produced a curious little deformed image with a hunch on its back, and exactly the colour of a three days' old Congo baby. Remembering the embalmed head, at first I almost thought that this black manikin was a real baby preserved in some similar manner. But seeing that it was not at all limber, and that it glistened a good deal like polished ebony, I concluded that it must be nothing but a wooden idol, which indeed it proved to be. For now the savage goes up to the empty fire-place, and removing the papered fire-board, sets up this little hunchbacked image, like a tenpin, between the andirons. The chimney jambs and all the bricks inside were very sooty, so that I thought this fire-place made a very appropriate little shrine or chapel for his Congo idol.

I now screwed my eyes hard towards the half hidden image to see what was next to follow. First he takes about a double handful of shavings out of his grego pocket, and places them carefully before the idol; then laying a bit of ship biscuit on top and applying the flame from the lamp, he kindled the shavings into a sacrificial blaze. Presently, after many hasty snatches into the fire, and still hastier withdrawals of his fingers, he at last succeeded in drawing out the biscuit; then blowing off the heat and ashes a little, he made a polite offer of it to the little negro. But the little devil did not seem to fancy such dry sort of fare at all; he never moved his lips.

All these strange antics were accompanied by still stranger guttural noises from the devotee, who seemed to be praying in a sing-song or else singing some pagan psalmody or other, during which his face twitched about in the most unnatural manner. At last extinguishing the fire, he took the idol up very unceremoniously, and bagged it again in his grego pocket as if he were a sportsman bagging a dead woodcock.

All these proceedings increased my uncomfortableness, and seeing him now exhibiting strong symptoms of concluding his business operations, and jumping into bed with me, I thought it was high time, now or never, to break the spell in which I had so long been bound.

But the interval I spent in deliberating what to say was a fatal one. Taking up his tomahawk from the table, he examined the head of it for an instant, and then holding it to the light, with his mouth at the handle, he puffed out great clouds of tobacco smoke. The next moment the light was extinguished, and this wild cannibal, tomahawk between his teeth, sprang into bed with me. I sang out, I could not help it now; and giving a grunt of astonishment he began feeling me.

Stammering out something, I knew not what, I rolled away from him against the wall, and then conjured him, whoever or whatever he might be, to keep quiet, and let me get up and light the lamp again. But his guttural responses satisfied me at once that he but ill comprehended my meaning.

'Who-e debel you?' – he at last said – 'you no speak-e, damme, I kill-e.' And so saying the lighted tomahawk began flourishing about me in the dark.

'Landlord, for God's sake, Peter Coffin!' shouted I. 'Landlord! Watch! Coffin! Angels! save me!'

'Speak-e! tell-ee me who-ee be, or dam-me, I kill-e!' again growled the cannibal, while his horrid flourishings of the tomahawk scattered the hot tobacco ashes about me till I thought my linen would get on fire. But thank heaven, at that moment the landlord came into the room light in hand, and leaping from the bed I ran up to him.

'Don't be afraid now,' said he, grinning again. 'Queequeg here wouldn't harm a hair of your head.'

'Stop your grinning,' shouted I, 'and why didn't you tell me that that infernal harpooneer was a cannibal?'

'I thought ye know'd it; didn't I tell ye, he was a peddlin' heads around town? – but turn flukes again and go to sleep. Queequeg, look here – you sabbee me, I sabbee you – this man sleepe you – you sabbee?'

'Me sabbee plenty' – grunted Queequeg, puffing away at his pipe and sitting up in bed. 'You gettee in,' he added, motioning to me with his tomahawk, and throwing the clothes to one side. He really did this in not only a civil but a really kind and charitable way. I stood looking at him a moment. For all his tattooings he was on the whole a clean, comely looking cannibal. What's all this fuss I have been making about, thought I – the man's a human being just as I am: he has just as much reason to fear me, as I have to be afraid of him. Better sleep with a sober cannibal than a drunken Christian.

'Landlord,' said I, 'tell him to stash his tomahawk there, or pipe, or whatever you call it; tell him to stop smoking, in short, and I will turn in with him. I don't fancy a man smoking in bed with me. It's dangerous. Besides, I aint insured.'

This being told to Queequeg, he at once complied, and again politely motioned me to get into bed – rolling over to one side as much as to say – I wont touch a leg of ye.

'Good night, landlord,' said I, 'you may go.' I turned in, and never slept better in my life.

CHAPTER 4

The Counterpane

Upon waking next morning, I found Queequeg's arm thrown over me in the most loving and affectionate manner. You had almost thought I had been his wife. The counterpane was of patchwork, full of odd little parti-coloured squares and triangles; and this arm of his tattooed all over with an interminable Cretan labyrinth of a figure, no two parts of which were of one precise shade – owing I suppose to his keeping his arm at sea unmethodically in sun and shade, his shirt sleeves irregularly rolled up at various times – this same arm of his, I say, looked for all the world like a strip of that same patchwork quilt. Indeed, partly lying on it as the arm did when I first awoke, I could hardly tell it from the quilt, and it was only by the sense of weight and pressure that I could tell that Queequeg was hugging me.

But at length all the past night's events soberly recurred, and then I lay only alive to the comical predicament. For though I tried to move his arm – unlock his bridegroom clasp – yet, sleeping as he was, he still hugged me tightly. I now strove to rouse him – 'Queequeg!' – but his only answer was a snore. I then rolled over, my neck feeling as if it were in a horse-collar; and suddenly felt a slight scratch. Throwing aside the counterpane, there lay the tomahawk sleeping by the savage's side, as if it were a hatchet-faced baby. A pretty pickle, truly, thought I; abed here with a cannibal and a tomahawk! 'Queequeg! – in the name of goodness, Queequeg, wake!' At length, by dint of much wriggling, and loud expostulations upon the unbecomingness of his hugging a fellow male in that matrimonial sort of style, I succeeded in extracting a grunt; and presently, he drew back his arm, shook himself all over like a Newfoundland dog just from the water, and sat up in bed, stiff as a pike-staff, looking at me, and rubbing his eyes as if he did not altogether remember how I came to be there. Meanwhile, I lay quietly eyeing him, having no serious misgivings now. At last he jumped out upon the floor, and by certain signs and sounds gave me to understand that, if it pleased me, he would dress first and then leave me to dress afterwards, leaving the whole apartment to myself. Thinks I, Queequeg, under the circumstances, this is a very civilized overture; but, the truth is, these savages have an innate sense of delicacy; it is marvellous how essentially polite they are. I pay this particular compliment to Queequeg, because he treated me with so much civility and consideration, while I was guilty of great rudeness; staring at him from the bed, and watching all his toilette motions; for the time my curiosity getting the better of my breeding. Nevertheless, a man like Queequeg you don't see every day.

He commenced dressing at top by donning his beaver hat, a very tall one, by the by, and then – still minus his trowsers – he hunted up his boots. What under the heavens he did it for, I cannot tell, but his next movement was to crush himself – boots in hand, and hat on – under the bed; when, from sundry violent gaspings and strainings, I inferred he was hard at work booting himself; though by no law of propriety that I ever heard of, is any man required to be private when putting on his boots. But Queequeg, do you see, was a creature in the transition state – neither caterpillar nor butterfly. He was just enough civilized to show off his outlandishness in the strangest possible manner. At last, he emerged with his hat very much dented and crushed down over his eyes, and began creaking and limping about the room as if not being much accustomed to boots.

Seeing, now, that there were no curtains to the window, and that the street being very narrow, the house opposite commanded a plain view into the room, and observing more and more the indecorous figure that Queequeg made, staving about with little else but his hat and boots on; I begged him to get into his pantaloons as soon as possible. He complied, and then proceeded to wash himself. At that time in the morning any Christian would have washed his face; but Queequeg, to my amazement, contented himself with restricting his ablutions to his chest, arms, and hands. He then donned his waistcoat, and taking up a piece of hard soap on the wash-stand centre-table, dipped it into water and commenced lathering his face. I was watching to see where he kept his razor, when lo and behold, he takes the harpoon from the bed corner, slips out the long wooden stock, unsheathes the head, whets it a little on his boot, and striding up to the bit of mirror against the wall, begins a vigorous scraping, or rather harpooning of his cheeks. Thinks I, Queequeg, this is using Rogers's best cutlery with a vengeance. Afterwards I wondered the less at this operation when I came to know of what fine steel the head of a harpoon is made, and how exceedingly sharp the long straight edges are always kept.

The rest of his toilet was soon achieved, and he proudly marched out of the room, wrapped up in his great pilot monkey jacket, sporting his harpoon like a marshal's baton.

CHAPTER 5

Breakfast

I quickly followed suit, and descending into the bar-room accosted the grinning landlord very pleasantly. I cherished no malice towards him, though he had been skylarking with me not a little in the matter of my bedfellow. However, a good laugh is a mighty good thing, and rather too scarce a good thing; the more's the pity. So, if any one man, in his own proper person, afford stuff for a good joke to anybody, let him not be backward, but let him cheerfully allow himself to spend and be spent in that way. And the man that has anything bountifully laughable about him, be sure there is more in that man than you perhaps think for.

The bar-room was now full of the boarders who had been dropping in the night previous, and whom I had not as yet had a good look at. They were nearly all whalemen; chief mates, and second mates, and third mates, and sea carpenters, and sea coopers, and sea blacksmiths, and harpooneers, and ship-keepers; a brown and brawny company, with bosky beards; an unshorn set, all wearing monkey jackets for morning gowns.

You could pretty plainly tell how long each one had been ashore. This young fellow's healthy cheek is like a sun-toasted pear in hue, and would seem to smell almost as musky; he cannot have been three days landed from his Indian voyage. That man next him looks a few shades lighter; you might say a touch of satin wood is in him. In the complexion of a third still lingers a tropic tawn, but slightly bleached withal; he doubtless has tarried whole weeks ashore. But who could show a cheek like Queequeg? which, barred with various tints, seemed like the Andes' western slope, to show forth in one array, contrasting climates, zone by zone.

'Grub, ho!' now cried the landlord, flinging open a door, and in we went to breakfast. They say that men who have seen the world thereby become quite at ease in manner, quite self-possessed in company. Not always, though: Ledyard, the great New England traveller, and Mungo Park, the Scotch one; of all men, they possessed the least assurance in the parlour. But perhaps the mere crossing of Siberia in a sledge drawn by dogs as Ledyard did, or the taking a long solitary walk on an empty stomach, in the negro heart of Africa, which was the sum of poor Mungo's performances – this kind of travel may not be the very best mode of attaining a high social polish.

These reflections just here are occasioned by the circumstance that after we were all seated at the table, and I was preparing to hear some good stories about whaling; to my no small surprise, nearly every man maintained a profound silence. And not only that, but they looked embarrassed. Yes, here were a set of seadogs, many of whom without the slightest bashfulness had boarded great whales on the high seas – entire strangers to them – and duelled them dead without winking; and yet, here they sat at a social breakfast table looking round as sheepishly at each other as though they had never been out of sight of some sheepfold among the Green Mountains. A curious sight; these bashful bears, these timid warrior whalemen!

But as for Queequeg – why, Queequeg sat there among them – at the head of the table, too, it so chanced; as cool as an icicle. To be sure his greatest admirer could not have cordially justified his bringing his harpoon into breakfast with him, and using it there without ceremony; reaching over the table with it, to the imminent jeopardy of many heads, and grappling the beefsteaks towards him. But that was certainly very coolly done by him, and every one knows that in most people's estimation, to do anything coolly is to do it genteelly.

We will not speak of all Queequeg's peculiarities here; how he eschewed coffee and hot rolls, and applied his undivided attention to beefsteaks, done rare. Enough, that when breakfast was over he withdrew like the rest into the public room, lighted his tomahawk-pipe, and was sitting there quietly digesting and smoking with his inseparable hat on, when I sallied out for a stroll.

CHAPTER 6

The Street

If I had been astonished at first catching a glimpse of so outlandish an individual as Queequeg circulating among the polite society of a civilized town, that astonishment soon departed upon taking my first daylight stroll through the streets of New Bedford.

In thoroughfares nigh the docks, any considerable seaport

will frequently offer to view the queerest looking nondescripts from foreign parts. Even in Broadway and Chestnut streets, Mediterranean mariners will sometimes jostle the affrighted ladies. Regent street is not unknown to Lascars and Malays; and at Bombay, in the Apollo Green, live Yankees have often scared the natives. But New Bedford beats all Water street and Wapping. In these last-mentioned haunts you see only sailors; but in New Bedford, actual cannibals stand chatting at street corners; savages outright; many of whom yet carry on their bones unholy flesh. It makes a stranger stare.

But, besides the Feegeeans, Tongatabooarrs, Erromanggoans, Pannangians, and Brighggians, and besides the wild specimens of the whaling-craft which unheeded reel about the streets, you will see other sights still more curious, certainly more comical. There weekly arrive scores of green Vermonters and New Hampshire men, all athirst for gain and glory in the fishery. They are mostly young, of stalwart frames; fellows who have felled forests, and now seek to drop the axe and snatch the whale-lance. Many are as green as the Green Mountains whence they came. In some things you would think them but a few hours old. Look there! that chap strutting round the corner. He wears a beaver hat and swallow-tailed coat, girdled with a sailor-belt and sheath-knife. Here comes another with a sou'-wester and a bombazine cloak.

No town-bred dandy will compare with a country-bred one – I mean a downright bumpkin dandy – a fellow that, in the dogdays, will mow his two acres in buckskin gloves for fear of tanning his hands. Now when a country dandy like this takes it into his head to make a distinguished reputation, and joins the great whale-fishery, you should see the comical things he does upon reaching the seaport. In bespeaking his sea-outfit, he orders bellbuttons to his waistcoats; straps to his canvas trowsers. Ah, poor Hay-Seed! how bitterly will burst those straps in the first howling gale, when thou art driven, straps, buttons, and all, down the throat of the tempest.

But think not that this famous town has only harpooneers, cannibals, and bumpkins to show her visitors. Not at all. Still New

Bedford is a queer place. Had it not been for us whalemen, that tract of land would this day perhaps have been in as howling condition as the coast of Labrador. As it is, parts of her back country are enough to frighten one, they look so bony. The town itself is perhaps the dearest place to live in, in all New England. It is a land of oil, true enough: but not like Canaan; a land, also, of corn and wine. The streets do not run with milk; nor in the spring-time do they pave them with fresh eggs. Yet, in spite of this, nowhere in all America will you find more patrician-like houses; parks and gardens more opulent, than in New Bedford. Whence came they? how planted upon this once scraggy scoria of a country?

Go and gaze upon the iron emblematical harpoons round yonder lofty mansion, and your question will be answered. Yes; all these brave houses and flowery gardens came from the Atlantic, Pacific, and Indian oceans. One and all, they were harpooned and dragged up from the bottom of the sea.

In New Bedford, fathers, they say, give whales for dowers to their daughters, and portion off their nieces with a few porpoises a-piece.

In summer time, the town is sweet to see; full of fine maples – long avenues of green and gold. And in August, high in air, the beautiful and bountiful horse-chestnuts, candelabra-wise, proffer the passer-by their tapering upright cones of congregated blossoms. So omnipotent is art; which in many a district of New Bedford has superinduced bright terraces of flowers upon the barren refuse rocks thrown aside at creation's final day. And the women of New Bedford, they bloom like their own red roses. But roses only bloom in summer; whereas the fine carnation of their cheeks is perennial as sunlight in the seventh heavens.

Elsewhere match that bloom of theirs, ye cannot, save in Salem, where they tell me the young girls breathe such musk, their sailor sweethearts smell them miles off shore, as though they were drawing nigh the odorous Moluccas instead of the Puritanic sands.

CHAPTER 7

The Chapel

In this same New Bedford there stands a Whaleman's Chapel, and few are the moody fishermen, shortly bound for the Indian Ocean or Pacific, who fail to make a Sunday visit to the spot. I am sure that I did not.

Returning from my first morning stroll, I again sallied out upon this special errand. The sky had changed from clear, sunny cold, to driving sleet and mist. Wrapping myself in my shaggy jacket of the cloth called bearskin, I fought my way against the stubborn storm. Entering, I found a small scattered congregation of sailors, and sailors' wives and widows. A muffled silence reigned, only broken at times by the shrieks of the storm. Each silent worshipper seemed purposely sitting apart from the other, as if each silent grief were insular and incommunicable. The chaplain had not yet arrived; and there these silent islands of men and women sat steadfastly eyeing several marble tablets, with black borders, masoned into the wall on either side the pulpit. Three of them ran something like the following, but I do not pretend to quote:

SACRED TO THE MEMORY OF
JOHN TALBOT,
WHO, AT THE AGE OF EIGHTEEN, WAS LOST
OVERBOARD NEAR THE ISLE OF DESOLATION, OFF
PATAGONIA
NOVEMBER 1ST, 1836.
THIS TABLET IS ERECTED TO HIS MEMORY
BY HIS SISTER.

SACRED TO THE MEMORY OF
ROBERT LONG, WILLIS ELLERY,
NATHAN COLEMAN, WALTER CANNY,
SETH MACY, AND SAMUEL GLEIG,
FORMING ONE OF THE BOATS' CREWS OF
THE SHIP ELIZA
WHO WERE TOWED OUT OF SIGHT BY A WHALE,
ON THE OFF-SHORE GROUND IN THE PACIFIC,
DECEMBER 31ST, 1839.
THIS MARBLE IS HERE PLACED BY THEIR SURVIVING
SHIPMATES.

SACRED TO THE MEMORY OF
THE LATE
CAPTAIN EZEKIEL HARDY,
WHO IN THE BOWS OF HIS BOAT WAS KILLED BY A
SPERM WHALE ON THE COAST OF JAPAN,
AUGUST 3RD, 1833.
THIS TABLET IS ERECTED TO HIS MEMORY BY
HIS WIDOW.

Shaking off the sleet from my ice-glazed hat and jacket, I seated myself near the door, and turning sideways was surprised to see Queequeg near me. Affected by the solemnity of the scene, there was a wondering gaze of incredulous curiosity in his countenance. This savage was the only person present who seemed to notice my entrance; because he was the only one who could not read, and, therefore, was not reading those frigid inscriptions on the wall. Whether any of the relatives of the seamen whose names appeared there were now among the congregation, I knew not; but so many are the unrecorded accidents in the fishery, and so plainly did several women present wear the countenance if not the trappings of some unceasing grief, that I feel sure that here before me were assembled those, in whose unhealing hearts the sight of those bleak tablets caused the old wounds to bleed afresh.

Oh! ye whose dead lie buried beneath the green grass; who standing among flowers can say – here, here lies my beloved; ye know not the desolation that broods in bosoms like these. What bitter blanks in those black-bordered marbles which cover no ashes! What deadly voids and unbidden infidelities in the lines that seem to gnaw upon all Faith, and refuse resurrections to the beings who have placelessly perished without a grave.

It needs scarcely to be told, with what feelings, on the eve of a Nantucket voyage, I regarded those marble tablets, and by the murky light of that darkened, doleful day read the fate of the whalemen who had gone before me. Yes, Ishmael, the same fate may be thine. But somehow I grew merry again. Delightful inducements to embark, fine chance for promotion, it seems – aye, a stove boat will make me an immortal by brevet. Yes, there is death in this business of whaling – a speechlessly quick chaotic bundling of a man into Eternity. But what then? Methinks we have hugely mistaken this matter of Life and Death. Methinks that what they call my shadow here on earth is my true substance. Methinks that in looking at things spiritual, we are too much like oysters observing the sun through the water, and thinking that thick water the thinnest of air. Methinks my body is but the lees of my better being. In fact take my body who will, take it I say, it is not me. And therefore three cheers for Nantucket; and come a stove boat and stove body when they will, for stave my soul, Jove himself cannot.

CHAPTER 8

A Bosom Friend

Returning to the Spouter-Inn from the Chapel, I found Queequeg there quite alone; he having left the Chapel before the benediction some time. He was sitting on a bench before the fire, with his feet on the stove hearth, and in one hand was holding close up to his face that little negro idol of his; peering hard into its face, and with a jack-knife gently whittling away at its nose, humming to himself in his heathenish way.

But being now interrupted, he put up the image; and pretty soon, going to the table, took up a large book there, and placing it on his lap began counting the pages with deliberate regularity; at every fiftieth page – as I fancied – stopping a moment, looking vacantly around him, and giving utterance to a gurgling whistle of astonishment. He would then begin again at the next fifty; seeming to commence at number one each time, as though he could not count more than fifty, and it was only by such a large number of fifties being found together, that his astonishment at the multitude of pages was excited.

With much interest I sat watching him. Savage though he was, and hideously marred about the face – at least to my taste – his countenance yet had a something in it which was by no means disagreeable. You cannot hide the soul. Through all his unearthly tattooings, I thought I saw the traces of a simple honest heart; and in his large, deep eyes, fiery black and bold, there seemed tokens of a spirit that would dare a thousand devils. And besides all this, there was a certain lofty bearing about the Pagan, which even his uncouthness could not altogether maim. He looked like a man who had never cringed and never had had a creditor. Whether it was, too, that his head being shaved, his forehead was drawn out in freer and brighter relief, and looked more expansive than it otherwise would, this I will not venture to decide; but certain it was his head was phrenologically an excellent one. It reminded me of General Washington's head, as seen in the popular busts of him. It had the same long regularly graded retreating slope from above the brows, which were likewise very projecting, like two long promontories thickly wooded on top. Queequeg was George Washington cannibalistically developed.

Whilst I was thus closely scanning him, half-pretending meanwhile to be looking out at the storm from the casement, he never heeded my presence, never troubled himself with so much as a single glance; but appeared wholly occupied with counting the pages of the marvellous book. Considering how sociably we had been sleeping together the night previous, and especially considering the affectionate arm I had found thrown over me upon waking in the morning, I thought this indifference of his very strange. But savages are strange beings; at times you do not know exactly how to take them. At first they are overawing; their calm self-collectedness of simplicity seems a Socratic wisdom. I had noticed also that Queequeg never consorted at all, or but very little, with the other seamen in the inn. All this struck me as mighty singular; yet, upon second thoughts, there was something almost sublime in it. Here was a man some twenty thousand miles from home, by the way of Cape Horn, that is – which was the only way he could get there – thrown among people as strange to him as though he were in the planet Jupiter; and yet he seemed entirely at his ease; preserving the utmost serenity; content with his own companionship; always equal to himself. Surely this was a touch of fine philosophy; though no doubt he had never heard there was such a thing as that. But, perhaps, to be true philosophers, we mortals should not be conscious of so living or so striving. So soon as I hear that such or such a man gives himself out for a philosopher, I conclude that, like the dyspeptic old woman, he must have 'broken his digester'.

As I sat there in that now lonely room; the fire burning low, in that mild stage when, after its first intensity has warmed the air, it then only glows to be looked at; the evening shades and phantoms gathering round the casements, and peering in upon us silent, solitary twain; the storm booming without in solemn swells; I began to be sensible of strange feelings. I felt a melting in me. No more my splintered heart and maddened hand were turned against the wolfish world. This soothing savage had redeemed it. There he sat, his very indifference speaking a nature in which there lurked no civilized hypocrisies and bland deceits. Wild he was; a very sight of sights to see; yet I began to feel myself mysteriously drawn towards him. And those same things that would have repelled most others, they were the very magnets that thus drew me. I'll try a pagan friend, thought I, since Christian kindness has proved but hollow courtesy. I drew my bench near him, and made some friendly signs and hints, doing my best to talk with him meanwhile. At first he little noticed these advances; but presently, upon my referring to his last night's hospitalities, he made out to ask me whether we were again to be bedfellows. I told him yes; whereat I thought he looked pleased, perhaps a little complimented.

We then turned over the book together, and I endeavoured to explain to him the purpose of the printing, and the meaning of the few pictures that were in it. Thus I soon engaged his interest; and from that we went to jabbering the best we could about the various outer sights to be seen in this famous town. Soon I proposed a social smoke; and, producing his pouch and tomahawk, he quietly offered me a puff. And then we sat exchanging puffs from that wild pipe of his.

This pleasant, genial smoke we had left us cronies. He seemed to take to me quite as naturally and unbiddenly as I to him; and when our smoke was over, he pressed his forehead against mine, clasped me round the waist, and said that henceforth we were married; meaning, in his country's phrase, that we were bosom friends; he would gladly die for me, if need should be. In a countryman, this sudden flame of friendship would have seemed far too premature, a thing to be much distrusted; but in this simple savage those old rules would not apply.

After supper, and another social chat and smoke, we went to our room together. He made me a present of his embalmed head; took out his enormous tobacco wallet, and groping under the tobacco, drew out some thirty dollars in silver; then spreading them on the table, and mechanically dividing them into two equal portions, pushed one of them towards me, and said it was mine. I was going to remonstrate; but he silenced me by pouring them into my trowsers' pockets. I let them stay. He then went about his evening prayers, took out his idol, and removed the paper fire-board. By certain signs and symptoms, I thought he seemed anxious for me to join him; but well knowing what was to follow, I deliberated a moment whether, in case he invited me, I would comply or otherwise.

I was a good Christian; born and bred in the bosom of the infallible Presbyterian Church. How then could I unite with this wild idolator in worshipping his piece of wood? But what is worship? thought I. Do you suppose now, Ishmael, that the magnanimous God of heaven and earth – pagans and all included – can possibly be jealous of an insignificant bit of black wood? Impossible! But what is worship? – to do the will of God – *that* is worship. And what is the will of God? – to do to my fellow man what I would have my fellow man to do to me – *that* is the will of God. Now, Queequeg is my fellow man. And what do I wish that this Queequeg would do to me? Why, unite with me in my particular Presbyterian form of worship. Consequently, I must then unite with him in his; ergo, I must turn idolator. So I kindled the shavings; helped prop up the innocent little idol; offered him burnt biscuit with Queequeg; salamed before him twice or thrice; kissed his nose; and that done, we undressed and went to bed, at peace with our own consciences and all the world. But we did not go to sleep without some little chat.

How it is I know not; but there is no place like a bed for confidential disclosures between friends. Man and wife, they say, there open the very bottom of their souls to each other; and some old couples often lie and chat over old times till nearly morning. Thus, then, in our hearts' honeymoon, lay I and Queequeg – a cosy, loving pair.

CHAPTER 9

Nightgown

We had lain thus in bed, chatting and napping at short intervals, and Queequeg now and then affectionately throwing his brown tattooed legs over mine, and then drawing them back; so entirely sociable and free and easy were we; when, at last, by reason of our confabulations, we felt like getting up again, though day-break was yet some way down the future.

Yes, we became very wakeful; so much so that our recumbent position began to grow wearisome, and by little and little we found ourselves sitting up; the clothes well tucked around us, leaning against the head-board with our four knees drawn up close together, and our two noses bending over them, as if our knee-pans were warming-pans. We felt very nice and snug, the more so since it was so chilly out of doors; indeed out of bedclothes too, seeing that there was no fire in the room. The more so, I say, because truly to enjoy bodily warmth, some small part of you must be cold, for there is no quality in this world that is not what it is merely by contrast. Nothing exists in itself. If you flatter yourself that you are all over comfortable, and have been so a long time, then you cannot be said to be comfortable any more. But if, like Queequeg and me in the bed, the tip of your nose or the crown of your head be slightly chilled, why then, indeed, in the general consciousness you feel most delightfully and unmistakably warm. For this reason a sleeping apartment should never be furnished with a fire, which is one of the luxurious discomforts of the rich. For the height of this sort of deliciousness is to have nothing but the blanket between you and your snugness and the cold of the outer air. Then you lie like the one warm spark in the heart of an arctic crystal.

We had been sitting in this crouching manner for some time, when all at once I thought I would open my eyes; for when

between sheets, whether by day or by night, and whether asleep
or awake, I have a way of always keeping my eyes shut, in order
the more to concentrate the snugness of being in bed. Because no
man can ever feel his own identity aright except his eyes be closed;
as if darkness were indeed the proper element of our essences,
though light be more congenial to our clayey part. Upon opening my eyes then, and coming out of my own pleasant and self-
created darkness into the coarse outer gloom of the unilluminated
twelve-o'clock-at-night, I experienced a revulsion. Nor did I at
all object to the hint from Queequeg that perhaps it were best to
strike a light, seeing that we were so wide awake; and besides he
felt a strong desire to have a few quiet puffs from his tomahawk.
Be it said, that though I had felt such a strong repugnance to his
smoking in the bed the night before, yet see how elastic our stiff
prejudices grow when love once comes to bend them. For now I
liked nothing better than to have Queequeg smoking by me, even
in bed, because he seemed to be full of such serene household joy
then. I was only alive to the condensed confidential comfortable-
ness of sharing a pipe and a blanket with a real friend. With our
shaggy jackets drawn about our shoulders, we now passed the
Tomahawk from one to the other, till slowly there grew over us
a blue hanging tester of smoke, illuminated by the flame of the
new-lit lamp.

Whether it was that this undulating tester rolled the savage
away to far distant scenes, I know not; but he now spoke of his
native island; and, eager to hear his history, I begged him to go
on and tell it. He gladly complied. Though at the time I but ill
comprehended not a few of his words, yet subsequent disclosures,
when I had become more familiar with his broken phraseology,
now enable me to present the whole story such as it may prove in
the mere skeleton I give.

CHAPTER 10

Biographical

Queequeg was a native of Kokovoko, an island far to the West and South. It is not down in any map; true places never are.

When a new-hatched savage running wild about his native woodlands in a grass clout, followed by the nibbling goats, as if he were a green sapling; even then, in Queequeg's ambitious soul, lurked a strong desire to see something more of Christendom than a specimen whaler or two. His father was a High Chief, a King; his uncle a High Priest; and on the maternal side he boasted aunts who were the wives of unconquerable warriors. There was excellent blood in his veins – royal stuff; though sadly vitiated, I fear, by the cannibal propensity he nourished in his untutored youth.

A Sag Harbour ship visited his father's bay, and Queequeg sought a passage to Christian lands. But the ship, having her full complement of seamen, spurned his suit; and not all the King his father's influence could prevail. But Queequeg vowed a vow. Alone in his canoe, he paddled off to a distant strait, which he knew the ship must pass through. On one side was a coral reef; on the other a low tongue of land, covered with mangrove thickets that grew out into the water. Hiding his canoe among these thickets, he sat down in the stern, paddle low in hand; and when the ship was gliding by, like a flash he darted out; gained her side; with one dash of his foot capsized and sank his canoe; climbed up the chains; and throwing himself at full length upon the deck, grappled a ring-bolt there, and swore not to let it go, though hacked in pieces.

In vain the captain threatened to throw him overboard; suspended a cutlass over his naked wrists; Queequeg was the son of a King, and Queequeg budged not. Struck by his desperate dauntlessness, the captain at last told him he might make himself at home. But this fine young savage – this sea Prince of Wales

– never saw the captain's cabin. They put him down among the sailors, and made a whaleman of him. But Queequeg disdained no seeming ignominy, if thereby he might happily gain the power of enlightening his untutored countrymen. For at bottom – so he told me – he was actuated by a profound desire to learn among the Christians, the arts whereby to make his people still happier than they were; and more than that, still better than they were. But, alas! the practices of whalemen soon convinced him that even Christians could be both miserable and wicked; infinitely more so, than all his father's heathens. Arrived at last in old Sag Harbour; and seeing what the sailors did there; and then going on to Nantucket, and seeing how they spent their wages in that place also, poor Queequeg gave it up for lost. Thought he, it's a wicked world in all meridians; I'll die a pagan.

And thus an old idolater at heart, he yet lived among these Christians, wore their clothes, and tried to talk their gibberish.

By hints, I asked him whether he did not propose going back, and having a coronation; since he might now consider his father dead and gone, he being very old and feeble at the last accounts. He answered no, not yet; and added that he was fearful Christianity, or rather Christians, had unfitted him for ascending the pure and undefiled throne of thirty pagan Kings before him. But by and by he would return – as soon as he felt himself baptized again. For the nonce, however, he proposed to sail about, and sow his wild oats in all four oceans.

I asked him what might be his immediate purpose, touching his future movements. He answered, to go to sea again, in his old vocation. Upon this, I told him that whaling was my own design, and informed him of my intention to sail out of Nantucket, as being the most promising port for an adventurous whaleman to embark from. He at once resolved to accompany me to that island, ship aboard the same vessel, get into the same watch, the same boat, the same mess with me, in short to share my every hap; with both my hands in his, boldly dip into the Potluck of both worlds. To all this I joyously assented; for besides the affection I now felt for Queequeg, he was an experienced harpooneer, and as such, could not fail to be of great usefulness to one, who, like me, was wholly ignorant of the mysteries of whaling.

His story being ended with his pipe's last dying puff, Queequeg embraced me, pressed his forehead against mine, and blowing out the light, we rolled over from each other, this way and that, and very soon were sleeping.

CHAPTER 11

Wheelbarrow

Next morning, Monday, after disposing of the embalmed head to a barber, for a block, I settled my own and comrade's bill; using, however, my comrade's money. The grinning landlord, as well as the boarders, seemed amazingly tickled at the sudden friendship which had sprung up between me and Queequeg – especially as Peter Coffin's cock and bull stories about him had previously so much alarmed me concerning the very person whom I now companied with.

We borrowed a wheelbarrow, and embarking our things, including my own poor carpet-bag, and Queequeg's canvas sack and hammock, away we went down to 'the Moss', the little Nantucket packet schooner moored at the wharf. As we were going along the people stared; not at Queequeg so much – for they were used to seeing cannibals like him in their streets – but at seeing him and me upon such confidential terms. But we heeded them not, going along wheeling the barrow by turns, and Queequeg now and then stopping to adjust the sheath on his harpoon barbs. I asked him why he carried such a troublesome thing with him ashore, and whether all whaling ships did not find their own harpoons. To this, in substance, he replied, that though what I hinted was true enough, yet he had a particular affection for his own harpoon, because it was of assured stuff, well tried in many a mortal combat, and deeply intimate with the hearts of whales. In short, like many inland reapers and mowers, who go into the farmers' meadows armed with their own scythes – though in no wise obliged to furnish them – even so, Queequeg, for his own private reasons, preferred his own harpoon.

Shifting the barrow from my hand to his, he told me a funny story about the first wheelbarrow he had ever seen. It was in Sag Harbour. The owners of his ship, it seems, had lent him one, in which to carry his heavy chest to his boarding house. Not to seem ignorant about the thing – though in truth he was entirely so, concerning the precise way in which to manage the barrow – Queequeg puts his chest upon it; lashes it fast; and then shoulders the barrow and marches up the wharf. 'Why,' said I, 'Queequeg, you might have known better than that, one would think. Didn't the people laugh?'

Upon this, he told me another story. The people of his island of Rokovoko, it seems, at their wedding feasts express the fragrant water of young cocoanuts into a large stained calabash like a punchbowl; and this punchbowl always forms the great central ornament on the braided mat where the feast is held. Now a certain grand merchant ship once touched at Rokovoko, and its commander – from all accounts, a very stately punctilious gentleman, at least for a sea captain – this commander was invited to the wedding feast of Queequeg's sister, a pretty young princess just turned of ten. Well; when all the wedding guests were assembled at the bride's bamboo cottage, this Captain matches in, and being assigned the post of honour, placed himself over against the punchbowl, and between the High Priest and his majesty the King, Queequeg's father. Grace being said – for those people have their grace as well as we – though Queequeg told me that unlike us, who at such times look downwards to our platters, they, on the contrary, copying the ducks, glance upwards to the great Giver of all feasts – Grace, I say, being said, the High Priest opens the banquet by the immemorial ceremony of the island; that is, dipping his consecrated and consecrating fingers into the bowl before the blessed beverage circulates. Seeing himself placed next the Priest, and noting the ceremony, and thinking himself – being Captain of a ship – as having plain precedence over a mere island King, especially in the King's own house – the Captain coolly proceeds to wash his hands in the punchbowl; taking it I suppose, for a huge finger-glass. 'Now,' said Queequeg, 'what you tink now? – Didn't our people laugh?'

At last, passage paid, and luggage safe, we stood on board the schooner. Hoisting sail, it glided down the Acushnet river. On one side, New Bedford rose in terraces of streets, their ice-covered trees all glittering in the clear, cold air. Huge hills and mountains of casks on casks were piled upon her wharves, and side by side the world-wandering whale ships lay silent and safely moored at last; while from others came a sound of carpenters and coopers, with blended noises of fires and forges to melt the pitch, all betokening that new cruises were on the start; that one most perilous and long voyage ended, only begins a second; and a second ended, only begins a third and so on, for ever and for aye. Such is the endlessness, yea, the intolerableness of all earthly effort.

Gaining the more open water, the bracing breeze waxed fresh; the little Moss tossed the quick foam from her bows, as a young colt his snortings. How I snuffed that Tartar air! – how I spurned that turnpike earth! – that common highway all over dented with the marks of slavish heels and hoofs; and turned me to admire the magnanimity of the sea which will permit no records.

At the same foam-fountain, Queequeg seemed to drink and reel with me. His dusky nostrils swelled apart; he showed his filed and pointed teeth. On, on we flew; and our offing gained, the Moss did homage to the blast; ducked and dived her brows as a slave before the Sultan. Sideways leaning, we sideways darted; every ropeyarn tingling like a wire; the two tall masts buckling like Indian canes in land tornadoes. So full of this reeling scene were we, as we stood by the plunging bowsprit, that for some time we did not notice the jeering glances of the passengers, a lubber-like assembly, who marvelled that two fellow beings should be so companionable; as though a white man were anything more dignified than a white-washed negro. But there were some boobies and bumpkins there, who, by their intense greenness, must have come from the heart and centre of all verdure. Queequeg caught one of these young saplings mimicking him behind his back. I thought the bumpkin's hour of doom was come. Dropping his harpoon, the brawny savage caught him in his arms, and by an almost miraculous dexterity and strength, sent him high up bodily into the air; then slightly tapping his stern in mid-somerset, the fellow landed with bursting lungs upon his feet, while Queequeg, turning his back upon him, lighted his tomahawk pipe and passed it to me for a puff.

'Capting! Capting!' yelled the bumpkin, running towards that officer; 'Capting, Capting, here's the devil.'

'Hallo, *you* sir,' cried the Captain, a gaunt rib of the sea, stalking up to Queequeg, 'what in thunder do you mean by that? Don't you know you might have killed that chap?'

'What him say?' said Queequeg, as he turned to me.

'He say,' said I, 'that you came near kill-e that man there,' pointing to the still shivering greenhorn.

'Kill-e,' cried Queequeg, twisting his tattooed face into an unearthly expression of disdain, 'ah! him bevy small-e fish-e; Queequeg no kill-e so small-e fish-e: Queequeg kill-e big whale!'

'Look you,' roared the Captain, 'I'll kill-e *you*, you cannibal, if you try any more of your tricks aboard here; so mind your eye.'

But it so happened just then, that it was high time for the Captain to mind his own eye. The prodigious strain upon the mainsail had parted the weather-sheet, and the tremendous boom was now flying from side to side, completely sweeping the entire after part of the deck. The poor fellow whom Queequeg had handled so roughly was swept overboard; all hands were in a panic; and to attempt snatching at the boom to stay it seemed madness. It flew from right to left, and back again, almost in one ticking of a watch, and every instant seemed on the point of snapping into splinters. Nothing was done, and nothing seemed capable of being done; those on deck rushed towards the bows, and stood eyeing the boom as if it were the lower jaw of an exasperated whale. In the midst of this consternation, Queequeg dropped deftly to his knees, and crawling under the path of the boom, whipped hold of a rope, secured one end to the bulwarks, and then flinging the other like a lasso, caught it round the boom as it swept over his head, and at the next jerk, the spar was that way trapped, and all was safe. The schooner was run into the wind, and while the hands were clearing away the stern boat, Queequeg, stripped to the waist, darted from the side with a long living arc of a leap. For three minutes or more he was seen swimming like a dog, throwing his long arms straight out before him through the freezing foam. I looked, but saw no one to be saved. The greenhorn had gone down. Shooting himself perpendicularly from the water, Queequeg now took an instant's glance around him, and dived down and disappeared. A few minutes more, and he rose again, one arm still striking out, and with the other dragging a lifeless form. The boat soon picked them up. The poor bumpkin was restored. All hands voted Queequeg a noble trump; the captain begged his pardon. From that hour I clove to Queequeg like a barnacle; yea, till poor Queequeg took his last long dive.

Was there ever such unconsciousness? He did not seem to think that he at all deserved a medal from the Humane and Magnanimous Societies. He only asked for water – fresh water – something to wipe the brine off; that done, he put on dry clothes, lighted his pipe, and leaning against the bulwarks, and mildly eyeing those around him, seemed to be saying to himself – 'It's a mutual, joint-stock world, in all meridians. We cannibals must help these Christians.'

CHAPTER 12

Nantucket

Nothing more happened worthy the mentioning; so, after a fine run, we safely arrived in Nantucket.

Nantucket! Take out your map and look at it. See what a real corner of the world it occupies; how it stands there, away off shore, more lonely than the Eddystone lighthouse. Look at it – a mere hillock, and elbow of sand; all beach, without a background. There is more sand there than you would use in twenty years as a substitute for blotting paper. Some gamesome wights will tell you that pieces of wood in Nantucket are carried about like bits of the true cross in Rome; that people there plant toadstools before their houses, to get under the shade in summer time; that one blade of grass makes an oasis, three blades in a day's walk a prairie; that they wear quicksand shoes, something like Laplander snowshoes; that they are so shut up, belted about, every way inclosed, surrounded, and made an utter island of by the ocean, that to their very chairs and tables small clams will sometimes be found adhering, as to the backs of sea turtles. But these extravaganzas only show that Nantucket is no Illinois.

What wonder, then, that these Nantucketers, born on a beach, should take to the sea for a livelihood! They first caught crabs and quohogs in the sand; grown bolder, they waded out with nets for mackerel; more experienced, they pushed off in boats and captured cod; and at last, launching a navy of great ships on the sea, explored this watery world; put an incessant belt of circumnavigations round it; peeped in at Bhering's Straits; and in all seasons and all oceans declared everlasting war with the mightiest animated mass that has survived the flood; most monstrous and most mountainous! That Himmalehan, salt-sea Mastodon, clothed with such portentousness of unconscious power, that his very panics are more to be dreaded than his most malicious assaults!

CHAPTER 13

Chowder

It was quite late in the evening when the little Moss came snugly to anchor, and Queequeg and I went ashore; so we could attend to no business that day, at least none but a supper and a bed. The landlord of the Spouter-Inn had recommended us to his cousin Hosea Hussey of the Try Pots, whom he asserted to be the proprietor of one of the best kept hotels in all Nantucket, and moreover he had assured us that cousin Hosea, as he called him, was famous for his chowders. But the directions he had given us about keeping a yellow warehouse on our starboard hand till we opened a white church to the larboard, and then keeping that on the larboard hand till we made a corner three points to the starboard, and that done, then ask the first man we met where the place was: these crooked directions of his very much puzzled us at first, especially as, at the outset, Queequeg insisted that the yellow warehouse must be left on the larboard hand, whereas I had understood Peter Coffin to say it was on the starboard. However, by dint of beating about a little in the dark, and now and then knocking up a peaceable inhabitant to inquire the way, we came to something which there was no mistaking.

Two enormous wooden pots painted black, and suspended by asses' ears, swung from the cross-trees of an old top-mast, planted in front of an old doorway. The horns of the cross-trees were sawed off on the other side, so that this old top-mast looked not a little like a gallows. I could not help staring at this gallows with a vague misgiving. A sort of crick was in my neck as I gazed up to the two remaining horns; yes, *two* of them, one for Queequeg and one for me. It's ominous, thinks I. A Coffin my Innkeeper upon landing in my first whaling port; tombstones staring at me in the whalemen's chapel; and here a gallows! and a pair of prodigious black pots too! Are these last throwing out oblique hints touching Tophet?

I was called from these reflections by the sight of a freckled woman with yellow hair and a yellow gown, standing in the porch of the inn, under a dull red lamp swinging there, carrying on a brisk scolding with a man in a purple shirt.

'Get along with ye,' said she to the man, 'or I'll be combing ye!'

'Come on, Queequeg,' said I, 'all right. There's Mrs Hussey.'

And so it turned out; Mr Hosea Hussey being from home, but leaving Mrs Hussey entirely competent to attend to all his affairs. Upon making known our desires for a supper and a bed, Mrs Hussey ushered us into a little room, and seating us at a table spread with the relics of a recently concluded repast, turned round to us and said – 'Clam or Cod?'

'What's that about Cods, ma'am?' said I.

'Clam or Cod?' she repeated.

'A clam for supper? a cold clam; is that what you mean, Mrs Hussey?' says I; 'but that's a rather cold and clammy reception in the winter time, ain't it, Mrs Hussey?'

But being in a great hurry to resume scolding the man in the purple shirt, and seeming to hear nothing but the word 'clam', Mrs Hussey hurried towards an open door leading to the kitchen, and bawling out 'clam for two', disappeared.

'Queequeg,' said I, 'do you think that we can make out a supper for us both on one clam?'

However, a warm savoury steam from the kitchen served to belie the apparently cheerless prospect before us. But when that smoking chowder came in, the mystery was delightfully explained. Oh, sweet friends! hearken to me. It was made of small juicy clams, scarcely bigger than hazel nuts, mixed with pounded ship biscuit, and salted pork cut up into little flakes; the whole enriched with butter, and plentifully seasoned with pepper and salt. Our appetites being sharpened by the frosty voyage, and in particular, Queequeg seeing his favourite fishing food before him, and the chowder being surpassingly excellent, we despatched it with great expedition: when leaning back a moment and bethinking me of Mrs Hussey's clam and cod announcement, I thought I would try a little experiment. Stepping to the kitchen door, I uttered the word 'cod' and resumed my seat. In a few moments the savoury steam came forth again, but with a different flavour, and in good time a fine cod-chowder was placed before us.

We resumed business; and while plying our spoons in the bowl, thinks I to myself, I wonder now if this here has any effect on the head? What's that stultifying saying about chowder-headed people? 'But look, Queequeg, ain't that a live eel in your bowl? Where's your harpoon?'

Fishiest of all fishy places was the Try Pots, which well deserved its name; for the pots there were always boiling chowders.

Chowder for breakfast, and chowder for dinner, and chowder for supper, till you began to look for fish-bones coming through your clothes. The area before the house was paved with clamshells. Mrs Hussey wore a polished necklace of codfish vertebrae; and Hosea Hussey had his account books bound in superior old shark-skin. There was a fishy flavour to the milk, too, which I could not at all account for, till one morning happening to take a stroll along the beach, I saw Hosea's brindled cow feeding on fish remnants, and marching along the sand with each foot in a cod's decapitated head, looking very slip-shod, I assure ye.

Supper concluded, we received a lamp, and directions from Mrs Hussey concerning the nearest way to bed; but as Queequeg was about to precede me up the stairs, the lady reached forth her arm, and demanded his harpoon; she allowed no harpoon in her chambers. 'Why not?' said I. 'Because it's dangerous,' says she. 'Ever since young Stiggs coming from that unfort'nt v'y'ge of his, when he was gone four years and a half, with only three barrels of *ile*, was found dead in my first floor back, with his harpoon in his side; ever since then I allow no boarders to take sich dangerous weepons in their rooms at night. So, Mr Queequeg, I will just take this here iron, and keep it for you till morning. But the chowder; clam or cod tomorrow for breakfast, men?'

'Both,' says I; 'and let's have a couple of smoked herring by way of variety.'

CHAPTER 14

The Ship

In bed we concocted our plans for the morrow. But to my surprise and no small concern, Queequeg now gave me to understand, that he had been diligently consulting Yojo – the name of his black little god – and Yojo had strongly insisted, that instead of our going together among the whaling-fleet in harbour, and in concert selecting our craft; instead of this, I say, Yojo earnestly enjoined that the selection of the ship should rest wholly with me, inasmuch as Yojo purposed befriending us; and, in order to do so, had already pitched upon a vessel, which, if left to myself, I, Ishmael, should infallibly light upon, and in that vessel I must immediately ship myself, for the present irrespective of Queequeg.

Now, I did not like that plan at all. I had not a little relied upon Queequeg's sagacity to point out the whaler best fitted to carry us and our fortunes securely. But as all my remonstrances produced no effect upon Queequeg, I was obliged to acquiesce. Next morning early, leaving Queequeg shut up with Yojo in our little bedroom – for it seemed that it was some sort of Lent or Ramadan, or day of fasting, humiliation, and prayer with Queequeg and Yojo that day; leaving Queequeg, then, fasting on his tomahawk pipe, and Yojo warming himself at his sacrificial fire of shavings, I sallied out among the shipping. After much prolonged sauntering and many random inquiries, I learnt that there were three ships up for three-years' voyages – the Devil-Dam, the Tit-bit, and the Pequod. *Devil-Dam*, I do not know the origin of; *Tit-bit* is obvious; *Pequod*, you will no doubt remember, was the name of a celebrated tribe of Massachusetts Indians, now extinct as the ancient Medes. I peered and pryed about the Devil-Dam; from her, hopped over to the Tit-bit; and, finally, going on board the Pequod, looked around her for a moment, and then decided that this was the very ship for us.

She was a ship of the old school, rather small if anything; with an old-fashioned claw-footed look about her. Long seasoned and weather-stained in the typhoons and calms of all four oceans, her old hull's complexion was darkened like a French grenadier's, who has alike fought in Egypt and Siberia. Her venerable bows looked bearded. Her masts – cut somewhere on the coast of Japan, where her original ones were lost overboard in a gale – her masts stood stiffly up like the spines of the three old kings of Cologne. Her ancient decks were worn and wrinkled, like the pilgrim-worshipped flag-stone in Canterbury Cathedral where Becket bled. But to all these her old antiquities, were added new and marvellous features, pertaining to the wild business that for more than half a century she had followed. Old Captain Peleg, many years her chief mate, before he commanded another vessel of his own, and now a retired seaman, and one of the principal owners of the Pequod – this old Peleg, during the term of his chief-mateship, had built upon her original grotesqueness, and inlaid it, all over, with a quaintness both of material and device, unmatched by anything except it be Thorkill-Hake's carved buckler or bedstead. She was apparelled like any barbaric Ethiopian emperor, his neck heavy with pendants of polished ivory. She was a cannibal of a craft, tricking herself forth in the chased bones of her enemies. All round, her unpanelled, open bulwarks were garnished like one continuous jaw, with the long sharp teeth of the Sperm Whale, inserted there for pins, to fasten her old hempen thews and tendons to. Those thews ran not through base blocks of landwood, but deftly travelled over sheaves of sea-ivory. Scorning a turnstile wheel at her reverend helm, she sported there a tiller; and that tiller was in one mass, curiously carved from the long narrow lower jaw of her hereditary foe. A noble craft, but somehow a most melancholy! All noble things are touched with that.

Now when I looked about the quarter-deck, for some one having authority, in order to propose myself as a candidate for the voyage, at first I saw nobody; but I could not well overlook a strange sort of tent, or rather wigwam, pitched a little behind the main-mast. It seemed only a temporary erection used in port. It was of a conical shape, some ten feet high; consisting of the long, huge slabs of limber black bone taken from the middle and highest part of the jaws of the Right Whale. Planted with their broad ends on the deck, a circle of these slabs laced together, mutually sloped towards each other, and at the apex united in a tufted point, where the loose hairy fibres waved to and fro like the topknot on some old Pottowottamie Sachem's head. A triangular opening faced towards the bows of the ship, so that the insider commanded a complete view forward.

And half concealed in this queer tenement, I at length found one who by his aspect seemed to have authority; and who, it being noon, and the ship's work suspended, was now enjoying respite from the burden of command. He was seated on an old-fashioned oaken chair wriggling all over with curious carving; and the bottom of which was formed of a stout interlacing of the same elastic stuff of which the wigwam was constructed.

The elderly man I saw was brown and brawny, like most old seamen, and heavily rolled up in blue pilot-cloth, cut in the Quaker style; only there was a fine and almost microscopic net-work of the minutest wrinkles interlacing round his eyes, which must have arisen from his continual sailings in many hard gales, and always looking to windward; for this causes the muscles about the eyes to become pursed together. Such eyewrinkles are very effectual in a scowl.

'Is this the captain of the Pequod?' said I.

'Supposing it be the captain of the Pequod, what dost thou want of him?' he demanded.

'I was thinking of shipping.'

'Thou wast, wast thou? I see thou art no Nantucketer – ever been in a stove boat?'

'No, sir, I never have.'

'Dost know nothing at all about whaling, I dare say – eh?'

'Nothing, sir; but I have no doubt I shall soon learn. I've been several voyages in the merchant service, and I—'

'Marchant service be damned. Talk not that lingo to me. Dost see that leg? – I'll take that leg away from thy stern, if ever thou talkest of the marchant service to me again. Marchant service indeed! I suppose now ye feel considerable proud of having served in those marchant ships. But flukes! man, what makes thee want to go a whaling, eh? – it looks a little suspicious, don't it, eh? – Hast not been a pirate, hast thou? – Didst not rob thy last Captain, didst thou? – Dost not think of murdering the officers when thou gettest to sea?'

I protested my innocence of these things. I saw that under the mask of these half humorous innuendoes, this old seaman, as an insulated Quakerish Nantucketer, was full of his insular prejudices.

'But what takes thee a-whaling? I want to know that before I think of shipping ye.'

'Well, sir, I want to see what whaling is. I want to see the world.'

'Want to see what whaling is, eh? Have ye clapped eye on Captain Ahab?'

'Who is Captain Ahab, sir?'

'Captain Ahab is the Captain of this ship.'

'I am mistaken then. I thought I was speaking to the Captain himself.'

'Thou art speaking to Captain Peleg, young man. It belongs to me and Captain Bildad to see the Pequod fitted out for the voyage, and supplied with all her needs, including crew. We are part owners and agents. But as I was going to say, if thou wanted to know what whaling is, as thou tellest ye do, I can put ye in a way of finding it out before ye bind yourself to it, past backing out. Clap eye on Captain Ahab, young man, and thou wilt find that he has only one leg.'

'What do you mean, sir? Was the other one lost by a whale?'

'Lost by a whale! Young man, come nearer to me: it was devoured, chewed up, crunched by the monstrousest parmacetty that ever chipped a boat! – ah, ah!'

I was a little alarmed by his energy, but said as calmly as I could, 'What you say is no doubt true enough, sir; but how could I know there was any peculiar ferocity in that particular whale, though indeed I might have inferred as much from the simple fact of the accident.'

'Look ye now, young man, thy lungs are a sort of soft, d'ye see; thou dost not talk shark a bit. *Sure*, ye've been to sea before now; sure of that?'

'Sir,' said I, 'I thought I told you that I had been four voyages in the merchant—'

'Hard down out of that! Mind what I said about the marchant service – don't aggravate me – I won't have it. But let us understand each other. I have given thee a hint about what whaling is; do ye yet feel inclined for it?'

'I do, sir.'

'Very good. Now, art thou the man to pitch a harpoon down a live whale's throat, and then jump after it? Answer, quick!'

'I am, sir, if it should be positively indispensable to do so; not to be got rid of, that is; which I don't take to be the fact.'

'Good again. Now then, thou not only wantest to go a-whaling, to find out by experience what whaling is, but ye also want to go in order to see the world? Was not that what ye said? Well then, just step forward there, and take a peep over the weather-bow, and then tell me what ye see there.'

Going forward and glancing over the weather-bow, I perceived that the ship swinging to her anchor with the flood-tide was now obliquely pointing towards the open ocean. The prospect was unlimited, but exceedingly monotonous and forbidding; not the slightest variety that I could see.

'Well, what's the report?' said Peleg when I came back; 'what did ye see?'

'Not much,' I replied – 'nothing but water; considerable horizon though, and there's a squall coming up, I think.'

'Well, what dost thou think then of seeing the world? Do ye wish to go round Cape Horn to see any more of it, eh? Can't ye see the world where you stand?'

I was a little staggered, but go a-whaling I must, and I would; and the Pequod was as good a ship as any – I thought the best – and all this I now repeated to Peleg. Seeing me so determined, he expressed his willingness to ship me.

'And thou mayest as well sign the papers right off,' he added – 'come along with ye.' And so saying, he led the way below deck into the cabin.

Seated on the transom was what seemed to me a most uncommon and surprising figure. It turned out to be Captain Bildad, who along with Captain Peleg was one of the largest owners of the vessel; the other shares being held by a crowd of old annuitants; widows, fatherless children, and chancery wards; each owning about the value of a timber head, or a foot of plank, or a nail or two in the ship. People in Nantucket invest their money in whaling vessels, the same way that you do yours in approved state stocks bringing in good interest.

Now, Bildad, like Peleg, and many other Nantucketers, was a Quaker, the island having been originally settled by that sect; and to this day its inhabitants in general retain in an uncommon measure the peculiarities of the Quaker, only variously and anomalously modified by things altogether alien and heterogeneous. For some of these same Quakers are the most sanguinary of all sailors and whale-hunters. They are fighting Quakers; they are Quakers with a vengeance.

So that there are instances among them of men, who, named with Scripture names – a singularly common fashion on the island – and in childhood naturally imbibing the stately dramatic thee and thou of the Quaker idiom; still, from the audacious, daring, and boundless adventure of their subsequent lives, strangely blend with these unoutgrown peculiarities, a thousand bold dashes of character, not unworthy a Scandinavian sea-king, or a poetical Pagan Roman. And when these things unite in a man of greatly superior natural force, who has also by the stillness and seclusion of many long night-watches in the remotest waters, and beneath constellations never seen here at the north, been led to think untraditionally and independently; receiving all nature's sweet or savage impressions fresh from her own virgin voluntary and confiding breast, and thereby chiefly, but with some help from accidental advantages, to learn a bold and nervous lofty language – that man makes one in a whole nation's census – a mighty pageant creature, formed for noble tragedies. Nor will it at all detract from him, dramatically regarded, if either by birth or other circumstances, he have what seems a half wilful over-ruling morbidness at the bottom of his nature. For all men tragically great are made so through a certain morbidness. Be sure of this, O young ambition, all mortal greatness is but disease.

Like Captain Peleg, Captain Bildad was a well-to-do, retired whaleman. But unlike Captain Peleg – who cared not a rush for what are called serious things – Captain Bildad had not only been originally educated according to the strictest sect of Nantucket

Quakerism, but all his subsequent ocean life, and the sight of many unclad, lovely island creatures, round the Horn – all that had not moved this native born Quaker one single jot. Still, for all this immutableness, was there some lack of common consistency about worthy Captain Peleg. Though refusing to bear arms against land invaders, yet himself had illimitably invaded the Atlantic and Pacific; and though a sworn foe to human bloodshed, yet had he spilled tuns upon tuns of Leviathan gore. How now in the contemplative evening of his days, the pious Bildad reconciled these things in the reminiscence, I do not know; but it did not seem to concern him much, and very probably he had long since come to the sage and sensible conclusion that a man's religion is one thing, and this practical world quite another.

Now Bildad, I am sorry to say, had the reputation of being an incorrigible old hunks, and in his sea-going days, a bitter, hard task-master. For a pious man, especially for a Quaker, he was certainly rather hard-hearted, to say the least. His own person was the exact embodiment of his utilitarian character. On his long, gaunt body, he carried no spare flesh, no superfluous beard, his chin having a soft, economical nap to it, like the worn nap of his broad-brimmed hat.

Such, then, was the person that I saw seated on the transom when I followed Captain Peleg down into the cabin. The space between the decks was small; and there, bolt upright, sat old Bildad, who always sat so, and never leaned, and this to save his coat tails. His broad-brim was placed beside him; his legs were stiffly crossed; his drab vesture was buttoned up to his chin; and spectacles on nose, he seemed absorbed in reading from a ponderous volume.

'Bildad,' cried Captain Peleg, 'at it again, Bildad, eh? Ye have been studying those Scriptures, now, for the last thirty years, to my certain knowledge. How far ye got, Bildad?'

As if long habituated to such profane talk from his old shipmate, Bildad quietly looked up, and seeing me, glanced again inquiringly towards Peleg.

'He says he's our man,' said Peleg, 'he wants to ship.'

'Dost thee?' said Bildad, in a hollow tone.

'I *dost*,' said I unconsciously, he was so intense a Quaker.

'What do ye think of him, Bildad?' said Peleg.

'He'll do,' said Bildad, eyeing me, and then went on spelling away at his book in a mumbling tone quite audible.

I thought him the queerest old Quaker I ever saw, especially as Peleg, his friend and old shipmate, seemed such a blusterer. But I said nothing, only looking round me sharply. Peleg now threw open a chest, and drawing forth the ship's articles, placed pen and ink before him, and seated himself at a little table. I began to think it was high time to settle with myself at what terms I would be willing to engage for the voyage. I was already aware that in the whaling business they paid no wages; but all hands, including the captain, received certain shares of the profits called *lays*, and that these lays were proportioned to the degree of importance pertaining to the respective duties of the ship's company. I was also aware that being a green hand at whaling, my own lay would not be very large; but considering that I was used to the sea, could steer a ship, splice a rope, and all that, I made no doubt that from all I had heard I should be offered at least the 275th lay – that is, the 275th part of the clear nett proceeds of the voyage, whatever that might amount to. And though the 275th lay was rather long lay, yet it was better than nothing; and if we had a lucky voyage, might pretty nearly pay for the clothing I would wear out on it, not to speak of my three years' beef and board, for which I would not have to pay one stiver.

It might be thought that this was a poor way to accumulate a princely fortune – and so it was, a very poor way indeed. But I am one of those that never take on about princely fortunes, and am quite content if the world is ready to board and lodge me, while I am putting up at this grim sign of the Thunder Cloud. Upon the whole, I thought that the 275th lay would be about the fair thing, but I did not know but what the stingy old Bildad might have a mighty deal to say about shipping hands. Now, old Bildad, to my no small surprise, never heeded us, but went on mumbling to himself out of his book, '*Lay* not up for yourselves treasures upon earth, where moth—'

'Well, Captain Bildad,' interrupted Peleg, 'what d'ye say, what lay shall we give this young man?'

'Thou knowest best,' was the sepulchral reply, 'the seven hundred and seventy-seventh wouldn't be too much, would it? – "where moth and rust do corrupt, but *lay*"—'

'Why, blast your eyes, Bildad,' cried Peleg, 'thou dost not want to swindle this young man! he must have more than that. I am going to put him down for the three hundredth, do ye hear that, Bildad! The three hundredth lay, I say.'

Bildad laid down his book, and turning towards him said, 'Captain Peleg, thou hast a generous heart; but thou must consider the duty thou owest to the other owners of this ship – widows and orphans, many of them – and that if we too abundantly reward the labours of this young man, we may be taking the bread from those widows and those orphans. The seven hundred and seventy-seventh lay, Captain Peleg.'

'Thou Bildad!' roared Peleg, starting up and clattering about the cabin. 'Blast ye, Captain Bildad, if I had followed thy advice in these matters, I would afore now had a conscience to lug about that would be heavy enough to founder the largest ship that ever sailed round Cape Horn. Whew!' he whistled at last – 'Now then, my young man, Ishmael's thy name, didn't ye say? Well then, down ye go here, Ishmael, for the three hundredth lay.'

'Captain Peleg,' said I, 'I have a friend with me who wants to ship too – shall I bring him down tomorrow?'

'To be sure,' said Peleg. 'Fetch him along, and we'll look at him. Has he ever whaled it any?'

'Killed more whales than I can count, Captain Peleg.'

'Well, bring him along then.'

And, after signing the papers, off I went. But I had not proceeded far, when I began to bethink me that the captain with whom I was to sail yet remained unseen by me; though, indeed, in many cases, a whale-ship will be completely fitted out, and receive all her crew on board, ere the captain makes himself visible; for sometimes these voyages are so prolonged, and the shore intervals at home so exceedingly brief, that if the captain have a family, or any absorbing concernment of that sort, he does not trouble himself much about his ship in port, but leaves her to the owners till all is ready for sea. However, it is always as well to have a look at him before irrevocably committing yourself into his hands. Turning back I accosted Captain Peleg, inquiring where Captain Ahab was to be found.

'And what dost thou want of Captain Ahab? It's all right enough; thou art shipped.'

'Yes, but I should like to see him.'

'But I don't think thou wilt be able to at present. I don't know exactly what's the matter with him; but he keeps close inside the house; a sort of sick, and yet he don't look so. In fact, he ain't sick; but no, he isn't well either. Any how, young man, he won't always see me, so I don't suppose he will thee. He's a queer man, Captain Ahab – so some think – but a good one. Oh, thou'lt like him well enough; no fear, no fear. He's a grand, ungodly, godlike man, Captain Ahab; doesn't speak much; but, when he does speak, then you may well listen. Mark ye, be forewarned; Ahab's above the common; Ahab's been in colleges, as well as 'mong the cannibals; been used to deeper wonders than the waves; fixed his fiery lance in mightier, stranger foes than whales. His lance! aye, the keenest and the surest that out of all our isle! Oh! he ain't Captain Bildad; no, and he ain't Captain Peleg; *he's Ahab*, boy; and Ahab of old, thou knowest, was a crowned king!'

'And a very vile one. When that wicked king was slain, the dogs, did they not lick his blood?'

'Come hither to me – hither, hither,' said Peleg, with a significance in his eye that almost startled me. 'Look ye, lad; never say that on board the Pequod. Never say it anywhere. Captain Ahab did not name himself. 'Twas a foolish, ignorant whim of his crazy, widowed mother, who died when he was only a twelvemonth old. And yet the old squaw Tistig, at Gay-Head, said that the name would somehow prove prophetic. And, perhaps, other fools like her may tell thee the same. I wish to warn thee. It's a lie. I know Captain Ahab well; I've sailed with him as mate years ago; I know what he is – a good man – not a pious, good man, like Bildad, but a swearing good man – something like me – only there's a good deal more of him. Aye, aye, I know that on the passage home he was a little out of his mind for a spell; but it was the sharp shooting pains in his bleeding stump that brought that about, as anyone might see. I know, too, that ever since he lost his leg last voyage by that accursed whale, he's been desperate moody, and savage sometimes; but that will all pass off. And once for all, let me tell thee and assure thee, young man, it's better to sail with a moody good captain than a laughing bad one. So good-bye to thee – and wrong not Captain Ahab, because he happens to have a wicked name. Besides, my boy, he has a wife – not three voyages wedded – a sweet, resigned girl. Think of that; by that sweet girl that old man has a child: hold ye then there can be any utter, hopeless harm in Ahab? No, no, my lad; stricken, blasted, if he be, Ahab has his humanities!'

CHAPTER 15

The Ramadan

As Queequeg's Ramadan, or Fasting and Humiliation, was to continue all day, I did not choose to disturb him till towards nightfall; for I cherish the greatest respect towards everybody's religious obligations, and could not find it in my heart to undervalue even a congregation of ants worshipping a toad-stool; or those other creatures in certain parts of our earth, who with a degree of footmanism quite unprecedented in other planets, bow down before the torso of a deceased landed proprietor merely on account of the inordinate possessions yet owned and rented in his name.

I say, we good Presbyterian Christians should be charitable in these things, and not fancy ourselves so vastly superior to other mortals, pagans and what not, because of their half-crazy conceits on these subjects. There was Queequeg, now, certainly entertaining the most absurd notions about Yojo and his Ramadan; but what of that? Queequeg seemed to be content; and there let him rest. All our arguing with him would not avail; let him be, I say: and Heaven have mercy on us all – Presbyterians and Pagans alike – for we are all somehow dreadfully cracked about the head, and sadly need mending.

CHAPTER 16

His Mark

As we were walking down the end of the wharf towards the ship, Queequeg carrying his harpoon, Captain Peleg in his gruff voice loudly hailed us from his wigwam, saying he let no cannibals on board, unless they previously produced their papers.

'What do you mean by that, Captain Peleg?' said I, now jumping on the bulwarks, and leaving my comrade standing on the wharf.

'I mean,' he replied, 'he must show his papers.'

'Yea,' said Captain Bildad in his hollow voice, sticking his head from behind Peleg's, out of the wigwam. 'He must show that he's converted. Son of darkness,' he added, turning to Queequeg, 'art thou at present in communion with any Christian church?'

'Why,' said I, 'he's a member of the first Congregational Church.' Here be it said, that many tattooed savages sailing in Nantucket ships at last come to be converted into the churches.

'First Congregational Church,' cried Bildad, 'what! that worships in Deacon Deuteronomy Coleman's meeting-house?', and so saying came out of the wigwam, and leaning stiffly over the bulwarks, took a good long look at Queequeg.

'How long hath he been a member?' he then said, turning to me; 'not very long, I rather guess, young man. Do tell, now,' cried Bildad, 'is this Philistine a regular member of Deacon Deuteronomy's meeting? I never saw him going there, and I pass it every Lord's day.'

'I don't know anything about Deacon Deuteronomy or his

meeting,' said I, 'all I know is, that Queequeg here is a born member of the First Congregational Church. He is a deacon himself, Queequeg is.'

'Young man,' said Bildad sternly, 'thou art skylarking with me – explain thyself, thou young Hittite. What church dost thee mean? answer me.'

Finding myself thus hard pushed, I replied, 'I mean, sir, the same ancient Catholic Church to which you and I, and Captain Peleg there, and Queequeg here, and all of us, and every mother's son and soul of us belong; the great and everlasting First Congregation of this whole worshipping world; we all belong to that; only some of us cherish some queer crotchets noways touching the grand belief; in *that* we all join hands.'

'Splice, thou mean'st *splice* hands,' cried Peleg, drawing nearer. 'Young man, you'd better ship for a missionary, instead of a foremast hand; I never heard a better sermon. Come aboard, come aboard; never mind about the papers. I say, tell Quohog there – what's that you call him? tell Quohog to step along. By the great anchor, what a harpoon he's got there! looks like good stuff that; and he handles it about right. I say, Quohog, or whatever your name is, did you ever stand in the head of a whale-boat? did you ever strike a fish?'

Without saying a word, Queequeg jumped upon the bulwarks, from thence into the bows of one of the whale-boats hanging to the side; and then bracing his left knee, and poising his harpoon, cried out in some such way as this:

'Cap'ain, you see him small drop tar on water dere? You see him? well, spose him one whale eye, well, den!' and taking sharp aim at it, he darted the iron right over old Bildad's broad brim, clean across the ship's decks, and struck the glistening tar spot out of sight.

'Now,' said Queequeg, quietly hauling in the line, 'spos-ee him whale-e eye; why, dad whale dead.'

'Quick,' said Peleg, who, aghast at the close vicinity of the flying harpoon, had retreated towards the cabin gangway. 'Quick, I say, you Bildad, and get the ship's papers. We must have Hedgehog there, I mean Quohog, in one of our boats. Look ye, Quohog, we'll give ye the ninetieth lay, and that's more than ever was given a harpooneer yet out of Nantucket.'

So down we went into the cabin, and to my great joy Queequeg was soon enrolled among the ship's company.

When all preliminaries were over and Peleg had got everything ready for signing, he turned to me and said, 'I guess, Quohog there don't know how to write, does he? I say, Quohog, blast ye! dost thou sign thy name or make thy mark?'

But at this question, Queequeg, who had twice or thrice before taken part in similar ceremonies, looked no ways abashed; but taking the offered pen, copied upon the paper, in the proper place, an exact counterpart of a queer round figure which was tattooed upon his arm.

CHAPTER 17

The Prophet

'Shipmates, have ye shipped in that ship?'

Queequeg and I had just left the Pequod, and were sauntering away from the water when the above words were put to us by a stranger, who levelled his massive forefinger at the vessel in question. He was but shabbily apparelled in faded jacket and patched trowsers; a rag of a black handkerchief investing his neck. A confluent small-pox had in all directions flowed over his face, and left it like the complicated ribbed bed of a torrent, when the rushing waters have been dried up.

'Have ye shipped in her?' he repeated.

'You mean the ship Pequod, I suppose,' said I, trying to gain a little more time for an uninterrupted look at him.

'Aye, the Pequod – that ship there,' he said.

'Yes,' said I, 'we have just signed the articles.'

'Anything down there about your souls?'

'About what?'

'Oh, perhaps you hav'n't got any,' he said quickly. 'No matter though, I know many chaps that hav'n't got any – good luck to 'em; and they are all the better off for it. A soul's a sort of a fifth wheel to a wagon.'

'What are you jabbering about, shipmate?' said I.

'*He's* got enough, though, to make up for all deficiencies of that sort in other chaps,' abruptly said the stranger, placing a nervous emphasis upon the word *he*.

'Queequeg,' said I, 'let's go; this fellow has broken loose from somewhere; he's talking about something and somebody we don't know.'

'Stop!' cried the stranger. 'Ye said true – ye hav'n't seen Old Thunder yet, have ye?'

'Who's Old Thunder?' said I, again riveted with the insane earnestness of his manner.

'Captain Ahab. Among some of us old sailor chaps, he goes by that name. Ye hav'n't seen him yet, have ye?'

'No, we hav'n't. He's sick they say, but is getting better, and will be all right again before long.'

'All right again before long!' laughed the stranger, with a derisive sort of laugh. 'Look ye; when Captain Ahab is all right, then this left arm of mine will be all right; not before.'

'What do you know about him?'

'What did they *tell* you about him? Say that!'

'They didn't tell much of anything about him; only I've heard that he's a good whale-hunter, and a good captain to his crew.'

'That's true, that's true. But you must jump when he gives an order. Step and growl; growl and go – that's the word with Captain Ahab. But nothing about that thing that happened to him off Cape Horn, long ago, when he lay like dead for three days and nights; nothing about that deadly skrimmage with the Spaniard afore the altar in Santa? – heard nothing about that, eh? Nothing about the silver calabash he spat into? And nothing about his losing his leg last voyage, according to the prophecy. Didn't ye hear a word about them matters and something more, eh? No, I don't think ye did; how could ye? Who knows it? Not all Nantucket, I guess. But hows'ever, ye've heard tell about the leg, and how he lost it, I dare say. Oh yes, *that* every one knows a'most – I mean they know he's only one leg; and that a parmacetti took the other off.'

'My friend,' said I, 'if you are speaking of Captain Ahab, of that ship there, the Pequod, then let me tell you, that I know all about the loss of his leg.'

'*All* about it, eh – sure you do? – all?'

'Pretty sure.'

With finger pointed and eye levelled at the Pequod, the stranger stood a moment; then starting a little, said: 'Ye've shipped, have ye? Names down on the papers? Well, well, what's signed, is signed; and what's to be, will be; and then again, perhaps it wont be, after all. Any how, it's all fixed and arranged a'ready; and some sailors or other must go with him, I suppose; as well these as any other men, God pity 'em! Morning to ye, shipmates, morning; the ineffable heavens bless ye; I'm sorry I stopped ye.'

'Look here, friend,' said I, 'if you have anything important to tell us, out with it; but if you are only trying to bamboozle us, you are mistaken in your game. It is the easiest thing in the world for a man to look as if he had a great secret in him. Come along, Queequeg, let's leave this crazy man. But stop, tell me your name, will you?'

'Elijah.'

Elijah! thought I, and we walked away, both commenting, after each other's fashion, upon this ragged old sailor; and agreed that he was a humbug, trying to be a bugbear.

CHAPTER 18

All Astir

A day or two passed, and there was great activity aboard the Pequod. Not only were the old sails being mended, but new sails were coming on board, and bolts of canvas, and coils of rigging; in short, everything betokened that the ship's preparations were hurrying to a close. Captain Peleg seldom or never went ashore: Bildad did all the purchasing and providing at the stores; and the men employed in the hold and on the rigging were working till long after night-fall.

Every one knows what a multitude of things – beds, saucepans, knives and forks, shovels and tongs, napkins, nut-crackers, and what not, are indispensable to the business of housekeeping. Just so with whaling, which necessitates a three-years' housekeeping upon the wide ocean, far from all grocers, coster-mongers, doctors, bakers, and bankers. And though this also holds true of merchant vessels, yet not by any means to the same extent as with whalemen. For besides the great length of the whaling voyage, the numerous articles peculiar to the prosecution of the fishery, and the impossibility of replacing them at the remote harbours usually frequented, it must be remembered, that of all ships, whaling vessels are the most exposed to accidents of all kinds, and especially to the destruction and loss of the very things upon which the success of the voyage most depends. Hence, the spare boats, spare spars, and spare lines and harpoons, and spare everythings, almost, but a spare Captain and duplicate ship.

At the period of our arrival at the Island, the heaviest storage of the Pequod had been almost completed; but for some time there was a continual fetching and carrying on board of divers odds and ends of things. Chief among those who did this fetching and carrying was Captain Bildad's sister, a lean old lady of a most determined and indefatigable spirit, but withal very kindhearted. At one time she would come on board with a jar of pickles for the steward's pantry; another time with a bunch of quills for the chief mate's desk, where he kept his log; a third time with a roll of flannel for the small of some one's rheumatic back. Never did any woman better deserve her name, which was Charity – Aunt Charity, as everybody called her.

But at last it was given out that next day the ship would sail. So next morning, Queequeg and I took a very early start.

CHAPTER 19

Going Aboard

It was nearly six o'clock, but only grey imperfect misty dawn, when we drew nigh the wharf.

'There are some sailors running ahead there, if I see right,' said I to Queequeg, 'she's off by sunrise, I guess; come on!'

'Avast!' cried a voice, whose owner at the same time coming close behind us, laid a hand upon both our shoulders, and then insinuating himself between us, stood peering from Queequeg to me. It was Elijah.

'Going aboard?'

'Hands off, will you,' said I.

'Lookee here,' said Queequeg, 'go 'way!'

'Aint going aboard, then?'

'Yes, we are,' said I, 'but what business is that of yours? Do you know, Mr Elijah, that I consider you a little impertinent?'

'No, no, no; I wasn't aware of that,' said Elijah, slowly and wonderingly.

'Elijah,' said I, 'you will oblige my friend and me by withdrawing. We are going to the Indian and Pacific oceans, and would prefer not to be detained.'

'Ye be, be ye? Coming back afore breakfast?'

'He's cracked, Queequeg,' said I, 'come on.'

'Holloa!' cried stationary Elijah, hailing us when we had removed a few paces.

'Never mind him,' said I, 'Queequeg, come on.'

But he stole up to us again, and suddenly clapping his hand on my shoulder, said – 'Did ye see anything looking like men going towards that ship a while ago?'

Struck by this plain matter-of-fact question, I answered, saying, 'Yes, I thought I did see four or five men; but it was too dim to be sure.'

'Very dim, very dim,' said Elijah. 'Morning to ye.'

Once more we quitted him; but once more he came softly after us; 'See if you can find 'em now, will ye?'

'Find who?'

'Morning to ye! morning to ye!' he rejoined, again moving off. 'Oh! I was going to warn ye against – but never mind, never mind – it's all one, all in the family too; sharp frost this morning, aint it? Good-bye to ye. Shan't see ye again very soon, I guess; unless it's before the Grand Jury.' And with these cracked words he finally departed, leaving me, for the moment, in no small wonderment at his frantic impudence.

At last, stepping on board the Pequod, we found everything in profound quiet, not a soul moving. The cabin entrance was locked within; the hatches were all on, and lumbered with coils of rigging. Going forward to the forecastle, we found the slide of the scuttle open. Seeing a light, we went down, and found only an old rigger there, wrapped in a tattered pea-jacket. He was thrown at whole length upon two chests, his face downwards and inclosed in his folded arms. The profoundest slumber slept upon him.

'Those sailors we saw, Queequeg, where can they have gone to?' said I, looking dubiously at the sleeper. But it seemed that, when on the wharf, Queequeg had not at all noticed what I now alluded to; hence I would have thought myself to have been optically deceived in that matter, were it not for Elijah's otherwise inexplicable question. But I beat the thing down and without more ado, sat quietly down.

Queequeg removed himself to just beyond the head of the sleeper, and lighted his tomahawk pipe. I sat at the feet. We kept the pipe passing over the sleeper, from one to the other. The strong vapour now began to tell upon him. He revolved over once or twice; then sat up and rubbed his eyes.

'Holloa!' he breathed at last, 'who be ye smokers?'

'Shipped men,' answered I, 'when does she sail?'

'Aye, aye, she sails today. The captain came aboard last night.'

'What Captain? – Ahab?'

'Who but him indeed?'

I was going to ask him further questions concerning Ahab, when we heard a noise on deck.

'Holloa! Starbuck's astir,' said the rigger. 'He's a lively chief mate, that; good man, and a pious; but all alive now, I must turn to.' So saying he went on deck, and we followed.

It was now clear sunrise. Soon the crew came on board in twos and threes; the riggers bestirred themselves; the mates were actively engaged; and several of the shore people were busy in bringing various last things on board.

Meanwhile Captain Ahab remained invisibly enshrined within his cabin.

CHAPTER 20

Merry Christmas

At length, towards noon, upon the final dismissal of the ship's riggers, and after the Pequod had been hauled out from the wharf, the two captains, Peleg and Bildad, issued from the cabin, and turning to the chief mate, Peleg said:

'Now, Mr Starbuck, Captain Ahab is all ready – just spoke to him – nothing more to be got from shore, eh? Well, call all hands, then. Muster 'em aft here – blast 'em!'

'No need of profane words, however great the hurry, Peleg,' said Bildad, 'but away with thee, friend Starbuck, and do our bidding.'

How now! Here upon the very point of starting for the voyage, Captain Peleg and Captain Bildad were going it with a high hand on the quarter-deck, just as if they were to be joint-commanders at sea, as well as to all appearances in port. And, as for Captain Ahab, no sign of him was yet to be seen. But then, the idea was that his presence was by no means necessary in getting the ship under weigh, and steering her well out to sea. Indeed, that was not at all his proper business, but the pilot's – so they said – therefore, Captain Ahab stayed below. And all this seemed natural enough.

But there was not much chance to think over the matter, for Captain Peleg was now all alive.

'Aft here, ye sons of bachelors,' he cried, as the sailors lingered at the main-mast. 'Mr Starbuck, drive 'em aft.'

'Strike the tent there!' – was the next order. As I hinted before, this whalebone marquee was never pitched except in port; and on board the Pequod the order to strike the tent was well known to be the next thing to heaving up the anchor.

'Man the capstan! Blood and thunder! – jump!' – was the next command, and the crew sprang for the handspikes. Now, in getting under weigh, the station generally occupied by the pilot is the forward part of the ship. And here Bildad, who, with Peleg, be it known, in addition to his other offices, was one of the licensed pilots of the port – he being suspected to have got himself made a pilot in order to save the Nantucket pilot-fee to all the ships he was concerned in, for he never piloted any other craft – Bildad, I say, might now be seen actively engaged in looking over the bows for the approaching anchor, and at intervals singing what seemed a dismal stave of psalmody, to cheer the hands at the windlass, who roared forth some sort of a chorus about the girls in Booble Alley.

Meantime, overseeing the other part of the ship, Captain Peleg ripped and swore astern in the most frightful manner. I almost thought he would sink the ship before the anchor could be got up.

At last the anchor was up, the sails were set, and off we glided. It was a short, cold Christmas; and as the short northern day merged into night, we found ourselves almost broad upon the wintry ocean, whose freezing spray cased us in ice, as in polished armour. The long rows of teeth on the bulwarks glistened in the moonlight; and like the white ivory tusks of some huge elephant, vast curving icicles depended from the bows.

Lank Bildad, as pilot, headed the first watch, and ever and anon, as the old craft deep dived into the green seas, and sent the shivering frost all over her, and the winds howled, and the cordage rang, his steady notes were heard –

'Sweet fields beyond the swelling flood,
    Stand dressed in living green.
So to the Jews old Canaan stood,
    While Jordan rolled between.'

Never did those sweet words sound more sweetly to me than then. They were full of hope and fruition. Spite of this frigid winter night in the boisterous Atlantic, spite of my wet feet and wetter jacket, there was yet, it then seemed to me, many a pleasant haven in store.

At last we gained such an offing, that the two pilots were needed no longer. The stout sail-boat that had accompanied us began ranging alongside.

It was curious and not unpleasing, how Peleg and Bildad were affected at this juncture, especially Captain Bildad. For loath to depart, yet; very loath to leave, for good, a ship bound on so long and perilous a voyage – beyond both stormy Capes; a ship in which some thousands of his hard earned dollars were invested; a ship, in which an old shipmate sailed as captain; a man almost as old as he; loath to say good-bye to a thing so every way brimful of every interest to him – poor old Bildad lingered long; paced the deck with anxious strides; and looked to windward; looked towards the wide and endless waters, only bounded by the far-off unseen Eastern Continents.

As for Peleg himself, there was a tear twinkling in his eye, when the lantern came too near. But, at last, he turned to his comrade, with a final sort of look about him – 'Captain Bildad – come, old shipmate, we must go. Back the main-yard there! Boat ahoy! Stand by to come close alongside, now! Careful, careful! – come, Bildad. Luck to ye, Starbuck – luck to ye, Mr Stubb – luck to ye, Mr Flask – good-bye, and good luck to ye all – and this day three years I'll have a hot supper smoking for ye in old Nantucket. Hurrah and away!'

'God bless ye, and have ye in His holy keeping, men,' murmured old Bildad, almost incoherently. 'I hope ye'll have fine weather now, so that Captain Ahab may soon be moving among ye – a pleasant sun is all he needs, and ye'll have plenty of them in the tropic voyage ye go. Be careful in the hunt, ye mates. Don't stave the boats needlessly, ye harpooneers; good white cedar plank is raised full three per cent within the year. Don't forget your prayers, either. Mr Starbuck, mind that cooper don't waste the spare staves. Oh! the sail-needles are in the green locker! Don't whale it too much a' Lord's days, men; but don't miss a fair chance either, that's rejecting Heaven's good gifts. Have an eye to the molasses tierce, Mr Stubb; it was a little leaky, I thought. If ye touch at the islands, Mr Flask, beware of fornication. Good-bye, good-bye! Don't keep that cheese too long down in the hold, Mr Starbuck; it'll spoil. Be careful with the butter—'

'Come, come, Captain Bildad; stop palavering – away!' and with that, Peleg hurried him over the side, and both dropped into the boat. Ship and boat diverged; the cold, damp night breeze blew between; a screaming gull flew overhead; the two hulls wildly rolled; we gave three heavy-hearted cheers, and blindly plunged like fate into the lone Atlantic.

CHAPTER 21

The Advocate

As Queequeg and I are now fairly embarked in this business of whaling; and as this business of whaling has somehow come to be regarded among landsmen as a rather unpoetical and disreputable pursuit; therefore, I am all anxiety to convince ye, ye landsmen, of the injustice hereby done to us hunters of whales.

In the first place, it may be deemed almost superfluous to establish the fact, that among people at large, the business of whaling is not accounted on a level with what are called the liberal professions. If a stranger were introduced into any miscellaneous metropolitan society, it would but slightly advance the general opinion of his merits, were he presented to the company as a harpooneer, say; and if in emulation of the naval officers he should append the initials S.W.F. (Sperm Whale Fishery) to his visiting card, such a procedure would be deemed pre-eminently presuming and ridiculous.

Doubtless one leading reason why the world declines honouring us whalemen is this: they think that, at best, our vocation amounts to a butchering sort of business. Butchers we are, that is true. But butchers, also, and butchers of the bloodiest badge have been all Martial Commanders whom the world invariably delights to honour. And as for the matter of the alleged uncleanliness of our business, ye shall soon be initiated into certain facts hitherto pretty generally unknown, and which, upon the whole, will triumphantly plant the sperm whale-ship at least among the cleanliest things of this tidy earth. But even granting the charge in question to be true; what disordered slippery decks of a whale-ship are comparable to the unspeakable carrion of those battle-fields from which so many soldiers return to drink in all ladies' plaudits? And if the idea of peril so much enhances the popular conceit of the soldier's profession; let me assure ye that many a veteran who has freely marched up to a battery, would recoil at the apparition of the Sperm Whale's vast tail, fanning into eddies the air over his head. For what are the comprehensible terrors of man compared with the interlinked terrors and wonders of God!

But, though the world scouts at us whale hunters, yet does it unwittingly pay us the profoundest homage; yea, an all-abounding adoration! for almost all the tapers, lamps, and candles that burn round the globe, burn, as before so many shrines, to our glory!

But look at this matter in other lights; weigh it in all sorts of scales; see what we whalemen are, and have been.

Why did the Dutch in De Witt's time have admirals of their whaling fleets? Why did Louis XVI of France, at his own personal expense, fit out whaling ships from Dunkirk, and politely invite to that town some score or two of families from our own island of

Nantucket? Why did Britain between the years 1750 and 1788 pay to her whalemen in bounties upwards of £1,000,000? And lastly, how comes it that we whalemen of America now outnumber all the rest of the banded whalemen in the world; sail a navy of upwards of seven hundred vessels; manned by eighteen thousand men; yearly consuming 4,000,000 of dollars; the ships worth, at the time of sailing, $20,000,000; and every year importing into our harbours a well reaped harvest of $7,000,000. How comes all this, if there be not something puissant in whaling?

But this is not the half; look again.

I freely assert, that the cosmopolite philosopher cannot, for his life, point out one single peaceful influence, which within the last sixty years has operated more potentially upon the whole broad world, than the high and mighty business of whaling. One way and another, it has begotten events so remarkable in themselves, and so continuously momentous in their sequential issues, that whaling may well be regarded as that Egyptian mother, who bore offspring themselves pregnant from her womb. It would be a hopeless, endless task to catalogue all these things. Let a handful suffice. For many years past the whale-ship has been the pioneer in ferreting out the remotest and least known parts of the earth. If American and European men-of-war now peacefully ride in once savage harbours, let them fire salutes to the honour and the glory of the whale-ship, which originally showed them the way, and first interpreted between them and the savages. They may celebrate as they will the heroes of Exploring Expeditions, your Cookes, your Krusensterns; but I say that scores of anonymous Captains have sailed out of Nantucket, that were as great, and greater than your Cooke and your Krusenstern. For in their succourless empty-handedness, they, in the heathenish sharked waters, and by the beaches of unrecorded, javelin islands, battled with virgin wonders and terrors that Cooke with all his marines and muskets would not willingly have dared. All that is made such a flourish of in the old South Sea Voyages, those things were but the lifetime commonplaces of our heroic Nantucketers. Ah, the world! Oh, the world!

Until the whale fishery rounded Cape Horn, no commerce but colonial, scarcely any intercourse but colonial, was carried on between Europe and the long line of the opulent Spanish provinces on the Pacific coast. It was the whaleman who first broke through the jealous policy of the Spanish crown, touching those colonies; and, if space permitted, it might be shown how from those whalemen eventuated the liberation of Peru, Chili, and Bolivia from the yoke of Old Spain, and the establishment of the eternal democracy in those parts.

That great America on the other side of the sphere, Australia, was given to the enlightened world by the whaleman. After its first blunder-born discovery by a Dutchman, all other ships long shunned those shores as pestiferously barbarous; but the whaleship touched there. The whale-ship is the true mother of that now mighty colony. Moreover, in the infancy of the first Australian settlement, the emigrants were several times saved from starvation by the benevolent biscuit of the whale-ship luckily dropping an anchor in their waters. The uncounted isles of all Polynesia confess the same truth, and do commercial homage to the whale-ship, that cleared the way for the missionary and the merchant, and in many cases carried the missionaries to their first destinations. If that double-bolted land, Japan, is ever to become hospitable, it is the whale-ship alone to whom the credit will be due; for already she is on the threshold.

But if, in the face of all this, you still declare that whaling has no noble associations connected with it, then am I ready to shiver fifty lances with you there, and unhorse you with a split helmet every time.

Whaling is not respectable.

Whaling not respectable? Whaling is imperial! By old English statutory law, the whale is declared 'a royal fish'.

There is no real dignity in whaling.

No dignity in whaling? The dignity of our calling the very heavens attest. Cetus is a constellation in the South! No more! Drive down your hat in presence of the Czar, and take it off to Queequeg! No more! I know a man that, in his lifetime, has taken three hundred and fifty whales. I account that man more honourable than that great captain of antiquity who boasted of taking as many walled towns.

And, as for me, if, by any possibility, there be any as yet undiscovered prime thing in me; if I shall ever deserve any real repute in that small but high hushed world which I might not be unreasonably ambitious of; if hereafter I shall do anything that, upon the whole, a man might rather have done than to have left undone; if, at my death, my executors, or more properly my creditors, find any precious MSS in my desk, then here I ascribe all the honour and glory to whaling; for a whale-ship was my Yale College and my Harvard.

CHAPTER 22

Knights and Squires

The chief mate of the Pequod was Starbuck, a native of Nantucket, and a Quaker by descent. He was a long, earnest man, and though born on an icy coast, seemed well adapted to endure hot latitudes, his flesh being hard as twice-baked biscuit. He must have been born in some time of general drought and famine. Only some thirty arid summers had he seen; those summers had dried up all his physical superfluousness. But this, his thinness, so to speak, seemed no more the token of wasting anxieties and cares, than it seemed the indication of any bodily blight. It was merely the condensation of the man. He was by no means ill-looking. His pure tight skin was an excellent fit; and closely wrapped up in it, and embalmed with inner health and strength, like a revivified Egyptian, this Starbuck seemed prepared to endure for long ages to come. Looking into his eyes, you seemed to see there the yet lingering images of those thousandfold perils he had calmly confronted through life. A staid, steadfast man, whose life for the most part was a telling pantomime of action, and not a tame chapter of sounds. Yet, for all his hardy sobriety and fortitude, there were certain qualities in him which at times affected, and in some cases seemed well nigh to overbalance all the rest. Uncommonly conscientious for a seaman, and endued with a deep natural reverence, the wild watery loneliness of his life did therefore strongly incline him to superstition; but to that sort of superstition, which in some organizations seems rather to spring, somehow, from intelligence than from ignorance. Outward portents and inward presentiments were his. And if at times these things bent the welded iron of his soul, much more did his faraway domestic memories of his young Cape wife and child tend to bend him still more from the original ruggedness of his nature, and open him still further to those latent influences which, in some honest-hearted men, restrain the gush of dare-devil daring, so often evinced by others in the more perilous vicissitudes of the fishery. 'I will have no man in my boat,' said Starbuck, 'who is not afraid of a whale.' By this, he seemed to mean that an utterly fearless man is a far more dangerous comrade than a coward.

'Aye, aye,' said Stubb, the second mate, 'Starbuck, there, is as careful a man as you'll find anywhere in this fishery.' But we shall ere long see what that word 'careful' precisely means when used by a man like Stubb, or almost any other whale hunter.

Starbuck was no crusader after perils; in him courage was not a sentiment; but a thing simply useful to him, and always at hand upon all mortally practical occasions. Besides, he thought, perhaps, that in this business of whaling, courage was one of the great staple outfits of the ship, like her beef and her bread, and not to be foolishly wasted. Wherefore he had no fancy for lowering for whales after sun-down; nor for persisting in fighting a fish that too much persisted in fighting him. For, thought Starbuck, I am here in this critical ocean to kill whales for my living, and not to be killed by them for theirs; and that hundreds of men had been so killed Starbuck well knew. What doom was his own father's? Where, in the bottomless deeps, could he find the torn limbs of his brother?

With memories like these in him, and, moreover, given to a

certain superstitiousness, as has been said; the courage of this Starbuck which could, nevertheless, still flourish, must indeed have been extreme.

CHAPTER 23

Knights and Squires

Stubb was the second mate. He was a native of Cape Cod; and hence was called a Cape-Cod-man. A happy-go-lucky; neither craven nor valiant; taking perils as they came with an indifferent air; and while engaged in the most imminent crisis of the chase, toiling away, calm and collected as a journeyman joiner engaged for the year. Good-humoured, easy, and careless, he presided over his whale-boat as if the most deadly encounter were but a dinner, and his crew all invited guests. He was as particular about the comfortable arrangement of his part of the boat, as an old stage-driver is about the snugness of his box. When close to the whale, in the very death-lock of the fight, he handled his unpitying lance coolly and off-handedly. He would hum over his old rigadig tunes while flank and flank with the most exasperated monster. Long usage had, for this Stubb, converted the jaws of death into an easy chair. What he thought of death itself, there is no telling. Whether he ever thought of it at all, might be a question; but, if he ever did chance to cast his mind that way, no doubt like a good sailor, he took it to be a sort of call of the watch to tumble aloft, and bestir themselves there, about something which he would find out when he obeyed the order, and not sooner.

What, perhaps with other things, made Stubb such an easygoing, unfearing man, so cheerily trudging off with the burden of life in a world full of grave peddlers, must have been his pipe. For, like his nose, his short, black little pipe was one of the regular features of his face. You would almost as soon have expected him to turn out of his bunk without his nose as without his pipe. He kept a whole row of pipes there ready loaded, stuck in a rack, within easy reach of his hand; and, whenever he turned in, he smoked them all out in succession, then loading them again to be in readiness anew. For, when Stubb dressed, instead of first putting his legs into his trowsers, he put his pipe into his mouth

The third mate was Flask, a native of Tisbury, in Martha's Vineyard. A short, stout, ruddy young fellow, very pugnacious concerning whales, who somehow seemed to think that the great Leviathans had personally and hereditarily affronted him; and therefore it was a sort of point of honour with him, to destroy them whenever encountered. So utterly lost was he to all sense of reverence for the many marvels of their majestic bulk and mystic ways; and so dead to anything like an apprehension of any possible danger from encountering them; that in his poor opinion, the wondrous whale was but a species of magnified mouse, or at least water-rat, requiring only a little circumvention and some small application of time and trouble in order to kill and boil. This ignorant, unconscious fearlessness of his made him a little waggish in the matter of whales; he followed these fish for the fun of it; and a three years' voyage round Cape Horn was only a jolly joke that lasted that length of time. As a carpenter's nails are divided into wrought nails and cut nails, so mankind may be similarly divided. Little Flask was one of the wrought ones; made to clinch tight and last long. They called him King-Post on board of the Pequod; because, in form, he could be well likened to the short, square timber known by that name in Arctic whalers; and which by the means of many radiating side timbers inserted into it, serves to brace the ship against the icy concussions of those battering seas.

Now these three mates were momentous men. They it was who by universal prescription commanded three of the Pequod's boats as headsmen. In that grand order of battle in which Captain Ahab would probably marshal his forces to descend on the whales, these three headsmen were as captains of companies.

And since in this famous fishery, each mate or headsman, like a Gothic Knight of old, is always accompanied by his boat-steerer or harpooneer, who in certain conjunctures provides him with a fresh lance, when the former one has been badly twisted, or elbowed in the assault; and moreover, as there generally subsists between the two a close intimacy and friendliness; it is therefore but meet, that in this place we set down who the Pequod's harpooneers were, and to what headsman each of them belonged.

First of all was Queequeg, whom Starbuck, the chief mate, had selected for his squire. But Queequeg is already known.

Next was Tashtego, an unmixed Indian from Gay Head, the most westerly promontory of Martha's Vineyard, where there still exists the last remnant of a village of red men, which has long supplied the neighbouring island of Nantucket with many of her most daring harpooneers. In the fishery, they usually go by the generic name of Gay-Headers. Tashtego's long, lean, sable hair, his high cheek bones, and black rounding eyes – for an Indian, Oriental in their largeness, but Antarctic in their glittering expression – all this sufficiently proclaimed him an inheritor of the unvitiated blood of those proud warrior hunters, who, in quest of the great New England moose, had scoured, bow in hand, the aboriginal forests of the main. But no longer snuffing in the trail of the wild beasts of the woodland, Tashtego now hunted in the wake of the great whales of the sea; the unerring harpoon of the son fitly replacing the infallible arrow of the sires. To look at the tawny brawn of his lithe snaky limbs, you would almost have credited the superstitions of some of the earlier Puritans, and half believed this wild Indian to be a son of the Prince of the Powers of the Air. Tashtego was Stubb's squire.

Third among the harpooneers was Daggoo, a gigantic, coal-black negro-savage, with a lion-like tread – an Ahasuerus to behold. Suspended from his ears were two golden hoops, so large that the sailors called them ring-bolts, and would talk of securing the top-sail halyards to them. In his youth Daggoo had voluntarily shipped on board of a whaler, lying in a lonely bay on his native coast. And never having been anywhere in the world but in Africa, Nantucket, and the pagan harbours most frequented by whalemen, Daggoo retained all his barbaric virtues, and erect as a giraffe, moved about the decks in all the pomp of six feet five in his socks. There was a corporeal humility in looking up at him; and a white man standing before him seemed a white flag come to beg truce of a fortress. This imperial negro, Ahasuerus Daggoo, was the Squire of little Flask, who looked like a chess-man beside him. As for the residue of the Pequod's company, be it said, that at the present day not one in two of the many thousand men before the mast employed in the American whale fishery are Americans born, though pretty nearly all the officers are. Herein it is the same with the American whale fishery as with the American army and military and merchant navies, and the engineering forces employed in the construction of the American Canals and Railroads. The same, I say, because in all these cases the native American liberally provides the brains, the rest of the world as generously supplying the muscles. No small number of these whaling seamen belong to the Azores, where the outward bound Nantucket whalers frequently touch to augment their crews from the hardy peasants of those rocky shores. In like manner, the Greenland whalers sailing out of Hull or London, put in at the Shetland Islands, to receive the full complement of their crew. Upon the passage homewards, they drop them there again. How it is, there is no telling, but Islanders seem to make the best whalemen. They were nearly all Islanders in the Pequod, *Isolatoes* too, I call such, not acknowledging the common continent of men, but each *Isolato* living on a separate continent of his own. Yet now, federated along one keel, what a set these Isolatoes were! An Anacharsis Clootz deputation from all the isles of the sea, and all the ends of the earth, accompanying Old Ahab in the Pequod to lay the world's grievances before that bar from which not very many of them ever come back. Black Little Pip – he never did – oh, no! he went before. On the grim Pequod's forecastle, ye shall ere long see him, beating his tambourine; prelusive of the eternal time, when sent for, to the great quarter-deck on high, he was bid strike in with angels, and beat his tambourine in glory; called a coward here, hailed a hero there!

CHAPTER 24

CHAPTER 24

Ahab

For several days after leaving Nantucket, nothing above hatches was seen of Captain Ahab. The mates regularly relieved each other at the watches, and for aught that could be seen to the contrary, they seemed to be the only commanders of the ship; only they sometimes issued from the cabin with orders so sudden and peremptory, that after all it was plain they but commanded vicariously. Yes, their supreme lord and dictator was there, though hitherto unseen by any eyes not permitted to penetrate into the now sacred retreat of the cabin.

Every time I ascended to the deck from my watches below, I instantly gazed aft to mark if any strange face were visible; for my first vague disquietude touching the unknown captain, now in the seclusion of the sea, became almost a perturbation. But whatever it was of apprehensiveness or uneasiness – to call it so – which I felt, yet whenever I came to look about me in the ship, it seemed against all warrantry to cherish such emotions. For though the harpooneers, with the great body of the crew, were a far more barbaric, heathenish, and motley set than any of the tame merchant-ship companies which my previous experiences had made me acquainted with, still I ascribed this – and rightly ascribed it – to the fierce uniqueness of the very nature of that wild Scandinavian vocation in which I had so abandonedly embarked. But it was especially the aspect of the three chief officers of the ship, the mates, which was most forcibly calculated to allay these misgivings, and induce confidence and cheerfulness in every presentment of the voyage. Three better, more likely sea-officers and men, each in his own different way, could not readily be found, and they were every one of them Americans; a Nantucketer, a Vineyarder, a Cape man. Now, it being Christmas when the ship shot from out her harbour, for a space we had biting Polar weather, though all the time running away from it to the southward; and by every degree and minute of latitude which we sailed, gradually leaving that merciless winter, and all its intolerable weather behind us. It was one of those less lowering, but still grey and gloomy enough mornings of the transition, when with a fair wind the ship was rushing through the water with a vindictive sort of leaping and melancholy rapidity, that as I mounted to the deck at the call of the forenoon watch, so soon as I levelled my glance towards the taffrail, foreboding shivers ran over me. Captain Ahab stood upon his quarter-deck.

There seemed no sign of common bodily illness about him, nor of the recovery from any. He looked like a man cut away from the stake, when the fire has overrunningly wasted all the limbs without consuming them, or taking away one particle from their compacted aged robustness. His whole high, broad form seemed made of solid bronze, and shaped in an unalterable mould, like Cellini's cast Perseus. Threading its way out from among his grey hairs, and continuing right down one side of his tawny scorched face and neck, till it disappeared in his clothing, you saw a slender rod-like mark, lividly whitish. It resembled that perpendicular seam sometimes made in the straight, lofty trunk of a great tree, when the upper lightning tearingly darts down it, and without wrenching a single twig, peels and grooves out the bark from top to bottom, ere running off into the soil, leaving the tree still greenly alive, but branded. Whether that mark was born with him, or whether it was the scar left by some desperate wound, no one could certainly say. But once Tashtego's senior, an old Gay-Head Indian among the crew, superstitiously asserted that not till he was full forty years old did Ahab become that way branded, and then it came upon him, not in the fury of any mortal fray, but in an elemental strife at sea. Yet, this wild hint seemed inferentially negatived, by what a grey Manxman insinuated, an old sepulchral man, who, having never before sailed out of Nantucket, had never ere this laid eye upon wild Ahab. Nevertheless, the old sea-traditions invested this old Manxman with preternatural powers of discernment. So that no white sailor contradicted him when he said that if ever Captain Ahab should be tranquilly laid out – which might hardly come to pass, he muttered – then, whoever should do that last office for the dead, would find a birthmark on him from crown to sole.

So powerfully did the whole grim aspect of Ahab affect me, and the livid brand which streaked it, that for the first few moments I hardly noted that not a little of this overbearing grimness was owing to the barbaric white leg upon which he partly stood. It had previously come to me that this ivory leg had at sea been fashioned from the polished bone of the Sperm Whale's jaw. 'Aye, he was dismasted off Japan,' said the Old Gay-Head Indian once; 'but like his dismasted craft, he shipped another mast without coming home for it. He has a quiver of 'em.'

I was struck with the singular posture he maintained. Upon each side of the Pequod's quarter-deck, and pretty close to the mizzen shrouds, there was an auger hole, bored about half an inch or so, into the plank. His bone leg steadied in that hole; one arm elevated, and holding by a shroud; Captain Ahab stood erect, looking straight out beyond the ship's ever-pitching prow. There was an infinity of firmest fortitude, a determinate, unsurrenderable wilfulness, in the fixed and fearless, forward dedication of that glance. Not a word he spoke; nor did his officers say aught to him; though by all their minutest gestures and expressions, they plainly showed the uneasy, if not painful, consciousness of being under a troubled master-eye. And not only that, but moody stricken Ahab stood before them with a crucifixion in his face; in all the nameless regal overbearing dignity of some mighty woe.

Ere long, he withdrew into his cabin. But after that morning, he was every day visible to the crew; either standing in his pivot-hole, or seated upon an ivory stool he had; or heavily walking the deck. As the sky grew less gloomy, he became still less and less a recluse; as if, when the ship had sailed from home, nothing but the dead wintry bleakness of the sea had then kept him so secluded. And, by and by, it came to pass, that he was almost continually in the air; but, as yet, for all that he said, or perceptibly did, on the at last sunny deck, he seemed as unnecessary there as another mast. But the Pequod was only making a passage now; not regularly cruising; nearly all whaling preparatives needing supervision the mates were fully competent to, so that there was little or nothing, out of himself, to employ or excite Ahab, now; and thus chase away, for that one interval, the clouds that layer upon layer were piled upon his brow.

Nevertheless, ere long, the warm, warbling persuasiveness of the pleasant, holiday weather we came to, seemed gradually to charm him from his mood. For, as when the red-cheeked, dancing girls, April and May, trip home to the wintry, misanthropic woods; even the barest, ruggedest, most thunder-cloven old oak will at least send forth some few green sprouts, to welcome such glad-hearted visitants; so Ahab did, in the end, a little respond to the playful allurings of that girlish air. More than once did he put forth the faint blossom of a look, which, in any other man, would have flowered out in a smile.

CHAPTER 25

Enter Ahab; to Him, Stubb

Some days elapsed, and ice and icebergs all astern, the Pequod now went rolling through the bright Quito spring, which, at sea, almost perpetually reigns on the threshold of the eternal August of the Tropic. The warmly cool, clear, ringing, perfumed, overflowing, redundant days, were as crystal goblets of Persian sherbet, heaped up – flaked up, with rose-water snow. The starred and stately nights seemed haughty dames in jewelled velvets, nursing at home in lonely pride, the memory of their absent conquering Earls, the golden helmeted suns! For sleeping man, 'twas hard to choose between such winsome days and such seducing nights. But all the witcheries of that unwaning weather did not merely lend new spells and potencies to the outward world. Inward they turned upon the soul, especially when the still mild hours of eve came on; then, memory shot her crystals as the clear ice most forms of noiseless twilights. And all these subtle agencies, more and more they wrought on Ahab's texture.

Old age is always wakeful; as if, the longer linked with life, the less man has to do with aught that looks like death. Among sea-commanders, the old greybeards will oftenest leave their berths to visit the night-cloaked deck. It was so with Ahab; only that now, of late, he seemed so much to live in the open air, that truly speaking, his visits were more to the cabin, than from the cabin to the planks. 'It feels like going down into one's tomb' – he would mutter to himself – 'for an old captain like me to be descending this narrow scuttle, to go to my grave-dug berth.'

So, almost every twenty-four hours, when the watches of the night were set, the silent steersman would watch the cabin-scuttle; and ere long the old man would emerge, griping at the iron banister. Some considering touch of humanity was in him; for he usually abstained from patrolling the quarter-deck; because to his wearied mates, seeking repose within six inches of his ivory heel, such would have been the reverberating crack and din of that bony step, that their dreams would have been of the crunching teeth of sharks. But once, the mood was on him too deep for common regardings; and as he was measuring the ship from taffrail to main-mast, Stubb, the odd second mate, came up from below, and with a certain unassured, deprecating humorousness, hinted that if Captain Ahab was pleased to walk the planks, then, no one could say nay; but there might be some way of muffling the noise; hinting something indistinctly and hesitatingly about a globe of tow, and the insertion into it, of the ivory heel. Ah! Stubb, thou did'st not know Ahab then.

'Am I a cannon-ball, Stubb,' said Ahab, 'that thou wouldst wad me that fashion? But go thy ways; I had forgot. Below to thy nightly grave; where such as ye sleep between shrouds, to use ye to the filling one at last. Down, dog, and kennel!'

Starting at the unforeseen concluding exclamation, Stubb was speechless a moment; then said excitedly, 'I am not used to be spoken to that way, sir; I do but less than half like it, sir.'

'Avast!' gritted Ahab between his set teeth, and violently moving away, as if to avoid some passionate temptation.

'No, sir; not yet,' said Stubb, emboldened, 'I will not tamely be called a dog, sir.'

'Then be called ten times a donkey, and a mule, and an ass, and begone, or I'll clear the world of thee!' As he said this, Ahab advanced upon him with such overbearing terrors in his aspect, that Stubb involuntarily retreated.

'I was never served so before without giving a hard blow for it,' muttered Stubb, as he found himself descending the cabin-scuttle. 'It's very queer. Stop, Stubb; somehow, now, I don't well know whether to go back and strike him, or – what's that? – down here on my knees and pray for him? Yes, that was the thought coming up in me; but it would be the first time I ever *did* pray. It's queer; very queer; and he's queer too; aye, take him fore and aft, he's about the queerest old man Stubb ever sailed with. Is he mad? He aint in his bed now, more than three hours out of the twenty-four; and he don't sleep then. Didn't that Dough-Boy, the steward, tell me that of a morning he always finds the old man's hammock clothes all rumpled and tumbled, and the sheets down at the foot, and the coverlid almost tied into knots, and the pillow a sort of frightful hot, as though a baked brick had been on it? A hot old man! I guess he's got what some folks ashore call a conscience; it's a kind of Tic-Dolly-row they say – worse nor a toothache. Well, well; I don't know what it is, but the Lord keep me from catching it. I wonder what he goes into the after hold for, every night, as Dough-Boy tells me he suspects; what's that for, I should like to know? Who's made appointments with him in the hold? Ain't that queer, now?'

CHAPTER 26

The Specksynder

Concerning the officers of the whale-craft, this seems as good a place as any to set down a little domestic peculiarity on shipboard, arising from the existence of the harpooneer class of officers. The large importance attached to the harpooneer's vocation is evinced by the fact, that originally in the old Dutch Fishery, two centuries and more ago, the command of a whale-ship was not wholly lodged in the person now called the captain, but was divided between him and an officer called the Specksynder. Literally this word means Fat-cutter; usage, however, in time made it equivalent to Chief Harpooneer. In those days, the captain's authority was restricted to the navigation and general management of the vessel: while over the whale-hunting department and all its concerns, the Specksynder or Chief Harpooneer reigned supreme. In the British Greenland Fishery, under the corrupted title of Specksioneer, this old Dutch official is still retained, but his former dignity is sadly abridged. Nevertheless, as upon the good conduct of the harpooneers the success of a whaling voyage largely depends, and since in the American Fishery he is not only an important officer in the boat, but under certain circumstances (night-watches on a whaling ground) the command of the ship's deck is also his; therefore the grand political maxim of the sea demands that he should nominally live apart from the men before the mast, and be in some way distinguished as their professional superior; though always, by them, familiarly regarded as their social equal.

Now, the grand distinction drawn between officer and man at sea is this – the first lives aft, the last forward. Hence, in whale-ships and merchantmen alike, the mates have their quarters with the captain; and so, too, in most of the American whalers the harpooneers are lodged in the after part of the ship. That is to say, they take their meals in the captain's cabin, and sleep in a place indirectly communicating with it.

Though the long period of a Southern whaling voyage (by far the longest of all voyages now or ever made by man), the peculiar perils of it, and the community of interest prevailing among a company, all of whom, high or low, depend for their profits, not upon fixed wages, but upon their common luck, together with their common vigilance, intrepidity, and hard work; though all these things do in some cases tend to beget a less rigorous discipline than in merchantmen generally; yet, never mind how much like an old Mesopotamian family these whalemen may, in some primitive instances, live together; for all that, the punctilious externals, at least, of the quarter-deck are seldom materially relaxed, and in no instance done away. Indeed, many are the Nantucket ships in which you will see the skipper parading his quarter-deck with an elated grandeur not surpassed in any military navy.

And though of all men the moody captain of the Pequod was the least given to that sort of shallowest assumption; and though the only homage he ever exacted was implicit, instantaneous obedience; though he required no man to remove the shoes from his feet ere stepping upon the quarter-deck; and though there were times when, owing to peculiar circumstances connected with events hereafter to be detailed, he addressed them in unusual terms, whether of condescension or *in terrorem* or otherwise; yet even Captain Ahab was by no means unobservant of the paramount forms and usages of the sea.

Nor, perhaps, will it fail to be eventually perceived, that behind those forms and usages, as it were, he sometimes masked himself; incidentally making use of them for other and more private ends than they were legitimately intended to subserve. That certain sultanism of his brain, which had otherwise in a good degree remained unmanifested; through those forms that same sultanism became incarnate in an irresistible dictatorship. For be a man's intellectual superiority what it will, it can never assume the practical, available supremacy over other men, without the aid of some sort of external arts and entrenchments, always, in themselves, more or less paltry and base. This it is, that for ever keeps God's true princes of the Empire from the world's hustings; and leaves the highest honours that this air can give, to those men who become famous more through their infinite inferiority to the choice hidden handful of the Divine Inert, than through their undoubted superiority over the dead level of the mass. Such large virtue lurks in these small things when extreme political superstitions invest them, that in some royal instances even to idiot imbecility they have imparted potency. But when, as in the case of Nicholas the Czar, the ringed crown of geographical empire encircles an imperial brain; then, the plebeian herds crouch abased before the tremendous centralization. Nor will the tragic dramatist who would depict mortal indomitableness in its fullest sweep and direct swing ever forget a hint, incidentally so important in his art, as the one now alluded to.

But Ahab, my Captain, still moves before me in all his Nantucket grimness and shagginess; and in this episode touching Emperors and Kings, I must not conceal that I have only to do with a poor old whale-hunter like him; and, therefore, all outward majestical trappings and housings are denied me. Oh, Ahab! what shall be grand in thee, it must needs be plucked at from the skies, and dived for in the deep, and featured in the unbodied air!

CHAPTER 27

The Cabin-table

It is noon; and Dough-Boy, the steward, thrusting his pale loaf-of-bread face from the cabin-scuttle, announces dinner to his lord and master; who, sitting in the lee quarter-boat, has just been taking an observation of the sun; and is now mutely reckoning the latitude on the smooth, medallion-shaped tablet, reserved for that daily purpose on the upper part of his ivory leg. From his complete inattention to the tidings, you would think that moody

Ahab had not heard his menial. But presently, catching hold of the mizzen shrouds, he swings himself to the deck, and in an even, unexhilarated voice, saying, 'Dinner, Mr Starbuck,' disappears into the cabin.

When the last echo of his sultan's step has died away, and Starbuck, the first Emir, has every reason to suppose that he is seated, then Starbuck rouses from his quietude, takes a few turns along the planks, and, after a grave peep into the binnacle, says, with some touch of pleasantness, 'Dinner, Mr Stubb,' and descends the scuttle. The second Emir lounges about the rigging awhile, and then slightly shaking the main brace, to see whether it be all right with that important rope, he likewise takes up the old burden, and with a rapid 'Dinner, Mr Flask,' follows after his predecessors.

But the third Emir, now seeing himself all alone on the quarter-deck, seems to feel relieved from some curious restraint; for, tipping all sorts of knowing winks in all sorts of directions, and kicking off his shoes, he strikes into a sharp but noiseless squall of a hornpipe right over the Grand Turk's head; and then, pitching his cap up into the mizzen-top for a shelf, he goes down rollicking, so far at least as he remains visible from the deck. But ere stepping into the cabin doorway below, he pauses, ships a new face altogether, and, then, independent, hilarious little Flask enters King Ahab's presence, in the character of Abjectus, or the Slave.

It is not the least among the strange things bred by the intense artificialness of sea-usages, that while in the open air of the deck some officers will, upon provocation, bear themselves boldly enough towards their commander; yet, ten to one, let those very officers the next moment go down to their customary dinner in that same commander's cabin, and straightway their inoffensive, not to say humble air towards him, as he sits at the head of the table; this is marvellous, sometimes most comical. What it is to be Caesar. It is a witchery of social czarship which there is no withstanding.

Over his ivory-inlaid table, Ahab presided like a mute, maned sea-lion on the white coral beach, surrounded by his war-like but still deferential cubs. In his own proper turn, each officer waited to be served. They were as little children before Ahab; and yet, in Ahab, there seemed not to lurk the smallest social arrogance. With one mind, their intent eyes all fastened upon the old man's knife, as he carved the chief dish before him. I do not suppose that for the world they would have profaned that moment with the slightest observation, even upon so neutral a topic as the weather. No! And when reaching out his knife and fork, between which the slice of beef was locked, Ahab thereby motioned Starbuck's plate towards him, the mate received his meat as though receiving alms; and cut it tenderly; and chewed it noiselessly; and swallowed it, not without circumspection. For, like the Coronation banquet at Frankfort, where the German Emperor profoundly dines with the seven Imperial Electors, so these cabin meals were eaten in awful silence; and yet at table old Ahab forbade not conversation; only he himself was dumb. What a relief it was to choking Stubb, when a rat made a sudden racket in the hold below. And poor little Flask, he was the little boy of this family party. His were the shinbones of the saline beef; his would have been the drumsticks. For Flask to have presumed to help himself, this must have seemed to him tantamount to larceny. Had he helped himself at that table, doubtless, never more would he have been able to hold his head up in this honest world; nevertheless, strange to say, Ahab never forbade him. And had Flask helped himself, the chances were Ahab had never so much as noticed it. Least of all did Flask presume to help himself to butter. Whether he thought the owners of the ship denied it to him, on account of its clotting his clear, sunny complexion; or whether he deemed that, on so long a voyage in such marketless waters, butter was at a premium, and therefore was not for him, a subaltern; however it was, Flask, alas! was a butterless man!

Another thing. Flask was the last person down at the dinner, and Flask is the first man up. Consider! If Stubb, who is but a peg higher than Flask, happens to have but a small appetite, and soon shows symptoms of concluding his repast, then Flask must bestir himself, he will not get more than three mouthfuls that day; for it is against holy usage for Stubb to precede Flask to the deck.

Therefore it was that Flask once admitted in private, that ever since he had arisen to the dignity of an officer, from that moment he had never known what it was to be otherwise than hungry, more or less. Peace and satisfaction, thought Flask, have for ever departed from my stomach. I am an officer; but, how I wish I could fist a bit of old-fashioned beef in the forecastle, as I used to when I was before the mast. There's the fruits of promotion now; there's the vanity of glory; there's the insanity of life! Besides, if it were so that any mere sailor of the Pequod had a grudge against Flask in Flask's official capacity, all that sailor had to do, in order to obtain ample vengeance, was to go aft at dinner-time, and get a peep at Flask through the cabin sky-light, sitting silly and dumfoundered before awful Ahab.

Now, Ahab and his three mates formed what may be called the first table in the Pequod's cabin. After their departure, taking place in inverted order to their arrival, the canvas cloth was cleared, or rather was restored to some hurried order by the pallid steward. And then the three harpooneers were bidden to the feast, they being its residuary legatees. In strange contrast to the hardly tolerable constraint and nameless invisible domineerings of the captain's table, was the entire care-free licence and ease, the almost frantic democracy of those inferior fellows the harpooneers. While their masters, the mates, seemed afraid of the sound of the hinges of their own jaws, the harpooneers chewed their food with such a relish that there was a report to it. They dined like lords; they filled their bellies like Indian ships all day loading with spices. Such portentous appetites had Queequeg and Tashtego, that to fill out the vacancies made by the previous repast, often the pale Dough-Boy was fain to bring on a great baron of salt-junk, seemingly quarried out of the solid ox. And if he were not lively about it, then Tashtego had an ungentlemanly way of accelerating him by darting a fork at his back, harpoonwise. And once Daggoo, seized with a sudden humour, assisted Dough-Boy's memory by snatching him up bodily, and thrusting his head into a great empty wooden trencher, while Tashtego, knife in hand, began laying out the circle preliminary to scalping him. He was naturally a very nervous, shuddering sort of little fellow, this bread-faced steward; the progeny of a bankrupt baker and a hospital nurse. And what with the standing spectacle of the black terrific Ahab, and the periodical tumultuous visitations of these three savages, Dough-Boy's whole life was one continual lip-quiver. Commonly, after seeing the harpooneers furnished with all things they demanded, he would escape from their clutches into his little pantry adjoining, and fearfully peep out at them through the blinds of its door, till all was over.

It was a sight to see Queequeg seated over against Tashtego, opposing his filed teeth to the Indian's; crosswise to them, Daggoo seated on the floor, for a bench would have brought his hearse-plumed head to the low carlines; at every motion of his colossal limbs, making the low cabin framework to shake, as when an African elephant goes passenger in a ship. Nor did the whetstone which the harpooneers carried in their pockets, for their lances and other weapons; and with which whetstones, at dinner, they would ostentatiously sharpen their knives; that grating sound did not at all tend to tranquillize poor Dough-Boy. How could he forget that in his Island days, Queequeg, for one, must certainly have been guilty of some murderous, convivial indiscretions. Alas! Dough-Boy! hard fares the white waiter who waits upon canni-bals. Not a napkin should he carry on his arm, but a buckler. In good time, though, to his great delight, the three salt-sea warriors would rise and depart; to his credulous, fable-mongering ears, all their martial bones jingling in them at every step, like Moorish scimitars in scabbards.

CHAPTER 28

The Mast-head

It was during the more pleasant weather, that in due rotation with the other seamen my first mast-head came round.

In most American whalemen the mast-heads are manned almost simultaneously with the vessel's leaving her port; even though she may have fifteen thousand miles, and more, to sail ere reaching her proper cruising ground. And if, after a three, four, or five years' voyage she is drawing nigh home with anything empty in her – say, an empty vial even – then, her mast-heads are kept manned to the last; and not till her skysail-poles sail in among the spires of the port, does she altogether relinquish the hope of capturing one whale more.

Now, afloat, the three mast-heads are kept manned from sunrise to sun-set; the seamen taking their regular turns (as at the helm), and relieving each other every two hours. In the serene weather of the tropics it is exceedingly pleasant the mast-head; nay, to a dreamy meditative man it is delightful. There you stand, a hundred feet above the silent decks, striding along the deep, as if the masts were gigantic stilts, while beneath you and between your legs, as it were, swim the hugest monsters of the sea, even as ships once sailed between the boots of the famous Colossus at old Rhodes. There you stand, lost in the infinite series of the sea, with nothing ruffled but the waves. The tranced ship indolently rolls; the drowsy trade winds blow; everything resolves you into languor. For the most part, in this tropic whaling life, a sublime uneventfulness invests you; you hear no news; read no gazettes; extras with startling accounts of commonplaces never delude you into unnecessary excitements; you hear of no domestic afflictions; bankrupt securities; fall of stocks; are never troubled with the thought of what you shall have for dinner – for all your meals for three years and more are snugly stowed in casks, and your bill of fare is immutable.

In one of those southern whalemen, on a long three or four years' voyage, as often happens, the sum of the various hours you spend at the mast-head would amount to several entire months. And it is much to be deplored that the place to which you devote so considerable a portion of the whole term of your natural life, should be so sadly destitute of anything approaching to a cosy inhabitiveness, or adapted to breed a comfortable localness of feeling, such as pertains to a bed, a hammock, a hearse, a sentry box, a pulpit, a coach, or any other of those small and snug contrivances in which men temporarily isolate themselves. Your most usual point of perch is the head of the t'gallant-mast, where you stand upon two thin parallel sticks (almost peculiar to whalemen) called the t'gallant cross-trees. Here, tossed about by the sea, the beginner feels about as cosy as he would standing on a bull's horns. To be sure, in cold weather you may carry your house aloft with you, in the shape of a watch-coat; but properly speaking the thickest watch-coat is no more of a house than the unclad body; for as the soul is glued inside of its fleshly tabernacle, and cannot freely move about in it, so a watch-coat is not so much of a house as it is a mere envelope, or additional skin encasing you.

Concerning all this, it is much to be deplored that the mast-heads of a southern whale-ship are unprovided with those enviable little tents or pulpits, called *crow's-nests*, in which the look-outs of a Greenland whaler are protected from the inclement weather of the frozen seas. In the fire-side narrative of Captain Sleet, entitled 'A Voyage among the Icebergs, in quest of the Greenland Whale, and incidentally for the re-discovery of the Lost Icelandic Colonies of Old Greenland'; in this admirable volume, all standers of mast-heads are furnished with a charmingly circumstantial account of the then recently invented *crow's-nest* of the Glacier, which was the name of Captain Sleet's good craft. He called it the *Sleet's crow's-nest*, in honour of himself; he being the original inventor and patentee and free from all ridiculous false delicacy. In shape, the Sleet's crow's-nest is something like a large tierce or pipe; it is open above, however, where it is furnished with a movable side-screen to keep to windward of your head in a hard gale. Being fixed on the summit of the mast, you ascend into it through a little trap-hatch in the bottom. On the after side, or side next the stem of the ship, is a comfortable seat, with a locker underneath for umbrellas, comforters, and coats. In front is a leather rack, in which to keep your speaking trumpet, pipe, telescope, and other nautical conveniences; that well replenished little case-bottle, so nicely tucked within easy reach, what a faithful friend and comforter it must have been.

But if we Southern whale-fishers are not so snugly housed aloft as Captain Sleet and his Greenland-men were; yet that disadvantage is greatly counterbalanced by the widely contrasting serenity of those seductive seas in which we South fishers mostly float. For one, I used to lounge up the rigging very leisurely, resting in the top to have a chat with Queequeg, or anyone else off duty whom I might find there.

Let me make a clean breast of it here, and frankly admit that I kept but sorry guard. With the problem of the universe revolving in me, how could I – being left completely to myself at such a thought-engendering altitude – how could I but lightly hold my obligations to observe all whale-ships' standing orders, 'Keep your weather eye open, and sing out every time'.

And let me in this place movingly admonish you, ye shipowners of Nantucket! Beware of enlisting in your vigilant fisheries any lad with lean brow and hollow eye, given to unseasonable meditativeness. Beware of such an one, I say: your whales must be seen before they can be killed; and this sunken-eyed young Platonist will tow you ten wakes round the world, and never make you one pint of sperm the richer. Nor are these monitions at all unneeded. For nowadays, the whale-fishery furnishes an asylum for many romantic and absent-minded young men, disgusted with the cares of earth, and seeking sentiment in tar and blubber. Childe Harold not unfrequently perches himself upon the mast-head of some luckless whale-ship, and in moody phrase ejaculates:

'Roll on, thou deep and dark blue ocean, roll!
Ten thousand blubber-hunters sweep over thee in vain.'

CHAPTER 29

The Quarter-deck

One morning shortly after breakfast, Ahab, as was his wont, ascended the cabin-gangway to the deck. There most sea-captains usually walk at that hour, as country gentlemen, after the same meal, take a few turns in the garden.

Soon his steady, ivory stride was heard, upon planks so familiar to his tread, that they were all over dented, like geological stones, with the peculiar mark of his walk. Did you fixedly gaze, too, upon that ribbed and dented brow; there also, you would see still stranger foot-prints – the foot-prints of his one unsleeping, ever-pacing thought.

But on the occasion in question, those dents looked deeper, even as his nervous step that morning left a deeper mark. And, so full of his thought was Ahab, that at every uniform turn that he made, you could almost see that thought turn in him as he turned, and pace in him as he paced.

'D'ye mark him, Flask?' whispered Stubb; 'the chick that's in him pecks the shell. T'will soon be out.'

The hours wore on; Ahab now shut up within his cabin; anon, pacing the deck. It drew near the close of day. Suddenly he came to a halt by the bulwarks, and inserting his bone leg into the auger-hole there, and with one hand grasping a shroud, he ordered Starbuck to send everybody aft.

'Sir!' said the mate, astonished at an order seldom or never given on ship-board except in some extraordinary case.

'Send everybody aft,' repeated Ahab. 'Mast-heads, there! come down!'

When the entire ship's company were assembled, and with curious and not wholly unapprehensive faces, were eyeing him, for he looked not unlike the weather horizon when a storm is coming up, Ahab, after rapidly glancing over the bulwarks, and then darting his eyes among the crew, started from his standpoint and resumed his heavy turns upon the deck. With bent head he continued to pace, unmindful of the wondering whispering among the men; till Stubb cautiously whispered to Flask, that Ahab must have summoned them there for the purpose of witnessing a pedestrian feat. But this did not last long. Vehemently pausing, he cried:

'What do ye do when ye see a whale, men?'

'Sing out for him!' was the impulsive rejoinder from a score of clubbed voices.

'Good!' cried Ahab, with a wild approval in his tones. 'And what do ye next, men?'

'Lower away, and after him!'

'And what tune is it ye pull to, men?'

'A dead whale or a stove boat!'

More and more strangely and fiercely glad and approving grew the countenance of the old man at every shout; while the mariners began to gaze curiously at each other, as if marvelling how it was that they themselves became so excited at such seemingly purposeless questions.

But, they were all eagerness again, as Ahab, now half-revolving in his pivot-hole, with one hand high up a shroud, and almost convulsively grasping it, addressed them thus:

'All ye mast-headers have before now heard me give orders about a white whale. Look ye! d'ye see this Spanish ounce of gold?' – holding up a broad bright coin to the sun – 'it is a sixteen dollar piece, men. D'ye see it? Mr Starbuck, hand me yon top-maul.'

While the mate was getting the hammer, Ahab, without speaking, was slowly rubbing the gold piece against the skirts of his jacket, as if to heighten its lustre, and without using any words was meanwhile lowly humming to himself, producing a sound so strangely muffled and inarticulate that it seemed the mechanical humming of the wheels of his vitality in him.

Receiving the top-maul from Starbuck, he advanced towards the main-mast with the hammer uplifted in one hand, exhibiting the gold with the other, and exclaiming: 'Whosoever of ye raises me a white-headed whale with a wrinkled brow and a crooked jaw;

whosoever of ye raises me that white-headed whale, with three holes punctured in his starboard fluke – look ye, whosoever of ye raises me that same white whale, he shall have this gold ounce, my boys!'

'Huzza! huzza!' cried the seamen, as with swinging tarpaulins they hailed the act of nailing the gold to the mast.

'It's a white whale, I say,' resumed Ahab, as he threw down the top-maul; 'a white whale. Skin your eyes for him; look sharp for white water; if ye see but a bubble, sing out.'

All this while Tashtego, Daggoo, and Queequeg had looked on with even more intense interest and surprise than the rest, and at the mention of the wrinkled brow and crooked jaw they had started as if each was separately touched by some specific recollection.

'Captain Ahab,' said Tashtego, 'that white whale must be the same that some call Moby-Dick.'

'Moby-Dick?' shouted Ahab. 'Do ye know the white whale then, Tash?'

'Does he fan-tail a little curious, sir, before he goes down?' said the Gay-Header deliberately.

'And has he a curious spout, too,' said Daggoo, 'very bushy and mighty quick, Captain Ahab?'

'And he have one, two, tree-oh! good many iron in him hide, too, Captain,' cried Queequeg, 'all twiske-tee be-twisk, like him-him' – faltering hard for a word, and screwing his hand round and round – 'like him-him—'

'Corkscrew!' cried Ahab, 'aye, Queequeg, the harpoons lie all twisted and wrenched in him; aye, Daggoo, his spout is a big one, like a whole shock of wheat, and white as a pile of our Nantucket wool; aye, Tashtego, and he fan-tails like a split jib in a squall. Death and devils! men, it is Moby-Dick ye have seen – Moby-Dick – Moby-Dick!'

'Captain Ahab,' said Starbuck, who, with Stubb and Flask, had been eyeing his superior with increasing surprise, but at last seemed struck with a thought which somewhat explained all the wonder. 'Captain Ahab, I have heard of Moby-Dick – but it was not Moby-Dick that took off thy leg?'

'Who told thee that?' cried Ahab; then pausing, 'Aye, Starbuck; aye, my hearties all round; it was Moby-Dick that dismasted me; Moby-Dick that brought me to this dead stump I stand on now. Aye, aye,' he shouted with a terrific, loud, animal sob, like that of a heart-stricken moose; 'Aye, aye! it was that accursed white whale that razeed me; made a poor pegging lubber of me for ever and a day!' Then tossing both arms, with measureless imprecations he shouted out: 'Aye, aye! and I'll chase him round Good Hope, and round the Horn, and round the Norway Maelstrom, and round perdition's flames before I give him up. And this is what ye have shipped for, men! to chase that white whale on both sides of land, and over all sides of earth, till he spouts black blood and rolls fin out. What say ye, men, will ye splice hands on it, now? I think ye do look brave.'

'Aye, aye!' shouted the harpooneers and seamen, running closer to the excited old man: 'A sharp eye for the White Whale; a sharp lance for Moby-Dick!'

'God bless ye,' he seemed to half sob and half shout. 'God bless ye, men. Steward! go draw the great measure of grog. But what's this long face about, Mr Starbuck; wilt thou not chase the white whale? art not game for Moby-Dick?'

'I am game for his crooked jaw, and for the jaws of Death too, Captain Ahab, if it fairly comes in the way of the business we follow; but I came here to hunt whales, not my commander's vengeance. How many barrels will thy vengeance yield thee even if thou gettest it, Captain Ahab? it will not fetch thee much in our Nantucket market.'

'Nantucket market! Hoot! But come closer, Starbuck; thou requirest a little lower layer. If money's to be the measurer, man, and the accountants have computed their great counting-house the globe, by girdling it with guineas, one to every three parts of an inch; then, let me tell thee, that my vengeance will fetch a great premium *here*!'

'He smites his chest,' whispered Stubb, 'what's that for? methinks it rings most vast, but hollow.'

'Vengeance on a dumb brute!' cried Starbuck, 'that simply

smote thee from blindest instinct! To be enraged with a dumb thing, Captain Ahab, seems blasphemous.'

'Hark ye yet again – the little lower layer. All visible objects, man, are but as pasteboard masks. But in each event – in the living act, the undoubted deed – there, some unknown but still reasoning thing puts forth the mouldings of its features from behind the unreasoning mask. If man will strike, strike through the mask! How can the prisoner reach outside except by thrusting through the wall? To me, the white whale is that wall, shoved near to me. Sometimes I think there's naught beyond. But 'tis enough. He tasks me; he heaps me; I see in him outrageous strength, with an inscrutable malice sinewing it. That inscrutable thing is chiefly what I hate; and be the white whale agent, or be the white whale principal, I will wreak that hate upon him. Talk not to me of blasphemy, man; I'd strike the sun if it insulted me. For could the sun do that, then could I do the other; since there is ever a sort of fair play herein, jealousy presiding over all creations. But not my master, man, is even that fair play. Who's over me? Truth hath no confines. Take off thine eye! more intolerable than fiends' glarings is a doltish stare! So, so; thou reddenest and palest; my head has melted thee to anger-glow. But look ye, Starbuck, what is said in heat, that thing unsays itself. There are men from whom warm words are small indignity. I meant not to incense thee. Let it go. Look! see yonder Turkish cheeks of spotted tawn – living, breathing pictures painted by the sun. The Pagan leopards – the unrecking and unworshipping things, that live; and seek, and give no reasons for the torrid life they feel! The crew, man, the crew! Are they not one and all with Ahab, in this matter of the whale? See Stubb! he laughs! See yonder Chilian! he snorts to think of it. Stand up amid the general hurricane, thy one tossed sapling cannot, Starbuck! And what is it? Reckon it. 'Tis but to help strike a fin; no wondrous feat for Starbuck. What is it more? From this one poor hunt, then, the best lance out of all Nantucket, surely he will not hang back, when every foremasthand has clutched a whetstone? Ah! constrainings seize thee; I see! the billow lifts thee! Speak, but speak! – Aye, aye! thy silence, then, *that* voices thee.

(*Aside*) Something shot from my dilated nostrils, he has inhaled it in his lungs. Starbuck now is mine; cannot oppose me now, without rebellion.'

'God keep me! – keep us all!' murmured Starbuck, lowly.

But in his joy at the enchanted, tacit acquiescence of the mate, Ahab did not hear his foreboding invocation; nor yet the low laugh from the hold; nor yet the presaging vibrations of the winds in the cordage; nor yet the hollow flap of the sails against the masts, as for a moment their hearts sank in. For Starbuck's downcast eyes lighted up with the stubbornness of life; the subterranean laugh died away; the winds blew on; the sails filled out; the ship heaved and rolled as before.

'The measure! the measure!' cried Ahab. Receiving the brimming pewter, and turning to the harpooneers, he ordered them to produce their weapons. Then ranging them before him near the capstan, with their harpoons in their hands, while his three mates stood at his side with their lances, and the rest of the ship's company formed a circle round the group; he stood for an instant searchingly eyeing every man of his crew. But those wild eyes met his, as the bloodshot eyes of the prairie wolves meet the eye of their leader, ere he rushes on at their head in the trail of the bison; but, alas! only to fall into the hidden snare of the Indian.

'Drink and pass!' he cried, handing the heavy charged flagon to the nearest seaman. 'The crew alone now drink. Round with it, round! Short draughts – long swallows, men; 'tis hot as Satan's hoof. So, so; it goes round excellently. It spiralizes in ye; forks out at the serpent-snapping eye. Well done; almost drained. That way it went, this way it comes. Hand it me – here's a hollow! Men, ye seem the years; so brimming life is gulped and gone. Steward, refill!

'Attend now, my braves, I have mustered ye all round this capstan; and ye mates, flank me with your lances; and ye harpooneers, stand there with your irons; and ye, stout mariners, ring me in, that I may in some sort revive a noble custom of my fisherman fathers before me. O men, you will yet see that – Ha! boy, come back? bad pennies come not sooner. Hand it me. Why, now, this

pewter had run brimming again, wer't not thou St Vitus' imp
– away, thou ague!

'Advance, ye mates! Cross your lances full before me. Well
done! let me touch the axis.' So saying, with extended arm, he
grasped the three level, radiating lances at their crossed centre;
while so doing, suddenly and nervously twitched them; meanwhile, glancing intently from Starbuck to Stubb; from Stubb to
Flask. It seemed as though, by some interior volition, he would
fain have shocked into them the same fiery emotion accumulated
within the Leyden jar of his own magnetic life. The three mates
quailed before his strong, sustained, and mystic aspect. Stubb and
Flask looked sideways from him; the honest eye of Starbuck fell
downright.

'In vain!' cried Ahab; 'but, maybe, 'tis well. For did ye three
but once take the full-forced shock, then mine own electric thing,
that had perhaps expired from out me. Perchance, too, it would
have dropped ye dead. Perchance ye need it not. Down lances!
And now, ye mates, I do appoint ye three cup bearers to my three
pagan kinsmen there – yon three most honourable gentlemen and
noblemen, my valiant harpooneers. Disdain the task? What, when
the great Pope washes the feet of beggars, using his tiara for ewer?
Oh, my sweet cardinals! your own condescension, *that* shall bend
ye to it. I do not order ye; ye will it. Cut your seizings and draw
the poles, ye harpooneers!'

Silently obeying the order, the three harpooneers now stood
with the detached iron part of their harpoons, some three feet
long, held, barbs up, before him.

'Stab me not with that keen steel! Cant them; cant them over!
know ye not the goblet end? Turn up the socket! So, so; now, ye
cup-bearers, advance. The irons! take them; hold them while I fill!'
Forthwith, he brimmed the harpoon sockets with the fiery waters
from the pewter.

'Now, three to three, ye stand. Commend the murderous
chalices! Bestow them, ye who are now made parties to this indis-
soluble league. Ha! Starbuck! but the deed is done! Yon ratifying
sun now waits to sit upon it. Drink, ye harpooneers! drink and

swear, ye men that man the deathful whale-boat's bow – Death to Moby-Dick! God hunt us all, if we do not hunt Moby-Dick to his death!' The long, barbed steel goblets were lifted; and to cries and maledictions against the white whale, the spirits were simultaneously quaffed down with a hiss. Starbuck paled, and turned, and shivered. Once more, and finally, the replenished pewter went the rounds among the frantic crew; when, waving his free hand to them, they all dispersed; and Ahab retired within his cabin.

CHAPTER 30

Dusk

[*By the main-mast; Starbuck leaning against it*]

My soul is more than matched; she's overmanned; and by a madman! Insufferable sting, that sanity should ground arms on such a field! But he drilled deep down, and blasted all my reason out of me! I think I see his impious end; but feel that I must help him to it. Will I, nill I, the ineffable thing has tied me to him; tows me with a cable I have no knife to cut. Horrible old man! Who's over him, he cries; – aye, he would be a democrat to all above; look, how he lords it over all below! Oh! I plainly see my miserable office – to obey, rebelling; and worse yet, to hate with touch of pity! For in his eyes I read some lurid woe would shrivel me up, had I it. Yet is there hope. Time and tide flow wide. The hated whale has the round watery world to swim in, as the small goldfish has its glassy globe. His heaven-insulting purpose, God may wedge aside. I would up heart, were it not like lead. But my whole clock's run down; my heart the all-controlling weight, I have no key to lift again.

[*A burst of revelry from the forecastle*]

Oh, God! to sail with such a heathen crew that have small touch of human mothers in them! Whelped somewhere by the sharkish sea. The white whale is their demigorgon. Hark! the infernal orgies! that revelry is forward! mark the unfaltering silence aft! Methinks it pictures life. Foremost through the sparkling sea shoots on the gay, embattled, bantering bow, but only to drag dark Ahab after it, where he broods within his sternward cabin, builded over the dead water of the wake, and further on, hunted by its wolfish gurglings. The long howl thrills me through! Peace! ye revellers, and set the watch! Oh, life! 'tis in an hour like this, with soul beat down and held to knowledge – as wild, untutored things are forced to feed – Oh, life! 'tis now that I do feel the latent horror in thee! but 'tis not me! that horror's out of me! and with the soft feeling of the human in me, yet will I try to fight ye, ye grim, phantom futures! Stand by me, hold me, bind me, O ye blessed influences!

CHAPTER 31

First Night-watch

FORE-TOP [*Stubb solus, and mending a brace*]

Ha! ha! ha! ha! hem! clear my throat! – I've been thinking over it ever since, and that ha, ha's the final consequence. Why so? Because a laugh's the wisest, easiest answer to all that's queer; and come what will, one comfort's always left – that unfailing comfort is, it's all predestinated. I heard not all his talk with Starbuck; but to my poor eye Starbuck then looked something as I the other evening felt. Be sure the old Mogul has fixed him, too. I twigged it, knew it; had had the gift, might readily have prophesied it – for when I clapped my eye upon his skull I saw it. Well, Stubb, *wise* Stubb – that's my title – well, Stubb, what of it, Stubb? Here's a carcase. I know not all that may be coming, but be it what it will, I'll go to it laughing. Such a waggish leering as lurks in all your horribles! I feel funny. Fa, la! lirra, skirra! What's my juicy little pear at home doing now? Crying its eyes out? Giving a party to the last arrived harpooneers, I dare say, gay as a frigate's pennant, and so am I – fa, la! lirra, skirra! Oh—

> We'll drink tonight with hearts as light,
> To love, as gay and fleeting
> As bubbles that swim, on the beaker's brim,
> And break on the lips while meeting.

A brave stave that – who calls? Mr Starbuck? Aye, aye, sir – (*Aside*) he's my superior, he has his too, if I'm not mistaken. Aye, aye, sir, just, through with this job – coming.

CHAPTER 32

Midnight, Forecastle

HARPOONEERS AND SAILORS

[*Foresail rises and discovers the watch standing, lounging, leaning, and lying in various attitudes, all singing in chorus*]

> Farewell and adieu to you, Spanish ladies!
> Farewell and adieu to you, ladies of Spain!
> Our captain's commanded.—

1ST NANTUCKET SAILOR

Oh, boys, don't be sentimental; it's bad for the digestion: Take a tonic, follow me!

[*Sings, and all follow*]

> Our captain stood upon the deck,
> A spy-glass in his hand,
> A viewing of those gallant whales
> That blew at every strand.

Oh, your tubs in your boats, my boys,
  And by your braces stand,
And we'll have one of those fine whales,
  Hand, boys, over hand!
So, be cheery, my lads! may your hearts never fail!
While the bold harpooneer is striking the whale!

MATE'S VOICE FROM THE QUARTER-DECK

Eight bells there, forward!

2ND NANTUCKET SAILOR

Avast the chorus! Eight bells there! d'ye hear, bell-boy? Strike the bell eight, thou Pip! thou blackling! and let me call the watch. I've the sort of mouth for that – the hogshead mouth. So, so, (*thrusts his head down the scuttle*), Star – bo-l-e-e-n-s, a-h-o-y! Eight bells there below! Tumble up!

DUTCH SAILOR

Grand snoozing tonight, maty; fat night for that. I mark this in our old Mogul's wine; it's quite as deadening to some as filliping to others. We sing; they sleep – aye, lie down there, like ground-tier butts. At 'em again! There, take this copper-pump, and hail 'em through it. Tell 'em to avast dreaming of their lasses. Tell 'em it's the resurrection; they must kiss their last, and come to judgement. That's the way – *that's* it; thy throat aint spoiled with eating Amsterdam butter.

FRENCH SAILOR

Hist, boys! let's have a jig or two before we ride to anchor in Blanket Bay. What say ye? There comes the other watch. Stand by all legs! Pip! little Pip! hurrah with your tambourine!

PIP [*Sulky and sleepy*]

Don't know where it is.

FRENCH SAILOR

Beat thy belly, then, and wag thy ears. Jig it, men, I say; merry's the word; hurrah! Damn me, won't you dance? Form, now, Indian-file, and gallop into the double-shuffle? Throw yourselves! Legs! legs!

ICELAND SAILOR

I don't like your floor, maty; it's too springy to my taste. I'm used to ice-floors. I'm sorry to throw cold water on the subject; but excuse me.

MALTESE SAILOR

Me too; where's your girls? Who but a fool would take his left hand by his right, and say to himself, how d'ye do? Partners! I must have partners!

SICILIAN SAILOR

Aye; girls and a green! – then I'll hop with ye; yea, turn grasshopper!

LONG-ISLAND SAILOR

Well, well, ye sulkies, there's plenty more of us. Hoe corn when you may, say I. All legs go to harvest soon. Ah! here comes the music; now for it!

AZORE SAILOR

[*Ascending, and pitching the tambourine up the scuttle*]

Here you are, Pip; and there's the windlass-bitts; up you mount! Now, boys!
[*The half of them dance to the tambourine; some go below; some sleep or lie among the coils of rigging. Oaths a-plenty*]

AZORE SAILOR [*Dancing*]

Go it, Pip! Bang it, bell-boy! Rig it, dig it, stig it, quig it, bell-boy! Make fire-flies; break the jinglers!

PIP

Jinglers, you say? – there goes another, dropped off; I pound it so.

CHINA SAILOR

Rattle thy teeth, then, and pound away; make a pagoda of thyself.

FRENCH SAILOR

Merry-mad! Hold up thy hoop, Pip, till I jump through it! Split jibs! tear yourselves!

TASHTEGO [*Quietly smoking*]

That's a white man; he calls that fun: humph! I save my sweat.

OLD MANX SAILOR

I wonder whether those jolly lads bethink them of what they are dancing over. I'll dance over your grave, I will – that's the bitterest threat of your night-women, that beat head-winds round corners. O Christ! to think of the green navies and the green-skulled crews! Well, well; belike the whole world's a ball, as you scholars have it; and so 'tis right to make one ball-room of it. Dance on, lads, you're young; I was once.

3RD NANTUCKET SAILOR

Spell oh! – whew! this is worse than pulling after whales in a calm – give us a whiff, Tash.
[*They cease dancing, and gather in clusters. Meantime the sky darkens – the wind rises*]

LASCAR SAILOR

By Brahma! boys, it'll be douse sail soon. The sky-born, hightide Ganges turned to wind! Thou showest thy black brow, Seeva!

MALTESE SAILOR [*Reclining and shaking his cap*]

It's the waves – the snow's caps turn to jig it now. They'll shake their tassels soon. Now would all the waves were women, then I'd go drown, and chassee with them evermore! There's naught so sweet on earth – heaven may not match it! – as those swift glances of warm, wild bosoms in the dance, when the over-arbouring arms hide such ripe, bursting grapes.

SICILIAN SAILOR [*Reclining*]

Tell me not of it! Hark ye, lad – fleet interlacings of the limbs – lithe swayings – coyings – flutterings! lip! heart! hip! all graze: unceasing touch and go! not taste, observe ye, else come satiety. Eh, Pagan? (*Nudging.*)

TAHITAN SAILOR [*Reclining on a mat*]

Hail, holy nakedness of our dancing girls! – the Heeva-Heeva! Ah! low veiled, high palmed Tahiti! I still rest me on thy mat, but the soft soil has slid! I saw thee woven in the wood, my mat! green the first day I brought ye thence; now worn and wilted quite. Ah me! – not thou nor I can bear the change! How then, if so be transplanted to yon sky? Hear I the roaring streams from Pirohitee's peak of spears, when they leap down the crags and drown the villages? – The blast! the blast! Up, spine, and meet it! (*Leaps to his feet.*)

PORTUGUESE SAILOR

How the sea rolls swashing 'gainst the side! Stand by for reefing, hearties! the winds are just crossing swords, pell-mell they'll go lunging presently.

DANISH SAILOR

Crack, crack, old ship! so long as thou crackest, thou holdest! Well done! The mate there holds ye to it stiffly. He's no more afraid than the isle fort at Cattegat, put there to fight the Baltic with storm-lashed guns, on which the sea-salt cakes!

4TH NANTUCKET SAILOR

He has his orders, mind ye that. I heard old Ahab tell him he must always kill a squall, something as they burst a waterspout with a pistol – fire your ship right into it!

ENGLISH SAILOR

Blood! but that old man's a grand old cove! We are the lads to hunt him up his whale!

ALL

Aye! Aye!

OLD MANX SAILOR

How the three pines shake! Pines are the hardest sort of tree to live when shifted to any other soil, and here there's none but the crew's cursed clay. Steady, helmsman! steady. This is the sort of weather when brave hearts snap ashore, and keeled hulls split at sea. Our captain has his birth-mark; look yonder, boys, there's another in the sky – lurid – like, ye see, all else pitch black.

DAGGOO

What of that? Who's afraid of black's afraid of me! I'm quarried out of it!

SPANISH SAILOR

(*Aside.*) He wants to bully, ah! – the old grudge makes me touchy.

(*Advancing.*) Aye, harpooneer, thy race is the undeniable dark side of mankind – devilish dark at that. No offence.

DAGGOO [*Grimly*]

None.

ST JAGO'S SAILOR

That Spaniard's mad or drunk. But that can't be, or else in his one case our old Mogul's fire-waters are somewhat long in working.

5TH NANTUCKET SAILOR

What's that I saw – lightning? Yes.

SPANISH SAILOR

No; Daggoo showing his teeth.

DAGGOO [*Springing*]

Swallow thine, mannikin! White skin, white liver!

SPANISH SAILOR [*Meeting him*]

Knife thee heartily! big frame, small spirit!

ALL

A row! a row! a row!

TASHTEGO [*With a whiff*]

A row a 'low, and a row aloft – Gods and men – both brawlers! Humph!

BELFAST SAILOR

A row! arrah a row! The Virgin be blessed, a row! Plunge in with ye!

ENGLISH SAILOR

Fair play! Snatch the Spaniard's knife! A ring, a ring!

OLD MANX SAILOR

Ready formed. There! the ringed horizon. In that ring Cain struck Abel. Sweet work, right work! No? Why then, God, mad'st thou the ring?

MATE'S VOICE FROM THE QUARTER-DECK

Hands by the halyards! in top-gallant sails! Stand by to reef top-sails!

ALL

The squall! the squall! jump, my jollies! (*They scatter.*)

PIP [*Shrinking under the windlass*]

Jollies? Lord help such jollies! Crish, crash! there goes the jib-stay! Blang-whang! God! Duck lower, Pip, here comes the royal yard! It's worse than being in the whirled woods, the last day of the year! Who'd go climbing after chestnuts now? But there they go, all cursing, and here I don't. Fine prospects to 'em; they're on the road to heaven. Hold on hard! Jimmini, what a squall! But those chaps there are worse yet – they are your white squalls, they. White squalls? white whale, shirr! shirr! Here have I heard all their chat just now, and the white whale – shirr! shirr! – but spoken of once! and only this evening – it makes me jingle all over like my tambourine – that anaconda of an old man swore 'em in to hunt him! Oh, thou big white God aloft there somewhere in yon darkness, have mercy on this small black boy down here; preserve him from all men that have no bowels to feel fear!

CHAPTER 33

Moby-Dick

I, Ishmael, was one of that crew; my shouts had gone up with the rest; my oath had been welded with theirs; and stronger I shouted, and more did I hammer and clinch my oath, because of the dread in my soul. A wild, mystical, sympathetical feeling was in me; Ahab's quenchless feud seemed mine. With greedy ears I learned the history of that murderous monster against whom I and all the others had taken our oaths of violence and revenge.

For some time past the unaccompanied, secluded White Whale had haunted those uncivilized seas mostly frequented by the Sperm Whale fishermen. But not all of them knew of his existence; only a few, comparatively, had knowingly given battle to Moby-Dick. Several vessels reported to have encountered a Sperm Whale of uncommon magnitude and malignity, which whale, after doing great mischief to his assailants, had completely escaped them. Yet, marked by various instances of great ferocity, cunning, and malice in the monster attacked, those who by accident ignorantly gave battle to Moby-Dick, such hunters, perhaps, were content to ascribe the peculiar terror he bred, more to the perils of the Sperm Whale fishery at large than to the individual cause.

In the beginning of the thing they had every one of them, almost, as boldly and fearlessly lowered for him, as for any other whale of that species. But at length, such calamities did ensue in these assaults – not restricted to sprained wrists and ankles, broken limbs, or devouring amputations – but fatal to the last degree of fatality; those repeated disastrous repulses, all accumulating and piling their terrors upon Moby-Dick; those things had gone far to shake the fortitude of many brave hunters, to whom the story of the White Whale had come.

Nor did wild rumours of all sorts fail to exaggerate, and still the more horrify the true histories of these deadly encounters. For not only do fabulous rumours naturally grow out of the very body of all surprising terrible events, even stripped of these surmisings, there was enough in the earthly make and incontestable character of the monster to strike the imagination with unwonted power. For, it was not so much his uncommon bulk that so much distinguished him from other Sperm Whales, but, as was elsewhere thrown out – a peculiar snow-white wrinkled forehead, and a high, pyramidical white hump. These were his prominent features; the tokens whereby, even in the limitless, uncharted seas, he revealed his identity, at a long distance, to those who knew him.

The rest of his body was so streaked, and spotted, and marbled with the same shrouded hue, that, in the end, he had gained his distinctive appellation of the White Whale; a name, indeed, literally justified by his vivid aspect, when seen gliding at high noon through a dark blue sea, leaving a milky-way wake of creamy foam, all spangled with golden gleamings. Nor was it his unwonted magnitude, nor his remarkable hue, nor yet his deformed lower jaw, that so much invested the whale with natural terror, as that unexampled, intelligent malignity which, according to specific accounts, he had over and over again evinced in his assaults. More than all, his treacherous retreats struck more of dismay than perhaps aught else. For, when swimming before his exulting pursuers, with every apparent symptom of alarm, he had several times been known to turn round suddenly, and, bearing down upon them, either stave their boats to splinters, or drive them back in consternation to their ship.

Already several fatalities had attended his chase. But though similar disasters, however little bruited ashore, were by no means unusual in the fishery, yet such seemed the White Whale's infernal aforethought of ferocity, that every dismembering or death that he caused was not wholly regarded as having been inflicted by an unintelligent agent.

Judge, then, to what pitches of inflamed, distracted fury the minds of his more desperate hunters were impelled, when amid the chips of chewed boats, and the sinking limbs of torn comrades, they swam out of the white curds of the whale's direful wrath into the serene, exasperating sunlight, that smiled on, as if at a birth or a bridal.

His three boats stove around him, and oars and men both whirling in the eddies; one captain, seizing the line-knife from his broken prow, had dashed at the whale, as an Arkansas duellist at his foe, blindly seeking with a six inch blade to reach the fathom-deep life of the whale. That captain was Ahab. And then it was, that suddenly sweeping his sickle-shaped lower jaw beneath him, Moby-Dick had reaped away Ahab's leg, as a mower a blade of grass in the field. No turbaned Turk, no hired Venetian or Malay, could have smote him with more seeming malice. Small reason was there to doubt, then, that ever since that almost fatal encounter, Ahab had cherished a wild vindictiveness against the whale, all the more fell for that in his frantic morbidness he at last came to identify with him, not only all his bodily woes, but all his intellectual and spiritual exasperations. The White Whale swam before him as the monomaniac incarnation of all those malicious agencies which some deep men feel eating in them, till they are left living on with half a heart and half a lung. That malignity, Ahab deliriously transferring to the abhorred White Whale, he pitted himself, all mutilated, against it. All that most maddens and torments; all that stirs up the lees of things; all truth with malice in it; all that cracks the sinews and cakes the brain; all the subtle demonisms of life and thought; all evil, to crazy Ahab, were visibly personified, and made practically assailable in Moby-Dick. He piled upon the whale's white hump the sum of all the general rage and hate felt by his whole race from Adam down; and then, as if his chest had been a mortar, he burst his hot heart's shell upon it.

CHAPTER 34

Hark!

'Hist! Did you hear that noise, Cabaco?'

It was the middle-watch: a fair moonlight; the seamen were standing in a cordon, extending from one of the fresh-water butts in the waist, to the scuttle-butt near the taffrail. In this manner, they passed the buckets to fill the scuttle-butt. Standing, for the most part, on the hallowed precincts of the quarter-deck, they were careful not to speak or rustle their feet. From hand to hand, the buckets went in the deepest silence, only broken by the occasional flap of a sail, and the steady hum of the unceasingly advancing keel.

It was in the midst of this repose, that Archy, one of the cordon, whose post was near the after-hatches, whispered to his neighbour, a Cholo, the words above.

'Hist! did you hear that noise, Cabaco?'

'Take the bucket, will ye, Archy? what noise d'ye mean?'

'There it is again – under the hatches – don't you hear it – a cough – it sounded like a cough.'

'Cough be damned! Pass along that return bucket.'

'There again – there it is! – it sounds like two or three sleepers turning over, now!'

'Caramba! have done, shipmate, will ye? It's the three soaked biscuits ye eat for supper turning over inside of ye – nothing else. Look to the bucket!'

'Say what ye will, shipmate; I've sharp ears.'

'Aye, you are the chap, aint ye, that heard the hum of the old Quakeress's knitting-needles fifty miles at sea from Nantucket; you're the chap.'

'Grin away; we'll see what turns up. Hark ye, Cabaco, there is somebody down in the after-hold that has not yet been seen on deck; and I suspect our old Mogul knows something of it too. I heard Stubb tell Flask, one morning watch, that there was something of that sort in the wind.'

'Tish! the bucket!'

CHAPTER 35

The Chart

Had you followed Captain Ahab down into his cabin, after the squall that took place on the night succeeding that wild ratification of his purpose with his crew, you would have seen him go to a locker in the transom, and bringing out a large wrinkled roll of yellowish sea charts, spread them before him on his screwed-down table. Then seating himself before it, you would have seen him intently study the various lines and shadings which there met his eye; and with slow but steady pencil trace additional courses over spaces that before were blank. At intervals, he would refer to piles of old log-books beside him, wherein were set down the seasons and places in which, on various former voyages of various ships, Sperm Whales had been captured or seen.

While thus employed, the heavy pewter lamp suspended in chains over his head continually rocked with the motion of the ship, and for ever threw shifting gleams and shadows of lines upon his wrinkled brow, till it almost seemed that while he himself was marking out lines and courses on the wrinkled charts, some invisible pencil was also tracing lines and courses upon the deeply marked chart of his forehead.

But it was not this night in particular that, in the solitude of his cabin, Ahab thus pondered over his charts. Almost every night they were brought out; almost every night some pencil marks were effaced, and others were substituted. For with the charts of all four oceans before him, Ahab was threading a maze of currents and eddies, with a view to the more certain accomplishment of that monomaniac thought of his soul.

Now, to any one not fully acquainted with the ways of the Leviathans, it might seem an absurdly hopeless task thus to seek out one solitary creature in the unhooped oceans of this planet. But not so did it seem to Ahab, who knew the sets of all tides and currents; and thereby calculating the driftings of the Sperm Whale's food; and, also, calling to mind the regular, ascertained seasons for hunting him in particular latitudes; could arrive at reasonable surmises, almost approaching to certainties, concerning the timeliest day to be upon this or that ground in search of his prey.

Besides, when making a passage from one feeding-ground to another, the Sperm Whales, guided by some infallible instinct – say, rather, secret intelligence from the Deity – mostly swim in *veins*, as they are called; continuing their way along a given ocean-line with such exactitude, that no ship ever sailed her course, by any chart, with one tithe of such marvellous precision. In these cases, the *vein* in which at these times he is said to swim generally embraces some few miles in width; but never exceeds the visual sweep from the whale-ship's mast-heads, when circumspectly gliding along this magic zone. The sum is, that at particular seasons within that breadth and along that path, migrating whales may with great confidence be looked for.

And hence not only at substantiated times, upon well known separate feeding-grounds, could Ahab hope to encounter his prey; but in crossing the widest expanses of water between those grounds he could, by his art, so place and time himself on his way, as even then not to be wholly without prospect of a meeting.

Though the Sperm Whales have their regular seasons for particular grounds, yet in general you cannot conclude that the herds which haunted such and such a latitude or longitude this year, say, will turn out to be identically the same with those that were found there the preceding season; though there are unquestionable instances where the contrary of this has proved true. And Ahab's chances of accomplishing his object have a particular set time and place conjoined in the one technical phrase – the Season-on-the-Line. For there and then, for several consecutive years, Moby-Dick had been periodically descried, lingering in those waters for awhile, as the sun, in its annual round, loiters for a predicted interval in any one sign of the Zodiac. There it was, too, that most of the deadly encounters with the White Whale had taken place; there the waves were storied with his deeds; there also was that tragic spot where the monomaniac old man had found the awful motive to his vengeance.

Now, the Pequod had sailed from Nantucket at the very beginning of the Season-on-the-Line. No possible endeavour then could enable her commander to make the great passage southwards, double Cape Horn, and then running down sixty degrees of latitude arrive in the equatorial Pacific in time to cruise there. Therefore, he must wait for the next ensuing season. Yet the premature hour of the Pequod's sailing had, perhaps, been correctly selected by Ahab, with a view to this very complexion of things. Because, an interval of three hundred and sixty-five days and nights was before him; an interval which, instead of impatiently enduring ashore, he would spend in a miscellaneous hunt; if by chance the White Whale, spending his vacation in seas far remote from his periodical feeding-grounds, should turn up his wrinkled brow off the Persian Gulf, or in the Bengal Bay, or China Seas, or in any other waters haunted by his race. So that Monsoons, Pampas, Nor-westers, Harmattans, Trades; any wind but the Levanter and Simoom might blow Moby-Dick into the zig-zag world-circle of the Pequod's circumnavigating wake.

But granting all this; yet, regarded discreetly and coolly, seems it not but a mad idea, this; that in the broad boundless ocean, one solitary whale, even if encountered, should be thought capable of individual recognition from his hunter, even as a white-bearded Mufti in the thronged thoroughfares of Constantinople? Yes. For the peculiar snow-white brow of Moby-Dick, and his snow-white hump, could not but be unmistakable. And have I not tallied the whale, Ahab would mutter to himself, as after poring over his charts till long after midnight he would throw himself back in reveries – tallied him, and shall he escape? His broad fins are bored, and scalloped out like a lost sheep's ear! And here, his mad mind would run on in a breathless race; till a weariness and faintness of pondering came over him; and in the open air of the deck he would seek to recover his strength. Ah, God! what trances of torments does that man endure who is consumed with one unachieved revengeful desire. He sleeps with clenched hands; and wakes with his bloody nails in his palms.

Crazy Ahab, scheming, unappeasedly steadfast hunter of the White Whale. God help thee, old man, thy thoughts have created a creature in thee; and he whose intense thinking thus makes him a Prometheus; a vulture feeds upon that heart for ever; that vulture the very creature he creates.

CHAPTER 36

Surmises

Though, consumed with the hot fire of his purpose, Ahab in all his thoughts and actions ever had in view the ultimate capture of Moby-Dick; though he seemed ready to sacrifice all mortal interests to that one passion; nevertheless it may have been that he was by nature and long habituation far too wedded to a fiery whaleman's ways, altogether to abandon the collateral prosecution of the voyage. Or at least if this were otherwise, there were not wanting other motives much more influential with him. It would be refining too much, perhaps, even considering his monomania, to hint that his vindictiveness towards the White Whale might have possibly extended itself in some degree to all Sperm Whales, and that the more monsters he slew by so much the more he multiplied the chances that each subsequently encountered whale would prove to be the hated one he hunted. But if such an hypothesis be indeed exceptionable, there were still additional considerations which, though not so strictly according with the wildness of his ruling passion, yet were by no means incapable of swaying him.

To accomplish his object Ahab must use tools; and of all tools used in the shadow of the moon, men are most apt to get out of order. He knew, for example, that however magnetic his ascendancy in some respects was over Starbuck, yet that ascendancy did not cover the complete spiritual man any more than mere corporeal superiority involves intellectual mastership; for to the purely spiritual, the intellectual but stand in a sort of corporeal relation. Starbuck's body and Starbuck's coerced will were Ahab's, so long as Ahab kept his magnet at Starbuck's brain; still he knew that for all this the chief mate, in his soul, abhorred his captain's quest, and could he, would joyfully disintegrate himself from it, or even frustrate it. It might be that a long interval would elapse ere the White Whale was seen. During that long interval Starbuck would ever be apt to fall into open relapses of rebellion against his captain's leadership, unless some ordinary, prudential, circumstantial influences were brought to bear upon him. Not only that, but the subtle insanity of Ahab respecting Moby-Dick was noways more significantly manifested than in his superlative sense and shrewdness in foreseeing that, for the present, the hunt should in some way be stripped of that strange imaginative impiousness which naturally invested it; that the full terror of the voyage must be kept withdrawn into the obscure background (for few men's courage is proof against protracted meditation unrelieved by action); that when they stood their long night-watches, his officers and men must have some nearer things to think of than Moby-Dick. For however eagerly the crew had hailed the announcement of his quest, yet all sailors of all sorts are more or less capricious and unreliable – they live in the varying outer weather, and they inhale its fickleness – and when retained for any object remote and blank in the pursuit, however promissory of life and passion in the end, it is above all things requisite that temporary interests and employments should intervene and hold them healthily suspended for the final dash.

Nor was Ahab unmindful of another thing. In times of strong emotion mankind disdain all base considerations; but such times are evanescent. The permanent constitutional condition of the

manufactured man, thought Ahab, is sordidness. Granting that
the White Whale fully incites the hearts of this my savage crew,
and playing round their savageness even breeds a certain gener-
ous knight-errantism in them, still, while for the love of it they
give chase to Moby-Dick, they must also have food for their more
common, daily appetites. For even the high lifted and chivalric
Crusaders of old times were not content to traverse two thousand
miles of land to fight for their holy sepulchre, without committing
burglaries, picking pockets, and gaining other pious perquisites by
the way. Had they been strictly held to their one final and romantic object – that final and romantic object, too many would have
turned from in disgust. I will not strip these men, thought Ahab,
of all hopes of cash – aye, cash. They may scorn cash now; but let
some months go by, and no perspective promise of it to them, and
then this same quiescent cash all at once mutinying in them, this
same cash would soon cashier Ahab.

Nor was there wanting still another precautionary motive more
related to Ahab personally. Having impulsively, it is probable, and
perhaps somewhat prematurely revealed the prime but private
purpose of the Pequod's voyage, Ahab was now entirely conscious
that, in so doing, he had indirectly laid himself open to the un-
answerable charge of usurpation; and with perfect impunity, both
moral and legal, his crew if so disposed, and to that end competent,
could refuse all further obedience to him, and even violently wrest
from him the command. From even the barely hinted imputation
of usurpation, and the possible consequences of such a suppressed
impression gaining ground, Ahab must of course have been most
anxious to protect himself. That protection could only consist in
his own predominating brain and heart and hand, backed by a
heedful, closely calculating attention to every minute atmospheric
influence which it was possible for his crew to be subjected to.

For all these reasons then, Ahab plainly saw that he must still
in a good degree continue true to the natural, nominal purpose of
the Pequod's voyage; observe all customary usages; and not only
that, but force himself to evince all his well known passionate
interest in the general pursuit of his profession. Be all this as it

may, his voice was now often heard hailing the three mast-heads and admonishing them to keep a bright look-out, and not omit reporting even a porpoise. This vigilance was not long without reward.

CHAPTER 37

The Mat-maker

It was a cloudy, sultry afternoon; the seamen were lazily lounging about the decks, or vacantly gazing over into the lead-coloured waters. Queequeg and I were mildly employed weaving what is called a sword-mat, for an additional lashing to our boat. So still and subdued and yet somehow preluding was all the scene, and such an incantation of revery lurked in the air, that each silent sailor seemed resolved into his own invisible self.

I was the attendant or page of Queequeg, while busy at the mat. As I kept passing and repassing the filling or woof of marline between the long yarns of the warp, using my own hand for the shuttle, and as Queequeg, standing sideways, ever and anon slid his heavy oaken sword between the threads, and idly looking off upon the water, carelessly and unthinkingly drove home every yarn, so a dreaminess did there then reign all over the ship and all over the sea, only broken by the intermitting dull sound of the sword.

Thus we were weaving and weaving away when I started at a sound so strange, long drawn, and musically wild and unearthly, that the ball of free will dropped from my hand, and I stood gazing up at the clouds whence that voice dropped like a wing. High aloft in the cross-trees was that mad Gay-Header, Tashtego. His body was reaching eagerly forward, his hand stretched out and at intervals he continued his cries.

As he stood hovering over you half suspended in air, so wildly and eagerly peering towards the horizon, you would have thought him some prophet or seer beholding the shadows of Fate, and by those wild cries announcing their coming.

'There she blows! there! there! there! she blows!'

'Where-away?'

'On the lee-beam, about two miles off! a school of them!'

Instantly all was commotion. The Sperm Whale blows as a clock ticks, with the same undeviating and reliable uniformity. And thereby whalemen distinguish this fish from other tribes of his genus.

'There go flukes!' was now the cry from Tashtego; and the whales disappeared.

'Quick, steward!' cried Ahab. 'Time! time!'

Dough-Boy hurried below, glanced at the watch, and reported the exact minute to Ahab. The ship was now kept away from the wind, and she went gently rolling before it. Tashtego reporting that the whales had gone down heading to leeward, we confidently looked to see them again directly in advance of our bows. For that singular craft at times evinced by the Sperm Whale when, sounding with his head in one direction, he nevertheless, while concealed beneath the surface, mills round, and swiftly swims off in the opposite quarter – this deceitfulness of his could not now be in action; for there was no reason to suppose that the fish seen by Tashtego had been in any way alarmed, or indeed knew at all of our vicinity. One of the men selected for shipkeepers – that is, those not appointed to the boats – by this time relieved the Indian at the main-mast head. The sailors at the fore and mizzen had come down; the line tubs were fixed in their places; the cranes were thrust out; the mainyard was backed, and the three boats swung over the sea like three samphire baskets over high cliffs. Outside of the bulwarks their eager crews with one hand clung to the rail, while one foot was expectantly poised on the gunwale. So look the long line of man-of-war's men about to throw themselves on board an enemy's ship.

But at this critical instant a sudden exclamation was heard that took every eye from the whale. With a start all glared at dark Ahab, who was surrounded by five dusky phantoms that seemed fresh formed out of air.

CHAPTER 38

The First Lowering

The phantoms, for so they then seemed, were flitting on the other side of the deck, and, with a noiseless celerity, were casting loose the tackles and bands of the boat which swung there. This boat had always been deemed one of the spare boats, though technically called the captain's, on account of its hanging from the starboard quarter. The figure that now stood by its bows was tall and swart, with one white tooth evilly protruding from its steel-like lips. A rumpled Chinese jacket of black cotton funereally invested him, with wide black trowsers of the same dark stuff. But strangely, crowning this ebonness was a glistening white plaited turban, the living hair braided and coiled round and round upon his head. Less swart in aspect, the companions of this figure were of that vivid, tiger-yellow complexion peculiar to some of the aboriginal natives of the Manillas – a race notorious for a certain diabolism of subtilty, and by some honest white mariners supposed to be the paid spies and secret confidential agents on the water of the devil, their lord, whose counting-room they suppose to be elsewhere.

While yet the wondering ship's company were gazing upon these strangers, Ahab cried out to the white-turbaned old man at their head, 'All ready there, Fedallah?'

'Ready,' was the half-hissed reply.

'Lower away then; d'ye hear?' shouting across the deck. 'Lower away there, I say.'

Such was the thunder of his voice, that spite of their amazement the men sprang over the rail; the sheaves whirled round in the blocks; with a wallow, the three boats dropped into the sea; while, with a dexterous, off-handed daring, unknown in any other vocation, the sailors goat-like leaped down the rolling ship's side into the tossed boats below.

Hardly had they pulled out from under the ship's lee, when a fourth keel, coming from the windward side, pulled round under the stern, and showed the five strangers rowing Ahab, who, standing erect in the stern, loudly hailed Starbuck, Stubb, and Flask, to spread themselves widely, so as to cover a large expanse of water. But with all their eyes again riveted upon the swart Fedallah and his crew, the inmates of the other boats obeyed not the command.

'Captain Ahab?—' said Starbuck.

'Spread yourselves,' cried Ahab; 'give way, all four boats. Thou, Flask, pull out more to leeward!'

'Aye, aye, sir,' cheerily cried little King-Post, sweeping round his great steering oar. 'Lay back!' addressing his crew. 'There! – there! – there again! There she blows right ahead, boys! – lay back!'

'Never heed yonder yellow boys, Archy.'

'Oh, I don't mind 'em, sir,' said Archy; 'I knew it all before now. Didn't I hear 'em in the hold? And didn't I tell Cabaco here of it? What say ye, Cabaco? They are stowaways, Mr Flask.'

'Pull, pull, my fine hearts-alive; pull, my children; pull, my little ones,' drawlingly and soothingly sighed Stubb to his crew, some of whom still showed signs of uneasiness. 'Why don't you break your backbones, my boys? What is it you stare at? Those chaps in yonder boat? Tut! They are only five more hands come to help us – never mind from where – the more the merrier. Pull, then, do pull; never mind the brimstone – devils are good fellows enough. So, so; there you are now; that's the stroke for a thousand pounds; that's the stroke to sweep the stakes! Hurrah for the gold cup of sperm oil, my heroes! Three cheers, men – all hearts alive! Easy, easy; don't be in a hurry – don't be in a hurry. Why don't you snap your oars, you rascals? Bite something, you dogs! So, so, so, then; softly, softly! That's it – that's it! long and strong. Give way there, give way! The devil fetch ye, ye rapscallions; ye are all asleep. Stop snoring, ye sleepers, and pull. Pull, will ye? pull, can't ye? pull, won't ye? Why in the name of gudgeons and ginger-cakes don't ye pull? – pull and break something! pull, and start your eyes out! Here!' whipping out the sharp knife from his girdle; 'every mother's son of ye draw his knife, and pull with the blade between his teeth. That's it – that's it. Now ye do something; that looks like it, my steel-bits. Start her – start her, my silver-spoons! Start her, marling-spikes!'

Stubb's exordium to his crew is given here at large, because he had rather a peculiar way of talking to them in general, and especially in inculcating the religion of rowing. But you must not suppose from this specimen of his sermonizings that he ever flew into downright passions with his congregation. Not at all; and therein consisted his chief peculiarity. He would say the most terrific things to his crew, in a tone so strangely compounded of fun and fury, and the fury seemed so calculated merely as a spice to the fun, that no oarsman could hear such queer invocations without pulling for dear life, and yet pulling for the mere joke of the thing. Besides he all the time looked so easy and indolent himself, so loungingly managed his steering-oar, and so broadly gaped – open-mouthed at times – that the mere sight of such a yawning commander, by sheer force of contrast, acted like a charm upon the crew. Then again, Stubb was one of those odd sort of humorists, whose jollity is sometimes so ambiguous, as to put all inferiors on their guard in the matter of obeying them.

In obedience to a sign from Ahab, Starbuck was now pulling obliquely across Stubb's bow; and when the two boats were pretty near to each other, Stubb hailed the mate.

'Mr Starbuck! a word with ye, sir, if ye please!'

'Halloa!' returned Starbuck, turning round not a single inch as he spoke; still earnestly but whisperingly urging his crew; his face set like a flint from Stubb's.

'What think ye of those yellow boys, sir!'

'Smuggled on board, somehow, before the ship sailed. (Strong, strong, boys!)' in a whisper to his crew, then speaking out loud again: 'A sad business, Mr Stubb! (seethe her, seethe her, my lads!) but never mind, Mr Stubb, all for the best. Let all your crew pull strong, come what will. (Spring, my men, spring!) There's hogsheads of sperm ahead, Mr Stubb, and that's what ye came for. (Pull, my boys!) Sperm, sperm's the play! This at least is duty; duty and profit hand in hand!'

'Aye, aye, I thought as much,' soliloquized Stubb, when the boats diverged, 'as soon as I clapt eye on 'em, I thought so. Aye, and that's what he went into the after hold for, so often, as Dough-Boy long suspected. They were hidden down there. The White Whale's at the bottom of it. Well, well, so be it! Can't be helped! All right! Give way, men! It ain't the White Whale today! Give way!'

Now the advent of these outlandish strangers at such a critical instant as the lowering of the boats from the deck, this had not unreasonably awakened a sort of superstitious amazement in some of the ship's company; but Archy's fancied discovery having some time previous got abroad among them, though indeed not credited then, this had in some small measure prepared them for the event. It took off the extreme edge of their wonder; and so what with all this and Stubb's confident way of accounting for their appearance, they were for the time freed from superstitious surmisings; though the affair still left abundant room for all manner of wild conjectures as to dark Ahab's precise agency in the matter from the beginning. For me, I silently recalled the mysterious shadows I had seen creeping on board the Pequod during the dim Nantucket dawn, as well as the enigmatical hintings of the unaccountable Elijah.

Meantime, Ahab, out of hearing of his officers, having sided the furthest to windward, was still ranging ahead of the other boats; a circumstance bespeaking how potent a crew was pulling him. Those tiger yellow creatures of his seemed all steel and whalebone; like five trip-hammers they rose and fell with regular strokes of strength, which periodically started the boat along the water like a horizontal burst boiler out of a Mississippi steamer. As for Fedallah, who was seen pulling the harpooneer oar, he had thrown aside his black jacket, and displayed his naked chest with the whole part of his body above the gunwale, clearly cut against the alternating depressions of the watery horizon; while at the other end of the boat Ahab, with one arm, like a fencer's, thrown half backward into the air, as if to counterbalance any tendency to trip; Ahab was seen steadily managing his steering oar as in a thousand boat lowerings ere the White Whale had torn him. All at once the outstretched arm gave a peculiar motion and then remained fixed, while the boat's five oars were seen simultaneously peaked. Boat and crew sat motionless on the sea. Instantly the three spread boats in the rear paused. The whales had irregularly settled bodily down into the blue, thus giving no distantly discernible token of the movement, though from his closer vicinity Ahab had observed it.

'Every man look out along his oars!' cried Starbuck. 'Thou, Queequeg, stand up!'

Nimbly springing up on the triangular raised box in the bow, the savage stood erect there, and with intensely eager eyes gazed off towards the spot where the chase had last been descried. Likewise upon the extreme stern of the boat where it was also triangularly platformed level with the gunwale, Starbuck himself was seen coolly and adroitly balancing himself to the jerking toss-ings of his chip of a craft, and silently eyeing the vast blue eye of the sea.

Not very far distant Flask's boat was also lying breathlessly still; its commander recklessly standing upon the top of the loggerhead, a stout sort of post rooted in the keel, and rising some two feet above the level of the stern platform. It is used for catching turns with the whale line. Its top is not more spacious than the palm of a man's hand, and standing upon such a base as that, Flask seemed perched at the mast-head of some ship which had sunk to all but her trucks. But little King-Post was small and short, and at the same time little King-Post was full of a large and tall ambition, so that this loggerhead stand-point of his did by no means satisfy King-Post.

'I can't see three seas off; tip us up an oar there, and let me on to that.'

Upon this, Daggoo, with either hand upon the gunwale to steady his way, swiftly slid aft, and then erecting himself volunteered his lofty shoulders for a pedestal.

'Good a mast-head as any, sir. Will you mount?'

'That I will, and thank ye very much, my fine fellow; only I wish you fifty feet taller.' Whereupon planting his feet firmly against two opposite planks of the boat, the gigantic negro, stooping a little, presented his flat palm to Flask's foot, and then putting Flask's hand on his hearse-plumed head and bidding him spring as he himself should toss, with one dexterous fling landed the little man high and dry on his shoulders. And here was Flask now standing, Daggoo with one lifted arm furnishing him with a breastband to lean against and steady himself by. At any time it is a strange sight to the tyro to see with what wondrous habitude of unconscious skill the whaleman will maintain an erect posture in his boat, even when pitched about by the most riotously perverse and cross-running seas. Still more strange to see him giddily perched upon the loggerhead itself, under such circumstances. But the sight of little Flask mounted upon gigantic Daggoo was yet more curious; for sustaining himself with a cool, indifferent, easy, unthought of, barbaric majesty, the noble negro to every roll of the sea harmoni-ously rolled his fine form. On his broad back, flaxen-haired Flask seemed a snow-flake. The bearer looked nobler than the rider.

Meanwhile Stubb, the third mate, betrayed no such far-gazing solicitudes. The whales might have made one of their regular soundings, not a temporary dive from mere fright; and if that were the case, Stubb, as his wont in such cases, it seems, was resolved to solace the languishing interval with his pipe. He withdrew it from his hatband, where he always wore it aslant like a feather. He loaded it, and rammed home the loading with his thumb-end; but hardly had he ignited his match across the rough sand-paper of his hand, when Tashtego, his harpooneer, whose eyes had been setting to windward like two fixed stars, suddenly dropped like light from his erect attitude to his seat, crying out in a quick frenzy of hurry, 'Down, down all, and give way! – there they are!'

To landsman, no whale, nor any sign of a herring, would have been visible at that moment; nothing but a troubled bit of green-ish white water, and thin scattered puffs of vapour hovering over it, and suffusingly blowing off to leeward, like the confused scud from white rolling billows. The air around suddenly vibrated and tingled, as it were, like the air over intensely heated plates of iron. Beneath this atmospheric waving and curling, and partially beneath a thin layer of water, also, the whales were swimming.

Seen in advance of all the other indications, the puffs of vapour they spouted seemed their forerunning couriers and detached flying outriders.

All four boats were now in keen pursuit of that one spot of troubled water and air. But it bade far to outstrip them; it flew on and on, as a mass of interblending bubbles borne down a rapid stream from the hills.

'Pull, pull, my good boys,' said Starbuck, in the intensest concentrated whisper to his men; while the sharp fixed glance from his eyes, darted straight ahead of the bow, almost seemed as two visible needles in two unerring binnacle compasses. He did not say much to his crew, though, nor did his crew say anything to him. Only the silence of the boat was at intervals startlingly pierced by one of his peculiar whispers, now harsh with command, now soft with entreaty.

How different the loud little King-Post. 'Sing out and say something, my hearties. Roar and pull, my thunderbolts! Beach me, beach me on their black backs, boys; only do that for me, and I'll sign over to you my Martha's Vineyard plantation, boys; including wife and children, boys. Lay me on – lay me on! O Lord, Lord! but I shall go stark, staring mad: See! see that white water!'

And so shouting, he pulled his hat from his head, and stamped up and down on it; then picking it up, flirted it far off upon the sea; and finally fell to rearing and plunging in the boat's stern like a crazed colt from the prairie.

'Look at that chap now,' philosophically drawled Stubb, who, with his short pipe, mechanically retained between his teeth, at a short distance, followed after – 'He's got fits, that Flask has. Fits? yes, give him fits – that's the very word – pitch fits into 'em. Merrily, merrily, hearts-alive. Pudding for supper, you know; merry's the word. Pull, babes – pull, sucklings – pull, all. But what the devil are you hurrying about? Softly, softly, and steadily, my men. Only pull, and keep pulling; nothing more. Crack all your backbones, and bite your knives in two – that's all. Take it easy – why don't ye take it easy, I say, and burst all your livers and lungs!'

But what it was that inscrutable Ahab said to that tiger-yellow crew of his – these were words best omitted here; for you live under the blessed light of the evangelical land. Only the infidel sharks in the audacious seas may give ear to such words, when, with tornado brow, and eyes of red murder, and foam-glued lips, Ahab leaped after his prey.

Meanwhile, all the boats tore on. The repeated specific allusions of Flask to 'that whale', as he called the fictitious monster which he declared to be incessantly tantalizing his boat's bow with its tail – these allusions of his were at times so vivid and lifelike, that they would cause some one or two of his men to snatch a fearful look over the shoulder. But this was against all rule; for the oarsmen must put out their eyes, and ram a skewer through their necks; usage pronouncing that they must have no organs but ears, and no limbs but arms, in these critical moments.

It was a sight full of quick wonder and awe! The vast swells of the omnipotent sea; the surging, hollow roar they made, as they rolled along the eight gunwales, like gigantic bowls in a boundless bowling-green; the brief suspended agony of the boat, as it would tip for an instant on the knife-like edge of the sharper waves, that almost seemed threatening to cut it in two; the sudden profound dip into the watery glens and hollows; the keen spurrings and goadings to gain the top of the opposite hill; the headlong, sled-like slide down its other side – all these, with the cries of the headsmen and harpooneers, and the shuddering gasps of the oarsmen, with the wondrous sight of the ivory Pequod bearing down upon her boats with outstretched sails, like a wild hen after her screaming brood; all this was thrilling. Not the raw recruit, marching from the bosom of his wife into the fever heat of his first battle; not the dead man's ghost encountering the first unknown phantom in the other world – neither of these can feel stranger and stronger emotions than that man does, who for the first time finds himself pulling into the charmed, churned circle of the hunted Sperm Whale.

The dancing white water made by the chase was now becoming more and more visible, owing to the increasing darkness of the dun cloud-shadows flung upon the sea. The jets of vapour no longer blended, but tilted everywhere to right and left; the whales seemed separating their wakes. The boats were pulled more apart; Starbuck giving chase to three whales running dead to leeward. Our sail was now set, and, with the still rising wind, we rushed along; the boat going with such madness through the water, that the lee oars could scarcely be worked rapidly enough to escape being torn from the row-locks.

Soon we were running through a suffusing wide veil of mist; neither ship nor boat to be seen.

'Give way, men,' whispered Starbuck, drawing still further aft the sheet of his sail; 'there is time to kill a fish yet before the squall comes. There's white water again! – close to! Spring!'

Soon after, two cries in quick succession on each side of us denoted that the other boats had got fast; but hardly were they overheard, when with a lightning-like hurtling whisper Starbuck said: 'Stand up!' and Queequeg, harpoon in hand, sprang to his feet.

Though not one of the oarsmen was then facing the life and death peril so close to them ahead, yet with their eyes on the intense countenance of the mate in the stern of the boat, they knew that the imminent instant had come; they heard, too, an enormous wallowing sound as of fifty elephants stirring in their litter. Meanwhile the boat was still booming through the mist, the waves curling and hissing around us like the erected crests of enraged serpents.

'That's his hump. *There*, *there*, give it to him!' whispered Starbuck.

A short rushing sound leaped out of the boat; it was the darted iron of Queequeg. Then all in one welded commotion came an invisible push from astern, while forward the boat seemed striking on a ledge; the sail collapsed and exploded; a gush of scalding vapour shot up near by; something rolled and tumbled like an earthquake beneath us. The whole crew were half suffocated as they were tossed helter-skelter into the white curdling cream of the squall. Squall, whale, and harpoon had all blended together; and the whale, merely grazed by the iron, escaped.

Though completely swamped, the boat was nearly unharmed. Swimming round it we picked up the floating oars, and lashing them across the gunwale, tumbled back to our places. There we sat up to our knees in the sea, the water covering every rib and plank, so that to our downward gazing eyes the suspended craft seemed a coral boat grown up to us from the bottom of the ocean.

The wind increased to a howl; the waves dashed their bucklers together; the whole squall roared, forked, and crackled around us like a white fire upon the prairie, in which, unconsumed, we were burning; immortal in these jaws of death! In vain we hailed the other boats; as well roar to the live coals down the chimney of a flaming furnace as hail those boats in that storm. Meanwhile the driving scud, rack, and mist grew darker with the shadows of night; no sign of the ship could be seen. The rising sea forbade all attempts to bale out the boat. The oars were useless as propellers, performing now the office of life-preservers. So, cutting the lashing of the waterproof match keg, after many failures Starbuck contrived to ignite the lamp in the lantern; then stretching it on a waif pole, handed it to Queequeg as the standard-bearer of this forlorn hope. There, then, he sat, holding up that imbecile candle in the heart of that almighty forlornness. There, then, he sat, the sign and symbol of a man without faith, hopelessly holding up hope in the midst of despair.

Wet, drenched through, and shivering cold, despairing of ship or boat, we lifted up our eyes as the dawn came on. The mist still spread over the sea, the empty lantern lay crushed in the bottom of the boat. Suddenly Queequeg started to his feet, hollowing his hand to his ear. We all heard a faint creaking, as of ropes and yards hitherto muffled by the storm. The sound came nearer and nearer; the thick mists were dimly parted by a huge, vague form. Affrighted, we all sprang into the sea as the ship at last loomed into view, bearing right down upon us within a distance of not much more than its length.

Floating on the waves we saw the abandoned boat, as for one instant it tossed and gaped beneath the ship's bows like a chip at the base of a cataract; and then the vast hull rolled over it, and it was seen no more till it came up weltering astern. Again we swam for it, were dashed against it by the seas, and were at last taken up and safely landed on board. Ere the squall came close to, the other boats had cut loose from their fish and returned to the ship in good time. The ship had given us up, but was still cruising, if haply it might light upon some token of our perishing – an oar or a lance pole.

CHAPTER 39

Ahab's Boat and Crew. Fedallah

'Who would have thought it, Flask!' cried Stubb; 'if I had but one leg you would not catch me in a boat, unless maybe to stop the plug-hole with my timber toe. Oh! he's a wonderful old man!'

'I don't think it so strange, after all, on that account,' said Flask. 'If his leg were off at the hip, now, it would be a different thing. That would disable him; but he has one knee, and good part of the other left, you know.'

'I don't know that, my little man; I never yet saw him kneel.'

Among whale-wise people it has often been argued whether, considering the paramount importance of his life to the success of the voyage, it is right for a whaling captain to jeopardize that life in the active perils of the chase.

But with Ahab the question assumed a modified aspect. Considering that the pursuit of whales is always under great and extraordinary difficulties; that every individual moment, indeed, then comprises a peril; under these circumstances is it wise for any maimed man to enter a whale-boat in the hunt? As a general thing, the joint-owners of the Pequod must have plainly thought not.

Ahab well knew that although his friends at home would think little of his entering a boat in certain comparatively harmless vicissitudes of the chase, for the sake of being near the scene of action and giving his orders in person, yet for Captain Ahab to have a boat actually apportioned to him as a regular headsman in the hunt – above all for Captain Ahab to be supplied with five extra men, as that same boat's crew, he well knew that such gener-ous conceits never entered the heads of the owners of the Pequod. Therefore he had not solicited a boat's crew from them, nor had he in any way hinted his desires on that head. Nevertheless he had taken private measures of his own touching all that matter. Until Cabaco's published discovery, the sailors had little foreseen it, though to be sure when, after being a little while out of port, all hands had concluded the customary business of fitting the whale-boats for service; when some time after this Ahab was now and then found bestirring himself in the matter of making thole-pins with his own hands for what was thought to be one of the spare boats, and even solicitously cutting the small wooden skewers, which when the line is running out are pinned over the groove in the bow: when all this was observed in him, and particularly his solicitude in having an extra coat of sheathing in the bottom of the boat, as if to make it better withstand the pointed pressure of his ivory limb; and also the anxiety he evinced in exactly shap-ing the thigh board, or clumsy cleat, as it is sometimes called, the horizontal piece in the boat's bow for bracing the knee against in darting or stabbing at the whale; when it was observed how often he stood up in that boat with his solitary knee fixed in the semi-circular depression in the cleat, and with the carpenter's chisel gouged out a little here and straightened it a little there; all these things, I say, had awakened much interest and curiosity at the time. But almost everybody supposed that this particular prepara-tive heedfulness in Ahab must only be with a view to the ultimate chase of Moby-Dick; for he had already revealed his intention to hunt that mortal monster in person. But such a supposition did by no means involve the remotest suspicion as to any boat's crew being assigned to that boat.

Now, with the subordinate phantoms, what wonder remained soon waned away; for in a whaler wonders soon wane. Besides, now and then such unaccountable odds and ends of strange nations come up from the unknown nooks and ash-holes of the earth to man these floating outlaws of whalers; and the ships themselves often pick up such queer castaway creatures found tossing about the open sea on planks, bits of wreck, oars, whale-boats, canoes, blown-off Japanese junks, and what not; that Beelzebub himself might climb up the side and step down into the cabin to chat with the captain, and it would not create any unsubduable excitement in the forecastle.

But be all this as it may, certain it is that while the subordinate phantoms soon found their place among the crew, though still as it were somehow distinct from them, yet that hair-turbaned Fedallah remained a muffled mystery to the last. Whence he came in a mannerly world like this, by what sort of unaccountable tie he soon evinced himself to be linked with Ahab's peculiar fortunes; nay, so far as to have some sort of a half-hinted influence; Heaven knows, but it might have been even authority over him; all this none knew. But one cannot sustain an indifferent air concerning Fedallah. He was such a creature as civilized, domestic people in the temperate zone only see in their dreams, and that but dimly; but the like of whom now and then glide among the unchanging Asiatic communities, especially the Oriental isles to the east of the continent – those insulated, immemorial, unalterable countries, which even in these modern days still preserve much of the ghostly aboriginalness of earth's primal generations, when the memory of the first man was a distinct recollection, and all men his descendants, unknowing whence he came, eyed each other as real phantoms, and asked of the sun and the moon why they were created and to what end; when though, according to Genesis, the angels indeed consorted with the daughters of men, the devils also, add the uncanonical Rabbins, indulged in mundane amours.

CHAPTER 40

The Spirit-spout

Days, weeks passed, and under easy sail, the ivory Pequod had slowly swept across four several cruising-grounds; that off the Azores; off the Cape de Verdes; on the Plate (so called), being off the mouth of the Rio de la Plata; and the Carrol Ground, an unstaked, watery locality, southerly from St Helena. It was while gliding through these latter waters that one serene and moonlight night, when all the waves rolled by like scrolls of silver; and, by their soft, suffusing seethings, made what seemed a silvery silence, not a solitude: on such a silent night a silvery jet was seen far in advance of the white bubbles at the bow. Lit up by the moon, it looked celestial; seemed some plumed and glittering god uprising from the sea. Fedallah first descried this jet. For of these moon-light nights, it was his wont to mount to the main-mast-head, and stand a look-out there, with the same precision as if it had been day. And yet, though herds of whales were seen by night, not one whaleman in a hundred would venture a lowering for them. You may think with what emotions, then, the seamen beheld this old Oriental perched aloft at such unusual hours; his turban and the moon, companions in one sky. But when, after spending his uniform interval there for several successive nights without utter-ing a single sound; when, after all this silence, his unearthly voice was heard announcing that silvery, moon-lit jet, every reclining mariner started to his feet as if some winged spirit had lighted in the rigging, and hailed the mortal crew. 'There she blows!' Had the trump of judgement blown, they could not have quivered more; yet still they felt no terror; rather pleasure. For though it was a most unwonted hour, yet so impressive was the cry, and so deliriously exciting, that almost every soul on board instinctively desired a lowering.

Walking the deck with quick, side-lunging strides, Ahab

commanded the t'gallant sails and royals to be set, and every stunsail spread. The best man in the ship must take the helm. Then, with every mast-head manned, the piled-up craft rolled down before the wind. The strange, upheaving, lifting tendency of the taffrail breeze filling the hollows of so many sails made the buoyant, hovering deck to feel like air beneath the feet; while still she rushed along, as if two antagonistic influences were struggling in her – one to mount direct to heaven, the other to drive yawingly to some horizontal goal. And had you watched Ahab's face that night, you would have thought that in him also two different things were warring. While his one live leg made lively echoes along the deck, every stroke of his dead limb sounded like a coffin-tap. On life and death this old man walked. But though the ship so swiftly sped, and though from every eye, like arrows, the eager glances shot, yet the silvery jet was no more seen that night. Every sailor swore he saw it once, but not a second time.

This midnight-spout had almost grown a forgotten thing, when, some days after, lo! at the same silent hour, it was again announced: again it was descried by all; but upon making sail to overtake it, once more it disappeared as if it had never been. And so it served us night after night, till no one heeded it but to wonder at it. Mysteriously jetted into the clear moonlight, or starlight, as the case might be; disappearing again for one whole day, or two days, or three; and somehow seeming at every repetition to be advancing still further and further in our van, this solitary jet seemed for ever alluring us on.

Nor with the immemorial superstition of their race, and in accordance with the preternaturalness, as it seemed, which in many things invested the Pequod, were there wanting some of the seamen who swore that whenever and wherever descried; at however remote times, or in however far apart latitudes and longitudes, that unnearable spout was cast by one self-same whale; and that whale, Moby-Dick. For a time, there reigned, too, a sense of peculiar dread at this flitting apparition, as if it were treacherously beckoning us on and on, in order that the monster might turn round upon us, and rend us at last in the remotest and most savage seas.

These temporary apprehensions, so vague but so awful, derived a wondrous potency from the contrasting serenity of the weather, in which, beneath all its blue blandness, some thought there lurked a devilish charm, as for days and days we voyaged along, through seas so wearily, lonesomely mild, that all space, in repugnance to our vengeful errand, seemed vacating itself of life before our urn-like prow.

But, at last, when turning to the eastward, the Cape winds began howling around us, and we rose and fell upon the long, troubled seas that are there; when the ivory-tusked Pequod sharply bowed to the blast, and gored the dark waves in her madness, till, like showers of silver chips, the foam-flakes flew over her bulwarks; then all this desolate vacuity of life went away, but gave place to sights more dismal than before.

Close to our bows, strange forms in the water darted hither and thither before us; while thick in our rear flew the inscrutable sea-ravens. And every morning, perched on our stays, rows of these birds were seen; and spite of our hootings, for a long time obstinately clung to the hemp, as though they deemed our ship some drifting, uninhabited craft; a thing appointed to desolation, and therefore fit roosting-place for their homeless selves. And heaved and heaved, still unrestingly heaved the black sea, as if its vast tides were a conscience; and the great mundane soul were in anguish and remorse for the long sin and suffering it had bred.

Cape of Good Hope, do they call ye? Rather Cape Tormentoto, as called of yore; for long allured by the perfidious silences that before had attended us, we found ourselves launched into this tormented sea, where guilty beings transformed into those fowls and these fish seemed condemned to swim on everlastingly without any haven in store, or beat that black air without any horizon. But calm, snow-white, and unvarying; still directing its fountain of feathers to the sky; still beckoning us on from before, the solitary jet would at times be descried.

During all this blackness of the elements, Ahab, though assuming for the time the almost continual command of the drenched and dangerous deck, manifested the gloomiest reserve; and more seldom than ever addressed his mates. In tempestuous times like these, after everything above and aloft has been secured, nothing more can be done but passively to await the issue of the gale. Then captain and crew become practical fatalists. So, with his ivory leg inserted into its accustomed hole, and with one hand firmly grasping a shroud, Ahab for hours and hours would stand gazing dead to windward, while an occasional squall of sleet or snow would all but congeal his very eyelashes together. Meantime, the crew, driven from the forward part of the ship by the perilous seas that burstingly broke over its bows, stood in a line along the bulwarks in the waist; and the better to guard against the leaping waves, each man had slipped himself into a sort of bowline secured to the rail, in which he swung as in a loosened belt. Few or no words were spoken; and the silent ship, as if manned by painted sailors in wax, day after day tore on through all the swift madness and gladness of the demoniac waves. By night the same muteness of humanity before the shrieks of the ocean prevailed; still in silence the men swung in the bowlines; still wordless Ahab stood up to the blast. Never could Starbuck forget the old man's aspect, when one night going down into the cabin to mark how the barometer stood, he saw him with closed eyes sitting straight in his floor-screwed chair; the rain and half-melted sleet of the storm from which he had some time before emerged still slowly dripping from the unremoved hat and coat. On the table beside him lay unrolled one of those charts of tides and currents which have previously been spoken of. His lantern swung from his tightly clenched hand. Though the body was erect, the head was thrown back so that the closed eyes were pointed towards the needle of the tell-tale that swung from a beam in the ceiling.

Terrible old man! thought Starbuck with a shudder, sleeping in this gale, still thou steadfastly eyest thy purpose.

CHAPTER 41

The Albatross

South-eastward from the Cape, off the distant Crozetts, a good cruising ground for Right Whalemen, a sail loomed ahead, the Goney (Albatross) by name. As she slowly drew nigh, from my lofty perch at the foremast-head, I had a good view of that sight so remarkable to a tyro in the far ocean fisheries – a whaler at sea, and long absent from home.

As if the waves had been fullers, this craft was bleached like the skeleton of a stranded walrus. All down her sides, this spectral appearance was traced with long channels of reddened rust, while all her spars and her rigging were like the thick branches of trees furred over with hoar-frost. Only her lower sails were set. A wild sight it was to see her long-bearded look-outs at those three mast-heads. They seemed clad in the skins of beasts, so torn and bepatched the raiment that had survived nearly four years of cruising. Standing in iron hoops nailed to the mast, they swayed and swung over a fathomless sea; and though, when the ship slowly glided close under our stem, we six men in the air came so nigh to each other that we might almost have leaped from the mast-heads of one ship to those of the other; yet, those forlorn-looking fishermen, mildly eyeing us as they passed, said not one word to our own look-outs, while the quarter-deck hail was being heard from below.

'Ship ahoy! Have ye seen the White Whale?'

But as the strange captain, leaning over the pallid bulwarks, was in the act of putting his trumpet to his mouth, it somehow fell from his hand into the sea; and the wind now rising amain, he in vain strove to make himself heard without it. Meantime his ship was still increasing the distance between. While in various silent ways the seamen of the Pequod were evincing their observance of this ominous incident at the first mere mention of the White Whale's name to another ship, Ahab for a moment paused; it almost seemed as though he would have lowered a boat to board the stranger, had not the threatening wind forbade. But taking advantage of his windward position, he again seized his trumpet, and knowing by her aspect that the stranger vessel was a Nantucketer and shortly bound home, he loudly hailed – 'Ahoy there! This is the Pequod, bound round the world! Tell them to address all future letters to the Pacific Ocean! and this time three years, if I am not at home, tell them to address them to—'

At that moment the two wakes were fairly crossed, and instantly, then, in accordance with their singular ways, shoals of small harmless fish, that for some days before had been placidly swimming by our side, darted away with what seemed shuddering fins, and ranged themselves fore and aft with the stranger's flanks. Though in the course of his continual voyagings Ahab must often before have noticed a similar sight, yet, to any monomaniac man, the veriest trifles capriciously carry meanings.

'Swim away from me, do ye?' murmured Ahab, gazing over into the water. There seemed but little in the words, but the tone conveyed more of deep helpless sadness than the insane old man had ever before evinced. But turning to the steersman, who thus far had been holding the ship in the wind to diminish her headway, he cried out in his old lion voice – 'Up helm! Keep her off round the world!'

Round the world! There is much in that sound to inspire proud feelings; but whereto does all that circumnavigation conduct? Only through numberless perils to the very point whence we started, where those that we left behind secure were all the time before us. Were this world an endless plain, and by sailing eastward we could for ever reach new distances, and discover sights more sweet and strange than any Cyclades or Islands of King Solomon, then there were promise in the voyage. But in pursuit of those far mysteries we dream of, or in tormented chase of that demon phantom that, some time or other, swims before all human hearts; while chasing such over this round globe, they either lead us on in barren mazes or midway leave us whelmed.

CHAPTER 42

The Gam

The ostensible reason why Ahab did not go on board of the whaler we had spoken was this: the wind and sea betokened storms. But even had this not been the case, he would not after all, perhaps, have boarded her – judging by his subsequent conduct on similar occasions – if so it had been that, by the process of hailing, he had obtained a negative answer to the question he put. For, as it eventually turned out, he cared not to consort, even for five minutes, with any stranger captain, except he could contribute some of that information he so absorbingly sought. But all this might remain inadequately estimated, were not something said here of the peculiar usages of whaling-vessels when meeting each other in foreign seas, and especially on a common cruising-ground.

If two strangers crossing the Pine Barrens in New York State, or the equally desolate Salisbury Plain in England; if casually encountering each other in such inhospitable wilds, these twain, for the life of them, cannot well avoid a mutual salutation; and stopping for a moment to interchange the news; and, perhaps, sitting down for a while and resting in concert: then, how much more natural that upon the illimitable Pine Barrens and Salisbury Plains of the sea, two whaling vessels descrying each other at the ends of the earth – off lone Fanning's Island, or the far away King's Mills; how much more natural, I say, that under such circumstances these ships should not only interchange hails, but come into still closer, more friendly and sociable contact. And especially would this seem to be a matter of course, in the case of vessels owned in one seaport, and whose captains, officers, and not a few of the men are personally known to each other; and consequently, have all sorts of dear domestic things to talk about. For the long absent ship, the outward-bounder, perhaps, has letters on board; at any rate, she will be sure to let her have some papers of a date a year or two later than the last one on her blurred and thumb-worn files. And in return for that courtesy, the outward-bound ship would receive the latest whaling intelligence from the cruising-ground to which she may be destined, a thing of the utmost importance to her. And in degree, all this will hold true concerning whaling vessels crossing each other's track on the cruising-ground itself, even though they are equally long absent from home. For one of them may have received a transfer of letters from some third, and now far remote vessel; and some of those letters may be for the people of the ship she now meets. Besides, they would exchange the whaling news, and have an agreeable chat. For not only would they meet with all the sympathies of sailors, but likewise with all the peculiar congenialities arising from a common pursuit and mutually shared privations and perils.

Nor would difference of country make any very essential difference; that is, so long as both parties speak one language, as is the case with Americans and English.

So, then, we see that of all ships separately sailing the sea, the whalers have most reason to be sociable – and they are so. Whereas, some merchant ships crossing each other's wake in the mid-Atlantic will oftentimes pass on without so much as a single word of recognition, mutually cutting each other on the high seas, like a brace of dandies in Broadway; and all the time indulging, perhaps, in finical criticism upon each other's rig. As for Men-of-War, when they chance to meet at sea, they first go through such a string of silly bowings and scrapings, such a ducking of ensigns, that there does not seem to be much right-down hearty good-will and brotherly love about it at all. As touching Slave-ships meeting, why, they are in such a prodigious hurry, they run away from each other as soon as possible. And as for Pirates, when they chance to cross each other's cross-bones, the first hail is – 'How many skulls?' – the same way that whalers hail – 'How many barrels?' And that question once answered, pirates straightway steer apart, for they are infernal villains on both sides, and don't like to see overmuch of each other's villanous likenesses.

But look at the godly, honest, unostentatious, hospitable,

sociable, free-and-easy whaler! What does the whaler do when she meets another whaler in any sort of decent weather? She has a '*Gam*', a thing so utterly unknown to all other ships that they never heard of the name even.

But what is a *Gam*? You might wear out your index-finger running up and down the columns of dictionaries, and never find the word. Dr Johnson never attained to that erudition; Noah Webster's ark does not hold it. Nevertheless, this same expressive word has now for many years been in constant use among some fifteen thousand true born Yankees. Certainly, it needs a definition, and should be incorporated into the Lexicon. With that view, let me learnedly define it.

GAM. NOUN – *A social meeting of two (or more) Whale-ships, generally on a cruising-ground; when, after exchanging hails, they exchange visits by boats' crews: the two captains remaining, for the time, on board of one ship, and the two chief mates on the other.*

There is another little item about Gamming which must not be forgotten here. All professions have their own little peculiarities of detail; so has the whale fishery. In a pirate, man-of-war, or slave-ship, when the captain is rowed anywhere in his boat, he always sits in the stern sheets on a comfortable, sometimes cushioned seat there, and often steers himself with a pretty little milliner's tiller decorated with gay cords and ribbons. But the whale-boat has no seat astern, no sofa of that sort whatever, and no tiller at all. High times indeed, if whaling captains were wheeled about the water on castors like gouty old aldermen in patent chairs. And as for a tiller, the whale-boat never admits of any such effeminacy; and therefore as in Gamming a complete boat's crew must leave the ship, and hence as the boat steerer or harpooneer is of the number, that subordinate is the steersman upon the occasion, and the captain, having no place to sit in, is pulled off to his visit all standing like a pine tree. And often you will notice that being conscious of the eyes of the whole visible world resting on him from the sides of the two ships, this standing captain is all alive to the importance of sustaining his dignity by maintaining his legs. Nor is this any very easy matter; for in his rear is the immense

projecting steering oar hitting him now and then in the small of
his back, the after-oar reciprocating by rapping his knees in front.
He is thus completely wedged before and behind, and can only expand himself sideways by settling down on his stretched legs; but
a sudden, violent pitch of the boat will often go far to topple him,
because length of foundation is nothing without corresponding
breadth. Merely make a spread angle of two poles, and you cannot
stand them up. Then, again, it would never do in plain sight of
the world's riveted eyes, it would never do, I say, for this strad-
dling captain to be seen steadying himself the slightest particle
by catching hold of anything with his hands; indeed, as token of
his entire, buoyant self-command, he generally carries his hands
in his trowsers' pockets; but perhaps being generally very large,
heavy hands, he carries them there for ballast. Nevertheless there
have occurred instances, well authenticated ones too, where the
captain has been known for an uncommonly critical moment or
two, in a sudden squall say – to seize hold of the nearest oarsman's
hair, and hold on there like grim death.

CHAPTER 43

Brit

Steering north-eastward from the Crozetts, we fell in with vast
meadows of brit, the minute, yellow substance, upon which the
Right Whale largely feeds. For leagues and leagues it undulated
round us, so that we seemed to be sailing through boundless fields
of ripe and golden wheat. On the second day, numbers of Right
Whales were seen, who, secure from the attack of a Sperm Whaler
like the Pequod, with open jaws sluggishly swam through the brit,
which, adhering to the fringing fibres of that wondrous Venetian
blind in their mouths, was in that manner separated from the
water that escaped at the lip.

As morning mowers, who side by side slowly and seethingly

advance their scythes through the long wet grass of marshy meads; even so these monsters swam, making a strange, grassy, cutting sound; and leaving behind them endless swaths of blue upon the yellow sea.

But it was only the sound they made as they parted the brit which at all reminded one of mowers. Seen from the mast-heads, especially when they paused and were stationary for a while, their vast black forms looked more like lifeless masses of rock than anything else. And as in the great hunting countries of India, the stranger at a distance will sometimes pass on the plains recumbent elephants without knowing them to be such, taking them for bare, blackened elevations of the soil; even so, often, with him, who for the first time beholds this species of the Leviathans of the sea. And even when recognized at last, their immense magnitude renders it very hard really to believe that such bulky masses of overgrowth can possibly be instinct, in all parts, with the same sort of life that lives in a dog or a horse.

CHAPTER 44

Squid

Slowly wading through the meadows of brit, the Pequod still held on her way north-eastward towards the island of Java; a gentle air impelling her keel, so that three tall tapering masts mildly waved to that languid breeze, as three mild palms on a plain. And still, at wide intervals in the silvery night, the lonely, alluring jet would be seen.

But one transparent blue morning, when a stillness almost pre-ternatural spread over the sea; when the long burnished sun-glade on the waters seemed a golden finger laid across them, enjoining some secrecy; when the slippered waves whispered together as they softly ran on; in this profound hush of the visible sphere a strange spectre was seen by Daggoo from the main-mast-head.

In the distance, a great white mass lazily rose, and rising higher and higher, and disentangling itself from the azure, at last gleamed before our prow like a snow-slide, new slid from the hills. Thus glistening for a moment, as slowly it subsided, and sank. Then once more arose, and silently gleamed. It seemed not a whale; and yet is this Moby-Dick? thought Daggoo. Again the phantom went down, but on re-appearing once more, with a stiletto-like cry that startled every man from his nod, the negro yelled out – 'There! there again! there she breaches! right ahead! The White Whale, the White Whale!'

Upon this, the seamen rushed to the yard-arms, as in swarming-time the bees rush to the boughs. Bare-headed in the sultry sun, Ahab stood on the bowsprit, and with one hand pushed far behind in readiness to wave his orders to the helmsman, cast his eager glance in the direction indicated aloft by the outstretched motion-less arm of Daggoo. No sooner did he distinctly perceive the white mass, than with a quick intensity he instantly gave orders for lowering.

The four boats were soon on the water; Ahab's in advance, and all swiftly pulling towards their prey. Soon it went down, and while, with oars suspended, we were awaiting its reappearance, lo! in the same spot where it sank, once more it slowly rose. Almost forgetting for the moment all thoughts of Moby-Dick, we now gazed at the most wondrous phenomenon which the secret seas have hitherto revealed to mankind. A vast pulpy mass, furlongs in length and breadth, of a glancing cream-colour, lay floating on the water, innumerable long arms radiating from its centre, and curling and twisting like a nest of anacondas, as if blindly to clutch at any hapless object within reach. No perceptible face or front did it have; no conceivable token of either sensation or instinct; but undulated there on the billows an unearthly, formless, chance-like apparition of life.

As with a low sucking sound it slowly disappeared again, Starbuck still gazing at the agitated waters where it had sunk, with a wild voice exclaimed – 'Almost rather had I seen Moby-Dick and fought him, than to have seen thee, thou white ghost!'

'What was it, sir?' said Flask.

'The great live Squid, which, they say, few whale-ships ever beheld, and returned to their ports to tell of it.'

But Ahab said nothing; turning his boat, he sailed back to the vessel; the rest as silently following.

Whatever superstitions the Sperm Whalemen in general have connected with the sight of this object, certain it is, that a glimpse of it being so very unusual, that circumstance has gone far to invest it with portentousness. So rarely is it beheld, that though one and all of them declare it to be the largest animated thing in the ocean, yet very few of them have any but the most vague ideas concerning its true nature and form; notwithstanding, they believe it to furnish to the Sperm Whale his only food. For though other species of whales find their food above water, and may be seen by man in the act of feeding, the spermaceti whale obtains his whole food in unknown zones below the surface; and only by inference is it that anyone can tell of what, precisely, that food consists. At times, when closely pursued, he will disgorge what are supposed to be the detached arms of the Squid; some of them thus exhibited exceeding twenty and thirty feet in length. They fancy that the monster to which these arms belonged ordinarily clings by them to the bed of the ocean; and that the Sperm Whale, unlike other species, is supplied with teeth in order to attack and tear it.

CHAPTER 45

The Line

With reference to the whaling scene shortly to be described, as well as for the better understanding of all similar scenes elsewhere presented, I have here to speak of the magical, sometimes horrible whale-line.

The line originally used in the fishery was of the best hemp, slightly vapoured with tar, not impregnated with it, as in the case of ordinary ropes; for while tar, as ordinarily used, makes the hemp more pliable to the rope-maker, and also renders the rope itself more convenient to the sailor for common ship use; yet, not only would the ordinary quantity too much stiffen the whale-line for the close coiling to which it must be subjected; but as seamen are beginning to learn, tar in general by no means adds to the rope's durability or strength, however much it may give it compactness and gloss.

Of late years the Manilla rope has in the American fishery almost entirely superseded hemp as a material for whale-lines; for, though not so durable as hemp, it is stronger, and far more soft and elastic; and I will add (since there is an aesthetics in all things), is much more handsome and becoming to the boat, than hemp. Hemp is a dusky, dark fellow, a sort of Indian; but Manilla is as a golden-haired Circassian to behold.

The whale-line is only two thirds of an inch in thickness. At first sight, you would not think it so strong as it really is. By experiment its one and fifty yarns will each suspend a weight of one hundred and twenty pounds; so that the whole rope will bear a strain nearly equal to three tons. In length, the common Sperm Whale-line measures something over two hundred fathoms. Towards the stern of the boat it is spirally coiled away in the tub so as to form one round, cheese-shaped mass of densely bedded 'sheaves', or layers of concentric spiralizations, without any hollow but the 'heart', or minute vertical tube formed at the axis of the cheese. As the least tangle or kink in the coiling would, in running out, infallibly take somebody's arm, leg, or entire body off, the utmost precaution is used in stowing the line in its tub. Some harpooneers will consume almost an entire morning in this business, carrying the line high aloft and then reeving it downwards through a block towards the tub, so as in the act of coiling to free it from all possible wrinkles and twists.

The tub, nearly three feet in diameter and of proportionate depth, makes a rather bulky freight for a craft whose planks are but one half-inch in thickness; for the bottom of the whale-boat is like critical ice, which will bear up a considerable distributed weight, but not very much of a concentrated one. When the painted canvas cover is clapped on the line-tub, the boat looks as if it were pulling off with a prodigious great wedding-cake to present to the whales.

Both ends of the line are exposed; the lower end terminating in an eye-splice or loop coming up from the bottom against the side of the tub, and hanging over its edge completely disengaged from everything. This arrangement of the lower end is necessary on two accounts. First: In order to facilitate the fastening to it of an additional line from a neighbouring boat, in case the stricken whale should sound so deep as to threaten to carry off the entire line originally attached to the harpoon. In these instances, the whale of course is shifted like a mug of ale, as it were, from the one boat to the other; though the first boat always hovers at hand to assist its consort. Second: This arrangement is indispensable for common safety's sake; for were the lower end of the line in any way attached to the boat, and were the whale then to run the line out to the end almost in a single, smoking minute as he sometimes does, he would not stop there, for the doomed boat would infallibly be dragged down after him into the profundity of the sea; and in that case no town-crier would ever find her again.

Before lowering the boat for the chase, the upper end of the line is taken aft from the tub, and passing round the loggerhead there, is again carried forward the entire length of the boat, resting crosswise upon the loom or handle of every man's oar, so that it jogs against his wrist in rowing; and also passing between the men, as they alternately sit at the opposite gunwales, to the leaded chocks or grooves in the extreme pointed prow of the boat, where a wooden pin or skewer the size of a common quill prevents it from slipping out. From the chocks it hangs in a slight festoon over the bows, and is then passed inside the boat again; and some ten or twenty fathoms (called box-line) being coiled upon the box in the bows, it continues its way to the gunwale still a little further aft, and is then attached to the short-warp – the rope which is immediately connected with the harpoon; but previous to that connexion, the short-warp goes through sundry mystifications too tedious to detail.

Thus the whale-line folds the whole boat in its complicated coils, twisting and writhing around it in almost every direction. All the oarsmen are involved in its perilous contortions; so that to the timid eye of the landsman, they seem as Indian jugglers, with the deadliest snakes sportively festooning their limbs. Nor can any son of mortal woman, for the first time, seat himself amid those hempen intricacies, and while straining his utmost at the oar, bethink him that at any unknown instant the harpoon may be darted, and all these horrible contortions be put in play like ringed lightnings; he cannot be thus circumstanced without a shudder that makes the very marrow in his bones to quiver in him like a shaken jelly. Yet habit – strange thing! what cannot habit accomplish? – Gayer sallies, more merry mirth, better jokes, and brighter repartees, you never heard over your mahogany, than you will hear over the half-inch white cedar of the whale-boat, when thus hung in hangman's nooses; and, like the six burghers of Calais before King Edward, the six men composing the crew pull into the jaws of death, with a halter around every neck, as you may say.

Perhaps a very little thought will now enable you to account for those repeated whaling disasters – some few of which are casually chronicled – of this man or that man being taken out of the boat by the line, and lost. For, when the line is darting out, to be seated then in the boat, is like being seated in the midst of the manifold whizzings of a steam-engine in full play, when every flying beam, and shaft, and wheel, is grazing you. It is worse; for you cannot sit motionless in the heart of these perils, because the boat is rocking like a cradle, and you are pitched one way and the other, without the slightest warning; and only by a certain self-adjusting buoyancy and simultaneousness of volition and action, can you escape being made a Mazeppa of, and run away with where the all-seeing sun himself could never pierce you out.

CHAPTER 46

Stubb Kills a Whale

If to Starbuck the apparition of the Squid was a thing of portents, to Queequeg it was quite a different object.

'When you see him 'quid,' said the savage, honing his harpoon in the bow of his hoisted boat, 'then you quick see him 'parm whale.'

The next day was exceedingly still and sultry, and with nothing special to engage them, the Pequod's crew could hardly resist the spell of sleep induced by such a vacant sea. For this part of the Indian Ocean through which we then were voyaging is not what whalemen call a lively ground; that is, it affords fewer glimpses of porpoises, dolphins, flying-fish, and other vivacious denizens of more stirring waters, than those off the Rio de la Plata, or the in-shore ground off Peru.

It was my turn to stand at the foremast-head; and with my shoulders leaning against the slackened royal shrouds, to and fro I idly swayed in what seemed an enchanted air. No resolution could withstand it; in that dreamy mood losing all consciousness, at last my soul went out of my body; though my body still continued to sway as a pendulum will, long after the power which first moved it is withdrawn.

Ere forgetfulness altogether came over me, I had noticed that the seamen at the main and mizen mast-heads were already drowsy. So that at last all three of us lifelessly swung from the spars, and for every swing that we made there was a nod from below from the slumbering helmsman. The waves, too, nodded their indolent crests; and across the wide trance of the sea, east nodded to west, and the sun over all.

Suddenly bubbles seemed bursting beneath my closed eyes; like vices my hands grasped the shrouds; some invisible, gracious agency preserved me; with a shock I came back to life. And lo!

close under our lee, not forty fathoms off, a gigantic Sperm Whale lay rolling in the water like the capsized hull of a frigate, his broad, glossy back, of an Ethiopian hue, glistening in the sun's rays like a mirror. But lazily undulating in the trough of the sea, and ever and anon tranquilly spouting his vapoury jet, the whale looked like a portly burgher smoking his pipe of a warm afternoon. But that pipe, poor whale, was thy last. As if struck by some enchanter's wand, the sleepy ship and every sleeper in it all at once started into wakefulness; and more than a score of voices from all parts of the vessel, simultaneously with the three notes from aloft, shouted forth the accustomed cry, as the great fish spouted the sparkling brine into the air.

'Clear away the boats! Luff!' cried Ahab. And obeying his own order, he dashed the helm down before the helmsman could handle the spokes.

The sudden exclamations of the crew must have alarmed the whale; and ere the boats were down, majestically turning, he swam away to the leeward, but with such a steady tranquillity, and making so few ripples as he swam, that thinking after all he might not as yet be alarmed, Ahab gave orders that not an oar should be used, and no man must speak but in whispers. So seated like Ontario Indians on the gunwales of the boats, we swiftly but silently paddled along; the calm not admitting of the noiseless sails being set. Presently, as we thus glided in chase, the monster perpendicularly flitted his tail forty feet into the air, and then sank out of sight like a tower swallowed up.

'There go flukes!' was the cry, an announcement immediately followed by Stubb's producing his match and igniting his pipe, for now a respite was granted. After the full interval of his sounding had elapsed, the whale rose again, and being now in advance of the smoker's boat, and much nearer to it than to any of the others, Stubb counted upon the honour of the capture. It was obvious, now, that the whale had at length become aware of his pursuers. All silence of cautiousness was therefore no longer of use. Paddles were dropped, and oars came loudly into play. And still puffing at his pipe, Stubb cheered on his crew to the assault.

Yes, a mighty change had come over the fish. All alive to his jeopardy, he was going 'head out'.

'Start her, start her, my men! Don't hurry yourselves; take plenty of time – but start her; start her like thunder-claps, that's all,' cried Stubb, spluttering out the smoke as he spoke. 'Start her, now; give 'em the long and strong stroke, Tashtego. Start her, Tash, my boy – start her, all; but keep cool, keep cool – cucumbers is the word – easy, easy – only start her like grim death and grinning devils, and raise the buried dead perpendicular out of their graves, boys – that's all. Start her!'

'Woo-hoo! Wa-hee!' screamed the Gay-Header in reply, raising some old war-whoop to the skies; as every oarsman in the strained boat involuntarily bounced forward with the one tremendous leading stroke which the eager Indian gave.

But his wild screams were answered by others quite as wild. 'Kee-hee! Kee-hee!' yelled Daggoo, straining forwards and backwards on his seat, like a pacing tiger in his cage.

'Ka-la! Koo-loo!' howled Queequeg, as if smacking his lips over a mouthful of Grenadier's steak. And thus with oars and yells the keels cut the sea. Meanwhile, Stubb retaining his place in the van, still encouraged his men to the onset, all the while puffing the smoke from his mouth. Like desperadoes they tugged and they strained, till the welcome cry was heard – 'Stand up, Tashtego! – give it to him!' The harpoon was hurled. 'Stern all!' The oarsmen back water; the same moment something went hot and hissing along every one of their wrists. It was the magical line. An instant before, Stubb had swiftly caught two additional turns with it round the loggerhead, whence, by reason of its increased rapid circlings, a hempen blue smoke now jetted up and mingled with the steady fumes from his pipe. As the line passed round and round the loggerhead; so also, just before reaching that point, it blisteringly passed through and through both of Stubb's hands, from which the hand-cloths, or squares of quilted canvas sometimes worn at these times, had accidentally dropped. It was like holding an enemy's sharp two-edged sword by the blade, and that enemy all the time striving to wrest it out of your clutch.

'Wet the line! wet the line!' cried Stubb to the tub oarsman (him seated by the tub) who, snatching off his hat, dashed the seawater into it. More turns were taken, so that the line began holding its place. The boat now flew through the boiling water like a shark all fins. Stubb and Tashtego here changed places – stem for stern – a staggering business truly in that rocking commotion.

From the vibrating line extending the entire length of the upper part of the boat, and from its now being more tight than a harp-string, you would have thought the craft had two keels – one cleaving the water, the other the air – as the boat churned on through both opposing elements at once. A continual cascade played at the bows; a ceaseless whirling eddy in her wake; and, at the slightest motion from within, even but of a little finger, the vibrating, cracking craft canted over her spasmodic gunwale into the sea. Thus they rushed; each man with might and main clinging to his seat, to prevent being tossed to the foam; and the tall form of Tashtego at the steering oar crouching almost double, in order to bring down his centre of gravity. Whole Atlantics and Pacifics seemed passed as they shot on their way, till at length the whale somewhat slackened his flight.

'Haul in – haul in!' cried Stubb to the bowsman! and, facing round towards the whale, all hands began pulling the boat up to him, while yet the boat was being towed on. Soon ranging up by his flank, Stubb, firmly planting his knee in the clumsy cleat, darted dart after dart into the flying fish; the boat alternately sterning out of the way of the whale's horrible wallow, and then ranging up for another fling.

The red tide now poured from all sides of the monster like brooks down a hill. His tormented body rolled not in brine but in blood, which bubbled and seethed for furlongs behind in their wake. The slanting sun playing upon this crimson pond in the sea, sent back its reflection into every face, so that they all glowed to each other like red men. And all the while, jet after jet of white smoke was agonizingly shot from the spiracle of the whale, and vehement puff after puff from the mouth of the excited headsman; as at every dart, hauling in upon his crooked lance (by the line attached to it), Stubb straightened it again and again, by a few rapid blows against the gunwale, then again and again sent it into the whale.

'Pull up – pull up!' he now cried to the bowsman, as the waning whale relaxed in his wrath. 'Pull up! – close to!' and the boat ranged along the fish's flank. When reaching far over the bow, Stubb slowly churned his long sharp lance into the fish, and kept it there, carefully churning and churning, as if cautiously seeking to feel after some gold watch that the whale might have swallowed, and which he was fearful of breaking ere he could hook it out. But that gold watch he sought was the innermost life of the fish. And now it is struck; for, starting from his trance into that unspeakable thing called his 'flurry', the monster horribly wallowed in his blood, overwrapped himself in impenetrable, mad, boiling spray, so that the imperilled craft, instantly dropping astern, had much ado blindly to struggle out from that frenzied twilight into the clear air of the day.

And now abating in his flurry, the whale once more rolled out into view; surging from side to side; spasmodically dilating and contracting his spout-hole, with sharp, cracking, agonized respirations. At last, gush after gush of clotted red gore, as if it had been the purple lees of red wine, shot into the frighted air; and falling back again, ran dripping down his motionless flanks into the sea. His heart had burst!

'He's dead, Mr Stubb,' said Daggoo.

'Yes; both pipes smoked out!' and withdrawing his own from his mouth, Stubb scattered the dead ashes over the water; and stood thoughtfully eyeing the vast corpse he had made.

CHAPTER 47

The Dart

A word concerning an incident in the last chapter. According to the invariable usage of the fishery, the whale-boat pushes off from the ship, with the headsman or whale-killer as temporary steersman, and the harpooneer or whale-fastener pulling the foremost oar, the one known as the harpooneer-oar. Now it needs a strong, nervous arm to strike the first iron into the fish; for often, in what is called a long dart, the heavy implement has to be flung to the distance of twenty or thirty feet. But however prolonged and exhausting the chase, the harpooneer is expected to pull his oar meanwhile to the uttermost; indeed, he is expected to set an example of superhuman activity to the rest, not only by incredible rowing, but by repeated loud and intrepid exclamations; and what it is to keep shouting at the top of one's compass, while all the other muscles are strained and half started – what that is none know but those who have tried it. For one, I cannot bawl very heartily and work very recklessly at one and the same time. In this straining, bawling state, then, with his back to the fish, all at once the exhausted harpooneer hears the exciting cry – 'Stand up, and give it to him!' He now has to drop and secure his oar, turn round on his centre half way, seize his harpoon from the crotch, and with what little strength may remain, he essays to pitch it somehow into the whale. No wonder, taking the whole fleet of whalemen in a body, that out of fifty fair chances for a dart, not five are successful; no wonder that so many harpooneers are madly cursed and disrated; no wonder that some of them actually burst their blood-vessels in the boat; no wonder that some Sperm Whalemen are absent four years with four barrels; no wonder that to many ship owners, whaling is but a losing concern; for it is the harpooneer that makes the voyage, and if you take the breath out of his body how can you expect to find it there when most wanted!

Again, if the dart be successful, then at the second critical instant, that is, when the whale starts to run, the boat-header and harpooneer likewise start to running fore and aft, to the imminent jeopardy of themselves and everyone else. It is then they change places; and the headsman, the chief officer of the little craft, takes his proper station in the bows of the boat.

Now, I care not who maintains the contrary, but all this is both foolish and unnecessary. The headsman should stay in the bows from first to last; he should both dart the harpoon and the lance, and no rowing whatever should be expected of him, except under circumstances obvious to any fisherman. I know that this would sometimes involve a slight loss of speed in the chase; but long experience in various whalemen of more than one nation has convinced me that in the vast majority of failures in the fishery, it has not by any means been so much the speed of the whale as the before described exhaustion of the harpooneer that has caused them. To insure the greatest efficiency in the dart, the harpooneers of this world must start to their feet from out of idleness, and not from out of toil.

CHAPTER 48

The Crotch

The crotch alluded to on a previous page deserves independent mention. It is a notched stick of a peculiar form, some two feet in length, which is perpendicularly inserted into the starboard gunwale near the bow, for the purpose of furnishing a rest for the wooden extremity of the harpoon, whose other naked, barbed end slopingly projects from the prow. Thereby the weapon is instantly at hand to its hurler, who snatches it up as readily from its rest as a backwoodsman swings his rifle from the wall. It is customary to have two harpoons reposing in the crotch, respectively called the first and second irons.

But these two harpoons, each by its own cord, are both connected with the line; the object being this: to dart them both, if possible, one instantly after the other into the same whale; so that if, in the coming drag, one should draw out, the other may still retain a hold. It is a doubling of the chances. But it very often happens that owing to the instantaneous, violent, convulsive running of the whale upon receiving the first iron, it becomes impossible for the harpooneer, however lightning-like in his movements, to pitch the second iron into him. Nevertheless, as the second iron is already connected with the line, and the line is running, hence that weapon must, at all events, be anticipatingly tossed out of the boat, somehow and somewhere; else the most terrible jeopardy would involve all hands. Tumbled into the water, it accordingly is in such cases; the spare coils of box line making this feat, in most instances, prudently practicable. But this critical act is not always unattended with the saddest and most fatal casualties.

Furthermore: you must know that when the second iron is thrown overboard, it thenceforth becomes a dangling, sharp-edged terror, skittishly curvetting about both boat and whale, entangling the lines, or cutting them, and making a prodigious sensation in all directions. Nor, in general, is it possible to secure it again until the whale is fairly captured and a corpse.

Consider, now, how it must be in the case of four boats all engaging one unusually strong, active, and knowing whale; when owing to these qualities in him, as well as to the thousand concurring accidents of such an audacious enterprise, eight or ten loose second irons may be simultaneously dangling about him. For, of course, each boat is supplied with several harpoons to bend on to the line should the first one be ineffectually darted without recovery. All these particulars are faithfully narrated here, as they will not fail to elucidate several most important, however intricate passages, in scenes hereafter to be painted.

CHAPTER 49

Stubb's Supper

Stubb's whale had been killed some distance from the ship. It was a calm; so, forming a tandem of three boats, we commenced the slow business of towing the trophy to the Pequod. And now, as we eighteen men with our thirty-six arms, and one hundred and eighty thumbs and fingers, slowly toiled hour after hour upon that inert, sluggish corpse in the sea; and it seemed hardly to budge at all, except at long intervals; good evidence was hereby furnished of the enormousness of the mass we moved. For, upon the great canal of Hang-Ho, or whatever they call it, in China, four or five labourers on the footpath will draw a bulky freighted junk at the rate of a mile an hour; but this grand argosy we towed heavily forged along, as if laden with pig-lead in bulk.

Darkness came on; but three lights up and down in the Pequod's main-rigging dimly guided our way; till drawing nearer we saw Ahab dropping one of several more lanterns over the bulwarks. Vacantly eyeing the heaving whale for a moment, he issued the usual orders for securing it for the night, and then handing his lantern to a seaman, went his way into the cabin, and did not come forward again until morning.

Though, in overseeing the pursuit of this whale, Captain Ahab had evinced his customary activity, to call it so; yet now that the creature was dead, some vague dissatisfaction, or impatience, or despair, seemed working in him; as if the sight of that dead body reminded him that Moby-Dick was yet to be slain; and though a thousand other whales were brought to his ship, all that would not one jot advance his grand, monomaniac object. Very soon you would have thought from the sound on the Pequod's decks, that all hands were preparing to cast anchor in the deep; for heavy chains are being dragged along the deck, and thrust rattling out of the port-holes. But by those clanking links, the vast corpse itself, not the ship, is to be moored. Tied by the head to the stern, and by the tail to the bows, the whale now lies with its black hull close to the vessel's, and seen through the darkness of the night, which obscured the spars and rigging aloft, the two – ship and whale – seemed yoked together like colossal bullocks, whereof one reclines while the other remains standing.

If moody Ahab was now all quiescence, at least so far as could be known on deck, Stubb, his second mate, flushed with conquest, betrayed an unusual but still good-natured excitement. Such an unwonted bustle was he in that the staid Starbuck, his official superior, quietly resigned to him for the time the sole management of affairs. One helping cause of all this liveliness in Stubb was soon made strangely manifest. Stubb was a high liver; he was somewhat intemperately fond of the whale as a flavourish thing to his palate.

'A steak, a steak, ere I sleep! You, Daggoo! overboard you go, and cut me one from his small!'

Here be it known, that though these wild fishermen do not, as a general thing, and according to the great military maxim, make the enemy defray the current expenses of the war (at least before realizing the proceeds of the voyage), yet now and then you find some of these Nantucketers who have a genuine relish for that particular part of the Sperm Whale designated by Stubb; comprising the tapering extremity of the body.

About midnight that steak was cut and cooked; and lighted by two lanterns of sperm oil, Stubb stoutly stood up to his spermaceti supper at the capstan-head, as if that capstan were a sideboard. Nor was Stubb the only banqueter on whale's flesh that night. Mingling their mumblings with his own mastications, thousands on thousands of sharks, swarming round the dead Leviathan, smackingly feasted on its fatness. The few sleepers below in their bunks were often startled by the sharp slapping of their tails against the hull, within a few inches of the sleepers' hearts. Peering over the side you could just see them wallowing in the sullen, black waters, and turning over on their backs as they scooped out huge globular pieces of the whale of the bigness of a human head.

Though amid all the smoking horror and diabolism of a seafight, sharks will be seen longingly gazing up to the ship's decks, like hungry dogs round a table where red meat is being carved, ready to bolt down every killed man that is tossed to them; and though, while the valiant butchers over the deck-table are thus cannibally carving each other's live meat with carving-knives all gilded and tasselled, the sharks, also, with their jewel-hilted mouths, are quarrelsomely carving away under the table at the dead meat; and though, were you to turn the whole affair upside down, it would still be pretty much the same thing, that is to say, a shocking sharkish business enough for all parties; and though sharks also are the invariable outriders of all slave ships crossing the Atlantic, systematically trotting alongside, to be handy in case a dead slave is to be decently buried; yet is there no conceivable time or occasion when you will find them in such countless numbers, and in gayer or more jovial spirits, than around a dead Sperm Whale, moored by night to a whale-ship. If you have never seen that sight, then suspend your decision about the propriety of devil-worship, and the expediency of conciliating the devil.

CHAPTER 50

The Whale as a Dish

That mortal man should feed upon the creature that feeds his lamp, and, like Stubb, eat him by his own light, as you may say, seems outlandish.

The fact is, that among his hunters at least, the whale would by all hands be considered a noble dish, were there not so much of him; but when you come to sit down before a meat-pie nearly one hundred feet long, it takes away your appetite. Only the most unprejudiced of men like Stubb nowadays partake of cooked whales; but the Esquimaux are not so fastidious. We all know how they live upon whales, and have rare old vintages of prime old train oil. Zogranda, one of their most famous doctors, recommends strips of blubber for infants, as being exceedingly juicy and nourishing. And this reminds me that certain Englishmen, who long ago were accidentally left in Greenland by a whaling vessel – that these men actually lived for several months on the mouldy scraps of whales which had been left ashore after trying out the blubber. Among the Dutch whalemen these scraps are called 'fritters'; which, indeed, they greatly resemble, being brown and crisp, and smelling something like old Amsterdam housewives' dough-nuts or oly-cooks, when fresh. They have such an eatable look that the most self-denying stranger can hardly keep his hands off.

But what further depreciates the whale as a civilized dish is his exceeding richness. He is the great prize ox of the sea, too fat to be delicately good. Look at his hump, which would be as fine eating as the buffalo's (which is esteemed a rare dish), were it not such a solid pyramid of fat. But the spermaceti itself, how bland and creamy that is; like the transparent, half-jellied, white meat of a cocoanut in the third month of its growth, yet far too rich to supply a substitute for butter. Nevertheless, many whalemen have a method of absorbing it into some other substance, and then partaking of it. In the long watches of the night it is a common thing for the seamen to dip their ship-biscuit into the huge oil-pots and let them fry there awhile. Many a good supper have I thus made.

In the case of a small Sperm Whale the brains are accounted a fine dish. The casket of the skull is broken into with an axe, and the two plump, whitish lobes being withdrawn (precisely resembling two large puddings), they are then mixed with flour, and cooked into a most delectable mess, in flavour somewhat resembling calves' head, which is quite a dish among some epicures; and everyone knows that some young bucks among the epicures, by continually dining upon calves' brains, by and by get to have a little brains of their own, so as to be able to tell a calf's head from their own heads; which, indeed, requires uncommon discrimination. And that is the reason why a young buck with an intelligent looking calf's head before him is somehow one of the saddest sights you can see. The head looks a sort of reproachfully at him, with an 'Et tu Brute!' expression.

CHAPTER 51

The Shark Massacre

When in the Southern Fishery, a captured Sperm Whale, after long and weary toil, is brought alongside late at night, it is not, as a general thing at least, customary to proceed at once to the business of cutting him in. For that business is an exceedingly laborious one; is not very soon completed; and requires all hands to set about it. Therefore, the common usage is to take in all sail; lash the helm a'lee; and then send everyone below to his hammock till daylight, with the reservation that, until that time, anchor-watches shall be kept; that is, two and two for an hour, each couple, the crew in rotation shall mount the deck to see that all goes well.

But sometimes, especially upon the Line in the Pacific, this plan will not answer at all; because such incalculable hosts of sharks gather round the moored carcase, that were he left so for six hours, say, on a stretch, little more than the skeleton would be visible by morning. In most other parts of the ocean, however, where these fish do not so largely abound, their wondrous voracity can be at times considerably diminished, by vigorously stirring them up with sharp whaling-spades, a procedure notwithstanding, which, in some instances, only seems to tickle them into still greater activity. But it was not thus in the present case with the Pequod's sharks; though any man unaccustomed to such sights, to have looked over her side that night, would have almost thought the whole round sea was one huge cheese, and those sharks the maggots in it.

Nevertheless, upon Stubb setting the anchor-watch after his supper was concluded; and when, accordingly, Queequeg and a forecastle seaman came on deck, no small excitement was created among the sharks; for immediately suspending the cutting stages over the side, and lowering three lanterns, so that they cast long gleams of light over the turbid sea, these two mariners, darting their long whaling-spades, kept up an incessant murdering of the sharks, by striking the keen steel deep into their skulls, seemingly their only vital part.

The whaling-spade used for cutting-in is made of the very best steel; is about the bigness of a man's spread hand; and in general shape, corresponds to the garden implement after which it is named; only its sides are perfectly flat, and its upper end considerably narrower than the lower. This weapon is always kept as sharp as possible; and when being used is occasionally honed, just like a razor. In its socket, a stiff pole, from twenty to thirty feet long, is inserted for a handle.

But in the foamy confusion of their mixed and struggling hosts, the marksmen could not always hit their mark; and this brought about new revelations of the incredible ferocity of the foe. They viciously snapped, not only at each other's disembowelments, but bent round, and bit their own; till those entrails seemed swallowed over and over again by the same mouth, to be oppositely voided by the gaping wound.

CHAPTER 52

Cutting In

It was a Saturday night, and such a Sabbath as followed! Ex officio professors of Sabbath breaking are all whalemen. The ivory Pequod was turned into what seemed a shamble; every sailor a butcher. You would have thought we were offering up ten thousand red oxen to the sea gods.

In the first place, the enormous cutting tackles, among other ponderous things comprising a cluster of blocks generally painted green, and which no single man can possibly lift – this vast bunch of grapes was swayed up to the main-top and firmly lashed to the lower mast-head, the strongest point anywhere above a ship's deck. The end of the hawser-like rope winding through these intricacies was then conducted to the windlass, and the huge lower block of the tackles was swung over the whale; to this block the great blubber hook, weighing some one hundred pounds, was attached. And now suspended in stages over the side, Starbuck and Stubb, the mates, armed with their long spades, began cutting a hole in the body for the insertion of the hook just above the nearest of the two side-fins. This done, a broad, semicircular line is cut round the hole, the hook is inserted, and the main body of the crew striking up a wild chorus, now commence heaving in one dense crowd at the windlass. When instantly, the entire ship careens over on her side; every bolt in her starts like the nailheads of an old house in frosty weather; she trembles, quivers, and nods her frighted mast-heads to the sky. More and more she leans over to the whale, while every gasping heave of the windlass is answered by a helping heave from the billows; till at last, a swift, startling snap is heard; with a great swash the ship rolls upwards and backwards from the whale, and the triumphant tackle rises into sight dragging after it the disengaged semicircular end of the first strip of blubber. Now as the blubber envelops the whale precisely as the rind does an orange, so is it stripped off from the body precisely as an orange is sometimes stripped by spiralizing it. For the strain constantly kept up by the windlass continually keeps the whale rolling over and over in the water, and as the blubber in one strip uniformly peels off along the line called the 'scarf', simultaneously cut by the spades of Starbuck and Stubb, the mates; and just as fast as it is thus peeled off, and indeed by that very act itself, it is all the time being hoisted higher and higher aloft till its upper end grazes the main-top; the men at the windlass then cease heaving, and for a moment or two the prodigious blood-dripping mass sways to and fro as if let down from the sky, and every one present must take good heed to dodge it when it swings, else it may box his ears and pitch him headlong overboard.

One of the attending harpooneers now advances with a long,

keen weapon called a boarding-sword, and watching his chance
he dexterously slices out a considerable hole in the lower part of
the swaying mass. Into this hole, the end of the second alternating great tackle is then hooked so as to retain a hold upon the
blubber, in order to prepare for what follows. Whereupon, this
accomplished swordsman, warning all hands to stand off, once
more makes a scientific dash at the mass, and with a few sidelong,
desperate, lunging slicings, severs it completely in twain; so that
while the short lower part is still fast, the long upper strip, called
a blanket-piece, swings clear, and is all ready for lowering. The
heavers forward now resume their song, and while the one tackle
is peeling and hoisting a second strip from the whale, the other is
slowly slackened away, and down goes the first strip through the
main hatchway right beneath, into an unfurnished parlour called
the blubber-room. Into this twilight apartment sundry nimble
hands keep coiling away the long blanket-piece as if it were a great
live mass of plaited serpents. And thus the work proceeds; the two
tackles hoisting and lowering simultaneously; both whale and
windlass heaving, the heavers singing, the blubber-room gentlemen coiling, the mates scarfing, the ship straining, and all hands
swearing occasionally, by way of assuaging the general friction.

CHAPTER 53

The Blanket

I have given no small attention to that not unvexed subject, the
skin of the whale.

The question is, what and where is the skin of the whale?
Already you know what his blubber is. That blubber is something
of the consistence of firm, close-grained beef, but tougher, more
elastic and compact, and ranges from eight or ten to twelve and
fifteen inches in thickness.

Now, however preposterous it may at first seem to talk of any creature's skin as being of that sort of consistence and thickness, yet in point of fact these are no arguments against such a presumption; because you cannot raise any other dense enveloping layer from the whale's body but that same blubber; and the outermost enveloping layer of any animal, if reasonably dense, what can that be but the skin?

True, from the unmarred dead body of the whale, you may scrape off with your hand an infinitely thin, transparent substance, somewhat resembling the thinnest shreds of isinglass, only it is almost as flexible and soft as satin; that is, previous to being dried, when it not only contracts and thickens, but becomes rather hard and brittle. What I am driving at here is this. That same infinitely thin, isinglass substance, which, I admit, invests the entire body of the whale, is not so much to be regarded as the skin of the creature, as the skin of the skin, so to speak; for it were simply ridiculous to say, that the proper skin of the tremendous whale is thinner and more tender than the skin of a new-born child.

Assuming the blubber to be the skin of the whale; then, when this skin, as in the case of a very large Sperm Whale, will yield the bulk of one hundred barrels of oil; and, when it is considered that, in quantity, or rather weight, that oil, in its expressed state, is only three fourths, and not the entire substance of the coat; some idea may hence be had of the enormousness of that animated mass, a mere part of whose mere integument yields such a lake of liquid as that. Reckoning ten barrels to the ton, you have ten tons for the net weight of only three quarters of the stuff of the whale's skin. Not the least among the many marvels he presents.

CHAPTER 54

The Funeral

'Haul in the chains! Let the carcase go astern!'

The vast tackles have now done their duty. The peeled white

body of the beheaded whale flashes like a marble sepulchre; though changed in hue, it has not perceptibly lost anything in bulk. It is still colossal. Slowly it floats more and more away, the water round it torn and splashed by the insatiate sharks, and the air above vexed with rapacious flights of screaming fowls, whose beaks are like so many insulting poniards in the whale. The vast white headless phantom floats further and further from the ship, and every rod that it so floats, what seem square roods of sharks and cubic roods of fowls augment the murderous din. For hours and hours from the almost stationary ship that hideous sight is seen. Beneath the unclouded and mild azure sky, upon the fair face of the pleasant sea, wafted by the joyous breezes, that great mass of death floats on and on, till lost in infinite perspectives.

There's a most doleful and most mocking funeral!

CHAPTER 55

The Sphynx

It should not have been omitted that previous to completely stripping the body of the Leviathan, he was beheaded. Now, the beheading of the Sperm Whale is a scientific anatomical feat, upon which experienced whale surgeons very much pride themselves: and not without reason.

Consider that the whale has nothing that can properly be called a neck; on the contrary, where his head and body seem to join, there, in that very place, is the thickest part of him. Remember, also, that the surgeon must operate from above, some eight or ten feet intervening between him and his subject, and that subject almost hidden in a discoloured, rolling, and oftentimes tumultuous and bursting sea. Bear in mind, too, that under these untoward circumstances he has to cut many feet deep in the flesh; and in that subterraneous manner, without so much as getting one single peep into the ever-contracting gash thus made, he must skilfully steer clear of all adjacent, interdicted parts, and exactly divide the spine at a critical point hard by its insertion into the skull. Do you not marvel, then, at Stubb's boast, that he demanded but ten minutes to behead a Sperm Whale?

When first severed, the head is dropped astern and held there by a cable till the body is stripped. That done, if it belong to a small whale it is hoisted on deck to be deliberately disposed of. But, with a full grown Leviathan this is impossible; for the Sperm Whale's head embraces nearly one third of his entire bulk, and completely to suspend such a burden as that were as vain a thing as to attempt weighing a Dutch barn in jewellers' scales.

The Pequod's whale being decapitated and the body stripped, the head was hoisted against the ship's side – about half way out of the sea, so that it might yet in great part be buoyed up by its native element. And there with the strained craft steeply leaning over to it, by reason of the enormous downward drag from the lower mast-head, and every yard-arm on that side projecting like a crane over the waves; there, that blood-dripping head hung to the Pequod's waist like the giant Holofernes's from the girdle of Judith.

When this last task was accomplished it was noon, and the seamen went below to their dinner. Silence reigned over the before tumultuous but now deserted deck. An intense copper calm, like a universal yellow lotus, was more and more unfolding its noiseless measureless leaves upon the sea. A short space elapsed, and up into this noiselessness came Ahab alone from his cabin. Taking a few turns on the quarter-deck, he paused to gaze over the side, then slowly getting into the main-chains he took Stubb's long spade – still remaining there after the whale's decapitation – and striking it into the lower part of the half-suspended mass, placed its other end crutch-wise under one arm, and so stood leaning over with eyes attentively fixed on this head.

It was a black and hooded head; and hanging there in the midst of so intense a calm, it seemed the Sphinx's in the desert. 'Speak, thou vast and venerable head,' muttered Ahab, 'speak, mighty head, and tell us the secret thing that is in thee. Of all divers, thou hast dived the deepest. That head upon which the upper sun now gleams, has moved amid this world's foundations. Where unrecorded names and navies rust, and untold hopes and anchors rot; where in her murderous hold this frigate earth is ballasted with bones of millions of the drowned; there, in that awful water-land, there was thy most familiar home. O head! thou hast seen enough to split the planets and make an infidel of Abraham, and not one syllable is thine!'

CHAPTER 56

The Monkey-rope

In the tumultuous business of cutting-in and attending to a whale, there is much running backwards and forwards among the crew. Now hands are wanted here, and then again hands are wanted there. There is no staying in any one place; for at one and the same time everything has to be done everywhere. It is much the same with him who endeavours the description of the scene. We must now retrace our way a little. It was mentioned that upon first breaking ground in the whale's back, the blubber-hook was inserted into the original hole there cut by the spades of the mates. But how did so clumsy and weighty a mass as that same hook get fixed in that hole? It was inserted there by my particular friend Queequeg, whose duty it was, as harpooneer, to descend upon the monster's back for the special purpose referred to. But in very many cases, circumstances require that the harpooneer shall remain on the whale till the whole flensing or stripping operation is concluded. The whale, be it observed, lies almost entirely submerged, excepting the immediate parts operated upon. So down there, some ten feet below the level of the deck, the poor harpooneer flounders about, half on the whale and half in the water, as the vast mass revolves like a tread-mill beneath him. On the occasion in question, Queequeg figured in the Highland costume

– a shirt and socks – in which to my eyes, at least, he appeared to uncommon advantage; and no one had a better chance to observe him, as will presently be seen.

Being the savage's bowsman, that is, the person who pulled the bow-oar in his boat (the second one from forward), it was my cheerful duty to attend upon him while taking that hard-scrabble scramble upon the dead whale's back. You have seen Italian organ-boys holding a dancing-ape by a long cord. Just so, from the ship's steep side, did I hold Queequeg down there in the sea, by what is technically called in the fishery a monkey-rope, attached to a strong strip of canvas belted round his waist.

It was a humorously perilous business for both of us. For, before we proceed further, it must be said that the monkey-rope was fast at both ends; fast to Queequeg's broad canvas belt, and fast to my narrow leather one. So that for better or for worse, we two, for the time, were wedded; and should poor Queequeg sink to rise no more, then both usage and honour demanded, that instead of cutting the cord, it should drag me down in his wake. So, then, an elongated Siamese ligature united us. Queequeg was my own inseparable twin brother; nor could I any way get rid of the dangerous liabilities which the hempen bond entailed.

So strongly and metaphysically did I conceive of my situation then, that while earnestly watching his motions, I seemed distinctly to perceive that my own individuality was now merged in a joint stock company of two: that my free will had received a mortal wound; and that another's mistake or misfortune might plunge innocent me into unmerited disaster and death. I jerked him now and then from between the whale and the ship, which would threaten to jam him. But handle Queequeg's monkey-rope heedfully as I would, sometimes he jerked it so, that I came very near sliding overboard. Nor could I possibly forget that, do what I would, I only had the management of one end of it.

I have hinted that I would often jerk poor Queequeg from between the whale and the ship – where he would occasionally fall, from the incessant rolling and swaying of both. But this was not the only jamming jeopardy he was exposed to. Unappalled by the massacre made upon them during the night, the sharks now freshly and more keenly allured by the before pent blood which began to flow from the carcase – the rabid creatures swarmed round it like bees in a beehive.

And right in among those sharks was Queequeg; who often pushed them aside with his floundering feet. A thing altogether incredible were it not that attracted by such prey as a dead whale, the otherwise miscellaneously carnivorous shark will seldom touch a man.

Nevertheless, it may well be believed that since they have such a ravenous finger in the pie, it is deemed but wise to look sharp to them. Accordingly, besides the monkey-rope, with which I now and then jerked the poor fellow from too close a vicinity to the maw of what seemed a peculiarly ferocious shark – he was provided with still another protection. Suspended over the side in one of the stages, Tashtego and Daggoo continually flourished over his head a couple of keen whale-spades, wherewith they slaughtered as many sharks as they could reach. This procedure of theirs, to be sure, was very disinterested and benevolent of them. They meant Queequeg's best happiness, I admit; but in their hasty zeal to befriend him, and from the circumstance that both he and the sharks were at times half hidden by the blood-mudded water, those indiscreet spades of theirs would come nearer amputating a leg than a tail. But poor Queequeg, I suppose, straining and gasping there with that great iron hook – poor Queequeg, I suppose, only prayed to his Yojo, and gave up his life into the hands of his gods. Well, well, my dear comrade and twin-brother, thought I, as I drew in and then slacked off the rope to every swell of the sea – what matters it, after all? Are you not the precious image of each and all of us men in this whaling world? That unsounded ocean you gasp in, is Life; those sharks, your foes; those spades, your friends; and what between sharks and spades you are in a sad pickle and peril.

But courage! there is good cheer in store for you, Queequeg. For now, as with blue lips and bloodshot eyes the exhausted savage at last climbs up the chains and stands all dripping and involuntarily

trembling over the side, the steward advances, and with a benevolent, consolatory glance hands him a dark flask. Strong spirits.

CHAPTER 57

Stubb and Flask Kill a Right Whale; and Then Have a Talk over Him

It must be borne in mind that all this time we have a Sperm Whale's
prodigious head hanging to the Pequod's side. But we must let it
continue hanging there a while till we can get a chance to attend to
it. For the present other matters press, and the best we can do now
for the head is to pray heaven the tackles may hold. Now, during
the past night and forenoon, the Pequod had gradually drifted
into a sea, which, by its occasional patches of yellow brit, gave
unusual tokens of the vicinity of Right Whales, a species of the
Leviathan that but few supposed to be at this particular time lurking anywhere near. And though all hands commonly disdained
the capture of those inferior creatures; and though the Pequod
was not commissioned to cruise for them at all; and though she
had passed numbers of them near the Crozetts without lowering
a boat; yet now that a Sperm Whale had been brought alongside
and beheaded, to the surprise of all, the announcement was made
that a Right Whale should be captured that day, if opportunity
offered.

Nor was this long wanting. Tall spouts were seen to leeward;
and two boats, Stubb's and Flask's, were detached in pursuit.
Pulling further and further away, they at last became almost invisible to the men at the mast-head. But suddenly in the distance,
they saw a great heap of tumultuous white water, and soon after
news came from aloft that one or both the boats must be fast.
An interval passed and the boats were in plain sight, in the act
of being dragged right towards the ship by the towing whale. So

close did the monster come to the hull, that at first it seemed as if he meant it malice; but suddenly going down in a maelstrom, within three rods of the planks, he wholly disappeared from view, as if diving under the keel. 'Cut, cut!' was the cry from the ship to the boats, which, for one instant, seemed on the point of being brought with a deadly dash against the vessel's side. But having plenty of line yet in the tubs, and the whale not sounding very rapidly, they paid out abundance of rope, and at the same time pulled with all their might so as to get ahead of the ship. For a few minutes the struggle was intensely critical; for while they still slacked out the tightened line in one direction, and still plied their oars in another, the contending strain threatened to take them under. But it was only a few feet advance they sought to gain. And they stuck to it till they did gain it; when instantly, a swift tremor was felt running like lightning along the keel, as the strained line, scraping beneath the ship, suddenly rose to view under her bows, snapping and quivering; and so flinging off its drippings, that the drops fell like bits of broken glass on the water, while the whale beyond also rose to sight, and once more the boats were free to fly. But the fagged whale abated his speed, and blindly altering his course, went round the stern of the ship towing the two boats after him, so that they performed a complete circuit.

Meantime, they hauled more and more upon their lines, till close flanking him on both sides, Stubb answered Flask with lance for lance; and thus round and round the Pequod the battle went, while the multitudes of sharks that had before swum round the Sperm Whale's body rushed to the fresh blood that was spilled, thirstily drinking at every new gash, as the eager Israelites did at the new bursting fountains that poured from the smitten rock.

At last his spout grew thick, and with a frightful roll and vomit, he turned upon his back a corpse.

While the two headsmen were engaged in making fast cords to his flukes, and in other ways getting the mass in readiness for towing, conversation ensued between them.

'I wonder what the old man wants with this lump of foul lard,' said Stubb, not without some disgust at the thought of having to do with so ignoble a Leviathan.

'Wants with it?' said Flask, coiling some spare line in the boat's bow, 'did you never hear that the ship which but once has a Sperm Whale's head hoisted on her starboard side, and at the same time a Right Whale's on the larboard; did you never hear, Stubb, that that ship can never capsize?'

'Why not?'

'I don't know, but I heard that gamboge ghost of a Fedallah saying so, and he seems to know all about ships' charms. But I sometimes think he'll charm the ship to no good. Did you ever notice how that tusk of his is a sort of carved into a snake's head, Stubb?'

'Sink him! I never look at him at all; but if ever I get a chance of a dark night, and he standing hard by the bulwarks, and no one by; look down there, Flask' – pointing into the sea with a peculiar motion of both hands – 'Aye, will I! Flask, I take that Fedallah to be the devil in disguise. Do you believe that cock and bull story about his having been stowed away on board ship? He's the devil, I say. The reason why you don't see his tail is because he tucks it up out of sight; he carries it coiled away in his pocket, I guess. Blast him! now that I think of it, he's always wanting oakum to stuff into his boots.'

'He sleeps in his boots, don't he? He hasn't got any hammock; but I've seen him lay of nights in a coil of rigging.'

'No doubt, and it's because of his cursed tail; he coils it down, do ye see, in the eye of the rigging.'

'What's the old man have so much to do with him for?'

'Striking up a swap or a bargain, I suppose.'

'Bargain? – about what?'

'Why, do ye see, the old man is hard bent after that White Whale, and the devil there is trying to come round him, and get him to swap away his silver watch, or his soul, or something of that sort, and then he'll surrender Moby-Dick.'

'Stubb, you are skylarking; how can Fedallah do that?'

'I don't know, Flask, but the devil is a curious chap, and a wicked one, I tell ye. But look sharp – aint you all ready there? Well, then, pull ahead, and let's get the whale alongside.'

'Such you were telling,' said Flask, when at last the two boats were slowly advancing with their burden towards the ship, 'that you meant to give Fedallah a sea-toss, if you got a good chance. Now, if he is going to live for ever, what good will it do to pitch him overboard – tell me that?'

'Give him a good ducking, anyhow.'

'But he'd crawl back.'

'Duck him again; and keep ducking him.'

'Suppose he should take it into his head to duck you, though – yes, and drown you – what then?'

'I should like to see him try it; I'd give him such a pair of black eyes that he wouldn't dare to show his face again for a long while, hereabouts where he sneaks so much. Damn the devil, Flask; do you suppose I'm afraid of the devil? Who's afraid of him, except the old governor who daresn't catch him and put him in double-darbies, as he deserves, but lets him go about kidnapping people; aye, and signed a bond with him, that all the people the devil kidnapped, he'd roast for him? There's a governor!'

'Do you suppose Fedallah wants to kidnap Captain Ahab?'

'Do I suppose it? You'll know it before long, Flask. But I am going now to keep a sharp look-out on him; and if I see anything very suspicious going on, I'll just take him by the nape of his neck, and say – Look here, Beelzebub, you don't do it; and if he makes any fuss, by the Lord I'll make a grab into his pocket for his tail, take it to the capstan, and give him such a wrenching and heaving, that his tail will come short off at the stump – do you see; and then, I rather guess when he finds himself docked in that fashion, he'll sneak off without the poor satisfaction of feeling his tail between his legs.'

'And what will you do with the tail, Stubb?'

'Do with it? Sell it for an ox whip when we get home – what else?'

'Now, do you mean what you say, and have been saying all along, Stubb?'

'Mean or not mean, here we are at the ship.'

The boats were here hailed, to tow the whale on the larboard side, where fluke chains and other necessaries were already prepared for securing him.

'Didn't I tell you so?' said Flask; 'yes, you'll soon see this Right Whale's head hoisted up opposite that parmaceti's.'

In good time, Flask's saying proved true. As before, the Pequod steeply leaned over towards the Sperm Whale's head; now, by the counterpoise of both heads, she regained her even keel; though sorely strained, you may well believe. So, when on one side you hoist in Locke's head, you go over that way; but now, on the other side, hoist in Kant's and you come back again; but in very poor plight. Thus, some minds for ever keep trimming boat. Oh, ye foolish! throw all these thunderheads overboard, and then you will float light and right.

In disposing of the body of a Right Whale, when brought alongside the ship, the same preliminary proceedings commonly take place as in the case of a Sperm Whale; only, in the latter instance, the head is cut off whole, but in the former the lips and tongue are separately removed and hoisted on deck, with all the well known black bone attached to what is called the crown-piece. But nothing like this, in the present case, had been done. The carcases of both whales had dropped astern; and the head-laden ship not a little resembled a mule carrying a pair of overburdening panniers.

Meantime, Fedallah was calmly eyeing the Right Whale's head, and ever and anon glancing from the deep wrinkles there to the lines in his own hand. And Ahab chanced so to stand, that the Parsee occupied his shadow; while, if the Parsee's shadow was there at all it seemed only to blend with and lengthen Ahab's. As the crew toiled, Laplandish speculations were bandied among them, concerning all these things.

CHAPTER 58

The Sperm Whale's Head –
Contrasted View

Here, now, are two great whales, laying their heads together; let us join them, and lay together our own. Of the grand order of folio Leviathans, the Sperm Whale and the Right Whale are by far the most noteworthy. They are the only whales regularly hunted by man. To the Nantucketer, they present the two extremes of all the known varieties of the whale. As the external difference between them is mainly observable in their heads; and as a head of each is this moment hanging from the Pequod's side; and as we may freely go from one to the other, by merely stepping across the deck – where, I should like to know, will you obtain a better chance to study practical cetology than here?

In the first place, you are struck by the general contrast between these heads. Both are massive enough in all conscience; but there is a certain mathematical symmetry in the Sperm Whale's which the Right Whale's sadly lacks. There is more character in the Sperm Whale's head. As you behold it, you involuntarily yield the immense superiority to him, in point of pervading dignity. In the present instance, too, this dignity is heightened by the pepper and salt colour of his head at the summit, giving token of advanced age and large experience. In short, he is what the fishermen technically call a 'grey-headed whale'.

Let us now note what is least dissimilar in these heads – namely, the two most important organs, the eye and the ear. Far back on the side of the head, and low down, near the angle of either whale's jaw, if you narrowly search, you will at last see a lashless eye, which you would fancy to be a young colt's eye; so out of all proportion is it to the magnitude of the head.

Now, from this peculiar sideway position of the whale's eyes, it is plain that he can never see an object which is exactly ahead, no more than he can one exactly astern. In a word, the position of the whale's eyes corresponds to that of a man's ears; and you may fancy, for yourself, how it would fare with you, did you sideways survey objects through your ears. You would find that you could only command some thirty degrees of vision in advance of the straight side-line of sight; and about thirty more behind it. If your bitterest foe were walking straight towards you, with dagger uplifted in broad day, you would not be able to see him, any more than if he were stealing upon you from behind. In a word, you would have two backs, so to speak; but, at the same time, also, two fronts (side fronts): for what is it that makes the front of a man – what, indeed, but his eyes?

Moreover, while in most other animals that I can now think of, the eyes are so planted as imperceptibly to blend their visual power, so as to produce one picture and not two to the brain; the peculiar position of the whale's eyes, effectually divided as they are by many cubic feet of solid head, which towers between them like a great mountain separating two lakes in valleys; this, of course, must wholly separate the impressions which each independent organ imparts. The whale, therefore, must see one distinct picture on this side, and another distinct picture on that side; while all between must be profound darkness and nothingness to him. Man may, in effect, be said to look out on the world from a sentry-box with two joined sashes for his window. But with the whale, these two sashes are separately inserted, making two distinct windows, but sadly impairing the view. This peculiarity of the whale's eyes is a thing always to be borne in mind in the fishery; and to be remembered by the reader in some subsequent scenes.

But the ear of the whale is full as curious as the eye. If you are an entire stranger to their race, you might hunt over these two heads for hours, and never discover that organ. The ear has no external leaf whatever; and into the hole itself you can hardly insert a quill, so wondrously minute is it. It is lodged a little behind the eye. With respect to their ears, this important difference is to be observed between the Sperm Whale and the Right. While the ear of the former has an external opening, that of the latter is entirely and evenly covered over with a membrane, so as to be quite imperceptible from without.

Is it not curious, that so vast a being as the whale should see the world through so small an eye, and hear the thunder through an ear which is smaller than a hare's? But if his eyes were broad as the lens of Herschel's great telescope; and his ears capacious as the porches of cathedrals; would that make him any longer of sight, or sharper of hearing? Not at all. Why then do you try to 'enlarge' your mind? Subtilize it.

Let us now with whatever levers and steam-engines we have at hand cant over the Sperm Whale's head, so that it may lie bottom up; then, ascending by a ladder to the summit, have a peep down the mouth; and were it not that the body is now completely separated from it, with a lantern we might descend into the great Kentucky Mammoth Cave of his stomach. But let us hold on here by this tooth, and look about us where we are. What a really beautiful and chaste-looking mouth! from floor to ceiling, lined, or rather papered with a glistening white membrane, glossy as bridal satins.

But come out now, and look at this portentous lower jaw, which seems like the long narrow lid of an immense snuff-box, with the hinge at one end, instead of one side. If you pry it up, so as to get it overhead, and expose its rows of teeth, it seems a terrific portcullis; and such, alas! it proves to many a poor wight in the fishery, upon whom these spikes fall with impaling force. But far more terrible is it to behold, when fathoms down in the sea, you see some sulky whale, floating there suspended, with his prodigious jaw, some fifteen feet long, hanging straight down at right-angles with his body, for all the world like a ship's jib-boom. This whale is not dead; he is only dispirited; out of sorts, perhaps; hypochondriac; and so supine, that the hinges of his jaw have relaxed, leaving him there in that ungainly sort of plight, a reproach to all his tribe, who must, no doubt, imprecate lock-jaws upon him.

In most cases this lower jaw – being easily unhinged by a practised artist – is disengaged and hoisted on deck for the purpose of extracting the ivory teeth, and furnishing a supply of that hard white whalebone with which the fishermen fashion all sorts of curious articles, including canes, umbrella-stocks, and handles to riding-whips. With a long, weary hoist the jaw is dragged on board, as if it were an anchor; and when the proper time comes – some few days after the other work – Queequeg, Daggoo, and Tashtego, being all accomplished dentists, are set to drawing teeth. With a keen cutting-spade, Queequeg lances the gums; then the jaw is lashed down to ringbolts, and a tackle being rigged from aloft, they drag out these teeth, as Michigan oxen drag stumps of old oaks out of wild wood-lands. There are generally forty-two teeth in all; in old whales, much worn down, but undecayed; nor filled after our artificial fashion. The jaw is afterwards sawn into slabs, and piled away like joists for building houses.

CHAPTER 59

The Right Whale's Head – Contrasted View

Crossing the deck, let us now have a good long look at the Right Whale's head.

As in general shape the noble Sperm Whale's head may be compared to a Roman war-chariot; so, at a broad view, the Right Whale's head bears a rather inelegant resemblance to a gigantic galliot-toed shoe. Two hundred years ago an old Dutch voyager likened its shape to that of a shoemaker's last. And in this same last or shoe, that old woman of the nursery tale, with the swarming brood, might very comfortably be lodged, she and all her progeny.

But as you come nearer to this great head it begins to assume different aspects, according to your point of view. If you stand on its summit and look at these two *f*-shaped spout-holes, you would take the whole head for an enormous bass-viol, and these spiracles, the apertures in its sounding-board. Then, again, if you fix your eye upon this strange, crested, comb-like incrustation on the top of the mass – this green, barnacled thing, which the Greenlanders call the 'crown', and the Southern fishers the 'bonnet' of the Right Whale; fixing your eyes solely on this, you would take the head for the trunk of some huge oak, with a bird's nest in its crotch. At any rate, when you watch those live crabs that nestle here on this bonnet, such an idea will be almost sure to occur to you; unless, indeed, your fancy has been fixed by the technical term 'crown' also bestowed upon it; in which case you will take great interest in thinking how this mighty monster is actually a diademed king of the sea, whose green crown has been put together for him in this marvellous manner. But if this whale be a king, he is a very sulky looking fellow to grace a diadem. Look at that hanging lower lip! what a huge sulk and pout is there! a sulk and pout, by carpenter's measurement, about twenty feet long and five feet deep; a sulk and pout that will yield you some 500 gallons of oil and more.

A great pity, now, that this unfortunate whale should be hare-lipped. The fissure is about a foot across. Over this lip, as over a slippery threshold, we now slide into the mouth. Upon my word were I at Mackinaw, I should take this to be the inside of an Indian wigwam. Good Lord! is this the road that Jonah went? The roof is about twelve feet high, and runs to a pretty sharp angle, as if there were a regular ridge-pole there; while these ribbed, arched, hairy sides present us with those wondrous, half vertical, scimi-tar-shaped slats of whalebone, say three hundred on a side, which depending from the upper part of the head or crown bone, form Venetian blinds. The edges of these bones are fringed with hairy fibres, through which the Right Whale strains the water, and in whose intricacies he retains the small fish, when open-mouthed he goes through the seas of brit in feeding time. In the central blinds of bone, as they stand in their natural order, there are certain curi-ous marks, curves, hollows, and ridges, whereby some whalemen calculate the creature's age, as the age of an oak by its circular rings.

In old times, there seem to have prevailed the most curious fancies concerning these blinds. One voyager in Purchas calls them the wondrous 'whiskers' inside of the whale's mouth; another, 'hogs' bristles'; a third old gentleman in Hackluyt uses the following elegant language: 'There are about two hundred and fifty fins growing on each side of his upper *chop*, which arch over his tongue on each side of his mouth.'

As every one knows, these same 'hogs' bristles', 'fins', 'whiskers', 'blinds', or whatever you please, furnish to the ladies their busks and other stiffening contrivances. But in this particular, the demand has long been on the decline. It was in Queen Anne's time that the bone was in its glory, the farthingale being then all the fashion. And as those ancient dames moved about gaily, though in the jaws of the whale, as you may say; even so, in a shower, do we nowadays fly under the same jaws for protection; the umbrella being a tent spread over the same bone.

But now forget all about blinds and whiskers for a moment, and, standing in the Right Whale's mouth, look around you afresh. Seeing all these colonnades of bone so methodically ranged about, would you not think you were inside of the great Haarlem organ, and gazing upon its thousand pipes? For a carpet to the organ we have a rug of the softest Turkey – the tongue, which is glued, as it were, to the floor of the mouth. It is very fat and tender, and apt to tear in pieces in hoisting it on deck. This particular tongue now before us; at a passing glance I should say it was a six-barreller; that is, it will yield you about that amount of oil. Ere this, you must have plainly seen the truth of what I started with – that the Sperm Whale and the Right Whale have almost entirely different heads.

Look your last, now, on these venerable hooded heads, while they yet lie together; for one will soon sink, unrecorded, in the sea; the other will not be very long in following.

Can you catch the expression of the Sperm Whale's there? It is the same he died with, only some of the longer wrinkles in the forehead seem now faded away. I think his broad brow to be full of a prairie-like placidity, born of a speculative indifference as to death. But mark the other head's expression. See that amazing lower lip, pressed by accident against the vessel's side, so as firmly to embrace the jaw. Does not this whole head seem to speak of an enormous practical resolution in facing death? This Right Whale I take to have been a Stoic; the Sperm Whale, a Platonian, who might have taken up Spinoza in his latter years.

CHAPTER 60

The Battering-ram

Ere quitting, for the nonce, the Sperm Whale's head, I would have you – as a sensible physiologist, simply – particularly remark its front aspect, in all its compacted collectedness. I would have you investigate it now with the sole view of forming to yourself some unexaggerated, intelligent estimate of whatever battering-ram power may be lodged there. Here is a vital point; for you must either satisfactorily settle this matter with yourself, or for ever remain an infidel as to one of the most appalling events perhaps anywhere to be found in all recorded history.

You observe that in the ordinary swimming position of the Sperm Whale, the front of his head presents an almost wholly vertical plane to the water; you observe that the lower part of that front slopes considerably backwards, so as to furnish more of a retreat for the long socket which receives the boom-like lower jaw; you observe that the mouth is entirely under the head. Moreover you observe that the whale has no external nose; and that what nose he has – his spout-hole – is on the top of his head; you observe that his eyes and ears are at the sides of his head, nearly one third of his entire length from the front. Wherefore, you must now have perceived that the front of the Sperm Whale's head is a dead, blind wall, without a single organ or tender prominence of any sort whatsoever. Furthermore, you are now to consider that only in the extreme, lower, backward sloping part of the front of the head is there the slightest vestige of bone; and not till you get near twenty feet from the forehead do you come to the full cranial development. So that this whole enormous boneless mass is as one wad. Finally, though, as will soon be revealed, its contents partly comprise the most delicate oil; yet, you are now to be apprised of the nature of the substance which so impregnably invests all that apparent effeminacy. In some previous place I have described to you how the blubber wraps the body of the whale, as the rind wraps an orange. Just so with the head; but with this difference: about the head this envelope, though not so thick, is of a boneless toughness, inestimable by any man who has not handled it. The severest pointed harpoon, the sharpest lance darted by the strong-est human arm, impotently rebounds from it. It is as though the forehead of the Sperm Whale were paved with horses' hoofs. I do not think that any sensation lurks in it.

Bethink yourself also of another thing. When two large, loaded Indiamen chance to crowd and crush towards each other in the docks, what do the sailors do? They do not suspend between them, at the point of coming contact, any merely hard substance, like iron or wood. No, they hold there a large, round wad of tow and cork, enveloped in the thickest and toughest of ox-hide. That bravely and uninjured takes the jam which would have snapped all their oaken handspikes and iron crow-bars. By itself this suf-ficiently illustrates the obvious fact I drive at. But supplementary to this, it has hypothetically occurred to me, that as ordinary fish possess what is called a swimming bladder in them, capable, at will, of distension or contraction; and as the Sperm Whale, as far as I know, has no such provision in him; considering, too, the otherwise inexplicable manner in which he now depresses his head altogether beneath the surface, and anon swims with it high elevated out of the water; considering the unobstructed elastic-ity of its envelope; considering the unique interior of his head; it has hypothetically occurred to me, I say, that those mystical lung-celled honeycombs there may possibly have some hitherto unknown and unsuspected connexion with the outer air, so as to be susceptible to atmospheric distension and contraction. If this be so, fancy the irresistibleness of that might, to which the most impalpable and destructive of all elements contributes.

Now, mark. Unerringly impelling this dead, impregnable, uninjurable wall, and this most buoyant thing within; there swims behind it all a mass of tremendous life, only to be adequately estimated as piled wood is – by the cord; and all obedient to one volition, as the smallest insect. So that when I shall hereafter detail to you all the specialities and concentrations of potency everywhere lurking in this expansive monster; when I shall show you some of his more inconsiderable braining feats; I trust you will have renounced all ignorant incredulity, and be ready to abide by this; that though the Sperm Whale stove a passage through the Isthmus of Darien, and mixed the Atlantic with the Pacific, you would not elevate one hair of your eye-brow.

CHAPTER 61

The Great Heidelburgh Tun

Now comes the Baling of the Case. But to comprehend it aright, you must know something of the curious internal structure of the thing operated upon. Regarding the Sperm Whale's head as a solid oblong, you may, on an inclined plane, sideways divide it into two quoins, whereof the lower is the bony structure, forming the cranium and jaws, and the upper an unctuous mass wholly free from bones; its broad forward end forming the expanded vertical apparent forehead of the whale. At the middle of the forehead horizontally subdivide this upper quoin, and then you have two almost equal parts, which before were naturally divided by an internal wall of a thick tendinous substance.

The lower subdivided part, called the junk, is one immense honeycomb of oil, formed by the crossing and re-crossing, into ten thousand infiltrated cells, of tough elastic white fibres throughout its whole extent. The upper part, known as the Case, may be regarded as the great Heidelburgh Tun of the Sperm Whale. And as that famous great tierce is mystically carved in front, so the whale's vast plaited forehead forms innumerable strange devices for the emblematical adornment of his wondrous tun. Moreover, as that of Heidelburgh was always replenished with the most excellent of the wines of the Rhenish valleys, so the tun of the whale contains by far the most precious of all his oily vintages; namely, the highly-prized spermaceti, in its absolutely pure, limpid, and odoriferous state. Nor is this precious substance found unalloyed in any other part of the creature. Though in life it remains perfectly fluid, yet, upon exposure to the air, after death, it soon begins to concrete; sending forth beautiful crystalline shoots, as when the first thin delicate ice is just forming in water. A large whale's case generally yields about five hundred gallons of sperm, though from unavoidable circumstances, considerable of it is spilled, leaks, and dribbles away, or is otherwise irrevocably lost in the ticklish business of securing what you can.

I know not with what fine and costly material the Heidelburgh Tun was coated within, but in superlative richness that coating could not possibly have compared with the silken pearl-coloured membrane, like the lining of a fine pelisse, forming the inner surface of the Sperm Whale's case.

It will have been seen that the Heidelburgh Tun of the Sperm Whale embraces the entire length of the entire top of the head; and since – as has been elsewhere set forth – the head embraces one third of the whole length of the creature, then setting that length down at eighty feet for a good sized whale, you have more than twenty-six feet for the depth of the tun, when it is lengthwise hoisted up and down against a ship's side.

As in decapitating the whale, the operator's instrument is brought close to the spot where an entrance is subsequently forced into the spermaceti magazine; he has, therefore, to be uncommonly heedful, lest a careless, untimely stroke should invade the sanctuary and wastingly let out its invaluable contents. It is this decapitated end of the head, also, which is at last elevated out of the water, and retained in that position by the enormous cutting tackles, whose hempen combinations, on one side, make quite a wilderness of ropes in that quarter. Thus much being said, attend now, I pray you, to that marvellous and – in this particular instance – almost fatal operation whereby the great Heidelburgh Tun is tapped.

CHAPTER 62

Cistern and Buckets

Nimble as a cat, Tashtego mounts aloft; and without altering his erect posture, runs straight out upon the overhanging main-yard-arm, to the part where it exactly projects over the hoisted Tun. He has carried with him a light tackle called a whip, consisting of only two parts, travelling through a single-sheaved block. Securing this block, so that it hangs down from the yard-arm, he swings one end of the rope, till it is caught and firmly held by a hand on deck. Then, hand-over-hand, down the other part, the Indian drops through the air, till dexterously he lands on the summit of the head. There – still high elevated above the rest of the company, to whom he vivaciously cries – he seems some Turkish Muezzin calling the good people to prayers from the top of a tower. A short-handled sharp spade being sent up to him, he diligently searches for the proper place to begin breaking into the Tun. In this business he proceeds very heedfully, like a treasure-hunter in some old house, sounding the walls to find where the gold is masoned in. By the time this cautious search is over, a stout iron-bound bucket, precisely like a well-bucket, has been attached to one end of the whip; while the other end, being stretched across the deck, is there held by two or three alert hands. These last now hoist the bucket within grasp of the Indian, to whom another person has reached up a very long pole. Inserting this pole into the bucket, Tashtego downward guides the bucket into the Tun, till it entirely disappears; then giving the word to the seamen at the whip, up comes the bucket again, all bubbling like a dairy-maid's pail of new milk. Carefully lowered from its height, the full-freighted vessel is caught by an appointed hand, and quickly emptied into a large tub. Then re-mounting aloft, it again goes through the same round until the deep cistern will yield no more. Towards the end, Tashtego has to ram his long pole harder and harder, and deeper and deeper into the Tun, until some twenty feet of the pole have gone down.

Now, the people of the Pequod had been baling some time in this way; several tubs had been filled with the fragrant sperm; when all at once a queer accident happened. Whether it was that Tashtego, that wild Indian, was so heedless and reckless as to let go for a moment his one-handed hold on the great cabled tackles suspending the head; or whether the place where he stood was so treacherous and oozy; or whether the Evil One himself would have it to fall out so, without stating his particular reasons; how it was exactly, there is no telling now; but, on a sudden, as the eightieth or ninetieth bucket came suckingly up – my God! poor Tashtego – like the twin reciprocating bucket in a veritable well – dropped head-foremost down into this great Tun of Heidelburgh, and with a horrible oily gurgling, went clean out of sight!

'Man overboard!' cried Daggoo, who amid the general consternation first came to his senses. 'Swing the bucket this way!' and putting one foot into it, so as the better to secure his slippery hand-hold on the whip itself, the hoisters ran him high up to the top of the head, almost before Tashtego could have reached its interior bottom. Meantime, there was a terrible tumult. Looking over the side, they saw the before lifeless head throbbing and heaving just below the surface of the sea, as if that moment seized with some momentous idea; whereas it was only the poor Indian unconsciously revealing by those struggles the perilous depth to which he had sunk. At this instant, while Daggoo, on the summit of the head, was clearing the whip – which had somehow got foul of the great cutting tackles – a sharp cracking noise was heard; and to the unspeakable horror of all, one of the two enormous hooks suspending the head tore out, and with a vast vibration the enormous mass sideways swung, till the drunk ship reeled and shook as if smitten by an iceberg. The one remaining hook, upon which the entire strain now depended, seemed every instant to be on the point of giving way; an event still more likely from the violent motions of the head.

'Come down, come down!' yelled the seamen to Daggoo, but with one hand holding on to the heavy tackles, so that if the head should drop, he would still remain suspended, the negro having cleared the foul line, rammed down the bucket into the now collapsed well, meaning that the buried harpooneer should grasp it, and so be hoisted out.

'In heaven's name, man,' cried Stubb, 'are you ramming home a cartridge there? – Avast! How will that help him; jamming that iron-bound bucket on top of his head? Avast, will ye!'

'Stand clear of the tackle!' cried a voice like the bursting of a rocket.

Almost in the same instant, with a thunder-boom, the enormous mass dropped into the sea, like Niagara's Table-Rock into the whirlpool; the suddenly relieved hull rolled away from it, to far down her glittering copper; and all caught their breath, as half swinging – now over the sailors' heads, and now over the water – Daggoo, through a thick mist of spray, was dimly beheld clinging to the pendulous tackles, while poor, buried-alive Tashtego was sinking utterly down to the bottom of the sea! But hardly had the blinding vapour cleared away, when a naked figure with a boarding-sword in its hand was for one swift moment seen hovering over the bulwarks. The next, a loud splash announced that my brave Queequeg had dived to the rescue. One packed rush was made to the side, and every eye counted every ripple, as moment followed moment, and no sign of either the sinker or the diver could be seen. Some hands now jumped into a boat alongside, and pushed a little off from the ship.

'Ha! ha!' cried Daggoo, all at once; and looking further off from the side, we saw an arm thrust upright from the blue waves; a sight strange to see, as an arm thrust forth from the grass over a grave.

'Both! both! – it is both!' – cried Daggoo again with a joyful shout; and soon after, Queequeg was seen boldly striking out with one hand, and with the other clutching the long hair of the Indian. Drawn into the waiting boat, they were quickly brought to the deck; but Tashtego was long in coming to, and Queequeg did not look very brisk.

Now, how had this noble rescue been accomplished? Why, diving after the slowly descending head, Queequeg with his keen sword had made side lunges near its bottom, so as to scuttle a large hole there; then dropping his sword, had thrust his long arm far inwards and upwards, and so hauled out our poor Tash by the head. He averred, that upon first thrusting in for him, a leg was presented; but well knowing that that was not as it ought to be and might occasion great trouble, he had thrust back the leg, and by a dexterous heave and toss, had wrought a somerset upon the Indian; so that with the next trial, he came forth in the good old way – head foremost. As for the great head itself, that was doing as well as could be expected.

And thus, through the courage and great skill in obstetrics of Queequeg, the deliverance, or rather, delivery of Tashtego, was successfully accomplished, in the teeth of the most apparently hopeless impediments; which is a lesson by no means to be forgotten. Midwifery should be taught in the same course with fencing and boxing, riding and rowing.

CHAPTER 63

The Praire

To scan the lines of his face, or feel the bumps on the head of this Leviathan; this is a thing which no Physiognomist or Phrenologist has as yet undertaken. Such an enterprise would seem almost as hopeful as for Lavater to have scrutinized the wrinkles on the Rock of Gibraltar, or for Gall to have mounted a ladder and manipulated the Dome of the Pantheon. Still, in that famous work of his, Lavater not only treats of the various faces of men, but also attentively studies the faces of horses, birds, serpents, and fish; and dwells in detail upon the modifications of expression discernible therein. Nor have Gall and his disciple Spurzheim failed to throw out some hints touching the phrenological characteristics of other beings than man. Therefore, though I am but ill qualified for a pioneer, in the application of these two semi-sciences to the whale, I will do my endeavour. I try all things; I achieve what I can.

Physiognomically regarded, the Sperm Whale is an anomalous creature. He has no proper nose. Nevertheless, Leviathan is of so mighty a magnitude, all his proportions are so stately, that the deficiency is no blemish at all. Nay, it is an added grandeur. As on your physiognomical voyage you sail round his vast head, your noble conceptions of him are never insulted by the reflection that he has a nose to be pulled. A pestilent conceit, which so often will insist upon obtruding even when beholding the mightiest royal beadle on his throne.

In some particulars, perhaps the most imposing physiognomical view to be had of the Sperm Whale, is that of the full front of his head. This aspect is Sublime.

In thought, a fine human brow is like the East when troubled with the morning. In the repose of the pasture, the curled brow of the bull has a touch of the grand in it. Pushing heavy cannon up mountain defiles, the elephant's brow is majestic. Human or animal, the mystical brow is as that great golden seal affixed by the German emperors to their decrees. It signifies – 'God: done this day by my hand.' But in most creatures, nay in man himself, very often the brow is but a mere strip of alpine land lying along the snow line. But in the great Sperm Whale, this high and mighty god-like dignity inherent in the brow is so immensely amplified, that gazing on it, in that full front view, you feel the Deity and the dread powers more forcibly than in beholding any other object in living nature. For you see no one point precisely; not one distinct feature is revealed; no nose, eyes, ears, or mouth; no face; he has none, proper; nothing but that one broad firmament of a forehead, pleated with riddles; dumbly lowering with the doom of boats, and ships, and men. Nor, in profile, does this wondrous brow diminish; though that way viewed, its grandeur does not domineer upon you so. In profile, you plainly perceive that horizontal, semi-crescentic depression in the forehead's middle, which, in man, is Lavater's mark of genius.

But how? Genius in the Sperm Whale? Has the Sperm Whale ever written a book, spoken a speech? No, his great genius is declared in his doing nothing particular to prove it. It is moreover declared in his pyramidical silence.

Champollion deciphered the wrinkled granite hieroglyphics. But there is no Champollion to decipher the Egypt of every man's and every being's face. Physiognomy, like every other human science, is but a passing fable. If then, Sir William Jones, who read in thirty languages, could not read the simplest peasant's face in its profounder and more subtle meanings, how may unlettered Ishmael hope to read the awful Chaldee of the Sperm Whale's brow? I but put that brow before you. Read it if you can.

CHAPTER 64

The Nut

If the Sperm Whale be physiognomically a Sphinx, to the phrenologist his brain seems that geometrical circle which it is impossible to square.

In the full-grown creature the skull will measure at least twenty feet in length. Unhinge the lower jaw, and the side view of this skull is as the side view of a moderately inclined plane resting throughout on a level base. But in life – as we have elsewhere seen – this inclined plane is angularly filled up, and almost squared by the enormous superincumbent mass of the junk and sperm. At the high end the skull forms a crater to bed that part of the mass; while under the long floor of this crater – in another cavity seldom exceeding ten inches in length and as many in depth – reposes the mere handful of this monster's brain. The brain is at least twenty feet from his apparent forehead in life; it is hidden away behind its vast outworks, like the innermost citadel within the amplified fortifications of Quebec.

CHAPTER 65

The Pequod Meets the Virgin

The predestinated day arrived, and we duly met the ship Jungfrau, Derick De Deer, master, of Bremen.

At one time the greatest whaling people in the world, the Dutch and Germans are now among the least; but here and there you still occasionally meet with their flag in the Pacific.

For some reason, the Jungfrau seemed quite eager to pay her respects. While yet some distance from the Pequod, she rounded to, and dropping a boat, her captain was impelled towards us, impatiently standing in the bows.

'What has he in his hand there?' cried Starbuck, pointing to something wavingly held by the German. 'Impossible! – a lamp-feeder!'

'Not that,' said Stubb, 'no, no, it's a coffee-pot, Mr Starbuck; he's coming off to make us our coffee, is the Yarman; don't you see that big tin can there alongside of him? – that's his boiling water. Oh! he's all right, is the Yarman.'

'Go along with you,' cried Flask, 'it's a lamp-feeder and an oil-can. He's out of oil, and has come a-begging.'

However curious it may seem for an oil-ship to be borrowing oil on the whale-ground, and however much it may invertedly contradict the old proverb about carrying coals to Newcastle, yet sometimes such a thing really happens; and in the present case Captain Derick De Deer did indubitably conduct a lamp-feeder as Flask did declare.

As he mounted the deck, Ahab abruptly accosted him, without at all heeding what he had in his hand; but in his broken lingo, the German soon evinced his complete ignorance of the White Whale; immediately turning the conversation to his lamp-feeder and oil-can, with some remarks touching his having to turn into his hammock at night in darkness – his last drop of Bremen oil being gone, and not a single flying-fish yet captured to supply the deficiency; concluding by hinting that his ship was indeed what in the fishery is technically called a clean one (that is, an empty one), well deserving the name of Jungfrau or the Virgin.

His necessities supplied, Derick departed; but he had not gained his ship's side, when whales were almost simultaneously raised from the mast-heads of both vessels; and so eager for the chase was Derick, that without pausing to put his oil-can and lamp-feeder aboard, he slewed round his boat and made after the Leviathan lamp-feeders.

Now, the game having risen to leeward, he and the other three German boats that soon followed him had considerably the start of the Pequod's keels. There were eight whales, an average pod. Aware of their danger, they were going all abreast with great speed straight before the wind. They left a great, wide wake, as though continually unrolling a great wide parchment upon the sea.

Full in this rapid wake, and many fathoms in the rear, swam a huge old bull, which by the yellowish incrustations overgrowing him, seemed afflicted with the jaundice, or some other infirmity. Whether this whale belonged to the pod seemed questionable; for it is not customary for such venerable Leviathans to be at all social. Nevertheless, he stuck to their wake, though indeed their back water must have retarded him. His spout was short, slow, and laborious; coming forth with a choking sort of gush, and spending itself in torn shreds, followed by strange subterranean commotions in him, which seemed to have egress at his other buried extremity, causing the waters behind him to upbubble.

'Who's got some paregoric?' said Stubb, 'he has the stomach-ache, I'm afraid. Lord, think of having half an acre of stomach-ache! It's the first foul wind I ever knew to blow from astern; but look, did ever whale yaw so before? it must be, he's lost his tiller.'

As an overladen Indiaman bearing down the Hindostan coast

with a deck load of frightened horses careens, buries, rolls, and wallows on her way; so did this old whale heave his aged bulk, and now and then partly turning over on his rib-ends, expose the cause of his devious wake in the unnatural stump of his starboard fin. Whether he had lost that fin in battle, or had been born without it, it were hard to say.

'Only wait a bit, old chap, and I'll give ye a sling for that wounded arm,' cried cruel Flask, pointing to the whale-line near him.

'Mind he don't sling thee with it,' cried Starbuck. 'Give way, or the German will have him.'

With one intent all the combined rival boats were pointed for this one fish, because not only was he the largest, and therefore the most valuable whale, but he was nearest to them. At this juncture, the Pequod's keels had shot by the three German boats last lowered; but Derick's boat still led the chase, though every moment neared by his foreign rivals. The only thing they feared was, that from being already so nigh to his mark, he would be enabled to dart his iron before they could overtake him. As for Derick, he seemed quite confident that this would be the case, and occasionally with a deriding gesture shook his lamp-feeder at the other boats.

'The ungracious and ungrateful dog!' cried Starbuck; 'he mocks and dares me with the very poor-box I filled for him not five minutes ago!' – then in his old intense whisper – 'give way, greyhounds! Dog to it!'

'I tell ye what it is, men' – cried Stubb to his crew – 'It's against my religion to get mad; but I'd like to eat that villanous Yarman – Pull – won't ye? Are ye going to let that rascal beat ye? Do ye love brandy? A hogshead of brandy, then, to the best man. Come, why don't some of ye burst a blood-vessel? Who's that been dropping an anchor overboard – we don't budge an inch – we're becalmed. Halloo, here's grass growing in the boat's bottom – and by the Lord, the mast there's budding. This won't do, boys. Look at that Yarman! The short and long of it is, men, will ye spit fire or not?'

'Oh! see the suds he makes!' cried Flask, dancing up and down

– 'What a hump – Oh, *do* pile on the beef – lays like a log! Oh! my lads, *do* spring – slap-jacks and quohogs for supper, you know, my lads – baked clams and muffins – oh, *do*, *do*, spring – he's a hundred barreller – don't lose him now – don't, oh, *don't*! see that Yarman – Oh! won't ye pull for your duff, my lads – such a sog! such a sogger! Don't ye love sperm? There goes three thousand dollars, men! – a bank! – a whole bank! The bank of England! – Oh, *do*, *do*, *do*! – What's that Yarman about now?'

At this moment Derick was in the act of pitching his lamp-feeder at the advancing boats, and also his oil-can; perhaps with the double view of retarding his rivals' way, and at the same time economically accelerating his own by the momentary impetus of the backward toss.

'The unmannerly Dutch dogger!' cried Stubb. 'Pull now, men, like fifty thousand line-of-battle-ship loads of red-haired devils. What d'ye say, Tashtego; are you the man to snap your spine in two-and-twenty pieces for the honour of old Gay-head? What d'ye say?'

'I say, pull like god-dam,' cried the Indian.

Fiercely, but evenly incited by the taunts of the German, the Pequod's three boats now began ranging almost abreast; and, so disposed, momentarily neared him. In that fine, loose, chivalrous attitude of the headsman when drawing near to his prey, the three mates stood up proudly, occasionally backing the after oarsman with an exhilarating cry of, 'There she slides, now! Hurrah for the white-ash breeze! Down with the Yarman! Sail over him!'

But so decided an original start had Derick had, that spite of all their gallantry, he would have proved the victor in this race, had not a righteous judgement descended upon him in a crab which caught the blade of his midship oarsman. While this clumsy lubber was striving to free his white-ash, and while, in consequence, Derick's boat was nigh to capsizing, and he thundering away at his men in a mighty rage – that was a good time for Starbuck, Stubb, and Flask. With a shout, they took a mortal start forwards, and slantingly ranged up on the German's quarter. An instant more, and all four boats were diagonally in the whale's immediate wake, while stretching from them, on both sides, was the foaming swell that he made.

It was a terrific, most pitiable, and maddening sight. The whale was now going head out, and sending his spout before him in a continual tormented jet; while his one poor fin beat his side in an agony of fright. Now to this hand, now to that, he yawed in his faltering flight, and still at every billow that he broke, he spasmodically sank in the sea, or sideways rolled towards the sky his one beating fin. This made the sight of him unspeakably pitiable; while still, in his amazing bulk, portcullis jaw, and omnipotent tail, there was enough to appal the stoutest man who so pitied.

Seeing now that but a very few moments more would give the Pequod's boats the advantage, and rather than be thus foiled of his game, Derick chose to hazard what to him must have seemed a most unusually long dart, ere the last chance would for ever escape.

But no sooner did his harpooneer stand up for the stroke, than all three tigers – Queequeg, Tashtego, Daggoo – instinctively sprang to their feet, and standing in a diagonal row, simultaneously pointed their barbs; and darted over the head of the German harpooneer, their three Nantucket irons entered the whale. Blinding vapours of foam and white-fire! The three boats, in the first fury of the whale's headlong rush, bumped the German's aside with such force, that both Derick and his baffled harpooneer were spilled out, and sailed over by the three flying keels.

'Don't be afraid, my butter-boxes,' cried Stubb, casting a passing glance upon them as he shot by; 'ye'll be picked up presently – all right – I saw some sharks astern – St Bernard's dogs, you know – relieve distressed travellers. Hurrah! this is the way to sail now. Every keel a sun-beam! Hurrah! – Here we go like three tin kettles at the tail of a mad cougar! Hurrah! this is the way a fellow feels when he's going to Davy Jones – all a rush down an endless inclined plane!'

But the monster's run was a brief one. Giving a sudden gasp, he tumultuously sounded. With a grating rush, the three lines flew round the loggerheads with such a force as to gouge deep grooves in them; while so fearful were the harpooneers that this rapid sounding would soon exhaust the lines, that using all their dexterous might, they caught repeated smoking turns with the rope to hold on; till at last – owing to the perpendicular strain from the lead-lined chocks of the boats, whence the three ropes went straight down into the blue – the gunwales of the bows were almost even with the water, while the three sterns tilted high in the air. And the whale soon ceasing to sound, for some time they remained in that attitude, fearful of expending more line, though the position was a little ticklish. But though boats have been taken down and lost in this way, yet it is this 'holding on', as it is called; this hooking up by the sharp barbs of his live flesh from the back; this it is that often torments the Leviathan into soon rising again to meet the sharp lance of his foes. Yet not to speak of the peril of the thing, it is to be doubted whether this course is always the best; for it is but reasonable to presume, that the longer the stricken whale stays under water, the more he is exhausted. Because, owing to the enormous surface of him – in a full grown Sperm Whale something less than 2000 square feet – the pressure of the water is immense. One whaleman has estimated it at the weight of twenty line-of-battle ships, with all their guns, and stores, and men on board.

As the three boats lay there on that gently rolling sea, gazing down into its eternal blue noon; and as not a single groan or cry of any sort, nay, not so much as a ripple or a bubble came up from its depths; what landsman would have thought, that beneath all that silence and placidity, the utmost monster of the seas was writhing in agony! Not eight inches of perpendicular rope were visible at the bows. Seems it credible that by three such thin threads the great Leviathan was suspended. Suspended? and to what? To three bits of board.

'Stand by, men; he stirs,' cried Starbuck, as the three lines suddenly vibrated in the water. The next moment, the boats gave a sudden bounce upwards, as a small icefield will, when a dense herd of white bears are scared from it into the sea.

'Haul in! Haul in!' cried Starbuck again; 'he's rising.'

The lines, of which, hardly an instant before, not one hand's breadth could have been gained, were now in long quick coils flung back all dripping into the boats, and soon the whale broke water within two ship's lengths of the hunters.

In most land animals there are certain valves or flood-gates in many of their veins, whereby when wounded, the blood is in some degree instantly shut off in certain directions. Not so with the whale; one of whose peculiarities it is, to have an entire non-valvular structure of the blood-vessels, so that when pierced even by so small a point as a harpoon, a deadly drain is at once begun upon his whole arterial system; and when this is heightened by the extraordinary pressure of water at a great distance below the surface, his life may be said to pour from him in incessant streams. Yet so vast is the quantity of blood in him, and so distant and numerous its interior fountains, that he will keep thus bleeding for a considerable period. Even now, when the boats pulled upon this whale, and perilously drew over his swaying flukes, and the lances were darted into him, they were followed by steady jets from the new made wound, which kept continually playing, while the natural spout-hole in his head was only at intervals sending its affrighted moisture into the air. From this last vent no blood yet came, because no vital part of him had thus far been struck. His life, as they significantly call it, was untouched.

As the boats now more closely surrounded him, the whole upper part of his form, with much of it that is ordinarily submerged, was plainly revealed. His eyes, or rather the places where his eyes had been, were beheld. From the points which the whale's eyes had once occupied, now protruded blind bulbs, horribly pitiable to see. But pity there was none. For all his old age, and his one arm, and his blind eyes, he must die the death and be murdered, in order to light the gay bridals and other merrymakings of men, and also to illuminate the solemn churches that preach unconditional inoffensiveness by all to all. Still rolling in his blood, at last he partially disclosed a strangely discoloured bunch or protuberance, the size of a bushel, low down on the flank.

'A nice spot,' cried Flask; 'let me prick him there once.'

'Avast!' cried Starbuck, 'there's no need of that!'

But humane Starbuck was too late. At the instant of the dart an ulcerous jet shot from this cruel wound, and goaded by it into more than sufferable anguish, the whale now spouting thick blood, with swift fury blindly darted at the craft, bespattering them and their crews all over with gore, capsizing Flask's boat and marring the bows. It was his death stroke. For so spent was he by loss of blood, that he helplessly rolled away from the wreck he had made; lay panting on his side, impotently flapped with his stumped fin, then over and over slowly revolved like a waning world; turned up the white secrets of his belly; lay like a log, and died.

Soon, while the crews were awaiting the arrival of the ship, the body showed symptoms of sinking with all its treasures unrifled. Immediately, by Starbuck's orders, lines were secured to it at different points, so that ere long every boat was a buoy; the sunken whale being suspended a few inches beneath them by the cords.

By heedful management, when the ship drew nigh, the whale was transferred to her side, and was strongly secured there by the stiffest fluke-chains, for it was plain that unless artificially upheld, the body would at once sink to the bottom.

It so chanced that almost upon first cutting into him with the spade, the entire length of a corroded harpoon was found imbedded in his flesh, on the lower part of the bunch before described. But as the stumps of harpoons are frequently found in the dead bodies of captured whales, with the flesh perfectly healed around them, and no prominence of any kind to denote their place; therefore, there must needs have been some other unknown reason in the present case fully to account for the ulceration alluded to. But still more curious was the fact of a lance-head of stone being found in him, not far from the buried iron, the flesh perfectly firm about it. Who had darted that stone lance? And when? It might have been darted by some Nor' West Indian long before America was discovered.

What other marvels might have been rummaged out of this monstrous cabinet there is no telling. But a sudden stop was put to further discoveries, by the ship's being unprecedentedly dragged over sideways to the sea, owing to the body's immensely increasing tendency to sink. However, Starbuck, who had the ordering of affairs, hung on to it to the last; hung on to it so resolutely, indeed, that when at length the ship would have been capsized, if still persisting in locking arms with the body; then, when the command was given to break clear from it, such was the immovable strain upon the timber-heads to which the fluke-chains and cables were fastened, that it was impossible to cast them off. Meantime everything in the Pequod was aslant. To cross to the other side of the deck was like walking up the steep gabled roof of a house. The ship groaned and gasped. Many of the ivory inlayings of her bulwarks and cabins were started from their places, by the unnatural dislocation. In vain handspikes and crows were brought to bear upon the fluke-chains, to pry them adrift from the timber-heads; and so low had the whale now settled that the submerged ends could not be at all approached, while every moment whole tons of ponderosity seemed added to the sinking bulk, and the ship seemed on the point of going over.

'Hold on, hold on, won't ye?' cried Stubb to the body, 'don't be in such a devil of a hurry to sink! By thunder, men, we must do something or go for it. No use prying there; avast, I say with your handspikes, and run one of ye for a prayer book and a pen-knife, and cut the big chains.'

'Knife? Aye, aye,' cried Queequeg, and seizing the carpenter's heavy hatchet, he leaned out of a port-hole, and steel to iron, began slashing at the largest fluke-chains. But a few strokes, full of sparks, were given, when the exceeding strain effected the rest. With a terrific snap, every fastening went adrift; the ship righted, the carcase sank.

Now, this occasional inevitable sinking of the recently killed Sperm Whale is a very curious thing; nor has any fisherman yet adequately accounted for it. Usually the dead Sperm Whale floats with great buoyancy, with its side or belly considerably elevated above the surface. If the only whales that thus sank were old, meagre, and broken-hearted creatures, their pads of lard diminished and all their bones heavy and rheumatic; then you might with some reason assert that this sinking is caused by an uncommon specific gravity in the fish so sinking, consequent upon this absence of buoyant matter in him. But it is not so. For young whales, in the highest health, and swelling with noble aspirations, prematurely cut off in the warm flush and May of life, with all their panting lard about them; even these brawny, buoyant heroes do sometimes sink.

It was not long after the sinking of the body that a cry was heard from the Pequod's mast-heads, announcing that the Jungfrau was again lowering her boats; though the only spout in sight was that of a Fin-Back, belonging to the species of uncapturable whales, because of its incredible power of swimming. Nevertheless, the Fin-Back's spout is so similar to the Sperm Whale's, that by unskilful fishermen it is often mistaken for it. And consequently Derick and all his host were now in valiant chase of this unnearable brute. The Virgin, crowding all sail, made after her four young keels, and thus they all disappeared far to leeward, still in bold, hopeful chase.

CHAPTER 66

Pitchpoling

To make them run easily and swiftly, the axles of carriages are anointed; and for much the same purpose, some whalers perform an analogous operation upon their boat; they grease the bottom. Nor is it to be doubted that as such a procedure can do no harm, it may possibly be of no contemptible advantage; considering that oil and water are hostile; that oil is a sliding thing, and that the object in view is to make the boat slide bravely. Queequeg believed strongly in anointing his boat, and one morning took more than customary pains in that occupation; crawling under its bottom, where it hung over the side, and rubbing in the unctuousness as though diligently seeking to insure a crop of hair from the craft's bald keel. He seemed to be working in obedience to some particular presentiment. Nor did it remain unwarranted by the event.

Towards noon whales were raised; but so soon as the ship sailed down to them, they turned and fled; a disordered flight, as of Cleopatra's barges from Actium.

Nevertheless, the boats pursued, and Stubb's was foremost. By great exertion, Tashtego at last succeeded in planting one iron; but the stricken whale, without at all sounding, still continued his horizontal flight, with added fleetness. Such unintermitted strainings upon the planted iron must sooner or later inevitably extract it. It became imperative to lance the flying whale, or be content to lose him. But to haul the boat up to his flank was impossible, he swam so fast and furious. What then remained?

Of all the wondrous devices and dexterities, the sleights of hand and countless subtleties, to which the veteran whaleman is so often forced, none exceed that fine manoeuvre with the lance called pitchpoling. Small sword, or broad sword, in all its exercises boasts nothing like it. It is indispensable only with an inveterate running whale; its grand fact and feature is the wonderful distance to which the long lance is accurately darted from a violently rocking, jerking boat, under extreme headway. Steel and wood included, the entire spear is some ten or twelve feet in length; the staff is much slighter than that of the harpoon, and also of a lighter material-pine. It is furnished with a small rope called a warp, by which it can be hauled back to the hand after darting.

But before going further, it is important to mention here, that though the harpoon may be pitchpoled in the same way with the lance, yet it is seldom done; and when done, is still less frequently successful, on account of the greater weight and inferior length of the harpoon as compared with the lance. As a general thing, therefore, you must first get fast to a whale, before any pitchpoling comes into play.

Look now at Stubb; a man who from his humorous, deliberate coolness and equanimity in the direst emergencies, was specially qualified to excel in pitchpoling. Look at him; he stands upright in the tossed bow of the flying boat; wrapt in fleecy foam, the towing whale is forty feet ahead. Handling the long lance lightly, glancing twice or thrice along its length to see if it be exactly straight, Stubb whistlingly gathers up the coil of the warp in one hand, so as to secure its free end in his grasp, leaving the rest unobstructed. Then holding the lance full before his waistband's middle, he levels it at the whale; when, covering him with it, he steadily depresses the butt-end in his hand, thereby elevating the point till the weapon stands fairly balanced upon his palm, fifteen feet in the air. Next moment, in a superb lofty arch the bright steel spans the foaming distance, and quivers in the life spot of the whale. Instead of sparkling water, he now spouts red blood.

'That drove the spigot out of him!' cries Stubb. ''Tis July's immortal Fourth; all fountains must run wine today! Would now, it were old Orleans whiskey, or old Ohio, or unspeakable old Monongahela! Then, Tashtego, lad, I'd have ye hold a canakin to the jet, and we'd drink round it! Yea, verily, hearts alive, we'd brew choice punch in the spread of his spout-hole there, and from that live punch-bowl quaff the living stuff!'

Again and again to such gamesome talk, the dexterous dart is repeated, the spear returning to its master like a greyhound held in skilful leash. The agonized whale goes into his flurry; the towline is slackened, and the pitchpoler dropping astern, folds his hands, and mutely watches the monster die.

CHAPTER 67

The Tail

Other poets have warbled the praises of the soft eye of the antelope, and the lovely plumage of the bird that never alights; less celestial, I celebrate a tail.

Reckoning the largest sized Sperm Whale's tail to begin at that point of the trunk where it tapers to about the girth of a man, it comprises upon its upper surface alone an area of at least fifty square feet. The compact round body of its root expands into two broad, firm, flat palms or flukes, gradually shoaling away to less than an inch in thickness. At the crotch or junction, these flukes slightly overlap, then sideways recede from each other like wings, leaving a wide vacancy between. In no living thing are the lines of beauty more exquisitely defined than in the crescentic borders of these flukes. At its utmost expansion in the full grown whale, the tail will considerably exceed twenty feet across.

The entire member seems a dense webbed bed of welded sinews; but cut into it, and you find that three distinct strata compose it – upper, middle, and lower. The fibres in the upper and lower layers are long and horizontal; those of the middle one, very short, and running crosswise between the outside layers. This triune structure, as much as anything else, imparts power to the tail.

But as if this vast local power in the tendinous tail were not enough, the whole bulk of the Leviathan is knit over with a warp and woof of muscular fibres and filaments, which passing on either side the loins and running down into the flukes, insensibly blend with them, and largely contribute to their might; so that in the tail the confluent measureless force of the whole whale seems concentrated to a point. Could annihilation occur to matter, this were the thing to do it.

Such is the subtle elasticity of the organ I treat of, that whether wielded in sport, or in earnest, or in anger, whatever be the mood it be in, its flexions are invariably marked by exceeding grace. Therein no fairy's arm can transcend it.

Five great motions are peculiar to it. First, when used as a fin for progression; second, when used as a mace in battle; third, in sweeping; fourth, in lobtailing; fifth, in peaking flukes.

First: Being horizontal in its position, the Leviathan's tail acts in a different manner from the tails of all other sea creatures. It never wriggles. In man or fish, wriggling is a sign of inferiority. To the whale, his tail is the sole means of propulsion. Scroll-wise coiled forwards beneath the body, and then rapidly sprung backwards, it is this which gives that singular darting, leaping motion to the monster when furiously swimming. His side-fins only serve to steer by.

Second: It is a little significant, that while one Sperm Whale fights another Sperm Whale only with his head and jaw, nevertheless, in his conflicts with man, he chiefly and contemptuously uses his tail. In striking at a boat, he swiftly curves away his flukes from it, and the blow is inflicted only by the recoil. If it be made in the unobstructed air, especially if it descend to its mark, the stroke is then simply irresistible. No ribs of man or boat can withstand it. Your only salvation lies in eluding it; but if it comes sideways through the opposing water, then partly owing to the light buoyancy of the whale-boat, and the elasticity of its materials, a cracked rib or a dashed plank or two, a sort of stitch in the side, is generally the most serious result. These submerged side blows are so often received in the fishery, that they are accounted mere child's play. Some one strips off a frock, and the hole is stopped.

Third: I cannot demonstrate it, but it seems to me, that in the whale the sense of touch is concentrated in the tail; for in this respect there is a delicacy in it equalled only by the daintiness of the elephant's trunk. This delicacy is chiefly evinced in the action of sweeping, when the whale with a certain soft slowness moves his immense flukes from side to side upon the surface of the sea; and if he feel but a sailor's whisker, woe to that sailor, whiskers and all. What tenderness there is in that preliminary touch!

Fourth: Stealing unawares upon the whale in the fancied security of the middle of solitary seas, you find him unbent from the vast corpulence of his dignity, and kitten-like, he plays on the ocean as if it were a hearth. But still you see his power in his play. The broad palms of his tail are flirted high into the air; then smiting the surface, the thunderous concussion resounds for miles. You would almost think a great gun had been discharged; and if you noticed the light wreath of vapour from the spiracle at his other extremity, you would think that that was the smoke from the touch-hole.

Fifth: As in the ordinary floating posture of the Leviathan the flukes lie considerably below the level of his back, they are then

Leabharlanna Fhine Gall

completely out of sight beneath the surface; but when he is about to plunge into the deeps, his entire flukes with at least thirty feet of his body are tossed erect in the air, and so remain vibrating a moment, till they downwards shoot out of view. Excepting the sublime *breach* – somewhere else to be described – this peaking of the whale's flukes is perhaps the grandest sight to be seen in all animated nature. Out of the bottomless profundities the gigantic tail seems spasmodically snatching at the highest heaven. Standing at the mast-head of my ship during a sunrise that crimsoned sky and sea, I once saw a large herd of whales in the east, all heading towards the sun, and for a moment vibrating in concert with peaked flukes. As it seemed to me at the time, such a grand embodiment of adoration of the gods was never beheld, even in Persia, the home of the fire worshippers. As Ptolemy Philopater testified of the elephant, I then testified of the whale, pronouncing him the most devout of all beings. For according to King Juba, the military elephants of antiquity often hailed the morning with their trunks uplifted in the profoundest silence.

The chance comparison in this chapter, between the whale and the elephant, should not tend to place those two on an equality. For as the mightiest elephant is but a terrier to Leviathan, so, compared with Leviathan's tail, his trunk is but the stalk of a lily. The most direful blow from the elephant's trunk were as the playful tap of a fan, compared with the measureless crush and crash of the Sperm Whale's ponderous flukes, which in repeated instances have one after the other hurled entire boats with all their oars and crews into the air, very much as an Indian juggler tosses his balls.

CHAPTER 68

The Grand Armada

The long and narrow peninsula of Malacca, extending south-eastward from the territories of Birmah, forms the most southerly point of all Asia. In a continuous line from that peninsula stretch the long islands of Sumatra, Java, Bally, and Timor; which, with many others, form a vast mole, or rampart, lengthwise connecting Asia with Australia, and dividing the long unbroken Indian Ocean from the thickly studded oriental archipelagoes. This rampart is pierced by several sally-ports for the convenience of ships and whales; conspicuous among which are the straits of Sunda and Malacca. By the straits of Sunda, chiefly, vessels bound to China from the west emerge into the China seas.

Time out of mind the piratical proas of the Malays, lurking among the low shaded coves and islets of Sumatra, have sallied out upon the vessels sailing through the straits, fiercely demanding tribute at the point of their spears. Though by the repeated bloody chastisements they have received at the hands of European cruisers, the audacity of these corsairs has of late been somewhat repressed; yet, even at the present day, we occasionally hear of English and American vessels, which, in those waters, have been remorselessly boarded and pillaged.

With a fair, fresh wind, the Pequod was now drawing nigh to these straits; Ahab purposing to pass through them into the Javan sea, and thence, cruising northwards, over waters known to be frequented here and there by the Sperm Whale, sweep inshore by the Philippine Islands, and gain the far coast of Japan, in time for the great whaling season there; where Ahab firmly counted upon giving battle to Moby-Dick, in the sea he was most known to frequent; and at a season when he might most reasonably be presumed to be haunting it.

But how now? in this zoned quest, does Ahab touch no land? does his crew drink air? Surely, he will stop for water. Nay. While other hulls are loaded down with alien stuff, to be transferred to foreign wharves, the world wandering whale-ship carries no cargo but herself and crew, their weapons and their wants. She carries years' water in her. Clear old prime Nantucket water; which, when three years afloat, the Nantucketer, in the Pacific, prefers to drink before the brackish fluid, but yesterday rafted off in casks, from the Peruvian or Indian streams. Hence it is, that, while other ships may have gone to China from New York, and back again, touching at a score of ports, the whale-ship, in all that interval, may not have sighted one grain of soil; her crew having seen no man but floating seamen like themselves.

Now, as many Sperm Whales had been captured off the western coast of Java, in the near vicinity of the Straits of Sunda; indeed, as most of the ground, roundabout, was generally recognized by the fishermen as an excellent spot for cruising; therefore, as the Pequod gained more and more upon Java Head, the look-outs were repeatedly hailed, and admonished to keep wide awake. But though the green palmy cliffs of the land soon loomed on the starboard bow, and with delighted nostrils the fresh cinnamon was snuffed in the air, yet not a single jet was descried. The ship had well nigh entered the straits, when the customary cheering cry was heard from aloft, and ere long a spectacle of singular magnificence saluted us.

But here be it premised, that owing to the unwearied activity with which of late they have been hunted over all four oceans, the Sperm Whales, instead of almost invariably sailing in small detached companies, as in former times, are now frequently met with in extensive herds. To this aggregation of the Sperm Whale into such immense caravans may be imputed the circumstance that even in the best cruising grounds you may now sometimes sail for weeks and months together, without being greeted by a single spout; and then be saluted by what sometimes seems thousands on thousands.

Broad on both bows, at the distance of some two or three miles, and forming a great semicircle, embracing one half of the level horizon, a continuous chain of whale-jets were up-playing and sparkling in the noon-day air.

Seen from the Pequod's deck, then, as she would rise on a high hill of the sea, this host of vapoury spouts, individually curling up into the air, and beheld through a blending atmosphere of bluish haze, showed like the thousand cheerful chimneys of some dense metropolis.

As marching armies approaching an unfriendly defile in the

mountains accelerate their march, even so did this vast fleet of whales now seem hurrying forward through the straits; gradually contracting the wings of their semicircle, and swimming on, in one solid, but still crescentic centre.

Crowding all sail the Pequod pressed after them; the harpooneers handling their weapons, and loudly cheering from the heads of their yet suspended boats. So with stun-sail piled on stun-sail, we sailed along, driving these Leviathans before us; when, of a sudden, the voice of Tashtego was heard, loudly directing attention to something in our wake.

Corresponding to the crescent in our van, we beheld another in our rear. It seemed formed of detached white vapours, rising and falling something like the spouts of the whales; only they did not so completely come and go; for they constantly hovered, without finally disappearing. Levelling his glass at this sight, Ahab quickly revolved in his pivot-hole, crying, 'Aloft there, and rig whips and buckets to wet the sails; Malays, sir, and after us!'

With glass under arm, Ahab to-and-fro paced the deck; in his forward turn beholding the monsters he chased, and in the after one the bloodthirsty pirates chasing *him*. And when he glanced upon the green walls of the watery defile in which the ship was then sailing, and bethought him that through that gate lay the route to his vengeance, and beheld, how that through that same gate he was now both chasing and being chased to his deadly end; and not only that, but a herd of remorseless wild pirates and inhuman atheistical devils were infernally cheering him on with their curses; – when all these conceits had passed through his brain, Ahab's brow was left gaunt and ribbed, like the black sand beach after some stormy tide has been gnawing it, without being able to drag the firm thing from its place.

But thoughts like these troubled very few of the reckless crew; and when, after steadily dropping and dropping the pirates astern, the Pequod at last shot by the vivid green Cockatoo Point on the Sumatra side, emerging at last upon the broad waters beyond; then, the harpooneers seemed more to grieve that the swift whales had been gaining upon the ship, than to rejoice that the ship had

so victoriously gained upon the Malays. But still driving on in the
wake of the whales, at length they seemed abating their speed;
gradually the ship neared them; and the wind now dying away,
word was passed to spring to the boats. But no sooner did the herd
become notified of the three keels that were after them, though
as yet a mile in their rear, than they rallied again, and forming in
close ranks and battalions, moved on with redoubled velocity.

Stripped to our shirts and drawers, we sprang to the white-ash,
and after several hours' pulling were almost disposed to renounce
the chase, when a general pausing commotion among the whales
gave animating token that they were now at last under the influence of that strange perplexity of inert irresolution, which, when
the fishermen perceive it in the whale, they say he is gallied. The
compact martial columns in which they had been hitherto swimming were now broken up in one measureless rout; and like King
Porus' elephants in the Indian battle with Alexander, they seemed
going mad with consternation. In all directions expanding in vast
irregular circles, and aimlessly swimming hither and thither, by
their short thick spoutings, they plainly betrayed their distraction
of panic. This was still more strangely evinced by those of their
number, who, completely paralysed as it were, helplessly floated
like water-logged dismantled ships on the sea.

Though many of the whales were in violent motion, yet as a
whole the herd neither advanced nor retreated, but collectively
remained in one place. As is customary in those cases, the boats
at once separated, each making for some one lone whale on the
outskirts of the shoal. In about three minutes' time, Queequeg's
harpoon was flung; the stricken fish darted blinding spray in our
faces, and then running away with us like light, steered straight for
the heart of the herd. Such a movement on the part of the whale
is in no wise unprecedented; yet does it present one of the more
perilous vicissitudes of the fishery. For as the swift monster drags
you deeper and deeper into the frantic shoal, you bid adieu to
circumspect life and only exist in a delirious throb.

But not a bit daunted, Queequeg steered us manfully; now sheer-
ing off from this monster directly across our route in advance;

now edging away from that, whose colossal flukes were suspended overhead, while all the time, Starbuck stood up in the bows, lance in hand, pricking out of our way whatever whales he could reach by short darts, for there was no time to make long ones.

All whale-boats carry certain curious contrivances, originally invented by the Nantucket Indians, called druggs. Two thick squares of wood of equal size are stoutly clenched together, so that they cross each other's grain at right angles; a line of considerable length is then attached to the middle of this block, and the other end of the line being looped, it can in a moment be fastened to a harpoon. It is chiefly among gallied whales that this drugg is used. For then, more whales are close round you than you can possibly chase at one time. But Sperm Whales are not every day encountered; while you may, then, you must kill all you can. And if you cannot kill them all at once, you must wing them, so that they can be afterwards killed at your leisure. Hence it is, that at times like these the drugg comes into requisition. Our boat was furnished with three of them. The first and second were successfully darted, and we saw the whales staggeringly running off, fettered by the enormous sidelong resistance of the towing drugg. They were cramped like malefactors with the chain and ball. But upon flinging the third, in the act of tossing overboard the clumsy wooden block, it caught under one of the seats of the boat, and in an instant tore it out and carried it away, dropping the oarsman in the boat's bottom as the seat slid from under him. On both sides the sea came in at the wounded planks, but we stuffed two or three drawers and shirts in, and so stopped the leaks for the time.

It had been next to impossible to dart these drugged-harpoons, were it not that as we advanced into the herd, our whale's way greatly diminished; moreover, that as we went still further and further from the circumference of commotion, the direful disorders seemed waning. So that when at last the jerking harpoon drew out, and the towing whale sideways vanished; then, with the tapering force of his parting momentum, we glided between two whales into the innermost heart of the shoal, as if from some mountain torrent we had slid into a serene valley lake. Here the storms in the roaring glens between the outermost whales were heard but not felt. In this central expanse the sea presented that smooth satin-like surface, called a sleek, produced by the subtle moisture thrown off by the whale in his more quiet moods. Yes, we were now in that enchanted calm which they say lurks at the heart of every commotion. And still in the distracted distance we beheld the tumults of the outer concentric circles, and saw successive pods of whales, eight or ten in each, swiftly going round and round, like multiplied spans of horses in a ring; and so closely shoulder to shoulder, that a Titanic circus-rider might easily have overarched the middle ones, and so have gone round on their backs. Owing to the density of the crowd of reposing whales, more immediately surrounding the embayed axis of the herd, no possible chance of escape was at present afforded us. We must watch for a breach in the living wall that hemmed us in; the wall that had only admitted us in order to shut us up. Keeping at the centre of the lake, we were occasionally visited by small tame cows and calves; the women and children of this routed host.

Like household dogs they came snuffling right up to our gunwales, and touching them; till it almost seemed that some spell had suddenly domesticated them. Queequeg patted their foreheads; Starbuck scratched their backs with his lance; but fearful of the consequences, refrained from darting it.

But far beneath this wondrous world upon the surface, another and still stranger world met our eyes as we gazed over the side. For, suspended in those watery vaults, floated the forms of the nursing mothers of the whales, and those that by their enormous girth seemed shortly to become mothers. The lake, as I have hinted, was to a considerable depth exceedingly transparent; and as human infants while suckling will calmly and fixedly gaze away from the breast, as if leading two different lives at the time; and while yet drawing mortal nourishment, be still spiritually feasting upon some unearthly reminiscence; even so did the young of these whales seem looking up towards us, but not at us, as if we were but a bit of Gulf-weed in their new-born sight. Floating on their sides, the mothers also seemed quietly eyeing us. One of

these little infants, that from certain queer tokens seemed hardly
a day old, might have measured some fourteen feet in length, and
some six feet in girth. He was a little frisky; though as yet his body
seemed scarce yet recovered from that irksome position it had so
lately occupied in the maternal reticule. The delicate side-fins, and
the palms of his flukes, still freshly retained the plaited crumpled
appearance of a baby's ears newly arrived from foreign parts.

'Line! line!' cried Queequeg, looking over the gunwale; 'him
fast! him fast! – Who line him! Who struck? – Two whale; one
big, one little!'

'What ails ye, man?' cried Starbuck.

'Look-e here,' said Queequeg pointing down. As when the
stricken whale, that from the tub has reeled out hundreds of fathoms of rope; as, after deep sounding, he floats up again, and shows
the slackened curling line buoyantly rising and spiralling towards
the air; so now, Starbuck saw long coils of the umbilical cord of
Madame Leviathan, by which the young cub seemed still tethered
to its dam. Not seldom in the rapid vicissitudes of the chase, this
natural line, with the maternal end loose, becomes entangled with
the hempen one, so that the cub is thereby trapped. Some of the
subtlest secrets of the seas seemed divulged to us in this enchanted
pond. We saw young Leviathan amours in the deep.

And thus, though surrounded by circle upon circle of conster-
nations and affrights, did these inscrutable creatures at the centre
freely and fearlessly indulge in all peaceful concernments; yea,
serenely revelled in dalliance and delight. But even so, amid the
tornadoed Atlantic of my being, do I myself still for ever centrally
disport in mute calm; and while ponderous planets of unwaning
woe revolve round me, deep down and deep inland there I still
bathe me in eternal mildness of joy.

Meanwhile, as we thus lay entranced, the occasional sudden
frantic spectacles in the distance evinced the activity of the other
boats, still engaged in drugging the whales on the frontier of the
host; or possibly carrying on the war within the first circle, where
abundance of room and some convenient retreats were afforded
them. But the sight of the enraged drugged whales now and then

blindly darting to and fro across the circles was nothing to what at last met our eyes. It is sometimes the custom when fast to a whale more than commonly powerful and alert, to seek to hamstring him, as it were, by sundering or maiming his gigantic tail-tendon. It is done by darting a short-handled cutting-spade, to which is attached a rope for hauling it back again. A whale wounded (as we afterwards learned) in this part, but not effectually, as it seemed, had broken away from the boat, carrying along with him half of the harpoon line; and in the extraordinary agony of the wound, he was now dashing among the revolving circles like the lone mounted desperado Arnold, at the battle of Saratoga, carrying dismay wherever he went.

But agonizing as was the wound of this whale, yet the peculiar horror with which he seemed to inspire the rest of the herd was owing to a cause which at first the intervening distance obscured from us. But at length we perceived that by one of the unimaginable accidents of the fishery, this whale had become entangled in the harpoon-line that he towed; he had also run away with the cutting-spade in him; and while the free end of the rope attached to that weapon had permanently caught in the coils of the harpoon-line round his tail, the cutting-spade itself had worked loose from his flesh. So that tormented to madness, he was now churning through the water, violently tossing the keen spade about him, wounding and murdering his own comrades.

This terrific object seemed to recall the whole herd from their stationary fright. First, the whales forming the margin of our lake began to crowd a little, and tumble against each other, as if lifted by half spent billows from afar; then the lake itself began faintly to heave and swell; the submarine bridal-chambers and nurseries vanished; in more and more contracting orbits the whales in the more central circles began to swim in thickening clusters. A low advancing hum was heard; and then like to the tumultuous masses of block-ice when the great river Hudson breaks up in Spring, the entire host of whales came tumbling upon their inner centre. Instantly Starbuck and Queequeg changed places; Starbuck taking the stern.

'Oars! Oars!' he intensely whispered, 'gripe your oars, and clutch your souls, now! My God, men, stand by! Shove him off, you Queequeg – the whale there! prick him! – hit him! Stand up – stand up, and stay so! Spring, men – pull, men; never mind their backs – scrape them! – scrape away!'

The boat was now all but jammed between two vast black bulks, leaving a narrow Dardanelles between their long lengths. But by desperate endeavour we at last shot into a temporary opening; then giving way rapidly, and at the same time earnestly watching for another outlet. After many similar hair-breadth escapes, we at last swiftly glided into what had just been one of the outer circles, but now crossed by random whales, all violently making for one centre. This lucky salvation was cheaply purchased by the loss of Queequeg's hat, who, while standing in the bows to prick the fugitive whales, had his hat taken clean from his head by the air-eddy made by the sudden tossing of a pair of broad flukes close by.

Riotous and disordered as the universal commotion now was, it soon resolved itself into what seemed a systematic movement; for having clumped together at last in one dense body, they then renewed their onward flight with augmented fleetness. Further pursuit was useless; but the boats still lingered in their wake to pick up what drugged whales might be dropped astern, and likewise to secure one which Flask had killed and waifed. The waif is a pennoned pole, two or three of which are carried by every boat; and which, when additional game is at hand, are inserted upright into the floating body of a dead whale, both to mark its place on the sea, and also as token of prior possession, should the boats of any other ship draw near.

The result of this lowering was somewhat illustrative of that sagacious saying in the fishery – the more whales the less fish. Of all the drugged whales only one was captured. The rest contrived to escape for the time, but only to be taken, as will hereafter be seen, by some other craft than the Pequod.

CHAPTER 69

Fast-fish and Loose-fish

The allusion to the waifs and waif-poles necessitates some account of the laws and regulations of the whale fishery, of which the waif may be deemed the grand symbol and badge.

It frequently happens that when several ships are cruising in company, a whale may be struck by one vessel, then escape, and be finally killed and captured by another vessel; and herein are indirectly comprised many minor contingencies, all partaking of this one grand feature. For example – after a weary and perilous chase and capture of a whale, the body may get loose from the ship by reason of a violent storm; and drifting far away to leeward, be retaken by a second whaler, who, in a calm, snugly tows it alongside, without risk of life or line. Thus the most vexatious and violent disputes would often arise between the fishermen, were there not some written or unwritten, universal, undisputed law applicable to all cases.

Perhaps the only formal whaling code authorized by legislative enactment was that of Holland. It was decreed by the States-General in A.D. 1695. But though no other nation has ever had any written whaling law, yet the American fishermen have been their own legislators and lawyers in this matter. They have provided a system which for terse comprehensiveness surpasses Justinian's Pandects and the By-laws of the Chinese Society for the Suppression of Meddling with other People's Business. Yes; these laws might be engraven on a Queen Anne's farthing, or the barb of a harpoon, and worn round the neck, so small are they.

I. A Fast-fish belongs to the party fast to it.

II. A Loose-fish is fair game for anybody who can soonest catch it.

But what plays the mischief with this masterly code is the

admirable brevity of it, which necessitates a vast volume of commentaries to expound it.

First: What is a Fast-fish? Alive or dead a fish is technically fast, when it is connected with an occupied ship or boat, by any medium at all controllable by the occupant or occupants. Likewise a fish is technically fast when it bears a waif, or any other recognized symbol of possession; so long as the party waifing it plainly evince their ability at any time to take it alongside, as well as their intention so to do. These are scientific commentaries; but the commentaries of the whalemen themselves sometimes consist in hard words and harder knocks. True, among the more upright and honourable whalemen allowances are always made for peculiar cases, where it would be an outrageous moral injustice for one party to claim possession of a whale previously chased or killed by another party. But others are by no means so scrupulous.

Some fifty years ago there was a curious case of whale-trover litigated in England, wherein the plaintiffs set forth that after a hard chase of a whale in the Northern seas; and when indeed they (the plaintiffs) had succeeded in harpooning the fish; they were at last, through peril of their lives, obliged to forsake not only their lines, but their boat itself. Ultimately the defendants (the crew of another ship) came up with the whale, struck, killed, seized, and finally appropriated it before the very eyes of the plaintiffs. And when those defendants were remonstrated with, their captain snapped his fingers in the plaintiffs' teeth, and assured them that by way of doxology to the deed he had done, he would now retain their line, harpoons, and boat, which had remained attached to the whale at the time of the seizure. Wherefore the plaintiffs now sued for the recovery of the value of their whale, line, harpoons, and boat.

Mr Erskine was counsel for the defendants; Lord Ellenborough was the judge. In the course of the defence, the witty Erskine went on to illustrate his position, by alluding to a recent crim. con. case, wherein a gentleman, after in vain trying to bridle his wife's viciousness, had at last abandoned her upon the seas of life; but in the course of years, repenting of that step, he instituted an action to recover possession of her. Erskine was on the other side; and he then supported it by saying, that though the gentleman had originally harpooned the lady, and had once had her fast, and only by reason of the great stress of her plunging viciousness, had at last abandoned her; yet abandon her he did, so that she became a Loose-fish; and therefore when a subsequent gentleman re-harpooned her, the lady then became that subsequent gentleman's property, along with whatever harpoon might have been found in her.

Now in the present case Erskine contended that the examples of the whale and the lady were reciprocally illustrative of each other.

These pleadings, and the counter pleadings, being duly heard, the very learned judge in set terms decided, to wit – That as for the boat, he awarded it to the plaintiffs, because they had merely abandoned it to save their lives; but that with regard to the controverted whale, harpoons, and line, they belonged to the defendants; the whale, because it was a Loose-fish at the time of the final capture; and the harpoons and line because when the fish made off with them, it acquired a property in those articles; and hence anybody who afterwards took the fish had a right to them. Now the plaintiffs afterwards took the fish; ergo, the aforesaid articles were theirs.

A common man looking at this decision of the very learned Judge might possibly object to it. But ploughed up to the primary rock of the matter, the two great principles laid down in the twin whaling laws previously quoted, and applied and elucidated by Lord Ellenborough in the above cited case; these two laws touching Fast-fish and Loose-fish, I say, will, on reflection, be found the fundamentals of all human jurisprudence; for notwithstanding its complicated tracery of sculpture, the Temple of the Law, like the Temple of the Philistines, has but two props to stand on.

Is it not a saying in every one's mouth, Possession is half of the law: that is, regardless of how the thing came into possession? But often possession is the whole of the law. What are the sinews and souls of Russian serfs and Republican slaves but Fast-fish, whereof possession is the whole of the law? What to the rapacious landlord is the widow's last mite but a Fast-fish? What is yonder undetected villain's marble mansion with a door-plate for a waif; what is that but a Fast-fish? What is the ruinous discount which Mordecai, the broker, gets from poor Woebegone, the bankrupt, on a loan to keep Woebegone's family from starvation; what is that ruinous discount but a Fast-fish? What is the Archbishop of Savesoul's income of £100,000 seized from the scant bread and cheese of hundreds of thousands of broken-backed labourers (all sure of heaven without any of Savesoul's help), what is that globular 100,000 but a Fast-fish? What are the Duke of Dunder's hereditary towns and hamlets but Fast-fish? What to that redoubted harpooneer, John Bull, is Ireland, but a Fast-fish? What to that apostolic lancer, Brother Jonathan, is Texas but a Fast-fish? And concerning all these, is not Possession the whole of the law?

But if the doctrine of Fast-fish be pretty generally applicable, the kindred doctrine of Loose-fish is still more widely so. That is internationally and universally applicable.

What was America in 1492 but a Loose-fish, in which Columbus struck the Spanish standard by way of waifing it for his royal master and mistress? What was Poland to the Czar? What Greece to the Turk? What India to England? What at last will Mexico be to the United States? All Loose-fish. What are the Rights of Man and the Liberties of the World but Loose-fish? What all men's minds and opinions but Loose-fish? What is the principle of religious belief in them but a Loose-fish? What to the ostentatious smuggling verbalists are the thoughts of thinkers but Loose-fish? What is the great globe itself but a Loose-fish? And what are you, reader, but a Loose-fish and a Fast-fish, too?

CHAPTER 70

The Pequod Meets the Rose-bud

It was a week or two after the last whaling scene recounted, and when we were slowly sailing over a sleepy, vapoury, midday sea, that a peculiar and not very pleasant smell was smelt in the sea.

'I will bet something now,' said Stubb, 'that somewhere hereabouts are some of those drugged whales we tickled the other day. I thought they would keel up before long.'

Presently, the vapours in advance slid aside; and there in the distance lay a ship, whose furled sails betokened that some sort of whale must be alongside. As we glided nearer, the stranger showed French colours from his peak; and by the eddying cloud of vulture sea-fowl that circled, and hovered, and swooped around him, it was plain that the whale alongside must be what the fishermen called a blasted whale, that is, a whale that has died unmolested on the sea, and so floated an unappropriated corpse. It may well be conceived, what an unsavoury odour such a mass must exhale; worse than an Assyrian city in the plague, when the living are incompetent to bury the departed. So intolerable indeed is it regarded by some, that no cupidity could persuade them to moor alongside of it. Yet are there those who will still do it; notwithstanding the fact that the oil obtained from such subjects is of a very inferior quality, and by no means of the nature of attar-of-rose.

Coming still nearer, we saw that the Frenchman had a second whale alongside; and this second whale seemed even more of a nosegay than the first. In truth, it turned out to be one of those problematical whales that seem to dry up and die with a sort of prodigious dyspepsia, or indigestion; leaving their defunct bodies almost entirely bankrupt of anything like oil. Nevertheless, in the proper place we shall see that no knowing fisherman will ever turn up his nose at such a whale as this, however much he may shun blasted whales in general.

The Pequod had now swept so nigh to the stranger, that Stubb vowed he recognized his cutting spade-pole entangled in the lines that were knotted round the tail of one whale.

'There's a pretty fellow, now,' he banteringly laughed, standing in the ship's bows, 'there's a jackal for ye! I well know that these Crappoes of Frenchmen are but poor devils in the fishery; sometimes lowering their boats for breakers, mistaking them for Sperm Whale spouts; yes, and sometimes sailing from their port with their hold full of boxes of tallow candles, and cases of snuffers, foreseeing that all the oil they will get won't be enough to dip the Captain's wick into; aye, we all know these things; but look ye, here's a Crappo that is content with our leavings, the drugged whale there, I mean; aye, and is content too with scraping the dry bones of that other precious fish he has there. Poor devil! I say, pass round a hat, some one, and let's make him a present of a little oil for dear charity's sake. For what oil he'll get from that drugged whale there, wouldn't be fit to burn in a jail; no, not in a condemned cell. And as for the other whale, why, I'll agree to get more oil by chopping up and trying out these three masts of ours, than he'll get from that bundle of bones; though, now that I think of it, it may contain something worth a good deal more than oil; yes, ambergris. I wonder now if our old man has thought of that. It's worth trying. Yes, I'm in for it'; and so saying he started for the quarter-deck.

By this time the faint air had become a complete calm; so that whether or no, the Pequod was now fairly entrapped in the smell, with no hope of escaping except by its breezing up again. Issuing from the cabin, Stubb now called his boat's crew, and pulled off for the stranger. Drawing across her bow, he perceived that in accordance with the fanciful French taste, the upper part of her stem-piece was carved in the likeness of a huge drooping stalk, was painted green, and for thorns had copper spikes projecting from it here and there; the whole terminating in a symmetrical folded bulb of a bright red colour. Upon her head boards, in large gilt letters, he read 'Bouton de Rose' – Rose-button, or Rose-bud; and this was the romantic name of this aromatic ship.

Though Stubb did not understand the *Bouton* part of the inscription, yet the word *rose*, and the bulbous figure-head put together, sufficiently explained the whole to him.

'A wooden rose-bud, eh?' he cried with his hand to his nose, 'that will do very well; but how like all creation it smells!'

Now in order to hold direct communication with the people on deck, he had to pull round the bows to the starboard side, and thus come close to the blasted whale; and so talk over it.

Arrived then at this spot, with one hand still to his nose, he bawled – 'Bouton-de-Rose, ahoy! are there any of you Bouton-de-Roses that speak English?'

'Yes,' rejoined a Guernsey-man from the bulwarks, who turned out to be the chief mate.

'Well, then, have you seen the White Whale?'

'*What* whale?'

'The *White* Whale – a Sperm Whale – Moby-Dick, have ye seen him?'

'Never heard of such a whale. Cachalot Blanche! White Whale – no.'

'Very good, then; good-bye now, and I'll call again in a minute.'

Then rapidly pulling back towards the Pequod, and seeing Ahab leaning over the quarter-deck rail awaiting his report, he moulded his two hands into a trumpet and shouted – 'No, sir! No!' Upon which Ahab retired, and Stubb returned to the Frenchman.

He now perceived that the Guernsey-man, who had just got into the chains, and was using a cutting-spade, had slung his nose in a sort of bag.

'What's the matter with your nose, there?' said Stubb. 'Broke it?'

'I wish it was broken, or that I didn't have any nose at all!' answered the Guernsey-man. 'But what are you holding *yours* for?'

'Oh, nothing! It's a wax nose; I have to hold it on. Fine day, aint it? Air rather gardeny, I should say; throw us a bunch of posies, will ye, Bouton-de-Rose?'

'What in the devil's name do you want here?' roared the Guernsey-man, flying into a sudden passion.

'Oh! keep cool – cool? yes, that's the word; why don't you pack those whales in ice while you're working at 'em? But joking aside, though; do you know, Rose-bud, that it's all nonsense trying to get any oil out of such whales? As for that dried up one, there, he hasn't a gill in his whole carcase.'

'I know that well enough; but the captain won't believe it; this is his first voyage; he was a Cologne manufacturer before. But come aboard, and mayhap he'll believe you, if he won't me; and so I'll get out of this dirty scrape.'

'Anything to oblige ye, my sweet and pleasant fellow,' rejoined Stubb, and with that he soon mounted to the deck. There a queer scene presented itself. The sailors, in tasselled caps of red worsted, were getting the heavy tackles in readiness for the whales. But they worked rather slow and talked very fast, and seemed in anything but a good humour. Now and then pairs of them would run up to the mast-head to get some fresh air. Some, thinking they would catch the plague, dipped oakum in coal-tar, and at intervals held it to their nostrils. Others, having broken the stems of their pipes almost short off at the bowl, were vigorously puffing tobacco-smoke, so that it constantly filled their olfactories.

Stubb was struck by a shower of outcries and anathemas proceeding from the captain's round-house abaft; and looking in that direction saw a fiery face thrust from behind the door, which was held ajar from within. This was the tormented surgeon, who, after in vain remonstrating against the proceedings of the day, had betaken himself to the captain's round-house (*cabinet* he called it) to avoid the pest; but still, could not help yelling out entreaties and indignations at times.

Marking all this, Stubb argued well for his scheme, and turning to the Guernsey-man had a little chat with him, during which the stranger mate expressed his detestation of his captain as a conceited ignoramus, who had brought them all into so un-savoury and unprofitable a pickle. Stubb further perceived that the Guernsey-man had not the slightest suspicion concerning the ambergris. He therefore held his peace on that head, but otherwise was quite frank and confidential with him, so that the two quickly concocted a little plan for both circumventing and satirizing the captain, without his distrusting their sincerity. According to this plan of theirs, the Guernsey-man, under cover of an interpreter's office, was to tell the captain what he pleased, but as coming from Stubb; and as for Stubb, he was to utter any nonsense that should come uppermost in him during the interview.

By this time their destined victim appeared from his cabin. He was a small and dark, but rather delicate looking man for a sea-captain, with large whiskers and moustache, however; and wore a red cotton velvet vest with watch-seals at his side. To this gentleman, Stubb was now politely introduced by the Guernsey-man, who at once ostentatiously put on the aspect of interpreting between them.

'What shall I say to him first?' said he.

'Why,' said Stubb, eyeing the velvet vest and the watch and seals, 'you may as well begin by telling him that he looks a sort of babyish to me, though I don't pretend to be a judge.'

'He says, Monsieur,' said the Guernsey-man, turning to his captain, 'that yesterday his ship spoke a vessel, whose captain and chief mate, with six sailors, had all died of a fever caught from a blasted whale they had brought alongside.'

Upon this the captain eagerly desired to know more.

'What now?' said the Guernsey-man to Stubb.

'Why, tell him that now I have eyed him carefully, I'm certain that he's no more fit to command a whale-ship than a St Jago monkey. In fact, tell him from me he's a baboon.'

'He vows and declares, Monsieur, that the other whale, the dried one, is far more deadly than the blasted one; in fine, Monsieur, he conjures us, as we value our lives, to cut loose from these fish.'

Instantly the captain ran forward, and in a loud voice commanded his crew to desist from hoisting the cutting-tackles, and at once cast loose the cables and chains confining the whales to the ship.

'What now?' said the Guernsey-man, when the captain had returned to them.

'Why, let me see; yes, you may as well tell him now that – that – in fact, tell him I've diddled him, and (aside to himself) perhaps somebody else.'

'He says, Monsieur, that he's very happy to have been of any service to us.'

Hearing this, the captain vowed that they were the grateful parties (meaning himself and mate) and concluded by inviting Stubb down into his cabin to drink a bottle of Bordeaux.

'Thank him heartily; but tell him it's against my principles to drink with the man I've diddled. In fact, tell him I must go.'

'He says, Monsieur, that his principles won't admit of his drinking; but that if Monsieur wants to live another day, then Monsieur had best drop all four boats, and pull the ship away from these whales, for it's so calm they won't drift.'

By this time Stubb was over the side, and getting into his boat, hailed the Guernsey-man to this effect – that having a long tow-line in his boat, he would do what he could to help them, by pulling out the lighter whale of the two from the ship's side. While the Frenchman's boats, then, were engaged in towing the ship one way, Stubb benevolently towed away at his whale the other way, ostentatiously slacking out a most unusually long tow-line.

Presently a breeze sprang up; Stubb feigned to cast off from the whale; hoisting his boats, the Frenchman soon increased his distance, while the Pequod slid in between him and Stubb's whale. Whereupon Stubb quickly pulled to the floating body, and hailing the Pequod to give notice of his intentions, at once proceeded to reap the fruit of his unrighteous cunning. Seizing his sharp boat-spade, he commenced an excavation in the body, a little behind the side fin. You would almost have thought he was digging a cellar there in the sea; and when at length his spade struck against the gaunt ribs, it was like turning up old Roman tiles and pottery buried in fat English loam. His boat's crew were all in high excitement, eagerly helping their chief, and looking as anxious as gold-hunters.

And all the time numberless fowls were diving, and ducking, and screaming, and fighting around them. Stubb was beginning to look disappointed, when suddenly from out the very heart of this plague, there stole a faint stream of perfume, which flowed through the tide of bad smells without being absorbed by it, as one river will flow into and then along with another, without at all blending with it for a time.

'I have it, I have it,' cried Stubb, with delight, striking something in the subterranean regions, 'a purse! a purse!'

Dropping his spade, he thrust both hands in, and drew out handfuls of something that looked like ripe Windsor soap, or rich mottled old cheese; very unctuous and savoury withal. You might easily dent it with your thumb; it is of a hue between yellow and ash colour. And this, good friends, is ambergris, worth a gold guinea an ounce to any druggist. Some six handfuls were obtained; but more was unavoidably lost in the sea, and still more, perhaps, might have been secured were it not for impatient Ahab's loud command to Stubb to desist, and come on board, else the ship would bid them good-bye.

CHAPTER 71

The Castaway

It was but some few days after encountering the Frenchman, that a most significant event befell the most insignificant of the Pequod's crew; an event most lamentable; and which ended in providing the sometimes madly merry and predestinated craft with a living and ever accompanying prophecy of whatever shattered sequel might prove her own.

Now, in the whale-ship, it is not every one that goes in the boats. Some few hands are reserved called ship-keepers, whose province it is to work the vessel while the boats are pursuing the whale. As a general thing, these ship-keepers are as hardy fellows as the men comprising the boats' crews. But if there happen to be an unduly slender, clumsy, or timorous wight in the ship, that wight is certain to be made a ship-keeper. It was so in the Pequod with the little negro Pippin by nick-name, Pip by abbreviation.

Pip, though over tender-hearted, was at bottom very bright, with that pleasant, genial, jolly brightness peculiar to his tribe; a tribe, which ever enjoy all holidays and festivities with finer, freer relish than any other race. For blacks, the year's calendar should show naught but three hundred and sixty-five Fourth of Julys and New Year's Days. Nor smile so, while I write that this little black was brilliant, for even blackness has its brilliancy; behold yon lustrous ebony, panelled in king's cabinets. But Pip loved life, and all life's peaceable securities; so that the panic-striking business in which he had somehow become entrapped had most sadly blurred his brightness.

It came to pass, that in the ambergris affair Stubb's after-oars-man chanced so to sprain his hand; and, temporarily, Pip was put into his place.

The first time Stubb lowered with him, Pip evinced much nerv-ousness; but happily, for that time, escaped close contact with the whale; and therefore came off not altogether discreditably; though Stubb, observing him, took care, afterwards, to exhort him to cherish his courageousness to the utmost, for he might often find it needful.

Now upon the second lowering, the boat paddled upon the whale; and as the fish received the darted iron, it gave its custom-ary rap, which happened, in this instance, to be right under poor Pip's seat. The involuntary consternation of the moment caused him to leap, paddle in hand, out of the boat; and in such a way, that part of the slack whale line coming against his chest, he breasted it overboard with him, so as to become entangled in it, when at last plumping into the water. That instant the stricken whale started on a fierce run, the line swiftly straightened; and presto! poor Pip came all foaming up to the chocks of the boat, remorselessly dragged there by the line, which had taken several turns around his chest and neck.

Tashtego stood in the bows. He was full of the fire of the hunt. Snatching the boat-knife from its sheath, he suspended its sharp edge over the line, and turning towards Stubb, exclaimed interrogatively, 'Cut?' Meantime Pip's blue, choked face plainly looked, Do, for God's sake! All passed in a flash. In less than half a minute, this entire thing happened.

'Damn him, cut!' roared Stubb; and so the whale was lost and Pip was saved.

So soon as he recovered himself, the poor little negro was assailed by yells and execrations from the crew. Tranquilly permitting these irregular cursings to evaporate, Stubb then in a plain, business-like, but still half humorous manner, cursed Pip officially; and that done, unofficially gave him much wholesome advice. The substance was, Never jump from a boat, Pip, except – but all the rest was indefinite, as the soundest advice ever is. Now, in general, *Stick to the boat* is your true motto in whaling; but cases will sometimes happen when *Leap from the boat* is still better. Moreover, as if perceiving at last that if he should give undiluted conscientious advice to Pip, he would be leaving him too wide a margin to jump in for the future, Stubb suddenly dropped all advice, and concluded with a peremptory command, 'Stick to the boat, Pip, or by the Lord, I won't pick you up if you jump; mind that. We can't afford to lose whales by the likes of you; a whale would sell for thirty times what you would, Pip, in Alabama. Bear that in mind, and don't jump any more.' Hereby perhaps Stubb indirectly hinted, that though man loved his fellow, yet man is a money-making animal, which propensity too often interferes with his benevolence.

But we are all in the hands of the Gods; and Pip jumped again. It was under very similar circumstances to the first performance; but this time he did not breast out the line; and hence, when the whale started to run, Pip was left behind on the sea, like a hurried traveller's trunk. Alas! Stubb was but too true to his word. It was a beautiful, bounteous, blue day; the spangled sea flatly stretching away to the horizon, like goldbeater's skin hammered out to the extremest. Bobbing up and down in that sea, Pip's ebon head showed like a head of cloves. No boat-knife was lifted when he fell so rapidly astern. Stubb's inexorable back was turned upon him; and the whale was winged. In three minutes, a whole mile of shoreless ocean was between Pip and Stubb. Out from the centre of the sea, poor Pip turned his crisp, curling, black head to the sun, another lonely castaway, though the loftiest and the brightest.

Now, in calm weather, to swim in the open ocean is as easy to the practised swimmer as to ride in a spring-carriage ashore. But the awful lonesomeness is intolerable. The intense concentration of self in the middle of such a heartless immensity, my God! who can tell it?

But had Stubb really abandoned the poor little negro to his fate? No; he did not mean to, at least. Because there were two boats in his wake, and he supposed, no doubt, that they would of course come up to Pip very quickly, and pick him up.

But it so happened, that those boats, without seeing Pip, suddenly spying whales close to them on one side, turned, and gave chase; and Stubb's boat was now so far away, and he and all his crew so intent upon his fish, that Pip's ringed horizon began to expand around him miserably. By the merest chance the ship itself at last rescued him; but from that hour the little negro went about the deck an idiot; such, at least, they said he was. The sea had jeeringly kept his finite body up, but drowned the infinite of his soul. Not drowned entirely, though. Rather carried down alive to wondrous depths, where strange shapes of the unwarped primal world glided to and fro before his passive eyes; and the miser-merman, Wisdom, revealed his hoarded heaps; and among the joyous, heartless, ever-juvenile eternities, Pip saw the multitudinous, God-omnipresent, coral insects, that out of the firmament of waters heaved the colossal orbs. He saw God's foot upon the treadle of the loom, and spoke it; and therefore his shipmates called him mad. So man's insanity is heaven's sense; and wandering from all mortal reason, man comes at last to that celestial thought, which, to reason, is absurd and frantic; and weal or woe, feels then uncompromised, indifferent as his God.

For the rest, blame not Stubb too hardly. The thing is common in that fishery; and in the sequel of the narrative, it will then be seen what like abandonment befell myself.

CHAPTER 72

A Squeeze of the Hand

That whale of Stubb's, so dearly purchased, was duly brought to the Pequod's side, where all those cutting and hoisting operations previously detailed were regularly gone through, even to the baling of the Heidelburgh Tun, or Case.

While some were occupied with this latter duty, others were employed in dragging away the larger tubs, so soon as filled with the sperm; and when the proper time arrived, this same sperm was carefully manipulated ere going to the try-works, of which anon.

It had cooled and crystallized to such a degree, that when, with several others, I sat down before a large Constantine's bath of it, I found it strangely concreted into lumps, here and there rolling about in the liquid part. It was our business to squeeze these lumps back into fluid. A sweet and unctuous duty! No wonder that in old times this sperm was such a favourite cosmetic. Such a clearer! such a sweetener! such a softener! After having my hands in it for only a few minutes, my fingers felt like eels.

As I sat there at my ease, cross-legged on the deck; under a blue tranquil sky; the ship under indolent sail, and gliding so serenely along; as I bathed my hands among those soft, gentle globules of infiltrated tissues, woven almost within the hour; as I snuffed up that uncontaminated aroma – literally and truly, like the smell of spring violets; I declare to you, that for the time I lived as in a musky meadow; while bathing in that bath, I felt divinely free from all ill-will, or petulance, or malice, of any sort whatsoever.

Would that I could keep squeezing that sperm for ever!

*

Now, while discoursing of sperm, it behooves to speak of other things akin to it, in the business of preparing the Sperm Whale for the try-works.

First comes white-horse, so called, which is obtained from the tapering part of the fish, and also from the thicker portions of his flukes. It is tough with congealed tendons – a wad of muscle – but still contains some oil. After being severed from the whale, the white-horse is first cut into portable oblongs ere going to the mincer.

Plum-pudding is the term bestowed upon certain fragmentary parts of the whale's flesh, here and there adhering to the blanket of blubber, and often participating to a considerable degree in its unctuousness. It is a most refreshing, convivial, beautiful object to behold. As its name imports, it is of an exceedingly rich, mottled tint, with a bestreaked snowy and golden ground, dotted with spots of the deepest crimson and purple. It is plums of rubies, in pictures of citron. Spite of reason, it is hard to keep yourself from eating it. I confess, that once I stole behind the foremast to try it. It tasted something as I should conceive a royal cutlet from the thigh of Louis le Gros might have tasted, supposing him to have been killed the first day after the venison season, and that particular venison season contemporary with an unusually fine vintage of the vineyards of Champagne.

But to descend into the blubber-room, and its inmates. When the proper time arrives for cutting up its contents, this apartment is a scene of terror to all tyros, especially by night. On one side, lit by a dull lantern, a space has been left clear for the workmen. They generally go in pairs – a pike-and-gaffman and a spademan. The whaling-pike is similar to a frigate's boarding-weapon of the same name. The gaff is something like a boat-hook. With his gaff, the gaffman hooks on to a sheet of blubber, and strives to hold it from slipping, as the ship pitches about. Meanwhile, the spade-man stands on the sheet itself, perpendicularly chopping it into the portable horse-pieces. This spade is sharp as hone can make it; the spademan's feet are shoeless; the thing he stands on will sometimes irresistibly slide away from him, like a sledge. If he cuts off one of his own toes, or one of his assistants', would you be very much astonished? Toes are scarce among veteran blubber-room men.

CHAPTER 73

The Cassock

Had you stepped on board the Pequod at a certain juncture of this post-mortemizing of the whale; and had you strolled forward nigh the windlass, pretty sure am I that you would have scanned with no small curiosity a very strange, enigmatical object, which you would have seen there. Not the wondrous cistern in the whale's head; not the prodigy of his unhinged lower jaw; not the miracle of his symmetrical tail; none of these would so surprise you, as half a glimpse of that unaccountable cone – longer than a Kentuckian is tall, nigh a foot in diameter at the base, and jet-black as Yojo, the ebony idol of Queequeg. And an idol, indeed, it is; or, rather, in old times, its likeness was. Such an idol as that found in the secret groves of Queen Maachah in Judea; and for worshipping which, king Asa, her son, did depose her, and destroyed the idol, and burnt it for an abomination at the brook Kedron, as darkly set forth in the 15th chapter of the first book of Kings.

Look at the sailor, called the mincer, who now comes along, and assisted by two allies, heavily backs the grandissimus, as the mariners call it, and with bowed shoulders, staggers off with it. Extending it upon the forecastle deck, he now proceeds cylindri-cally to remove its dark pelt, as an African hunter the pelt of a boa. This done he turns the pelt inside out, like a pantaloon leg; gives it a good stretching, so as almost to double its diameter; and at last hangs it, well spread, in the rigging, to dry. Ere long, it is taken down; when removing some three feet of it, towards the pointed extremity, and then cutting two slits for arm-holes at the other end, he lengthwise slips himself bodily into it. The mincer now stands before you invested in the full canonicals of his calling. Immemorial to all his order, this investiture alone will adequately protect him, while employed in the peculiar functions of his office.

That office consists in mincing the horse-pieces of blubber for the pots; an operation which is conducted at a curious wooden horse, planted endwise against the bulwarks, and with a capacious tub beneath it, into which the minced pieces drop, fast as the sheets from a rapt orator's desk. Arrayed in decent black; occupying a conspicuous pulpit; intent on bible leaves; what a candidate for an archbishoprick, what a lad for a Pope were this mincer!

'Bible leaves! Bible leaves!' This is the invariable cry from the mates to the mincer. It enjoins him to be careful and cut his work into as thin slices as possible, inasmuch as by so doing the business of boiling out the oil is much accelerated, and its quantity considerably increased, besides perhaps improving it in quality.

CHAPTER 74

The Try-works

Besides her hoisted boats, an American whaler is outwardly distinguished by her try-works. She presents the curious anomaly of the most solid masonry joining with oak and hemp in constituting the completed ship. It is as if from the open field a brick-kiln were transported to her planks.

The try-works are planted between the foremast and main-mast, the most roomy part of the deck. The timbers beneath are of a peculiar strength, fitted to sustain the weight of an almost solid mass of brick and mortar, some ten feet by eight square, and five in height. The foundation does not penetrate the deck, but the masonry is firmly secured to the surface by ponderous knees of iron bracing it on all sides, and screwing it down to the timbers. On the flanks it is cased with wood, and at top completely covered by a large, sloping, battened hatchway. Removing this hatch we expose the great try-pots, two in number, and each of several barrels' capacity. When not in use, they are kept remarkably clean. Sometimes they are polished with soapstone and sand, till they shine within like silver punch-bowls. During the night-watches some cynical old sailors will crawl into them and coil themselves away there for a nap. While employed in polishing them – one man in each pot, side by side – many confidential communications are carried on, over the iron lips. It is a place also for profound mathematical meditation. It was in the left hand try-pot of the Pequod, with the soapstone diligently circling round me, that I was first indirectly struck by the remarkable fact, that in geometry all bodies gliding along the cycloid, my soapstone for example, will descend from any point in precisely the same time.

Removing the fire-board from the front of the try-works, the bare masonry of that side is exposed, penetrated by the two iron mouths of the furnaces, directly underneath the pots. These mouths are fitted with heavy doors of iron. The intense heat of the fire is prevented from communicating itself to the deck, by means of a shallow reservoir extending under the entire inclosed surface of the works. By a tunnel inserted at the rear, this reservoir is kept replenished with water as fast as it evaporates. There are no external chimneys; they open direct from the rear wall. And here let us go back for a moment.

It was about nine o'clock at night that the Pequod's try-works were first started on this present voyage. It belonged to Stubb to oversee the business.

'All ready there? Off hatch, then, and start her. You cook, fire the works.' This was an easy thing, for the carpenter had been thrusting his shavings into the furnace throughout the passage. Here be it said that in a whaling voyage the first fire in the try-works has to be fed for a time with wood. After that no wood is used, except as a means of quick ignition to the staple fuel. In a word, after being tried out, the crisp, shrivelled blubber, now called scraps or fritters, still contains considerable of its unctuous properties. These fritters feed the flames. Like a plethoric burning

martyr, or a self-consuming misanthrope, once ignited, the whale
supplies his own fuel and burns by his own body. Would that he
consumed his own smoke! for his smoke is horrible to inhale,
and inhale it you must, and not only that, but you must live in
it for the time. It has an unspeakable, wild, Hindoo odour about
it, such as may lurk in the vicinity of funereal pyres. It smells like
the left wing of the day of judgement; it is an argument for the
pit.

By midnight the works were in full operation. We were clear
from the carcase; sail had been made; the wind was freshening; the
wild ocean darkness was intense. But that darkness was licked up
by the fierce flames, which at intervals forked forth from the sooty
flues, and illuminated every lofty rope in the rigging, as with the
famed Greek fire. The burning ship drove on, as if remorselessly
commissioned to some vengeful deed.

The hatch, removed from the top of the works, now afforded a
wide hearth in front of them. Standing on this were the Tartarean
shapes of the pagan harpooneers, always the whale-ship's stokers.
With huge pronged poles they pitched hissing masses of blubber
into the scalding pots, or stirred up the fires beneath, till the snaky
flames darted, curling, out of the doors to catch them by the feet.
The smoke rolled away in sullen heaps. To every pitch of the ship
there was a pitch of the boiling oil, which seemed all eagerness
to leap into their faces. Opposite the mouth of the works, on the
further side of the wide wooden hearth, was the windlass. This
served for a sea-sofa. Here lounged the watch, when not otherwise
employed, looking into the red heat of the fire, till their eyes felt
scorched in their heads. Their tawny features, now all begrimed
with smoke and sweat, their matted beards, and the contrasting
barbaric brilliancy of their teeth, all these were strangely revealed
in the capricious emblazonings of the works. As they narrated
to each other their unholy adventures, their tales of terror told
in words of mirth; as their uncivilized laughter forked upwards
out of them, like the flames from the furnace; as to and fro, in
their front, the harpooneers wildly gesticulated with their huge
pronged forks and dippers; as the wind howled on, and the sea

leaped, and the ship groaned and dived, and yet steadfastly shot her red hell further and further into the blackness of the sea and the night, and scornfully champed the white bone in her mouth, and viciously spat round her on all sides; then the rushing Pequod, freighted with savages, and laden with fire, and burning a corpse, and plunging into that blackness of darkness, seemed the material counterpart of her monomaniac commander's soul.

So seemed it to me, as I stood at her helm, and for long hours silently guided the way of this fire-ship on the sea.

CHAPTER 75

Stowing Down and Clearing Up

Already has it been related how the great Leviathan is afar off descried from the mast-head; how he is chased over the watery moors, and slaughtered in the valleys of the deep; how he is then towed alongside and beheaded; and how (on the principle which entitled the headsman of old to the garments in which the beheaded was killed) his great padded surtout becomes the property of his executioner; how, in due time, he is condemned to the pots, and, like Shadrach, Meshach, and Abednego, his spermaceti, oil, and bone pass unscathed through the fire; but now it remains to conclude the last chapter of this part of the description by rehearsing – singing, if I may – the romantic proceeding of decanting off his oil into the casks and striking them down into the hold, where once again Leviathan returns to his native profundities, sliding along beneath the surface as before; but, alas! never more to rise and blow.

While still warm, the oil, like hot punch, is received into the six-barrel casks; and while, perhaps, the ship is pitching and rolling this way and that in the midnight sea, the enormous casks are slewed round and headed over, end for end, and sometimes perilously scoot across the slippery deck, like so many land slides, till at last man-handled and stayed in their course; and all round the hoops, rap, rap, go as many hammers as can play upon them, for now, *ex officio*, every sailor is a cooper.

At length, when the last pint is casked, and all is cool, then the great hatchways are unsealed, the bowels of the ship are thrown open, and down go the casks to their final rest in the sea. This done, the hatches are replaced, and hermetically closed, like a closet walled up.

In the sperm fishery, this is perhaps one of the most remarkable incidents in all the business of whaling. One day the planks stream with freshets of blood and oil; on the sacred quarter-deck enormous masses of the whale's head are profanely piled; great rusty casks lie about, as in a brewery yard; the smoke from the try-works has besooted all the bulwarks; the mariners go about suffused with unctuousness; the entire ship seems great Leviathan himself; while on all hands the din is deafening.

But a day or two after, you look about you, and prick your ears in this self-same ship; and were it not for the tell-tale boats and try-works, you would all but swear you trod some silent merchant vessel, with a most scrupulously neat commander. The unmanufactured sperm oil possesses a singularly cleansing virtue. This is the reason why the decks never look so white as just after what they call an affair of oil. Besides, from the ashes of the burned scraps of the whale, a potent ley is readily made; and whenever any adhesiveness from the back of the whale remains clinging to the side, that ley quickly exterminates it. Hands go diligently along the bulwarks, and with buckets of water and rags restore them to their full tidiness. The soot is brushed from the lower rigging. All the numerous implements which have been in use are likewise faithfully cleansed and put away. The great hatch is scrubbed and placed upon the try-works, completely hiding the pots; every cask is out of sight; all tackles are coiled in unseen nooks; and when by the combined and simultaneous industry of almost the entire ship's company, the whole of this conscientious duty is at last concluded, then the crew themselves proceed to their own ablutions; shift themselves from top to toe; and finally issue to the immaculate deck, fresh and all aglow, as bridegrooms new-leaped from out the daintiest Holland.

Now, with elated step, they pace the planks in twos and threes, and humorously discourse of parlours, sofas, carpets, and fine cambrics; propose to mat the deck; think of having hangings to the top; object not to taking tea by moonlight on the piazza of the forecastle. To hint to such musked mariners of oil, and bone, and blubber, were little short of audacity. They know not the thing you distantly allude to. Away, and bring us napkins!

But mark: aloft there, at the three mast-heads, stand three men intent on spying out more whales, which, if caught, infallibly will again soil the old oaken furniture, and drop at least one small grease-spot somewhere. Yes; and many is the time, when, after the severest uninterrupted labours, which know no night; continuing straight through for ninety-six hours; when from the boat, where they have swelled their wrists with all day rowing on the Line, they step to the deck only to carry vast chains, and heave the heavy windlass, and cut and slash, yea, and in their very sweatings to be smoked and burned anew by the combined fires of the equatorial sun and the equatorial try-works; when, on the heel of all this, they have finally bestirred themselves to cleanse the ship, and make a spotless dairy room of it; many is the time the poor fellows, just buttoning the necks of their clean frocks, are startled by the cry of 'There she blows!' and away they fly to fight another whale. Oh! my friends, but this is man-killing! Yet this is life. For hardly have we mortals cleansed ourselves and learned to live here in clean tabernacles of the soul; hardly is this done, when – *There she blows!* – the ghost is spouted up, and away we sail to fight some other world, and go through young life's old routine again.

Oh! the metempsychosis! Oh! Pythagoras, that in bright Greece, two thousand years ago, did die, so good, so wise, so mild; I sailed with thee along the Peruvian coast last voyage – and, foolish as I am, taught thee, a green simple boy, how to splice a rope!

CHAPTER 76

Leg and Arm. The Pequod, of Nantucket, Meets the Samuel Enderby, of London

'Ship, ahoy! Hast seen the White Whale?'

So cried Ahab, once more hailing a ship showing English colours, bearing down under the stern. Trumpet to mouth, the old man was standing in his hoisted quarter-boat, his ivory leg plainly revealed to the stranger captain, who was carelessly reclining in his own boat's bow. He was a darkly-tanned, burly, good-natured, fine-looking man, of sixty or thereabouts, dressed in a spacious roundabout, that hung round him in festoons of blue pilot-cloth; and one empty arm of this jacket streamed behind him.

'Hast seen the White Whale?'

'See you this?' and withdrawing it from the folds that had hidden it, he held up a white arm of Sperm Whale bone, terminating in a wooden head like a mallet.

'Man my boat!' cried Ahab, impetuously, and tossing about the oars near him – 'Stand by to lower!'

In less than a minute, he and his crew were dropped to the water, and were soon alongside of the stranger. But in the excitement of the moment, Ahab had forgotten that since the loss of his leg he had never once stepped on board of any vessel at sea but his own, and then it was always by an ingenious and very handy mechanical contrivance peculiar to the Pequod. Now, it is no very easy matter for anybody – except those who are almost hourly used to it, like whalemen – to clamber up a ship's side from a boat on the open sea; for the great swells now lift the boat high up towards the bulwarks, and then instantaneously drop it half way down to the kelson. So, deprived of one leg, and the strange ship of course being altogether unsupplied with the kindly invention,

Ahab now found himself abjectly reduced to a clumsy landsman again.

It has before been hinted, perhaps, that every little untoward circumstance that befell him, and which indirectly sprang from his luckless mishap, almost invariably irritated or exasperated Ahab. And in the present instance, all this was heightened by the sight of the two officers of the strange ship, leaning over the side, by the perpendicular ladder of nailed cleats there, and swinging towards him a pair of ornamented manropes; for at first they did not seem to bethink them that a one-legged man must be too much of a cripple to use their sea bannisters. But this awkwardness only lasted a minute, because the strange captain cried out, 'I see, I see! – avast heaving there! Jump, boys, and swing over the cutting-tackle.'

As good luck would have it, they had had a whale alongside a day or two previous, and the great tackles were still aloft, and the massive curved blubber-hook, now clean and dry, was still attached to the end. This was quickly lowered to Ahab, who at once slid his solitary thigh into the curve of the hook, and then giving the word, held himself fast, and at the same time also helped to hoist his own weight, by pulling hand-over-hand upon one of the running parts of the tackle. Soon he was carefully swung inside the high bulwarks, and gently landed upon the capstan head. With his ivory arm frankly thrust forth in welcome, the other captain advanced, and Ahab, putting out his ivory leg, and crossing the ivory arm (like two sword-fish blades) cried out in his walrus way, 'Aye, aye, hearty! let us shake bones together! – an arm and a leg! – an arm that never can shrink, d'ye see; and a leg that never can run. Where did'st thou see the White Whale?'

'The White Whale,' said the Englishman, pointing his ivory arm towards the East; 'There I saw him, on the Line, last season.'

'And he took that arm off, did he?' asked Ahab, now sliding down from the capstan, and resting on the Englishman's shoulder, as he did so.

'Aye, he was the cause of it, at least; and that leg, too?'

'Spin me the yarn,' said Ahab; 'how was it?'

'It was the first time in my life that I ever cruised on the Line,' began the Englishman. 'Well, one day we lowered for a pod of four or five whales, and my boat fastened to one of them; a circus horse he was, too, that went milling and milling round so, that my boat's crew could only trim dish, by sitting all their sterns on the outer gunwale. Presently up breaches from the bottom of the sea a bouncing great whale, with a milky-white head and hump, all crows' feet and wrinkles.'

'It was he, it was he!' cried Ahab.

'And harpoons sticking in near his starboard fin.'

'Aye, aye – they were mine – *my* irons,' cried Ahab, exultingly – 'but on!'

'Give me a chance, then,' said the Englishman, good-hu-mouredly. 'Well, this old great-grandfather, with the white head and hump, runs all afoam into the pod, and goes to snapping furiously at my fast-line.'

'Aye, I see! – wanted to part it; free the fast-fish – an old trick – I know him.'

'How it was exactly,' continued the one-armed commander, 'I do not know; but in biting the line, it got foul of his teeth, caught there somehow; but we didn't know it then; so that when we afterwards pulled on the line, bounce we came plump on to his hump! instead of the other whale's that went off to windward, all fluking. Seeing how matters stood, and what a noble great whale it was – the noblest and biggest I ever saw, sir, in my life – I resolved to capture him, spite of the boiling rage he seemed to be in. And thinking the hap-hazard line would get loose, or the tooth it was tangled to might draw; seeing all this, I say, I jumped into my first mate's boat – Mr Mounttop's here – which, d'ye see, was gunwale and gunwale with mine, then; and snatching the first harpoon, let this old great-grandfather have it. But, Lord, look you, sir, the next instant I was blind as a bat – both eyes out – all befogged and bedeadened with black foam – the whale's tail looming straight up out of it, perpendicular in the air, like a marble steeple. No use sterning all, then; but as I was groping at midday, with a blind-ing sun, all crown-jewels; as I was groping, I say, after the second iron, to toss it overboard – down comes the tail like a Lima tower, cutting my boat in two, leaving each half in splinters; and, flukes first, the white hump backed through the wreck, as though it was all chips. We all struck out. To escape his terrible flailings, I seized hold of my harpoon-pole sticking in him, and for a moment clung to that. But a combing sea dashed me off, and at the same instant, the fish went down like a flash; and the barb of that cursed second iron towing along near me caught me here' (clapping his hand just below his shoulder); 'yes, caught me just here, I say, and bore me down to Hell's flames, I was thinking; when, when, all of a sudden, thank the good God, the barb ript its way along the flesh – clear along the whole length of my arm – came out nigh my wrist, and up I floated.'

'What became of the White Whale?' now cried Ahab, who thus far had been impatiently listening.

'Oh!' cried the one-armed captain, 'Oh, yes! Well; after he sounded, we didn't see him again for some time; in fact, as I before hinted, I didn't then know what whale it was that had served me such a trick, till some time afterwards, when coming back to the Line, we heard about Moby-Dick – as some call him – and then I knew it was he.'

'Did'st thou cross his wake again?'

'Twice.'

'But could not fasten?'

'Didn't want to try to: aint one limb enough? And I'm thinking Moby-Dick doesn't bite so much as he swallows. No more White Whales for me. There would be great glory in killing him, I know that; and there is a ship-load of precious sperm in him, but, hark ye, he's best let alone; don't you think so, Captain?' – glancing at the ivory leg.

'He is. But he will still be hunted, for all that. What is best let alone, that accursed thing is not always what least allures. He's all a magnet! How long since thou saw'st him last? Which way heading?'

'Bless my soul and curse the foul fiend's. This man's blood – it's at the boiling point. He was heading east, I think.'

Fedallah slid over the bulwarks to take the boat's steering oar, and Ahab, swinging the cutting-tackle towards him, commanded the ship's sailors to stand by to lower.

In a moment he was standing in the boat's stern, and the Manilla men were springing to their oars. In vain the English captain hailed him. With back to the stranger ship, and face set like a flint, Ahab stood upright till alongside of the Pequod.

CHAPTER 77

The Cabin. Ahab and Starbuck

According to usage they were pumping the ship; and lo! no inconsiderable oil came up with the water; the casks below must have sprung a bad leak. Much concern was shown; and Starbuck went down to report this unfavourable affair.

Now, from the South and West the Pequod was drawing nigh to Formosa and the Bashee Isles, between which lies one of the tropical outlets from the China waters into the Pacific. And so Starbuck found Ahab with a general chart of the oriental archipelagoes spread before him; and another separate one representing the long eastern coasts of the Japanese islands – Niphon, Matsmai, and Sikoke. The wondrous old man, with his back to the gangway door, was wrinkling his brow, and tracing his old courses again.

'Who's there?' hearing the footstep at the door, but not turning round to it. 'On deck! Begone!'

'Captain Ahab mistakes; it is I. The oil in the hold is leaking, sir. We must up Burtons and break out.'

'Up Burtons and break out? Heave-to here for a week to tinker a parcel of old hoops?'

'Either do that, sir, or waste in one day more oil than we may make good in a year. What we come twenty thousand miles to get is worth saving, sir.'

'So it is, so it is; if we get it.'

'I was speaking of the oil in the hold, sir.'

'And I was not speaking or thinking of that at all. Begone! Let it leak! I'm all aleak myself. Aye! leaks in leaks! not only full of leaky casks, but those leaky casks are in a leaky ship; and that's a far worse plight than the Pequod's, man. Yet I don't stop to plug my leak; for who can find it in the deep-loaded hull; or how hope to plug it, even if found, in this life's howling gale? Starbuck! I'll not have the Burtons hoisted.'

'What will the owners say, sir?'

'Let the owners stand on Nantucket beach and outyell the Typhoons. What cares Ahab? Owners, owners? Look ye, the only real owner of anything is its commander; and hark ye, my conscience is in this ship's keel. – On deck!'

'Captain Ahab,' said the reddening mate, moving further into the cabin; 'A better man than I might well pass over in thee what he would quickly enough resent in a younger man; aye, and in a happier, Captain Ahab.'

'Devils! Dost thou then so much as dare to critically think of me? – On deck!'

'Nay, sir, not yet; I do entreat. And I do dare, sir – to be forbearing! Shall we not understand each other better than hitherto, Captain Ahab?'

Ahab seized a loaded musket from the rack, and pointing it towards Starbuck, exclaimed: 'There is one God that is Lord over the earth, and one Captain that is lord over the Pequod. On deck!'

For an instant in the flashing eyes of the mate, and his fiery cheeks, you would have almost thought that he had really received the blaze of the levelled tube. But, mastering his emotion, he calmly, as he quitted the cabin, paused for an instant and said: 'Thou hast outraged, not insulted me, sir; but for that I ask thee not to beware of Starbuck; thou wouldst but laugh; but let Ahab beware of Ahab; beware of thyself, old man.'

'He waxes brave, but nevertheless obeys; most careful bravery that!' murmured Ahab, as Starbuck disappeared. 'What's that he said – Ahab beware of Ahab – there's something there!' Then unconsciously using the musket for a staff, with an iron brow he paced to and fro in the little cabin; but presently the thick plaits of his forehead relaxed, and returning the gun to the rack, he went to the deck.

'Thou art but too good a fellow, Starbuck,' he said lowly to the mate; then raising his voice to the crew: 'Furl the t'gallant-sails, and close-reef the top-sails, fore and aft; back the mainyard; up Burtons, and break out in the main-hold.'

It were perhaps vain to surmise exactly why it was, that as respecting Starbuck, Ahab thus acted. It may have been a flash of honesty in him; or mere prudential policy which, under the circumstance, imperiously forbade the slightest symptom of open disaffection, however transient, in the important chief officer of his ship. However it was, his orders were executed; and the Burtons were hoisted.

CHAPTER 78

Queequeg in his Coffin

Upon searching, it was found that the casks last struck into the hold were perfectly sound, and that the leak must be further off. So deep did they go; and so ancient, and corroded, and weedy the aspect of the lowermost puncheons, that you almost looked next for some mouldy corner-stone cask containing coins of Captain Noah, with copies of the posted placards, vainly warning the infatuated old world from the flood. Tierce after tierce, too, of water, and bread, and beef, and shooks of staves, and iron bundles of hoops, were hoisted out, till at last the piled decks were hard to get about; and the hollow hull echoed under foot, and reeled and rolled in the sea like an air-freighted demijohn. Top-heavy was the ship as a dinnerless student with all Aristotle in his head.

Now, at this time it was that my poor pagan companion, and fast bosom-friend, Queequeg, was seized with a fever, which brought him nigh to his endless end.

Be it said, that in this vocation of whaling, sinecures are unknown; dignity and danger go hand in hand; till you get to be Captain, the higher you rise the harder you toil. So with poor Queequeg, who, as harpooneer, must not only face all the rage of the living whale, but – as we have elsewhere seen – mount his dead back in a rolling sea; and finally descend into the gloom of the hold, and bitterly sweating all day in that subterraneous confinement, resolutely manhandle the clumsiest casks and see to their stowage. To be short, among whalemen, the harpooneers are the holders, so called.

Poor Queequeg! when the ship was about half disembowelled, you should have stooped over the hatchway, and peered down upon him there; where, stripped to his woollen drawers, the tattooed savage was crawling about amid that dampness and slime like a green spotted lizard at the bottom of a well. And a well, or an ice-house, it somehow proved to him, poor pagan; where, strange to say, for all the heat of his sweatings, he caught a terrible chill which lapsed into a fever; and at last, after some days' suffering, laid him in his hammock, close to the very sill of the door of death. How he wasted and wasted away in those few long-lingering days, till there seemed but little left of him but his frame and tattooing. But as all else in him thinned, and his cheek-bones grew sharper, his eyes, nevertheless, seemed growing fuller and fuller; they became of a strange softness of lustre; and mildly but deeply looked out at you there from his sickness, a wondrous testimony to that immortal health in him which could not die, or be weakened. An awe that cannot be named would steal over you as you sat by the side of this waning savage, and saw the drawing near of Death.

Not a man of the crew but gave him up; and, as for Queequeg himself, what he thought of his case was forcibly shown by a curious favour he asked. He called one to him in the grey morning watch, and taking his hand, said that while in Nantucket he had chanced to see certain little canoes of dark wood, like the rich war-wood of his native isle; and upon inquiry, he had learned that all whalemen who died in Nantucket were laid in those same dark canoes, and that the fancy of being so laid had much pleased him; for it was not unlike the custom of his own race, who, after embalming a dead warrior, stretched him out in his canoe, and so left him to be floated away to the starry archipelagoes; for not only do they believe that the stars are isles, but that far beyond all visible horizons, their own mild, uncontinented seas interflow with the blue heavens; and so form the white breakers of the milky way.

Now, when this strange circumstance was made known aft, the carpenter was at once commanded to do Queequeg's bidding. There was some heathenish, coffin-coloured old lumber aboard, which, upon a long previous voyage, had been cut from the aboriginal groves of the Lackaday islands, and from these dark planks the coffin was recommended to be made. No sooner was the carpenter apprised of the order, than taking his rule, he forthwith, with all the indifferent promptitude of his character, proceeded into the forecastle and took Queequeg's measure with great accuracy, regularly chalking Queequeg's person as he shifted the rule.

'Ah! poor fellow! he'll have to die now,' ejaculated the Long Island sailor.

This done, he marshalled the planks and his tools, and to work. When the last nail was driven, and the lid duly planed and fitted, he lightly shouldered the coffin and went forward with it, inquiring whether they were ready for it yet.

Overhearing the indignant but half-humorous cries with which the people on deck began to drive the coffin away, Queequeg, to every one's consternation, commanded that the thing should be instantly brought to him.

Leaning over in his hammock, Queequeg long regarded the coffin with an attentive eye. He then called for his harpoon, had the wooden stock drawn from it, and then had the iron part placed in the coffin along with one of the paddles of his boat. All by his own request, also, biscuits were then ranged round the sides within: a flask of fresh water was placed at the head, and a small bag of woody earth scraped up in the hold at the foot; and a piece of sail-cloth being rolled up for a pillow, Queequeg now entreated to be lifted into his final bed, that he might make trial of its comforts, if any it had. He lay without moving a few minutes, then told one to go to his bag and bring out his little god, Yojo. Then crossing his arms on his breast with Yojo between, he called for the coffin lid (hatch he called it) to be placed over him. The head part turned over with a leather hinge, and there lay Queequeg in his coffin with little but his composed countenance in view. 'Rarmai' (it will do; it is easy), he murmured at last, and signed to be replaced in his hammock.

But ere this was done, Pip drew nigh to him where he lay, and with soft sobbings, took him by the hand; in the other, holding his tambourine.

'Poor rover! will ye never have done with all this weary roving? where go ye now? But if the currents carry ye to those sweet Antilles where the beaches are only beat with water-lilies, will ye do one little errand for me? Seek out one Pip, who's now been missing long: I think he's in those far Antilles. If ye find him, then comfort him; for he must be very sad; for look! he's left his tambourine behind; I found it. Rig-a-dig, dig, dig! Now, Queequeg, die; and I'll beat ye your dying march.'

'I have heard,' murmured Starbuck, gazing down the scuttle, 'that in violent fevers, men, all ignorance, have talked in ancient tongues; and that when the mystery is probed, it turns out always that in their wholly forgotten childhood those ancient tongues had been really spoken in their hearing by some lofty scholars. So, to my fond faith, poor Pip, in this strange sweetness of his lunacy, brings heavenly vouchers of all our heavenly homes. Where learned he that, but there? – Hark! he speaks again: but more wildly now.'

'Form two and two! Let's make a General of him! Ho, where's his harpoon? Lay it across here. Rig-a-dig, dig, dig! huzza! Oh for a game cock now to sit upon his head and crow! Queequeg dies game! – mind ye that; Queequeg dies game! take ye good heed of that; Queequeg dies game! I say; game, game, game! but base little Pip, he died a coward; died all a'shiver; out upon Pip! Hark ye; if ye find Pip, tell all the Antilles he's a runaway; a coward, a coward, a coward! Tell them he jumped from a whale-boat! I'd never beat my tambourine over base Pip, and hail him General, if he were once more dying here. No, no! shame upon all cowards – shame upon them! Let 'em go drown like Pip, that jumped from a whale-boat. Shame! shame!'

During all this, Queequeg lay with closed eyes. Pip was led away, and the sick man was replaced in his hammock.

But now that he had apparently made every preparation for death, Queequeg suddenly rallied; soon there seemed no need of the carpenter's box: and thereupon, when some expressed their delighted surprise, he, in substance, said that the cause of his sudden convalescence was this; at a critical moment, he had just recalled a little duty ashore, which he was leaving undone; and therefore had changed his mind about dying: he could not die yet. They asked him, then, whether to live or die was a matter of his own sovereign will and pleasure. He answered, certainly. In a word, it was Queequeg's conceit, that if a man made up his mind to live, mere sickness could not kill him: nothing but a whale, or a gale, or some violent, ungovernable, unintelligent destroyer of that sort.

Now, there is this noteworthy difference between savage and civilized; that while a sick, civilized man may be six months convalescing, generally speaking, a sick savage is almost half-well again in a day. So, in good time my Queequeg gained strength; and at length after sitting on the windlass for a few indolent days (but eating with a vigorous appetite) he suddenly leaped to his feet, threw out arms and legs, gave himself a good stretching, yawned a little bit, and then springing into the head of his hoisted boat, and poising a harpoon, pronounced himself fit for a fight.

With a wild whimsiness, he now used his coffin for a sea-chest. Many spare hours he spent, in carving the lid with all manner of grotesque figures and drawings; and it seemed that hereby he was striving, in his rude way, to copy parts of the twisted tattooing on his body. And this tattooing had been the work of a departed prophet and seer of his island, who, by those hieroglyphic marks, had written out on his body a complete theory of the heavens and the earth, and a mystical treatise on the art of attaining truth; so that Queequeg in his own proper person was a riddle to unfold; a wondrous work in one volume; but whose mysteries not even himself could read, though his own live heart beat against them; and these mysteries were therefore destined in the end to moulder away with the living parchment whereon they were inscribed, and so be unsolved to the last. And this thought it must have been which suggested to Ahab that wild exclamation of his, when one morning turning away from surveying poor Queequeg – 'Oh, devilish tantalization of the gods!'

CHAPTER 79

The Pacific

When gliding by the Bashee isles we emerged at last upon the great South Sea; were it not for other things, I could have greeted my dear Pacific with uncounted thanks, for now the long supplication of my youth was answered; that serene ocean rolled eastwards from me a thousand leagues of blue.

There is one knows not what sweet mystery about this sea, whose gently awful stirrings seem to speak of some hidden soul beneath; like those fabled undulations of the Ephesian sod over the buried Evangelist St John. And meet it is, that over these sea-pastures, wide-rolling watery prairies and Potters' Fields of all four continents, the waves should rise and fall, and ebb and flow unceasingly; for here, millions of mixed shades and shadows, drowned dreams, somnambulisms, reveries; all that we call lives and souls, lie dreaming, dreaming, still; tossing like slumberers in their beds; the ever-rolling waves but made so by their restlessness.

To any meditative Magian rover, this serene Pacific, once beheld, must ever after be the sea of his adoption. It rolls the mid-most waters of the world, the Indian Ocean and Atlantic being but its arms. The same waves wash the moles of the new-built Californian towns, but yesterday planted by the recentest race of men, and lave the faded but still gorgeous skirts of Asiatic lands, older than Abraham; while all between float milky-ways of coral isles, and low-lying, endless, unknown Archipelagoes, and impenetrable Japans. Thus this mysterious, divine Pacific zones the world's whole bulk about; makes all coasts one bay to it; seems the tide-beating heart of earth. Lifted by those eternal swells, you needs must own the seductive god, bowing your head to Pan.

But few thoughts of Pan stirred Ahab's brain, as standing like an iron statue at his accustomed place beside the mizzen rigging, with one nostril he unthinkingly snuffed the sugary musk from the Bashee isles (in whose sweet woods mild lovers must be walking), and with the other consciously inhaled the salt breath of the new found sea; that sea in which the hated White Whale must even then be swimming. Launched at length upon these almost final waters, and gliding towards the Japanese cruising-ground, the old man's purpose intensified itself. His firm lips met like the lips of a vice; the delta of his forehead's veins swelled like overladen brooks; in his very sleep, his ringing cry ran through the vaulted hull, 'Stern all! the White Whale spouts thick blood!'

CHAPTER 80

The Forge

With matted beard, and swathed in a bristling shark-skin apron, about midday, Perth the begrimed, blistered old blacksmith was standing between his forge and anvil, the latter placed upon an iron-wood log, with one hand holding a pike-head in the coals, and with the other at his forge's lungs, when Captain Ahab came along, carrying in his hand a small rusty-looking leathern bag. While yet a little distance from the forge, moody Ahab paused; till at last, Perth, withdrawing his iron from the fire, began hammering it upon the anvil – the red mass sending off the sparks in thick hovering flights, some of which flew close to Ahab.

'Are these thy Mother Carey's chickens, Perth? they are always flying in thy wake; birds of good omen, too, but not to all; look here, they burn; but thou – thou liv'st among them without a scorch.'

'Because I am scorched all over, Captain Ahab,' answered Perth, resting for a moment on his hammer; 'I am past scorching; not easily can'st thou scorch a scar.'

'Well, well; no more. Thy shrunk voice sounds too calmly, sanely woeful to me. In no Paradise myself, I am impatient of all misery in others that is not mad. Thou should'st go mad, blacksmith; say, why dost thou not go mad? How can'st thou endure without being mad? Do the heavens yet hate thee, that thou can'st not go mad? – What wert thou making there?'

'Welding an old pike-head, sir; there were seams and dents in it.'

'And can'st thou make it all smooth again, blacksmith, after such hard usage as it had?'

'I think so, sir.'

'And I suppose thou can'st smooth almost any seams and dents; never mind how hard the metal, blacksmith?'

'Aye, sir, I think I can; all seams and dents but one.'

'Look ye here, then,' cried Ahab, passionately advancing, and leaning with both hands on Perth's shoulders; 'look ye here – *here* – can ye smooth out a seam like this, blacksmith,' sweeping one hand across his ribbed brow; 'if thou could'st, blacksmith, glad enough would I lay my head upon thy anvil, and feel thy heaviest hammer between my eyes. Answer! Can'st thou smooth this seam?'

'Oh! that is the one, sir! Said I not all seams and dents but one?'

'Aye, blacksmith, it is the one; aye, man, it is unsmoothable; for though thou only see'st it here in my flesh, it has worked down into the bone of my skull – *that* is all wrinkles! But, away with child's play; no more gaffs and pikes today. Look ye here!' jingling the leathern bag, as if it were full of gold coins. 'I, too, want a harpoon made; one that a thousand yoke of fiends could not part, Perth; something that will stick in a whale like his own fin-bone. There's the stuff,' flinging the pouch upon the anvil. 'Look ye, blacksmith, the gathered nail-stubs of the steel shoes of racing horses.'

'Horse-shoe stubs, sir? Why, Captain, thou hast here the best and stubbornest stuff we blacksmiths ever work.'

'I know it, old man. Quick! forge me the harpoon. And forge me first twelve rods for its shank; then wind, and twist, and hammer these twelve together like the yarns and strands of a tow-line. Quick! I'll blow the fire.'

When at last the twelve rods were made, Ahab tried them, one by one, by spiralling them, with his own hand, round a long, heavy iron bolt. 'A flaw!' rejecting the last one. 'Work that over again, Perth.'

This done, Perth was about to begin welding the twelve into one, when Ahab stayed his hand, and said he would weld his own iron. As, then, with regular, gasping hems, he hammered on the anvil, Perth passing to him the glowing rods, one after the other, and the hard pressed forge shooting up its intense straight flame, the Parsee passed silently, and bowing over his head towards the fire, seemed invoking some curse or some blessing on the toil.

'What's that bunch of lucifers dodging about there for?' muttered Stubb, looking on from the forecastle. 'That Parsee smells fire like a fusee; and smells of it himself, like a hot musket's powder-pan.'

At last the shank, in one complete rod, received its final heat; and as Perth plunged it all hissing into the cask of water near by, the scalding steam shot up into Ahab's bent face.

'Would'st thou brand me, Perth? Have I been but forging my own branding-iron, then?'

'Pray God, not that; yet I fear something, Captain Ahab. Is not this harpoon for the White Whale?'

'For the white fiend! But now for the barbs; thou must make

them thyself, man. Here are my razors – the best of steel; here, and make the barbs sharp as the needle-sleet of the Icy Sea.'

Fashioned at last into an arrowy shape, and welded by Perth to the shank, the steel soon pointed the end of the iron; and as the blacksmith was about giving the barbs their final heat, prior to tempering them, he cried to Ahab to place the water-cask near.

'No, no – no water for that; I want it of the true death-temper. Ahoy, there! Tashtego, Queequeg, Daggoo! What say ye, pagans! Will ye give me as much blood as will cover this barb?' holding it high up. A cluster of dark nods replied, Yes. Three punctures were made in the heathen flesh, and the White Whale's barbs were then tempered.

'Ego non baptizo te in nomine patris, sed in nomine diaboli!' deliriously howled Ahab, as the malignant iron scorchingly devoured the baptismal blood.

Now, mustering the spare poles from below, and selecting one of hickory, Ahab fitted the end to the socket of the iron. A coil of new tow-line was then unwound, and some fathoms of it taken to the windlass, and stretched to a great tension. Pressing his foot upon it, till the rope hummed like a harp-string, then eagerly bending over it, and seeing no strandings, Ahab exclaimed, 'Good! and now for the seizings.'

At one extremity the rope was unstranded, and the separate spread yarns were all braided and woven round the socket of the harpoon; the pole was then driven hard up into the socket; from the lower end the rope was traced half way along the pole's length, and firmly secured so, with intertwistings of twine. This done, pole, iron, and rope – like the Three Fates – remained inseparable, and Ahab moodily stalked away with the weapon; the sound of his ivory leg, and the sound of the hickory pole, both hollowly ringing along every plank. But ere he entered his cabin, a light, unnatural, half-bantering, yet most piteous sound was heard. Oh, Pip! thy wretched laugh, thy idle but unresting eye; all thy strange mummeries not unmeaningly blended with the black tragedy of the melancholy ship, and mocked it!

CHAPTER 81

The Gilder

Penetrating further and further into the heart of the Japanese cruising ground, the Pequod was soon all astir in the fishery. Often, in mild, pleasant weather, for twelve, fifteen, eighteen, and twenty hours on the stretch, they were engaged in the boats, steadily pulling, or sailing, or paddling after the whales, or for an interlude of sixty or seventy minutes calmly awaiting their uprising; though with but small success for their pains.

At such times, under an abated sun; afloat all day upon smooth, slow heaving swells; seated in his boat, light as a birch canoe; and so sociably mixing with the soft waves themselves, that like hearthstone cats they purr against the gunwale; these are the times of dreamy quietude, when beholding the tranquil beauty and brilliancy of the ocean's skin, one forgets the tiger heart that pants beneath it; and would not willingly remember, that this velvet paw but conceals a remorseless fang.

Nor did such soothing scenes, however temporary, fail of at least as temporary an effect on Ahab. But if these secret golden keys did seem to open in him his own secret golden treasuries, yet did his breath upon them prove but tarnishing.

And that same day, too, gazing far down from his boat's side into that same golden sea, Starbuck lowly murmured:

'Loveliness unfathomable, as ever lover saw in his young bride's eye! – Tell me not of thy teeth-tiered sharks, and thy kidnapping cannibal ways. Let faith oust fact; let fancy oust memory; I look deep down and do believe.'

CHAPTER 82

The Whale Watch

Next day, whales were seen and four were slain; and one of them by Ahab. It was far down the afternoon; and when all the spearings of the crimson fight were done: and floating in the lovely sunset sea and sky, sun and whale both stilly died together.

The four whales slain that evening had died wide apart; one, far to windward; one, less distant, to leeward; one ahead; one astern. These last three were brought alongside ere nightfall; but the windward one could not be reached till morning; and the boat that had killed it lay by its side all night; and that boat was Ahab's.

The waif-pole was thrust upright into the dead whale's spout-hole; and the lantern hanging from its top cast a troubled flickering glare upon the black, glossy back, and far out upon the midnight waves, which gently chafed the whale's broad flank, like soft surf upon a beach.

Ahab and all his boat's crew seemed asleep but the Parsee; who crouching in the bow, sat watching the sharks, that spectrally played round the whale, and tapped the light cedar planks with their tails. A sound like the moaning in squadrons over Asphaltites of unforgiven ghosts of Gomorrah ran shuddering through the air.

Started from his slumbers, Ahab saw the Parsee; and hooped round by the gloom of the night they seemed the last men in a flooded world. 'I have dreamed it again,' said he.

'Of the hearses? Have I not said, old man, that neither hearse nor coffin can be thine?'

'And who are hearsed that die on the sea?'

'But I said, old man, that ere thou couldst die on this voyage, two hearses must verily be seen by thee on the sea; the first not made by mortal hands; and the visible wood of the last one must be grown in America.'

'Aye, aye! a strange sight that, Parsee: a hearse and its plumes floating over the ocean with the waves for the pallbearers. Ha! Such a sight we shall not soon see.'

'Believe it or not, thou can'st not die till it be seen.'

'And what was that saying about thyself?'

'Though it come to the last, I shall still go before thee thy pilot.'

'And when thou art so gone before – if that ever befall – then ere I can follow, thou must still appear to me, to pilot me still? Was it not so? Well, then, did I believe all ye say, oh my pilot! I have here two pledges that I shall yet slay Moby-Dick and survive it.'

'Take another pledge, old man,' said the Parsee, as his eyes lighted up like fire-flies – 'Hemp only can kill thee.'

'The gallows, ye mean. I am immortal then, on land and on sea,' cried Ahab, with a laugh of derision; 'Immortal on land and on sea!'

Both were silent again, as one man. The grey dawn came on, and the slumbering crew arose from the boat's bottom, and ere noon the dead whale was brought to the ship.

CHAPTER 83

The Quadrant

It was hard upon high noon; and Ahab, seated in the bows of his high-hoisted boat, was about taking his wonted daily observation of the sun to determine his latitude.

Now, in that Japanese sea, the days in summer are as freshets of effulgences. The sky looks lacquered; clouds there are none; the horizon floats; and this nakedness of unrelieved radiance is as the insufferable splendours of God's throne. Well that Ahab's quadrant was furnished with coloured glasses, through which to take sight of that solar fire. So, swinging his seated form to the roll of the ship, and with his astrological-looking instrument placed to his eye, he remained in that posture for some moments to catch the precise instant when the sun should gain its precise meridian. Meantime while his whole attention was absorbed, the Parsee was kneeling beneath him on the ship's deck, and with face thrown up like Ahab's, was eyeing the same sun with him; only the lids of his eyes half hooded their orbs, and his wild face was subdued to an earthly passionlessness. At length the desired observation was taken; and with his pencil upon his ivory leg, Ahab soon calculated what his latitude must be at that precise instant. Then falling into a moment's revery, he again looked up towards the sun and murmured to himself: 'Thou sea-mark! thou high and mighty Pilot! thou tellest me truly where I *am* – but can'st thou cast the least hint where I *shall* be? Or can'st thou tell where some other thing besides me is this moment living? Where is Moby-Dick? These eyes of mine look into the very eye that is even now beholding him; aye, and into the eye that is even now equally beholding the objects on the unknown, thither side of thee, thou sun!'

Then gazing at his quadrant, he pondered again, and muttered: 'Foolish toy! babies' plaything of haughty admirals, and commodores, and captains; the world brags of thee, of thy cunning and might; but what after all can'st thou do, but tell the poor, pitiful point, where thou thyself happenest to be on this wide planet, and the hand that holds thee: no! not one jot more! Thou can'st not tell where one drop of water or one grain of sand will be tomorrow noon; and yet with thy impotence thou insultest the sun! Science! Curse thee, thou vain toy; and cursed be all the things that cast man's eyes aloft to that heaven, whose live vividness but scorches him, as these old eyes are even now scorched with thy light, O sun! Level by nature to this earth's horizon are the glances of man's eyes; not shot from the crown of his head, as if God had meant him to gaze on his firmament. Curse thee, thou quadrant!' dashing it to the deck, 'no longer will I guide my earthly way by thee; the level ship's compass, and the level dead-reckoning, by log and by line; *these* shall conduct me, and show me my place on the sea. Aye,' lighting from the boat to the deck, 'thus I trample on thee, thou paltry thing that feebly pointest on high; thus I split and destroy thee!'

As the frantic old man thus spoke and thus trampled with his live and dead feet, a sneering triumph that seemed meant for Ahab, and a fatalistic despair that seemed meant for himself – these passed over the motionless Parsee's face.

CHAPTER 84

The Candles

Warmest climes but nurse the cruellest fangs: the tiger of Bengal crouches in spiced groves of ceaseless verdure. Skies the most effulgent but basket the deadliest thunders: gorgeous Cuba knows tornadoes that never swept tame northern lands. So, too, it is, that in these resplendent Japanese seas the mariner encounters the direst of all storms, the Typhoon. It will sometimes burst from out that cloudless sky, like an exploding bomb upon a dazed and sleepy town.

Towards evening of that day, the Pequod was torn of her canvas, and bare-poled was left to fight a Typhoon which had struck her directly ahead. When darkness came on, sky and sea roared and split with the thunder, and blazed with the lightning, that showed the disabled masts fluttering here and there with the rags which the first fury of the tempest had left for its after sport.

Holding by a shroud, Starbuck was standing on the quarter-deck; at every flash of the lightning glancing aloft, to see what additional disaster might have befallen the intricate hamper there; while Stubb and Flask were directing the men in the higher hoisting and firmer lashing of the boats. But all their pains seemed naught. Though lifted to the very top of the cranes, the windward quarter boat (Ahab's) did not escape. A great rolling sea, dashing high up against the reeling ship's high teetering side, stove in the boat's bottom at the stern, and left it again, all dripping through like a sieve.

'Bad work, bad work! Mr Starbuck,' said Stubb, regarding the wreck, 'but the sea will have its way.'

'Here!' cried Starbuck, 'markest thou not that the gale comes from the eastward, the very course Ahab is to run for Moby-Dick? the very course he swung to this day noon? The gale that now hammers at us, we can turn it into a fair wind that will drive us towards home. Yonder, to windward, all is blackness of doom; but to leeward, homeward! see it lightens up there; but not with the lightning.'

At that moment in one of the intervals of profound darkness, a voice was heard at his side; and almost at the same instant a volley of thunder peals rolled overhead.

'Who's there?'

'Old Thunder!' said Ahab, groping his way along the bulwarks to his pivot-hole; but suddenly finding his path made plain to him by elbowed lances of fire.

Now, as the lightning-rod to a spire on shore is intended to carry off the perilous fluid into the soil; so the kindred rod which at sea some ships carry to each mast is intended to conduct it into the water. But as this conductor must descend to considerable depth, that its end may avoid all contact with the hull, the lower parts of a ship's lightning-rods are not always overboard; but are generally made in long slender links, so as to be the more readily hauled up into the chains outside, or thrown down into the sea, as occasion may require.

'The rods! The rods!' cried Starbuck to the crew, suddenly admonished to vigilance by the vivid lightning that had just been darting flambeaux, to light Ahab to his post. 'Are they overboard? drop them over, fore and aft. Quick!'

'Avast!' cried Ahab; 'let's have fair play here, though we be the weaker side. Yet I'll contribute to raise rods on the Himmalehs and Andes, that all the world may be secured; but out on privileges! Let them be, sir.'

'Look aloft!' cried Starbuck. 'The St Elmo's Lights (corpus

sancti) corposants! the corposants!'

All the yard-arms were tipped with a pallid fire; and touched at each tri-pointed lightning-rod-end with three tapering white flames, each of the three tall masts was silently burning in that sulphurous air, like three gigantic wax tapers before an altar. Over a seething sea, God's burning finger has been laid on the ship.

While this pallidness was burning aloft, few words were heard from the enchanted crew; who in one thick cluster stood on the forecastle, all their eyes gleaming in that pale phosphorescence, like a far away constellation of stars. Relieved against the ghostly light, the gigantic jet negro, Daggoo, loomed up to thrice his real stature, and seemed the black cloud from which the thunder had come. The parted mouth of Tashtego revealed his shark-white teeth, which strangely gleamed as if they too had been tipped by corposants; while lit up by the preternatural light, Queequeg's tattooing burned like Satanic blue flames on his body.

The tableau all waned at last with the pallidness aloft; and once more the Pequod and every soul on her decks were wrapped in a pall. A moment or two passed, when Starbuck, going forward, pushed against some one. It was Stubb.

'Look ye, Mr Starbuck – but it's too dark to look. Hear me, then: I take that mast-head flame we saw for a sign of good luck; for those masts are rooted in a hold that is going to be chock a' block with sperm-oil, d'ye see; and so, all that sperm will work up into the masts, like sap in a tree. Yes, our three masts will yet be as three spermaceti candles – that's the good promise we saw.'

At that moment Starbuck caught sight of Stubb's face slowly beginning to glimmer into sight. Glancing upwards, he cried: 'See! See!' and once more the high tapering flames were beheld with what seemed redoubled supernaturalness in their pallor.

'The corposants have mercy on us all,' cried Stubb, again.

At the base of the main-mast, full beneath the doubloon and the flame, the Parsee was kneeling in Ahab's front, but with his head bowed away from him; while near by, from the arched and overhanging rigging, where they had just been engaged securing a spar, a number of the seamen, arrested by the glare, now cohered together, and hung pendulous, like a knot of numbed wasps from a drooping, orchard twig. In various enchanted attitudes, others remained rooted to the deck; but all their eyes upcast.

'Aye, aye, men!' cried Ahab. 'Look up at it; mark it well; the white flame but lights the way to the White Whale! Hand me those main-mast links there; I would fain feel this pulse, and let mine beat against it; blood against fire! So.'

Then turning, the last link held fast in his left hand, he put his foot upon the Parsee; and with fixed upward eye, and high-flung right arm, he stood erect before the lofty tri-pointed trinity of flames.

'Oh! thou clear spirit of clear fire, whom on these seas I as Persian once did worship, till in the sacramental act so burned by thee, that to this hour I bear the scar; I now know thee, thou clear spirit, and I now know that thy right worship is defiance. To neither love nor reverence wilt thou be kind; and e'en for hate thou can'st but kill; and all are killed. No fearless fool now fronts thee. I own thy speechless, placeless power; but to the last gasp of my earthquake life will dispute its unconditional, unintegral mastery in me. While I earthly live, the queenly personality lives in me, and feels her royal rights. Oh, thou clear spirit, of thy fire thou madest me, and like a true child of fire, I breathe it back to thee.'

[*Sudden, repeated flashes of lightning; the nine flames leap lengthwise to thrice their previous height; Ahab, with the rest, closes his eyes, his right hand pressed hard upon them.*]

'I own thy speechless, placeless power; said I not so? Nor was it wrung from me; nor do I now drop these links. Thou can'st blind; but I can then grope. Thou can'st consume; but I can then be ashes. The lightning flashes through my skull; mine eye-balls ache and ache; my whole beaten brain seems as beheaded, and rolling on some stunning ground. Oh, oh! Yet blindfold, yet will I talk to thee. Light though thou be, thou leapest out of darkness; but I am darkness leaping out of light, leaping out of thee! Oh, thou foundling fire. Leap! leap up, and lick the sky! I leap with thee; I burn with thee; would fain be welded with thee; defyingly I worship thee!'

'The boat!' cried Starbuck, 'look at thy boat, old man!'

Ahab's harpoon, the one forged at Perth's fire, remained firmly lashed in its conspicuous crotch, so that it projected beyond his whale-boat's bow; but the sea that had stove its bottom had caused the loose leather sheath to drop off; and from the keen steel barb there now came a levelled flame of pale, forked fire. As the silent harpoon burned there like a serpent's tongue, Starbuck grasped Ahab by the arm – 'God, God is against thee, old man; forbear! t'is an ill voyage! ill begun, ill continued; let me square the yards, while we may, old man, and make a fair wind of it homewards, to go on a better voyage than this.'

Overhearing Starbuck, the panic-stricken crew instantly ran to the braces – though not a sail was left aloft. But dashing the rattling lightning links to the deck, and snatching the burning harpoon, Ahab waved it like a torch among them; swearing to transfix with it the first sailor that but cast loose a rope's end. Petrified by his aspect, and still more shrinking from the fiery dart that he held, the men fell back in dismay, and Ahab again spoke:

'All your oaths to hunt the White Whale are as binding as mine; and heart, soul, and body, lungs and life, old Ahab is bound. And that ye may know to what tune this heart beats; look ye here; thus I blow out the last fear!' And with one blast of his breath he extinguished the flame.

As in the hurricane that sweeps the plain, men fly the neighbourhood of some lone, gigantic elm, whose very height and strength but render it so much the more unsafe, because so much the more a mark for thunderbolts; so at those last words of Ahab's many of the mariners did run from him in a terror of dismay.

CHAPTER 85

The Musket

During the most violent shocks of the Typhoon, the man at the Pequod's jaw-bone tiller had several times been reelingly hurled to the deck by its spasmodic motions, even though preventer tackles had been attached to it – for they were slack – because some play to the tiller was indispensable. In a severe gale like this, while the ship is but a tossed shuttle-cock to the blast, it is by no means uncommon to see the needles in the compasses go round and round. It was thus with the Pequod's; it is a sight that hardly anyone can behold without some sort of unwonted emotion.

Some hours after midnight, the Typhoon abated so much, that through the strenuous exertions of Starbuck and Stubb – one engaged forward and the other aft – the shivered remnants of the jib and fore and main-top-sails were cut adrift from the spars, and went eddying away to leeward.

The three corresponding new sails were now bent and reefed, and a storm-trysail was set further aft; so that the ship soon went through the water with some precision again; and the course – for the present, East-south-east – which he was to steer, if practicable, was once more given to the helmsman. For during the violence of the gale, he had only steered according to its vicissitudes. But as he was now bringing the ship as near her course as possible, watching the compass meanwhile, lo! a good sign! the wind seemed coming round astern; aye, the foul breeze became fair!

In compliance with the standing order of his commander – to report immediately, and at any one of the twenty-four hours, any decided change in the affairs of the deck – Starbuck had no sooner trimmed the yards to the breeze – however reluctantly and gloomily – than he mechanically went below to apprise Captain Ahab of the circumstance.

Ere knocking at his state-room, he involuntarily paused before it a moment. The cabin lamp – taking long swings this way and that – was casting fitful shadows upon the old man's bolted door – a thin one, with fixed blinds inserted, in place of upper panels. The loaded muskets in the rack were shiningly revealed, as they stood upright against the forward bulkhead. Starbuck was an honest, upright man; but out of Starbuck's heart, at that instant, there evolved an evil thought; but so blent with its neutral or good accompaniments that for the instant he hardly knew it for itself.

'He would have shot me once,' he murmured, 'yes, there's the very musket that he pointed at me; let me touch it – lift it. Strange, that I, who have handled so many deadly lances, strange, that I should shake so now. Loaded? I must see. Aye, aye; and powder in the pan; that's not good. Best spill it? – wait. I'll cure myself of this. I'll hold the musket boldly while I think. I come to report a fair wind to him. But how fair? Fair for death and doom – *that's* fair for Moby-Dick. It's a fair wind that's only fair for that accursed fish. The very tube he pointed at me! – the very one; *this* one – I hold it here; he would have killed me with the very thing I handle now. Aye and he would fain kill all his crew. Has he not dashed his heavenly quadrant? and in these same perilous seas, gropes he not his way by mere dead reckoning of the error-abounding log? and in this very Typhoon, did he not swear that he would have no lightning-rods? But shall this crazed old man be tamely suffered to drag a whole ship's company down to doom with him? – Yes, it would make him the wilful murderer of thirty men and more, if this ship come to any deadly harm. If, then, he were this instant – put aside, that crime would not be his. Ha! is he muttering in his sleep? Yes, just there – in there, he's sleeping. Sleeping? aye, but still alive, and soon awake again. I can't withstand thee, then, old man. Not reasoning; not remonstrance; not entreaty wilt thou hearken to. Flat obedience to thy own flat commands, this is all thou breathest. Aye, and say'st the men have vow'd thy vow; say'st all of us are Ahabs. Great God forbid! – But is there no other way? no lawful way? Make him a prisoner to be taken home? What! hope to wrest this old man's living power from his own living hands? Only a fool would try it. What, then, remains? The land is hundreds of leagues away, and locked Japan the nearest. I stand alone here upon an open sea, with two oceans and a whole continent between me and law. Aye, aye, 'tis so. Would I be a murderer, then, if'—— and slowly, stealthily, he placed the loaded musket's end against the door.

'On this level, Ahab's hammock swings within; his head this way. A touch, and Starbuck may survive to hug his wife and child again. – Oh, Mary! Mary! – boy! boy! boy! – But if I wake thee not to death, old man, who can tell to what unsounded deeps Starbuck's body this day week may sink, with all the crew! Great God, where art thou? Shall I? shall I?—— The wind has gone down and shifted, sir; the fore and main topsails are reefed and set; she heads her course.'

'Stern all! Oh Moby-Dick, I clutch thy heart at last!'

Such were the sounds that now came hurtling from out the old man's tormented sleep, as if Starbuck's voice had caused the long dumb dream to speak. The yet levelled musket shook like a drunkard's arm against the panel; Starbuck seemed wrestling with an angel; but turning from the door, he placed the death-tube in its rack, and left the place.

'He's too sound asleep, Mr Stubb; go thou down, and wake him, and tell him. I must see to the deck here. Thou know'st what to say.'

CHAPTER 86

The Needle

Next morning the not-yet-subsided sea rolled in long slow billows of mighty bulk, and striving in the Pequod's gurgling track, pushed her on like giants' palms outspread. The strong, unstaggering breeze abounded so, that sky and air seemed vast outbellying sails; the whole world boomed before the wind. Muffled in the full morning light, the invisible sun was only known by the spread intensity of his place; where his bayonet rays moved on in stacks.

Long maintaining an enchanted silence, Ahab stood apart. But suddenly he hurried towards the helm, huskily demanding how the ship was heading.

'East-sou-east, sir,' said the frightened steersman.

'Thou liest!' smiting him with his clenched fist. 'Heading East at this hour in the morning, and the sun astern?'

Upon this every soul was confounded; for the phenomenon just then observed by Ahab had unaccountably escaped every one else.

Thrusting his head half way into the binnacle, Ahab caught one glimpse of the compasses; his uplifted arm slowly fell; for a moment he almost seemed to stagger. Standing behind him Starbuck looked, and lo! the two compasses pointed East, and the Pequod was as infallibly going West.

But ere the first wild alarm could get out abroad among the crew, the old man with a rigid laugh exclaimed, 'I have it! Mr Starbuck, last night's thunder turned our compasses – that's all. Thou hast before now heard of such a thing, I take it.'

'Aye; but never before has it happened to me, sir,' said the pale mate, gloomily.

Deliberately standing before the binnacle, and eyeing the trans-pointed compasses, the old man, with the sharp of his extended hand, now took the precise bearing of the sun, and satisfied that the needles were exactly inverted, shouted out his orders for the ship's course to be changed accordingly. The yards were hard up; and once more the Pequod thrust her undaunted bows into the opposing wind.

Meanwhile, whatever were his own secret thoughts, Starbuck said nothing, but quietly he issued all requisite orders; while Stubb and Flask – who seemed then to be sharing his feelings – likewise unmurmuringly acquiesced. As for the men, though some of them lowly rumbled, their fear of Ahab was greater than their fear of Fate. But as ever before, the pagan harpooneers remained almost wholly unimpressed.

For a space the old man walked the deck in rolling reveries. But

chancing to slip with his ivory heel, he saw the crushed copper
sight-tubes of the quadrant he had the day before dashed to the
deck.

'Thou poor, proud heaven-gazer and sun's pilot! yesterday I
wrecked thee, and today the compasses would fain have wrecked
me. So, so. But Ahab is lord over the level load-stone yet. Mr
Starbuck – a lance without the pole; a top-maul, and the smallest
of the sail-maker's needles. Quick!'

Accessory, perhaps, to the impulse dictating the thing he was
now about to do were certain prudential motives, whose object
might have been to revive the spirits of his crew by a stroke of
his subtile skill, in a matter so wondrous as that of the inverted
compasses. Besides, the old man well knew that to steer by trans-
pointed needles, though clumsily practicable, was not a thing to
be passed over by superstitious sailors, without some shudderings
and evil portents.

'Men,' said he, steadily turning upon the crew, as the mate
handed him the things he had demanded, 'my men, the thunder
turned old Ahab's needles; but out of this bit of steel Ahab can
make one of his own, that will point as true as any.'

Abashed glances of servile wonder were exchanged by the
sailors, as this was said; and with fascinated eyes they awaited
whatever magic might follow. But Starbuck looked away.

With a blow from the top-maul Ahab knocked off the steel head
of the lance, and then handing to the mate the long iron rod remaining, bade him hold it upright, without its touching the deck.
Then, with the maul, after repeatedly smiting the upper end of this
iron rod, he placed the blunted needle endwise on the top of it, and
less strongly hammered that, several times, the mate still holding
the rod as before. Then going through some small strange motions
with it – whether indispensable to the magnetizing of the steel,
or merely intended to augment the awe of the crew, is uncertain
– he called for linen thread; and moving to the binnacle, slipped
out the two reversed needles there, and horizontally suspended
the sail-needle by its middle, over one of the compass-cards. At
first, the steel went round and round, quivering and vibrating at

either end; but at last it settled to its place, when Ahab, who had been intently watching for this result, stepped frankly back from the binnacle, and pointing his stretched arm towards it, exclaimed – 'Look ye, for yourselves, if Ahab be not lord of the level load-stone! The sun is East, and that compass swears it!'

One after another they peered in, for nothing but their own eyes could persuade such ignorance as theirs, and one after another they slunk away. In his fiery eyes of scorn and triumph, you then saw Ahab in all his fatal pride.

CHAPTER 87

The Life-buoy

Steering now south-eastward by Ahab's levelled steel, and her progress solely determined by Ahab's level log and line, the Pequod held on her path towards the Equator. Making so long a passage through such unfrequented waters, descrying no ships, and ere long, sideways impelled by unvarying trade winds, over waves monotonously mild; all these seemed the strange calm things preluding some riotous and desperate scene.

At last, when the ship drew near to the outskirts, as it were, of the equatorial fishing-ground, and in the deep darkness that goes before the dawn, was sailing by a cluster of rocky islets, the watch – then headed by Flask – was startled by a cry so plaintively wild and unearthly – like half-articulated wailings of the ghosts of all Herod's murdered Innocents – that one and all, they started from their reveries, and for the space of some moments stood, or sat, or leaned all transfixedly listening, while that wild cry remained within hearing. The Christian or civilized part of the crew said it was mermaids, and shuddered; but the pagan harpooneers re-mained unappalled. Yet the grey Manxman – the oldest mariner of all – declared that the wild thrilling sounds that were heard were the voices of newly drowned men in the sea.

Below in his hammock, Ahab did not hear of this till grey dawn, when he came to the deck; it was then recounted to him by Flask, not unaccompanied with hinted dark meanings. He hollowly laughed, and thus explained the wonder.

Those rocky islands the ship had passed were the resort of great numbers of seals, and some young seals that had lost their dams, or some dams that had lost their cubs, must have risen nigh the ship and kept company with her, crying and sobbing with their human sort of wail. But this only the more affected some of them, because most mariners cherish a very superstitious feeling about seals, arising not only from their peculiar tones when in distress, but also from the human look of their round heads and semi-intelligent faces, seen peeringly uprising from the water alongside. In the sea, under certain circumstances, seals have more than once been mistaken for men.

But the bodings of the crew were destined to receive a most plausible confirmation in the fate of one of their number that morning. At sun-rise this man went from his hammock to his mast-head at the fore; and whether it was that he was not yet half waked from his sleep (for sailors sometimes go aloft in a transition state), whether it was thus with the man, there is now no telling; but, be that as it may, he had not been long at his perch, when a cry was heard – a cry and a rushing – and looking up, they saw a falling phantom in the air; and looking down, a little tossed heap of white bubbles in the blue of the sea.

The life-buoy – a long slender cask – was dropped from the stern, where it always hung obedient to a cunning spring; but no hand rose to seize it, and the sun having long beat upon this cask it had shrunken, so that it slowly filled, and the parched wood also filled at its every pore; and the studded iron-bound cask followed the sailor to the bottom, as if to yield him his pillow, though in sooth but a hard one.

And thus the first man of the Pequod that mounted the mast to look out for the White Whale, on the White Whale's own peculiar ground; that man was swallowed up in the deep. But few, perhaps, thought of that at the time. Indeed, in some sort, they were not grieved at this event, at least as a portent; for they regarded it, not as a foreshadowing of evil in the future, but as the fulfilment of an evil already presaged. They declared that now they knew the reason of those wild shrieks they had heard the night before. But again the old Manxman said nay.

The lost life-buoy was now to be replaced; Starbuck was directed to see to it; but as no cask of sufficient lightness could be found, and as in the feverish eagerness of what seemed the approaching crisis of the voyage, all hands were impatient of any toil but what was directly connected with its final end, whatever that might prove to be; therefore, they were going to leave the ship's stern unprovided with a buoy, when by certain strange signs and inuendoes Queequeg hinted a hint concerning his coffin.

'A life-buoy of a coffin!' cried Starbuck, starting.

'Rather queer, that, I should say,' said Stubb.

'It will make a good enough one,' said Flask, 'the carpenter here can arrange it easily.'

'Bring it up; there's nothing else for it,' said Starbuck, after a melancholy pause. 'Rig it, carpenter; do not look at me so – the coffin, I mean. Dost thou hear me? Rig it.'

'And shall I nail down the lid, sir?' moving his hand as with a hammer.

'Aye.'

'And shall I caulk the seams, sir?' moving his hand as with a caulking-iron.

'Aye.'

'And shall I then pay over the same with pitch, sir?' moving his hand as with a pitch-pot.

'Away! what possesses thee to this? Make a life-buoy of the coffin, and no more. Mr Stubb, Mr Flask, come forward with me.'

'He goes off in a huff. The whole he can endure; at the parts he baulks. Now I don't like this. I don't like it at all. But heigh-ho! I'll do the job, now, tenderly. I'll have me – let's see – how many in the ship's company, all told? But I've forgotten. Any way, I'll have me thirty separate, Turk's-headed life-lines, each three feet long hanging all round to the coffin. Then, if the hull go down, there'll be thirty lively fellows all fighting for one coffin, a sight not seen very often beneath the sun!'

CHAPTER 88

The Pequod Meets the Rachel

Next day, a large ship, the Rachel, was descried, bearing directly down upon the Pequod, all her spars thickly clustering with men. At the time the Pequod was making good speed through the water; but as the broad-winged windward stranger shot nigh to her, the boastful sails all fell together as blank bladders that are burst, and all life fled from the smitten hull.

'Bad news; she brings bad news,' muttered the old Manxman. But ere her commander, who, with trumpet to mouth, stood up in his boat; ere he could hopefully hail, Ahab's voice was heard.

'Hast seen the White Whale?'

'Aye, yesterday. Have ye seen a whale-boat adrift?'

Throttling his joy, Ahab negatively answered this unexpected question; and would then have fain boarded the stranger, when the stranger captain himself, having stopped his vessel's way, was seen descending her side. A few keen pulls, and his boat-hook soon clinched the Pequod's main-chains, and he sprang to the deck. Immediately he was recognized by Ahab for a Nantucketer he knew. But no formal salutation was exchanged.

'Where was he? – not killed! – not killed!' cried Ahab, closely advancing. 'How was it?'

It seemed that somewhat late on the afternoon of the day previous, while three of the stranger's boats were engaged with a shoal of whales, which had led them some four or five miles from the ship; and while they were yet in swift chase to windward, the white hump and head of Moby-Dick had suddenly loomed up out of the blue water, not very far to leeward; whereupon, the fourth rigged boat – a reserved one – had been instantly lowered in chase. After a keen sail before the wind, this fourth boat – the swiftest keeled of all – seemed to have succeeded in fastening – at least, as well as the man at the mast-head could tell anything about it. In the distance he saw the diminished dotted boat; and then a swift gleam of bubbling white water; and after that nothing more; whence it was concluded that the stricken whale must have indefinitely run away with his pursuers, as often happens. There was some apprehension, but no positive alarm, as yet. The recall signals were placed in the rigging; darkness came on; and forced to pick up her three far to windward boats – ere going in quest of the fourth one in the precisely opposite direction – the ship had not only been necessitated to leave that boat to its fate till near midnight, but, for the time, to increase her distance from it. But the rest of her crew being at last safe aboard, she crowded all sail – stun-sail on stun-sail – after the missing boat; kindling a fire in her try-pots for a beacon; and every other man aloft on the look-out. But though when she had thus sailed a sufficient distance to gain the presumed place of the absent ones when last seen; though she then paused to lower her spare boats to pull all around her; and not finding anything, had again dashed on; again paused, and lowered her boats; and though she had thus continued doing till day light; yet not the least glimpse of the missing keel had been seen.

The story told, the stranger Captain immediately went on to reveal his object in boarding the Pequod. He desired that ship to unite with his own in the search; by sailing over the sea some four or five miles apart, on parallel lines, and so sweeping a double horizon, as it were.

'I will wager something now,' whispered Stubb to Flask, 'that some one in that missing boat wore off that Captain's best coat; mayhap, his watch – he's so cursed anxious to get it back. Who ever heard of two pious whale-ships cruising after one missing whale-boat in the height of the whaling season? See, Flask, only see how pale he looks – pale in the very buttons of his eyes – look – it wasn't the coat – it must have been the—'

'My boy, my own boy is among them. For God's sake – I beg, I conjure' – here exclaimed the stranger Captain to Ahab, who thus far had but icily received his petition. 'For eight-and-forty hours let me charter your ship – I will gladly pay for it, and roundly pay for it – if there be no other way – for eight-and-forty hours only – only that – you must, oh, you must, and you *shall* do this thing.'

'His son!' cried Stubb, 'oh, it's his son he's lost! I take back the coat and watch – what says Ahab? We must save that boy.'

'He's drowned with the rest on 'em, last night,' said the old Manx sailor standing behind them; 'I heard; all of ye heard their spirits.'

Now, what made this incident of the Rachel's the more melancholy was that the captain's son is a little lad, but twelve years old, whose father with the earnest but unmisgiving hardihood of a Nantucketer's paternal love had thus early sought to initiate him in the perils and wonders of a vocation almost immemorially the destiny of all his race. Nor does it unfrequently occur, that Nantucket captains will send a son of such tender age away from them, for a protracted three or four years' voyage in some other ship than their own; so that their first knowledge of a whaleman's career shall be unenervated by any chance display of a father's natural but untimely partiality, or undue apprehensiveness and concern. Meantime, now the stranger was still beseeching his poor boon of Ahab; and Ahab still stood like an anvil, receiving every shock, but without the least quivering of his own.

'I will not go,' said the stranger, 'till you say *aye* to me. Do to me as you would have me do to you in the like case. For *you* too have a boy, Captain Ahab – though but a child, and nestling safely at home now – a child of your old age too – Yes, yes, you relent; I see it – run, run, men, now, and stand by to square in the yards.'

'Avast,' cried Ahab – 'touch not a rope-yarn'; then in a voice that prolongingly moulded every word – 'Captain Gardiner, I will not do it. Even now I lose time. Good-bye, good-bye. God bless ye, man, and may I forgive myself, but I must go. Mr Starbuck, look at the binnacle watch, and in three minutes from this present instant warn off all strangers: then brace forward again, and let the ship sail as before.'

Hurriedly turning, with averted face, he descended into his cabin, leaving the strange captain transfixed at this unconditional and utter rejection of his so earnest suit. But starting from his enchantment, Gardiner silently hurried to the side; more fell than stepped into his boat, and returned to his ship.

Soon the two ships diverged their wakes; and long as the strange vessel was in view, she was seen to yaw hither and thither at every dark spot, however small, on the sea. This way and that her yards were swung round; starboard and larboard, she continued to tack; now she beat against a head sea; and again it pushed her before it; while all the while, her masts and yards were thickly clustered with men, as three tall cherry trees, when the boys are cherrying among the boughs.

But by her still halting course and winding, woeful way, you plainly saw that this ship that so wept with spray still remained without comfort. She was Rachel, weeping for her children, because they were not.

CHAPTER 89

The Hat

And now that at the proper time and place, after so long and wide a preliminary cruise, Ahab – all other whaling waters swept – seemed to have chased his foe into an ocean-fold, to slay him the more securely there; now that he found himself hard by the very latitude and longitude where his tormenting wound had been inflicted; now that a vessel had been spoken which on the very day preceding had actually encountered Moby-Dick; and now that all his successive meetings with various ships contrastingly concurred to show the demoniac indifference with which the White Whale tore his hunters, whether sinning or sinned against; now it was that there lurked a something in the old man's eyes, which it was hardly sufferable for feeble souls to see. As the unsetting polar

star, which through the livelong, arctic, six months' night sustains
its piercing, steady, central gaze; so Ahab's purpose now fixedly
gleamed down upon the constant midnight of the gloomy crew.

Alike, joy and sorrow, hope and fear, seemed ground to finest
dust, and powdered, for the time, in the clamped mortar of Ahab's
iron soul. Like machines, they dumbly moved about the deck, ever
conscious that the old man's despot eye was on them.

Nor, at any time, by night or day could the mariners now step
upon the deck, unless Ahab was before them; his hat slouched
heavily over his eyes; so that however motionless he stood, however the days and nights were added on, that he had not swung in
his hammock; yet hidden beneath that slouching hat, they could
never tell unerringly whether, for all this, his eyes were really
closed at times: or whether he was still intently scanning them; no
matter, though he stood so in the scuttle for a whole hour on the
stretch, and the unheeded night-damp gathered in beads of dew
upon that stone-carved coat and hat. The clothes that the night
had wet, the next day's sunshine dried upon him; and so, day after
day, and night after night; he went no more beneath the planks;
whatever he wanted from the cabin that thing he sent for.

He ate in the same open air; he never reaped his beard; which
darkly grew all gnarled, as unearthed roots of trees blown over.
But though his whole life was now become one watch on deck;
and though the Parsee's watch was without intermission as his
own; yet these two never seemed to speak – one man to the other
– unless at long intervals some passing unmomentous matter
made it necessary.

But Ahab, at the first faintest glimmering of the dawn, his iron
voice was heard from aft – 'Man the mast-heads!' – and all through
the day, till after sunset and after twilight, the same voice every
hour, at the striking of the helmsman's bell, was heard – 'What
d'ye see? – sharp! sharp!'

But when three or four days had slided by, after meeting the
children-seeking Rachel; and no spout had yet been seen; the
monomaniac old man seemed distrustful of his crew's fidelity; at
least, of nearly all except the pagan harpooneers; he seemed to

doubt, even, whether Stubb and Flask might not willingly overlook the sight he sought.

'I will have the first sight of the whale myself,' he said. 'Aye! Ahab must have the doubloon!' and with his own hands he rigged a nest of basketed bowlines; and sending a hand aloft, with a single sheaved block, to secure to the main-mast head, he received the two ends of the downward-reeved rope; and attaching one to his basket prepared a pin for the other end, in order to fasten it at the rail. This done, with that end yet in his hand and standing beside the pin, he looked round upon his crew, sweeping from one to the other; pausing his glance long upon Daggoo, Queequeg, Tashtego; but shunning Fedallah; and then settling his firm relying eye upon the chief mate, said, 'Take the rope, sir – I give it into thy hands, Starbuck.' Then arranging his person in the basket, he gave the word for them to hoist him to his perch, Starbuck being the one who secured the rope at last; and afterwards stood near it. And thus, with one hand clinging round the royal mast, Ahab gazed abroad upon the sea for miles and miles – ahead, astern, this side, and that – within the wide expanded circle commanded at so great a height.

Now, the first time Ahab was perched aloft; ere he had been there ten minutes; one of those red-billed savage sea-hawks which so often fly incommodiously close round the manned mast-heads of whalemen in these latitudes; one of these birds came wheeling and screaming round his head in a maze of untrackably swift circlings. Then it darted a thousand feet straight up into the air; then spiralized downwards, and went eddying again round his head.

But with his gaze fixed upon the dim and distant horizon, Ahab seemed not to mark this wild bird; nor, indeed, would anyone else have marked it much, it being no uncommon circumstance; only now almost the least heedful eye seemed to see some sort of cunning meaning in almost every sight.

'Your hat, your hat, sir!' suddenly cried the Sicilian seaman, who being posted at the mizzen-mast-head, stood directly behind Ahab, though somewhat lower than his level, and with a deep gulf of air dividing them.

But already the sable wing was before the old man's eyes; the long hooked bill at his head: with a scream, the black hawk darted away with his prize.

Ahab's hat was never restored; the wild hawk flew on and on with it; far in advance of the prow: and at last disappeared; while from the point of that disappearance, a minute black spot was dimly discerned, falling from that vast height into the sea.

CHAPTER 90

The Pequod Meets the Delight

The intense Pequod sailed on; the rolling waves and days went by; the life-buoy-coffin still lightly swung; and another ship, most miserably misnamed the Delight, was descried. As she drew nigh, all eyes were fixed upon her broad beams, called shears, which, in some whaling-ships, cross the quarter-deck at the height of eight or nine feet; serving to carry the spare, unrigged, or disabled boats.

Upon the stranger's shears were beheld the shattered, white ribs, and some few splintered planks, of what had once been a whale-boat; but you now saw through this wreck, as plainly as you see through the peeled, half-unhinged, and bleaching skeleton of a horse.

'Hast seen the White Whale?'

'Look!' replied the hollow-cheeked captain from his taffrail; and with his trumpet he pointed to the wreck.

'Hast killed him?'

'The harpoon is not yet forged that will ever do that,' answered the other, sadly glancing upon a rounded hammock on the deck, whose gathered sides some noiseless sailors were busy in sewing together.

'Not forged!' and snatching Perth's levelled iron from the crotch, Ahab held it out, exclaiming – 'Look ye, Nantucketer; here in this hand I hold his death! Tempered in blood, and tempered by lightning are these barbs; and I swear to temper them triply in that hot place behind the fin, where the White Whale most feels his accursed life!'

'Then God keep thee, old man – see'st thou that' – pointing to the hammock – 'I bury but one of five stout men, who were alive only yesterday; but were dead ere night. Only that one I bury; the rest were buried before they died; you sail upon their tomb.' Then turning to his crew – 'Are ye ready there? place the plank then on the rail, and lift the body; so, then – Oh! God' – advancing towards the hammock with uplifted hands – 'may the resurrection and the life—'

'Brace forward! Up helm!' cried Ahab like lightning to his men.

But the suddenly started Pequod was not quick enough to escape the sound of the splash that the corpse soon made as it struck the sea; not so quick, indeed, but that some of the flying bubbles might have sprinkled her hull with their ghostly baptism.

As Ahab now glided from the dejected Delight, the strange life-buoy hanging at the Pequod's stern came into conspicuous relief.

'Ha! yonder! look yonder, men!' cried a foreboding voice in her wake. 'In vain, oh, ye strangers, ye fly our sad burial; ye but turn us your taffrail to show us your coffin!'

CHAPTER 91

The Symphony

Slowly crossing the deck from the scuttle, Ahab leaned over the side, and watched how his shadow in the water sank and sank to his gaze, the more and more that he strove to pierce the profundity. But the lovely aromas in that enchanted air did at last seem to dispel, for a moment, the cankerous thing in his soul. That glad, happy air, that winsome sky, did at last stroke and caress him; the

step-mother world, so long cruel – forbidding – now threw affectionate arms round his stubborn neck, and did seem to joyously
sob over him, as if over one, that however wilful and erring, she
could yet find it in her heart to save and to bless. From beneath
his slouched hat Ahab dropped a tear into the sea; nor did all the
Pacific contain such wealth as that one wee drop.

Starbuck saw the old man; saw him, how he heavily leaned over
the side; and he seemed to hear in his own true heart the measureless sobbing that stole out of the centre of the serenity around.
Careful not to touch him, or be noticed by him, he yet drew near
to him, and stood there.

Ahab turned.

'Starbuck!'

'Sir.'

'Oh, Starbuck! it is a mild, mild wind, and a mild looking sky.
On such a day – very much such a sweetness as this – I struck
my first whale – a boy-harpooneer of eighteen! Forty years of
continual whaling! forty years of privation, and peril, and storm-
time! forty years on the pitiless sea! For forty years I have fed
upon dry salted fare – fit emblem of the dry nourishment of my
soul! – when the poorest landsman has had fresh fruit to his daily
hand, and broken the world's fresh bread to my mouldy crusts
– away, whole oceans away, from that young girl-wife I wedded
past fifty, and sailed for Cape Horn the next day, leaving but one
dent in my marriage pillow – wife? wife? – rather a widow with
her husband alive! Aye, I widowed that poor girl when I married
her, Starbuck; and then, the madness, the frenzy, the boiling
blood and the smoking brow, with which, for a thousand lowerings old Ahab has furiously, foamingly chased his prey – more
a demon than a man! – aye, aye! what a forty years' fool has old
Ahab been! Close! Stand close to me, Starbuck; let me look into
a human eye; it is better than to gaze into sea or sky; better than
to gaze upon God. By the green land; by the bright hearth-stone!
this is the magic glass, man; I see my wife and my child in thine
eye. No, no; stay on board, on board! – lower not when I do;
when branded Ahab gives chase to Moby-Dick. That hazard shall

not be thine. No, no! not with the far away home I see in that eye!'

'Oh, my Captain! my Captain! noble soul! grand old heart, after all! why should any one give chase to that hated fish! Away with me! let us fly these deadly waters! let us home! Wife and child, too, are Starbuck's – wife and child of his brotherly, sisterly, play-fellow youth; even as thine, sir, are the wife and child of thy loving, longing, paternal old age! Away! let us away! – this instant let me alter the course! How cheerily, how hilariously, O my Captain, would we bowl on our way to see old Nantucket again! I think, sir, they have some such mild blue days, even as this, in Nantucket.'

'They have, they have. I have seen them – some summer days in the morning. About this time – yes, it is his noon nap now – the boy vivaciously wakes; sits up in bed; and his mother tells him of me, of cannibal old me; how I am abroad upon the deep, but will yet come back to dance him again.'

''Tis my Mary, my Mary herself! She promised that my boy, every morning, should be carried to the hill to catch the first glimpse of his father's sail! Yes, yes! no more! it is done! we head for Nantucket! Come, my Captain, study out the course, and let us away! See, see! the boy's face from the window! the boy's hand on the hill!'

But Ahab's glance was averted; like a blighted fruit tree he shook, and cast his last, cindered apple to the soil.

'What is it, what nameless, inscrutable, unearthly thing is it; what cozening, hidden lord and master, and cruel, remorseless emperor commands me; that against all natural lovings and longings, I so keep pushing, and crowding, and jamming myself on all the time; recklessly making me ready to do what in my own proper, natural heart, I durst not so much as dare? Is Ahab, Ahab? Is it I, God, or who, that lifts this arm? And all the time, lo! that smiling sky, and this unsounded sea! But it is a mild, mild wind, and a mild looking sky; and the airs smells now, as if it blew from a far-away meadow; they have been making hay somewhere under the slopes of the Andes, Starbuck, and the mowers are sleeping among the new-mown hay. Sleeping? Aye, toil we how we may, we all sleep at last on the field. Sleep? Aye, and rust amid greenness; as last year's scythes flung down, and left in the half-cut swaths – Starbuck!'

But blanched to a corpse's hue with despair, the mate had stolen away.

Ahab crossed the deck to gaze over on the other side; but started at two reflected, fixed eyes in the water there. Fedallah was motionlessly leaning over the same rail.

CHAPTER 92

The Chase – First Day

That night, in the mid-watch, the old man suddenly thrust out his face fiercely, snuffing up the sea air as a sagacious ship's dog will, in drawing nigh to some barbarous isle. He declared that a whale must be near. Soon that peculiar odour, sometimes to a great distance given forth by the living Sperm Whale, was palpable to all the watch; nor was any mariner surprised when, after inspecting the compass, and then the dog-vane, and then ascertaining the precise bearing of the odour as nearly as possible, Ahab rapidly ordered the ship's course to be slightly altered, and the sail to be shortened.

The acute policy dictating these movements was sufficiently vindicated at daybreak, by the sight of a long sleek on the sea directly and lengthwise ahead, smooth as oil, and resembling in the pleated watery wrinkles bordering it the polished metallic-like marks of some swift tide-rip, at the mouth of a deep, rapid stream.

'Man the mast-heads! Call all hands!'

Thundering with the butts of three clubbed handspikes on the forecastle deck, Daggoo roused the sleepers with such judgement claps that they seemed to exhale from the scuttle, so instantaneously did they appear with their clothes in their hands.

'What d'ye see?' cried Ahab, flattening his face to the sky.

'Nothing, nothing, sir!' was the sound hailing down in reply.

'T'gallant sails! – stun-sails! alow and aloft, and on both sides!'

All sail being set, he now cast loose the life-line, reserved for swaying him to the main royal-mast-head; and in a few moments they were hoisting him thither, when, while but two thirds of the way aloft, and while peering ahead through the horizontal vacancy between the main-top-sail and top-gallant-sail, he raised a gull-like cry in the air, 'There she blows! – there she blows! A hump like a snow-hill! It is Moby-Dick!'

Fired by the cry which seemed simultaneously taken up by the three look-outs, the men on deck rushed to the rigging to behold the famous whale they had so long been pursuing. Ahab had now gained his final perch, some feet above the other look-outs, Tashtego standing just beneath him on the cap of the top-gallant-mast, so that the Indian's head was almost on a level with Ahab's heel. From this height the whale was now seen some mile or so ahead, revealing his high sparkling hump, and regularly jetting his silent spout into the air. To the credulous mariners it seemed the same silent spout they had so long ago beheld in the moonlit Atlantic and Indian Oceans.

'And did none of ye see it before?' cried Ahab, hailing the perched men all around him. 'No, the doubloon is mine, Fate reserved the doubloon for me, *I* only; none of ye could have raised the White Whale first. There she blows! there she blows! – there she blows! There again! – there again!' he cried, in long-drawn, lingering, methodic tones, attuned to the gradual prolongings of the whale's visible jets. 'He's going to sound! In stun-sails! Down top-gallant-sails! Stand by three boats. Mr Starbuck, remember, stay on board, and keep the ship. Helm there! Luff, luff a point! So; steady, man, steady! There go flukes! No, no; only black water! All ready the boats there? Stand by, stand by! Lower me, Mr Starbuck; lower, lower, quick, quicker!' and he slid through the air to the deck.

'He is heading straight to leeward, sir,' cried Stubb, 'right away from us; cannot have seen the ship yet.'

'Be dumb, man! Stand by the braces! Hard down the

helm! brace up! Shiver her! – shiver her! So; well that! Boats, boats!'

Soon all the boats but Starbuck's were dropped; all the boat-sails set – all the paddles plying; with rippling swiftness, shooting to leeward; and Ahab heading the onset. A pale, death-glimmer lit up Fedallah's sunken eyes; a hideous motion gnawed his mouth.

Like noiseless nautilus shells, their light prows sped through the sea; but only slowly they neared the foe. As they neared him, the ocean grew still more smooth; seemed drawing a carpet over its waves; seemed a noon-meadow, so serenely it spread. At length the breathless hunter came so nigh his seemingly unsuspecting prey, that his entire dazzling hump was distinctly visible, sliding along the sea and continually set in a revolving ring of finest, fleecy, greenish foam. He saw the vast, involved wrinkles of the slightly projecting head beyond. Before it, far out on the soft Turkish-rugged waters, went the glistening white shadow from his broad, milky forehead, a musical rippling playfully accompanying the shade; and behind, the blue waters interchangeably flowed over into the moving valley of his steady wake; and on either hand bright bubbles arose and danced by his side. But these were broken again by the light toes of hundreds of gay fowl softly feathering the sea, alternate with their fitful flight; and like to some flag-staff rising from the painted hull of an argosy, the tall but shattered pole of a recent lance projected from the White Whale's back; and at intervals one of the cloud of soft-toed fowls hovering, and to and fro skimming like a canopy over the fish, silently perched and rocked on this pole, the long tail feathers streaming like pennons.

A gentle joyousness – a mighty mildness of repose in swiftness – invested the gliding whale as he swam. No wonder there had been some among the hunters who namelessly transported and allured by all this serenity, had ventured to assail it; but had fatally found that quietude but the vesture of tornadoes. Yet calm, enticing calm, oh, whale! thou glidest on, to all who for the first time eye thee, no matter how many in that same way thou may'st have bejuggled and destroyed before.

And thus, through the serene tranquillities of the tropical sea, among waves whose hand-clappings were suspended by exceeding rapture, Moby-Dick moved on, still withholding from sight the full terrors of his submerged trunk, entirely hiding the wrenched hideousness of his jaw. But soon the fore part of him slowly rose from the water; for an instant his whole marbleized body formed a high arch, like Virginia's Natural Bridge, and warningly waving his bannered flukes in the air, the grand god revealed himself, sounded, and went out of sight. Hoveringly halting, and dipping on the wing, the white sea-fowls longingly lingered over the agitated pool that he left.

With oars apeak, and paddles down, the sheets of their sails adrift, the three boats now stilly floated, awaiting Moby-Dick's reappearance.

'An hour,' said Ahab, standing rooted in his boat's stern; and he gazed beyond the whale's place, towards the dim blue spaces and wide wooing vacancies to leeward. It was only an instant; for again his eyes seemed whirling round in his head as he swept the watery circle. The breeze now freshened; the sea began to swell.

'The birds! – the birds!' cried Tashtego. In long Indian file, as when herons take wing, the white birds were now all flying towards Ahab's boat; and when within a few yards began fluttering over the water there, wheeling round and round, with joyous, expectant cries. Their vision was keener than man's; Ahab could discover no sign in the sea. But suddenly as he peered down and down into its depths, he profoundly saw a white living spot no bigger than a white weasel, with wonderful celerity uprising, and magnifying as it rose, till it turned, and then there were plainly revealed two long crooked rows of white, glistening teeth, floating up from the undiscoverable bottom. It was Moby-Dick's open mouth and scrolled jaw; his vast, shadowed bulk still half blending with the blue of the sea. The glittering mouth yawned beneath the boat like an open-doored marble tomb; and giving one sidelong sweep with his steering oar, Ahab whirled the craft aside from this tremendous apparition. Then, calling upon Fedallah to change places with him, went forward to the bows, and seizing Perth's harpoon, commanded his crew to grasp their oars and stand by to stern.

Now, by reason of this timely spinning round the boat upon its axis, its bow, by anticipation, was made to face the whale's head while yet under water. But as if perceiving this stratagem, Moby-Dick, with that malicious intelligence ascribed to him, sidelingly transplanted himself, as it were, in an instant, shooting his pleated head lengthwise beneath the boat.

Through and through; through every plank and each rib, it thrilled for an instant, the whale obliquely lying on his back, in the manner of a biting shark, slowly and feelingly taking its bows full within his mouth, so that the long, narrow, scrolled lower jaw curled high up into the open air, and one of the teeth caught in a row-lock. The bluish pearl-white of the inside of the jaw was within six inches of Ahab's head, and reached higher than that. In this attitude the White Whale now shook the slight cedar as a mildly cruel cat her mouse. With unastonished eyes Fedallah gazed, and crossed his arms; but the tiger-yellow crew were tumbling over each other's heads to gain the uttermost stern.

And now, while both elastic gunwales were springing in and out, as the whale dallied with the doomed craft in this devilish way; and from his body being submerged beneath the boat, he could not be darted at from the bows, for the bows were almost inside of him, as it were; and while the other boats involuntarily paused, as before a quick crisis impossible to withstand, then it was that monomaniac Ahab, furious with this tantalizing vicinity of his foe, which placed him all alive and helpless in the very jaws he hated; frenzied with all this, he seized the long bone with his naked hands, and wildly strove to wrench it from its gripe. As now he thus vainly strove, the jaw slipped from him; the frail gunwales bent in, collapsed, and snapped, as both jaws, like an enormous shears, sliding further aft, bit the craft completely in twain, and locked themselves fast again in the sea, midway between the two floating wrecks. These floated aside, the broken ends drooping, the crew at the stern-wreck clinging to the gunwales, and striving to hold fast to the oars to lash them across.

At that preluding moment, ere the boat was yet snapped, Ahab, the first to perceive the whale's intent, by the crafty upraising of his head, a movement that loosed his hold for the time; at that moment his hand had made one final effort to push the boat out of the bite. But only slipping further into the whale's mouth, and tilting over sideways as it slipped, the boat had shaken off his hold on the jaw; spilled him out of it, as he leaned to the push; and so he fell flat-faced upon the sea.

Ripplingly withdrawing from his prey, Moby-Dick now lay at a little distance, vertically thrusting his oblong white head up and down in the billows; and at the same time slowly revolving his whole spindled body; so that when his vast wrinkled forehead rose – some twenty or more feet out of the water – the now rising swells, with all their confluent waves, dazzlingly broke against it; vindictively tossing their shivered spray still higher into the air. So, in a gale, the but half baffled Channel billows recoil from the base of the Eddystone, only triumphantly to overleap its summit with their scud.

But soon resuming his horizontal attitude, Moby-Dick swam swiftly round and round the wrecked crew; sideways churning the water in his vengeful wake, as if lashing himself up to still another and more deadly assault. The sight of the splintered boat seemed to madden him, as the blood of grapes and mulberries cast before Antiochus's elephants in the book of Maccabees. Meanwhile Ahab, half smothered in the foam of the whale's insolent tail, and too much of a cripple to swim – though he could still keep afloat, even in the heart of such a whirlpool as that; helpless Ahab's head was seen, like a tossed bubble which the least chance shock might burst. From the boat's fragmentary stern, Fedallah incuriously and mildly eyed him; the clinging crew, at the other drifting end, could not succour him; more than enough was it for them to look to themselves. For so revolvingly appalling was the White Whale's aspect, and so planetarily swift the ever-contracting circles he made, that he seemed horizontally swooping upon them. And though the other boats, unharmed, still hovered hard by; still they dared not pull into the eddy to strike, lest that should be the signal for the instant destruction of the jeopardized castaways, Ahab and all; nor in that case could they themselves hope to escape. With straining eyes, then, they remained on the outer edge of the direful zone, whose centre had now become the old man's head.

Meantime, from the beginning all this had been descried from the ship's mast-heads; and squaring her yards, she had borne down upon the scene; and was now so nigh, that Ahab in the water hailed her – 'Sail on the' – but that moment a breaking sea dashed on him from Moby-Dick, and whelmed him for the time. But struggling out of it again, and chancing to rise on a towering crest, he shouted – 'Sail on the whale! – Drive him off!'

The Pequod's prows were pointed; and breaking up the charmed circle, she effectually parted the White Whale from his victim. As he sullenly swam off, the boats flew to the rescue.

Dragged into Stubb's boat with blood-shot, blinded eyes, the white brine caking in his wrinkles; the long tension of Ahab's bodily strength did crack, and helplessly he yielded to his body's doom: for a time, lying all crushed in the bottom of Stubb's boat, like one trodden under foot of herds of elephants. Far inland, nameless wails came from him, as desolate sounds from out ravines.

But this intensity of his physical prostration did but so much the more abbreviate it. In an instant's compass, great hearts sometimes condense to one deep pang, the sum total of those shallow pains kindly diffused through feebler men's whole lives. And so, such hearts, though summary in each one suffering; still, if the gods decree it, in their life-time aggregate a whole age of woe, wholly made up of instantaneous intensities; for even in their pointless centres, those noble natures contain the entire circumferences of inferior souls.

'The harpoon,' said Ahab, half way rising, and draggingly leaning on one bended arm – 'is it safe?'

'Aye, sir, for it was not darted; this is it,' said Stubb, showing it.

'Lay it before me; any missing men?'

'One, two, three, four, five; there were five oars, sir, and here are five men.'

'That's good. – Help me, man; I wish to stand. So, so, I see him! there! there! going to leeward still; what a leaping spout! – Hands off from me! The eternal sap runs up in Ahab's bones again! Set the sail; out oars; the helm!'

It is often the case that when a boat is stove, its crew, being picked up by another boat, help to work that second boat; and the chase is thus continued with what is called double-banked oars. It was thus now. But the added power of the boat did not equal the added power of the whale, for he seemed to have treble-banked his every fin; swimming with a velocity which plainly showed, that if now, under these circumstances, pushed on, the chase would prove an indefinitely prolonged, if not a hopeless one; nor could any crew endure for so long a period, such an unintermitted, intense straining at the oar; a thing barely tolerable only in some one brief vicissitude. The ship itself, then, as it sometimes happens, offered the most promising intermediate means of overtaking the chase. Accordingly, the boats now made for her, and were soon swayed up to their cranes – the two parts of the wrecked boat having been previously secured by her – and then hoisting everything to her side, and stacking her canvas high up, and sideways outstretching it with stun-sails, like the double-jointed wings of an albatross; the Pequod bore down in the leeward wake of Moby-Dick. At the well known, methodic intervals, the whale's glittering spout was regularly announced from the manned mast-heads; and when he would be reported as just gone down, Ahab would take the time, and then pacing the deck, binnacle-watch in hand, so soon as the last second of the allotted hour expired, his voice was heard – 'Whose is the doubloon now? D'ye see him?' and if the reply was, No, sir! straightway he commanded them to lift him to his perch. In this way the day wore on; Ahab, now aloft and motionless; anon, unrestingly pacing the planks.

As he was thus walking, uttering no sound, except to hail the men aloft, or to bid them hoist a sail still higher, or to spread one to a still greater breadth – thus to and fro pacing, beneath his slouched hat, at every turn he passed his own wrecked boat, which had been dropped upon the quarter-deck, and lay there reversed;

broken bow to shattered stern. At last he paused before it; and as in an already over-clouded sky fresh troops of clouds will sometimes sail across, so over the old man's face there now stole some such added gloom as this.

Stubb saw him pause; and perhaps intending, not vainly, though, to evince his own unabated fortitude, and thus keep up a valiant place in his captain's mind, he advanced, and eyeing the wreck exclaimed – 'The thistle the ass refused; it pricked his mouth too keenly, sir; ha! Ha!'

'What soulless thing is this that laughs before a wreck? Man, man! did I not know thee brave as fearless fire (and as mechanical) I could swear thou wert a poltroon. Groan nor laugh should be heard before a wreck.'

'Aye, sir,' said Starbuck drawing near, ''tis a solemn sight; an omen, and an ill one.'

'Omen? omen? – the dictionary! If the gods think to speak outright to man, they will honourably speak outright; not shake their heads, and give an old wives' darkling hint. Begone! Ye two are the opposite poles of one thing; Starbuck is Stubb reversed, and Stubb is Starbuck; and ye two are all mankind; and Ahab stands alone among the millions of the peopled earth, nor gods nor men his neighbours! Cold, cold – I shiver! – How now? Aloft there! D'ye see him? Sing out for every spout, though he spout ten times a second!'

The day was nearly done; only the hem of his golden robe was rustling. Soon, it was almost dark, but the look-out men still remained unset.

'Can't see the spout now, sir; – too dark' – cried a voice from the air.

'How heading when last seen?'

'As before, sir – straight to leeward.'

'Good! he will travel slower now 'tis night. Down royals and top-gallant stun-sails, Mr Starbuck. We must not run over him before morning; he's making a passage now, and may heave-to a while. Helm there! keep her full before the wind! Aloft! come down! – Mr Stubb, send a fresh hand to the foremast head, and see it manned till morning.' Then advancing towards the doubloon in the main-mast – 'Men, this gold is mine, for I earned it; but I shall let it abide here till the White Whale is dead; and then, whosoever of ye first raises him, upon the day he shall be killed, this gold is that man's; and if on that day I shall again raise him, then, ten times its sum shall be divided among all of ye! Away now! – the deck is thine, sir.'

And so saying, he placed himself half way within the scuttle, and slouching his hat, stood there till dawn, except when at intervals rousing himself to see how the night wore on.

CHAPTER 93

The Chase – Second Day

At day-break, the three mast-heads were punctually manned afresh.

'D'ye see him?' cried Ahab, after allowing a little space for the light to spread.

'See nothing, sir.'

'Turn up all hands and make sail! he travels faster than I thought for – the top-gallant sails! – aye, they should have been kept on her all night. But no matter – 'tis but resting for the rush.'

The ship tore on; leaving such a furrow in the sea as when a cannon-ball, missent, becomes a plough-share and turns up the level field.

'By salt and hemp!' cried Stubb, 'but this swift motion of the deck creeps up one's legs and tingles at the heart. This ship and I are two brave fellows! – Ha! ha! Some one take me up, and launch me, spine-wise, on the sea – for by live-oaks! my spine's a keel. Ha, ha! we go the gait that leaves no dust behind!'

'There she blows – she blows! – she blows! – right ahead!' was now the mast-head cry.

'Aye, aye!' cried Stubb, 'I knew it – ye can't escape – blow on and split your spout, O whale! the mad fiend himself is after ye! blow your trump – blister your lungs! – Ahab will dam off your blood, as a miller shuts his water-gate upon the stream!'

And Stubb did but speak out for well nigh all that crew. The frenzies of the chase had by this time worked them bubblingly up, like old wine worked anew. Whatever pale fears and forebodings some of them might have felt before; these were not only now kept out of sight through the growing awe of Ahab, but they were broken up, and on all sides routed, as timid prairie hares that scatter before the bounding bison. The hand of Fate had snatched all their souls; and by the stirring perils of the previous day; the rack of the past night's suspense; the fixed, unfearing, blind, reckless way in which their wild craft went plunging towards its flying mark; by all these things, their hearts were bowled along. The wind that made great bellies of their sails, and rushed the vessel on by arms invisible as irresistible; this seemed the symbol of that unseen agency which so enslaved them to the race.

They were one man, not thirty. For as the one ship that held them all; though it was put together of all contrasting things – oak, and maple, and pine wood; iron, and pitch, and hemp – yet all these ran into each other in the one concrete hull, which shot on its way, both balanced and directed by the long central keel; even so, all the individualities of the crew, this man's valour, that man's fear; guilt and guiltiness, all varieties were welded into oneness, and were all directed to that fatal goal which Ahab their one lord and keel did point to.

The rigging lived. The mast-heads, like the tops of tall palms, were outspreadingly tufted with arms and legs. Clinging to a spar with one hand, some reached forth the other with impatient wavings; others, shading their eyes from the vivid sunlight, sat far out on the rocking yards; all the spars in full bearing of mortals, ready and ripe for their fate. Ah! how they still strove through that infinite blueness to seek out the thing that might destroy them!

'Why sing ye not out for him, if ye see him?' cried Ahab, when, after the lapse of some minutes since the first cry, no more had been heard. 'Sway me up, men; ye have been deceived; not Moby-Dick casts one odd jet that way, and then disappears.'

It was even so; in their headlong eagerness, the men had mistaken some other thing for the whale-spout, as the event itself soon proved; for hardly had Ahab reached his perch; hardly was the rope belayed to its pin on deck, when he struck the key-note to an orchestra, that made the air vibrate as with the combined discharges of rifles. The triumphant halloo of thirty buckskin lungs was heard, as – much nearer to the ship than the place of the imaginary jet, less than a mile ahead – Moby-Dick bodily burst into view! For not by any calm and indolent spoutings; not by the peaceable gush of that mystic fountain in his head, did the White Whale now reveal his vicinity; but by the far more wondrous phenomenon of breaching. Rising with his utmost velocity from the furthest depths, the Sperm Whale thus booms his entire bulk into the pure element of air, and piling up a mountain of dazzling foam, shows his place to the distance of seven miles and more. In those moments, the torn, enraged waves he shakes off seem his mane; in some cases, this breaching is his act of defiance.

'There she breaches! there she breaches!' was the cry, as in his immeasurable bravadoes the White Whale tossed himself salmon-like to heaven. So suddenly seen in the blue plain of the sea, and relieved against the still bluer margin of the sky, the spray that he raised, for the moment, intolerably glittered and glared like a glacier; and stood there gradually fading and fading away from its first sparkling intensity, to the dim mistiness of an advancing shower in a vale.

'Aye, breach your last to the sun, Moby-Dick!' cried Ahab, 'thy hour and thy harpoon are at hand! – Down! down all of ye, but one man at the fore. The boats! – stand by!'

Unmindful of the tedious rope-ladders of the shrouds, the men, like shooting stars, slid to the deck, by the isolated back-stays and halyards; while Ahab, less dartingly, but still rapidly was dropped from his perch.

'Lower away,' he cried, so soon as he had reached his boat – a spare one, rigged the afternoon previous. 'Mr Starbuck, the ship is thine – keep away from the boats, but keep near them. Lower, all!'

As if to strike a quick terror into them, by this time being the first assailant himself, Moby-Dick had turned, and was now coming for the three crews. Ahab's boat was central; and cheering his men, he told them he would take the whale head-and-head, that is, pull straight up to his forehead, – a not uncommon thing; for when within a certain limit, such a course excludes the coming onset from the whale's sidelong vision. But ere that close limit was gained, and while yet all three boats were plain as the ship's three masts to his eye; the White Whale churning himself into furious speed, almost in an instant as it were, rushing among the boats with open jaws, and a lashing tail, offered appalling battle on every side; and heedless of the irons darted at him from every boat, seemed only intent on annihilating each separate plank of which those boats were made. But skilfully manoeuvred, incessantly wheeling like trained chargers in the field, the boats for a while eluded him; though, at times, but by a plank's breadth; while all the time, Ahab's unearthly slogan tore every other cry but his to shreds.

But at last in his untraceable evolutions, the White Whale so crossed and recrossed, and in a thousand ways entangled the slack of the three lines now fast to him, that they foreshortened, and, of themselves, warped the devoted boats towards the planted irons in him; though now for a moment the whale drew aside a little, as if to rally for a more tremendous charge. Seizing that opportunity, Ahab first paid out more line: and then was rapidly hauling and jerking in upon it again – hoping that way to disencumber it of some snarls – when lo! – a sight more savage than the embattled teeth of sharks!

Caught and twisted – corkscrewed in the mazes of the line, loose harpoons and lances, with all their bristling barbs and points, came flashing and dripping up to the chocks in the bows of Ahab's boat. Only one thing could be done. Seizing the boat-knife, he critically reached within – through – and then, without – the rays of steel; dragged in the line beyond, passed it, inboard, to the bowsman, and then, twice sundering the rope near the chocks – dropped the intercepted faggot of steel into the sea; and was all fast again. That instant, the White Whale made a sudden rush among the remaining tangles of the other lines; by so doing, irresistibly dragged the more involved boats of Stubb and Flask towards his flukes; dashed them together like two rolling husks on a surf-beaten beach, and then, diving down into the sea, disappeared in a boiling maelstrom, in which, for a space, the odorous cedar chips of the wrecks danced round and round, like the grated nutmeg in a swiftly stirred bowl of punch.

While the two crews were yet circling in the waters, reaching out after the revolving line-tubs, oars, and other floating furniture, while aslope little Flask bobbed up and down like an empty vial, twitching his legs upwards to escape the dreaded jaws of sharks; and Stubb was lustily singing out for some one to ladle him up; and while the old man's line – now parting – admitted of his pulling into the creamy pool to rescue whom he could – in that wild simultaneousness of a thousand concreted perils, Ahab's yet unstricken boat seemed drawn up towards heaven by invisible wires – as, arrow-like, shooting perpendicularly from the sea, the White Whale dashed his broad forehead against its bottom, and sent it, turning over and over, into the air; till it fell again – gunwale downwards – and Ahab and his men struggled out from under it, like seals from a sea-side cave.

The first uprising momentum of the whale – modifying its direction as he struck the surface – involuntarily launched him along it, to a little distance from the centre of the destruction he had made; and with his back to it, he now lay for a moment slowly feeling with his flukes from side to side; and when ever a stray oar, bit of plank, the least chip or crumb of the boats touched his skin, his tail swiftly drew back, and came sideways smiting the sea. But soon, as if satisfied that his work for that time was done, he pushed his pleated forehead through the ocean, and trailing after him the intertangled lines, continued his leeward way at a traveller's methodic pace.

As before, the attentive ship having descried the whole fight, again came bearing down to the rescue, and dropping a boat, picked up the floating mariners, tubs, oars, and whatever else could be caught at, and safely landed them on her decks. Some sprained shoulders, wrists, and ankles; livid contusions; wrenched harpoons and lances; inextricable intricacies of rope; shattered oars and planks; all these were there; but no fatal or even serious ill seemed to have befallen any one. As with Fedallah the day before, so Ahab was now found grimly clinging to his boat's broken half, which afforded a comparatively easy float; nor did it so exhaust him as the previous day's mishap.

But when he was helped to the deck, all eyes were fastened upon him; as instead of standing by himself he still half-hung upon the shoulder of Starbuck, who had thus far been the foremost to assist him. His ivory leg had been snapped off, leaving but one short sharp splinter.

'Aye aye, Starbuck, 'tis sweet to lean sometimes, be the leaner who he will; and would old Ahab had leaned oftener than he has.'

'But no bones broken, sir, I hope,' said Stubb with true concern.

'Aye! and all splintered to pieces, Stubb! – d'ye see it. But even with a broken bone, old Ahab is untouched; and I account no living bone of mine one jot more me, than this dead one that's lost. Nor White Whale, nor man, nor fiend, can so much as graze old Ahab in his own proper and inaccessible being. Can any lead touch yonder floor, any mast scrape yonder roof? – Aloft there! which way?'

'Dead to leeward, sir.'

'Up helm, then; pile on the sail again, ship-keepers! down the rest of the spare boats and rig them – Mr Starbuck away, and muster the boat's crews.'

'Let me first help thee towards the bulwarks, sir.'

'Oh, oh, oh! how this splinter gores me now! Accursed fate! that the unconquerable captain in the soul should have such a craven mate!'

'Sir?'

'My body, man, not thee. Give me something for a cane – there, that shivered lance will do. Muster the men. Surely I have not seen him yet. By heaven it cannot be! – missing? – quick! call them all.'

The old man's hinted thought was true. Upon mustering the company, the Parsee was not there.

'The Parsee!' cried Stubb – 'he must have been caught in—'

'The black vomit wrench thee! – run all of ye above, alow, cabin, forecastle – find him – not gone – not gone!'

But quickly they returned to him with the tidings that the Parsee was nowhere to be found.

'Aye, sir,' said Stubb – 'caught among the tangles of your line – I thought I saw him dragging under.'

'*My* line! my line? Gone? – gone? What means that little word? – What death-knell rings in it, that old Ahab shakes as if he were the belfry. The harpoon, too! – toss over the litter there – d'ye see it? – the forged iron, men, the White Whale's – no, no, no – blistered fool! this hand did dart it! – 'tis in the fish! Aloft there! Keep him nailed – Quick! – all hands to the rigging of the boats – collect the oars – harpooneers! the irons, the irons! – hoist the royals higher – a pull on all the sheets! – helm there! steady, steady for your life! I'll ten times girdle the unmeasured globe; yea and dive straight through it, but I'll slay him yet!'

'Great God! but for one single instant show thyself,' cried Starbuck; 'never, never wilt thou capture him, old man – In Jesus' name no more of this, that's worse than devil's madness. Two days chased; twice stove to splinters; thy very leg once more snatched from under thee; thy evil shadow gone – all good angels mobbing thee with warnings: what more wouldst thou have? – Shall we keep chasing this murderous fish till he swamps the last man? Shall we be dragged by him to the bottom of the sea? Shall we be towed by him to the infernal world? Oh, oh – Impiety and blasphemy to hunt him more!'

'Starbuck, of late I've felt strangely moved to thee; ever since that hour we both saw – thou know'st what, in one another's eyes. But in this matter of the whale, be the front of thy face to me as the palm of this hand – a lipless, unfeatured blank. Ahab is for ever Ahab, man. This whole act's immutably decreed. 'Twas rehearsed by thee and me a billion years before this ocean rolled. Fool! I am the Fates' lieutenant; I act under orders. Look thou, underling! that thou obeyest mine. Stand round me, men. Ye see an old man cut down to the stump; leaning on a shivered lance; propped up on a lonely foot. 'Tis Ahab – his body's part; but Ahab's soul's a centipede, that moves upon a hundred legs. I feel strained, half stranded, as ropes that tow dismasted frigates in a gale; and I may look so. But ere I break, ye'll hear me crack; and till ye hear that, know that Ahab's hawser tows his purpose yet. Believe ye, men, in the things called omens? Then laugh aloud, and cry encore! For ere they drown, drowning things will twice rise to the surface; then rise again, to sink for evermore. So with Moby-Dick – two days he's floated – tomorrow will be the third. Aye, men, he'll rise once more – but only to spout his last! D'ye feel brave men, brave?'

'As fearless fire,' cried Stubb.

'And as mechanical,' muttered Ahab. Then as the men went forward, he muttered on: 'The things called omens! And yesterday I talked the same to Starbuck there, concerning my broken boat. Oh! how valiantly I seek to drive out of others' hearts what's clinched so fast in mine! – The Parsee – the Parsee! – gone, gone? and he was to go before: but still was to be seen again ere I could perish – How's that? – There's a riddle now might baffle all the lawyers backed by the ghosts of the whole line of judges: like a hawk's beak it pecks my brain. *I'll, I'll* solve it, though!'

When dusk descended, the whale was still in sight to leeward. So once more the sail was shortened, and everything passed nearly as on the previous night; only, the sound of hammers, and the hum of the grindstone was heard till nearly daylight, as the men toiled by lanterns in the complete and careful rigging of the spare boats and sharpening their fresh weapons for the morrow. Meantime, of the broken keel of Ahab's wrecked craft the carpenter made him another leg; while still as on the night before, slouched Ahab stood fixed within his scuttle; his hid, heliotrope glance anticipatingly gone backward on its dial; sat due eastward for the earliest sun.

CHAPTER 94

The Chase – Third Day

The morning of the third day dawned fair and fresh, and once more the solitary night-man at the fore-mast-head was relieved by crowds of the daylight look-outs, who dotted every mast and almost every spar.

'D'ye see him?' cried Ahab; but the whale was not yet in sight.

'In his infallible wake, though; but follow that wake, that's all. Helm there; steady, as thou goest, and hast been going. What a lovely day again! were it a new-made world, and made for a summer-house to the angels, and this morning the first of its throwing open to them, a fairer day could not dawn upon that world. Here's food for thought, had Ahab time to think; but Ahab never thinks; he only feels, feels, feels; *that's* tingling enough for mortal man! to think's audacity. God only has that right and privilege. Thinking is, or ought to be, a coolness and a calmness; and our poor hearts throb, and our poor brains beat too much for that. And yet, I've sometimes thought my brain was very calm – frozen calm, this old skull cracks so, like a glass in which the contents turned to ice, and shiver it. And still this hair is growing now; this moment growing, and heat must breed it; but no, it's like that sort of common grass that will grow anywhere, between the earthy clefts of Greenland ice or in Vesuvius lava. How the wild winds blow it; they whip it about me as the torn shreds of split sails lash the tossed ship they cling to. A vile wind that has no doubt blown ere this through prison corridors and cells, and wards of hospitals, and ventilated them, and now comes blowing hither as innocent as fleeces. Out upon it! – it's tainted. Were I the wind, I'd blow no more on such a wicked, miserable world. I'd crawl somewhere to a cave, and slink there. And yet, 'tis a noble and heroic thing, the wind! who ever conquered it? In every fight it has the last and bitterest blow. Run tilting at it, and you but run through it. Ha! a coward wind that strikes stark naked men, but will not stand to receive a single blow. Even Ahab is a braver thing – a nobler thing than that. Would now the wind but had a body; but all the things that most exasperate and outrage mortal man, all these things are bodiless, but only bodiless as objects, not as agents. There's a most special, a most cunning, oh, a most malicious difference! And yet, I say again, and swear it now, that there's something all glorious and gracious in the wind. These warm Trade Winds, at least, that in the clear heavens blow straight on, in strong and steadfast, vigorous mildness; and veer not from their mark, however the baser currents of the sea may turn and tack, and mightiest Mississippies of the land swift and swerve about, uncertain where to go at last. And by the eternal Poles! these same Trades that so directly blow my good ship on; these Trades, or something like them – something so unchangeable, and full as strong, blow my keeled soul along! To it! Aloft there! What d'ye see?'

'Nothing, sir.'

'Nothing! and noon at hand! The doubloon goes a-begging! See the sun! Aye, aye, it must be so. I've oversailed him. How, got the start? Aye, he's chasing *me* now; not I, *him* – that's bad; I might have known it, too. Fool! the lines – the harpoons he's towing. Aye, aye, I have run him by last night. About! about! Come down, all of ye, but the regular look-outs! Man the braces!'

Steering as she had done, the wind had been somewhat on the Pequod's quarter, so that now being pointed in the reverse direction, the braced ship sailed hard upon the breeze as she rechurned the cream in her own white wake.

'Against the wind he now steers for the open jaw,' murmured Starbuck to himself, as he coiled the new hauled main-brace upon the rail. 'God keep us, but already my bones feel damp within me, and from the inside wet my flesh. I misdoubt me that I disobey my God in obeying him!'

'Stand by to sway me up!' cried Ahab, advancing to the hempen basket. 'We should meet him soon.'

'Aye, aye, sir,' and straightway Starbuck did Ahab's bidding, and once more Ahab swung on high. A whole hour now passed;

gold-beaten out to ages. Time itself now held long breaths with keen suspense. But at last, some three points off the weather bow, Ahab descried the spout again, and instantly from the three mast-heads three shrieks went up as if the tongues of fire had voiced it.

'Forehead to forehead I meet thee, this third time, Moby-Dick! On deck there! – brace sharper up; crowd her into the wind's eye. He's too far off to lower yet, Mr Starbuck. The sails shake! Stand over that helmsman with a top-maul! So, so; he travels fast, and I must down. But let me have one more good round look aloft here at the sea; there's time for that. An old, old sight, and yet somehow so young; aye, and not changed a wink since I first saw it, a boy, from the sand-hills of Nantucket! The same! – the same! – the same to Noah as to me. There's a soft shower to leeward. Such lovely leewardings! They must lead somewhere – to something else than common land, more palmy than the palms. Leeward! the White Whale goes that way; look to windward, then; the better if the bitterer quarter. But good-bye, good-bye, old mast-head! What's this? – green? aye, tiny mosses in these warped cracks. No such green weather stains on Ahab's head! There's the difference now between man's old age and matter's. But aye, old mast, we both grow old together; sound in our hulls, though, are we not, my ship? Aye, minus a leg, that's all. By heaven this dead wood has the better of my live flesh every way. I can't compare with it; and I've known some ships made of dead trees outlast the lives of men made of the most vital stuff of vital fathers. What's that he said? he should still go before me, my pilot; and yet to be seen again? But where? Will I have eyes at the bottom of the sea, supposing I descend those endless stairs? and all night I've been sailing from him, wherever he did sink to. Aye, aye, like many more thou told'st direful truth as touching thyself, O Parsee; but, Ahab, there thy shot fell short. Good-bye, mast-head – keep a good eye upon the whale, the while I'm gone. We'll talk tomorrow, nay, tonight, when the White Whale lies down there, tied by head and tail.'

He gave the word; and still gazing round him, was steadily lowered through the cloven blue air to the deck.

In due time the boats were lowered; but as standing in his

shallop's stern, Ahab just hovered upon the point of the descent, he waved to the mate, – who held one of the tackle-ropes on deck – and bade him pause.

'Starbuck!'

'Sir?'

'For the third time my soul's ship starts upon this voyage, Starbuck.'

'Aye, sir, thou wilt have it so.'

'Some ships sail from their ports, and ever afterwards are missing, Starbuck!'

'Truth, sir: saddest truth.'

'Some men die at ebb tide; some at low water; some at the full of the flood – and I feel now like a billow that's all one crested comb, Starbuck. I am old – shake hands with me, man.'

Their hands met; their eyes fastened; Starbuck's tears the glue.

'Oh, my captain, my captain! – noble heart – go not – go not! – see, it's a brave man that weeps; how great the agony of the persuasion then!'

'Lower away!' – cried Ahab, tossing the mate's arm from him. 'Stand by the crew!'

In an instant the boat was pulling round close under the stern.

'The sharks! the sharks!' cried a voice from the low cabin window there; 'O master, my master, come back!'

But Ahab heard nothing; for his own voice was high-lifted then; and the boat leaped on. Yet the voice spake true; for scarce had he pushed from the ship, when numbers of sharks, seemingly rising from out the dark waters beneath the hull, maliciously snapped at the blades of the oars, every time they dipped in the water; and in this way accompanied the boat with their bites. It is a thing not uncommonly happening to the whale-boats in those swarming seas; the sharks at times apparently following them in the same prescient way that vultures hover over the banners of marching regiments in the east. But these were the first sharks that had been observed by the Pequod since the White Whale had been first descried; and whether it was that Ahab's crew were all such tiger-yellow barbarians, and therefore their flesh more musky to the senses of the sharks – a matter sometimes well known to affect them – however it was, they seemed to follow that one boat without molesting the others.

'Heart of wrought steel!' murmured Starbuck gazing over the side, and following with his eyes the receding boat – 'can'st thou yet ring boldly to that sight? – lowering thy keel among ravening sharks, and followed by them, open-mouthed to the chase; and this the critical third day? – For when three days flow together in one continuous intense pursuit, be sure the first is the morning, the second the noon, and the third the evening and the end of that thing – be that end what it may. Oh! my God! what is this that shoots through me, and leaves me so deadly calm, yet expectant – fixed at the top of a shudder! Future things swim before me, as in empty outlines and skeletons; all the past is somehow grown dim. Mary, girl! thou fadest in pale glories behind me; boy! I seem to see but thy eyes grown wondrous blue. Strangest problems of life seem clearing; but clouds sweep between – Is my journey's end coming? My legs feel faint; like his who has footed it all day. Feel thy heart – beats it yet? – Stir thyself, Starbuck! – stave it off – move, move! speak aloud! Mast-head there! See ye my boy's hand on the hill? – Crazed – aloft there! – keep thy keenest eye upon the boats: mark well the whale! – Ho! again! – drive off that hawk! see! he pecks – he tears the vane' – pointing to the red flag flying at the main-truck – 'Ha! he soars away with it! – Where's the old man now? see'st thou that sight, oh Ahab! – shudder, shudder!'

The boats had not gone very far, when by a signal from the mast-heads – a downward pointed arm – Ahab knew that the whale had sounded; but intending to be near him at the next rising, he held on his way a little sideways from the vessel; the becharmed crew maintaining the profoundest silence, as the head-beat waves hammered and hammered against the opposing bow.

'Drive, drive in your nails, oh ye waves! to their uttermost heads drive them in! ye but strike a thing without a lid; and no coffin and no hearse can be mine: and hemp only can kill me! Ha! ha!'

Suddenly the waters around them slowly swelled in broad circles; then quickly upheaved, as if sideways sliding from a submerged berg of ice, swiftly rising to the surface. A low rumbling sound was heard; a subterraneous hum; and then all held their breaths; as bedraggled with trailing ropes, and harpoons, and lances, a vast form shot lengthwise, but obliquely from the sea. Shrouded in a thin drooping veil of mist, it hovered for a moment in the rainbowed air; and then fell swamping back into the deep.

Crushed thirty feet upwards, the waters flashed for an instant like heaps of fountains, then brokenly sank in a shower of flakes, leaving the circling surface creamed like new milk round the marble trunk of the whale.

'Give way!' cried Ahab to the oarsmen, and the boats darted forward to the attack; but maddened by yesterday's fresh irons that corroded in him, Moby-Dick seemed combinedly possessed by all the angels that fell from heaven. The wide tiers of welded tendons overspreading his broad white forehead looked knitted together; as head on, he came churning his tail among the boats; and once more flailed them apart; spilling out the irons and lances from the two mates' boats, and dashing in one side of the upper part of their bows, but leaving Ahab's almost without a scar.

While Daggoo and Queequeg were stopping the strained planks; and as the whale swimming out from them turned, and showed one entire flank as he shot by them again; at that moment a quick cry went up. Lashed round and round to the fish's back; pinioned in the turns upon turns in which, during the past night, the whale had reeled the involutions of the lines around him, the half torn body of the Parsee was seen; his sable raiment frayed to shreds; his distended eyes turned full upon old Ahab.

The harpoon dropped from his hand.

'Befooled, befooled!' – drawing in a long lean breath – 'Aye, Parsee! I see thee again. Aye, and thou goest before; and this, this then is the hearse that thou didst promise. But I hold thee to the last letter of thy word. Where is the second hearse? Away, mates, to the ship! those boats are useless now; repair them if ye can in time, and return to me; if not, Ahab is enough to die – Down, men! the first thing that but offers to jump from this boat I stand in, that thing I harpoon. Ye are not other men, but my arms and my legs; and so obey me. Where's the whale? gone down again?'

But he looked too nigh the boat; for as if bent upon escaping with the corpse he bore, and as if the particular place of the last encounter had been but a stage in his leeward voyage, Moby-Dick was now again steadily swimming forward; and had almost passed the ship – which thus far had been sailing in the contrary direction to him, though for the present her headway had been stopped. He seemed swimming with his utmost velocity, and now only intent upon pursuing his own straight path in the sea.

'Oh! Ahab,' cried Starbuck, 'not too late is it, even now, the third day, to desist. See! Moby-Dick seeks thee not. It is thou, thou, that madly seekest him!'

Setting sail to the rising wind, the lonely boat was swiftly impelled to leeward, by both oars and canvas. And at last when Ahab was sliding by the vessel, so near as plainly to distinguish Starbuck's face as he leaned over the rail, he hailed him to turn the vessel about, and follow him, not too swiftly, at a judicious inter-val. Glancing upwards, he saw Tashtego, Queequeg, and Daggoo, eagerly mounting to the three mast-heads; while the oarsmen were rocking in the two staved boats which had but just been hoisted to the side, and were busily at work in repairing them. One after the other, through the portholes, as he sped, he also caught flying glimpses of Stubb and Flask, busying themselves on deck among bundles of new irons and lances. As he saw all this; as he heard the hammers in the broken boats; far other hammers seemed driving a nail into his heart. But he rallied. And now marking that the vane or flag was gone from the main-mast-head, he shouted to Tashtego, who had just gained that perch, to descend again for another flag, and a hammer and nails, and so nail it to the mast.

Whether fagged by the three days' running chase, and the resist-ance to his swimming in the knotted hamper he bore; or whether it was some latent deceitfulness and malice in him: whichever was true, the White Whale's way now began to abate, as it seemed, from the boat so rapidly nearing him once more; though indeed the whale's last start had not been so long a one as before. And still as Ahab glided over the waves the unpitying sharks accompanied him; and so pertinaciously stuck to the boat; and so continually bit at the plying oars, that the blades became jagged and crunched, and left small splinters in the sea, at almost every dip.

'Heed them not! those teeth but give new rowlocks to your oars. Pull on! 'tis the better rest, the shark's jaw than the yielding water.'

'But at every bite, sir, the thin blades grow smaller and smaller!'

'They will last long enough! pull on! – But who can tell' – he muttered – 'whether these sharks swim to feast on the whale or on Ahab? – But pull on! Aye, all alive, now – we near him. The helm! take the helm; let me pass' – and so saying, two of the oarsmen helped him forward to the bows of the still flying boat.

At length as the craft was cast to one side, and ran ranging along with the White Whale's flank, he seemed strangely oblivious of its advance – as the whale sometimes will – and Ahab was fairly within the smoky mountain mist, which, thrown off from the whale's spout, curled round his great, Monadnock hump; he was even thus close to him; when, with body arched back, and both arms lengthwise high-lifted to the poise, he darted his fierce iron, and his far fiercer curse into the hated whale. As both steel and curse sank to the socket, as if sucked into a morass, Moby-Dick sideways writhed; spasmodically rolled his nigh flank against the bow, and, without staving a hole in it, so suddenly canted the boat over, that had it not been for the elevated part of the gunwale to which he then clung, Ahab would once more have been tossed into the sea. As it was, three of the oarsmen – who foreknew not the precise instant of the dart, and were therefore unprepared for its effects – these were flung out; but so fell, that in an instant two of them clutched the gunwale again, and rising to its level on a combing wave, hurled themselves bodily inboard again; the third man helplessly dropping astern, but still afloat and swimming.

Almost simultaneously, with a mighty volition of ungraduated, instantaneous swiftness, the White Whale darted through the weltering sea. But when Ahab cried out to the steersman to take new turns with the line, and hold it so; and commanded the crew to turn round on their seats, and tow the boat up to the mark; the moment the treacherous line felt that doubt strain and tug, it snapped in the empty air!

'What breaks in me? Some sinew cracks! – 'tis whole again; oars! Oars! Burst in upon him!'

Hearing the tremendous rush of the sea-crashing boat, the whale wheeled round to present his blank forehead at bay; but in that evolution, catching sight of the nearing black hull of the ship; seemingly seeing in it the source of all his persecutions; bethinking it – it may be – a larger and nobler foe; of a sudden, he bore down upon its advancing prow, smiting his jaws amid fiery showers of foam.

Ahab staggered; his hand smote his forehead. 'I grow blind; hands! stretch out before me that I may yet grope my way. Is't night?'

'The whale! The ship!' cried the cringing oarsmen.

'Oars! oars! Slope downwards to thy depths, O sea, that ere it be for ever too late, Ahab may slide this last, last time upon his mark! I see: the ship! the ship! Dash on, my men! Will ye not save my ship?'

But as the oarsmen violently forced their boat through the sledge-hammering seas, the before whale-smitten bow-ends of two planks burst through, and in an instant almost, the temporarily disabled boat lay nearly level with the waves; its half-wading, splashing crew, trying hard to stop the gap and bale out the pouring water.

Meantime, for that one beholding instant, Tashtego's masthead hammer remained suspended in his hand; and the red flag, half-wrapping him as with a plaid, then streamed itself straight out from him, as his own forward-flowing heart; while Starbuck and Stubb, standing upon the bowsprit beneath, caught sight of the down-coming monster just as soon as he.

'The whale, the whale! Up helm, up helm! Oh, all ye sweet powers of air, now hug me close! Let not Starbuck die, if die he must, in a woman's fainting fit. Up helm, I say – ye fools, the jaw! the jaw! Is this the end of all my bursting prayers? all my life-long fidelities? Oh, Ahab, Ahab, lo, thy work. Steady! helmsman, steady. Nay, nay! Up helm again! He turns to meet us! Oh, his unappeasable brow drives on towards one, whose duty tells him he cannot depart. My God, stand by me now!'

'Stand not by me, but stand under me, whoever you are that will now help Stubb; for Stubb, too, sticks here. I grin at thee, thou grinning whale! Who ever helped Stubb, or kept Stubb awake, but Stubb's own unwinking eye? And now poor Stubb goes to bed upon a mattress that is all too soft; would it were stuffed with brushwood! I grin at thee, thou grinning whale! Look ye, sun, moon, and stars! I call ye assassins of as good a fellow as ever spouted up his ghost. For all that, I would yet ring glasses with ye, would ye but hand the cup! Oh, oh! oh, oh! thou grinning whale, but there'll be plenty of gulping soon! Why fly ye not, O Ahab! For me, off shoes and jacket to it; let Stubb die in his drawers! A most mouldy and over salted death, though; cherries! cherries! cherries! Oh, Flask, for one red cherry ere we die!'

'Cherries? I only wish that we were where they grow. Oh, Stubb, I hope my poor mother's drawn my part-pay ere this; if not, few coppers will now come to her, for the voyage is up.'

From the ship's bows, nearly all the seamen now hung inactive; hammers, bits of plank, lances, and harpoons, mechanically retained in their hands, just as they had darted from their various employments; all their enchanted eyes intent upon the whale, which from side to side strangely vibrating his predestinating head, sent a broad band of overspreading semicircular foam before him as he rushed. Retribution, swift vengeance, eternal malice were in his whole aspect, and spite of all that mortal man could do, the solid white buttress of his forehead smote the ship's starboard bow, till men and timbers reeled. Some fell flat upon their faces. Like dislodged trucks, the heads of the harpooneers aloft shook on their bull-like necks. Through the breach, they heard the waters pour, as mountain torrents down a flume.

'The ship! The hearse! – the second hearse!' cried Ahab from the boat; 'its wood could only be American!'

Diving beneath the settling ship, the whale ran quivering along its keel; but turning under water, swiftly shot to the surface again – far off the other bow, but within a few yards of Ahab's boat, where, for a time, he lay quiescent.

'I turn my body from the sun. What ho, Tashtego! let me hear thy hammer. Oh! ye three unsurrendered spires of mine; thou uncracked keel; and only god-bullied hull; thou firm deck, and haughty helm, and Pole-pointed prow – death-glorious ship! must ye then perish, and without me? Am I cut off from the last fond pride of meanest shipwrecked captains? Oh, lonely death on lonely life! Oh, now I feel my topmost greatness lies in my topmost grief. Ho, ho! from all your furthest bounds, pour ye now in, ye bold billows of my whole foregone life, and top this one piled comber of my death! Towards thee I roll, thou all-destroying but unconquering whale; to the last I grapple with thee; from hell's heart I stab at thee; for hate's sake I spit my last breath at thee. Sink all coffins and all hearses to one common pool! and since neither can be mine, let me then tow to pieces, while still chasing thee, though tied to thee, thou damned whale! *Thus*, I give up the spear!'

The harpoon was darted; the stricken whale flew forward; with igniting velocity the line ran through the groove – ran foul. Ahab stooped to clear it; he did clear it; but the flying turn caught him round the neck, and voicelessly as Turkish mutes bowstring their victim, he was shot out of the boat, ere the crew knew he was gone. Next instant, the heavy eye-splice in the rope's final end flew out of the stark-empty tub, knocked down an oarsman, and smiting the sea, disappeared in its depths.

For an instant, the tranced boat's crew stood still; then turned, 'The ship? Great God, where is the ship?' Soon they through dim, bewildering mediums saw her sidelong fading phantom, as in the gaseous Fata Morgana; only the uppermost masts out of water; while fixed by infatuation, or fidelity, or fate, to their once lofty perches, the pagan harpooneers still maintained their sinking lookouts on the sea. And now, concentric circles seized the lone boat itself, and all its crew, and each floating oar, and every lance-pole, and spinning, animate and inanimate, all round and round in one vortex, carried the smallest chip of the Pequod out of sight.

But as the last whelmings intermixingly poured themselves over the sunken head of the Indian at the main-mast, leaving a few inches of the erect spar yet visible, together with long streaming yards of the flag, which calmly undulated, with ironical coincidings, over the destroying billows they almost touched – at that instant, a red arm and a hammer hovered backwardly uplifted in the open air, in the act of nailing the flag faster and yet faster to the subsiding spar. A sky-hawk that tauntingly had followed the main-truck downwards from its natural home among the stars, pecking at the flag, and incommoding Tashtego there; this bird now chanced to intercept its broad fluttering wing between the hammer and the wood; and simultaneously feeling that ethereal thrill, the submerged savage beneath, in his death-gasp, kept his hammer frozen there; and so the bird of heaven, with archangelic shrieks, and his imperial beak thrust upwards, and his whole captive form folded in the flag of Ahab, went down with his ship, which, like Satan, would not sink to hell till she had dragged a living part of heaven along with her, and helmeted herself with it.

Now small fowls flew screaming over the yet yawning gulf; a sullen white surf beat against its steep sides; then all collapsed, and the great shroud of the sea rolled on as it rolled five thousand years ago.

Epilogue

'AND I ONLY AM ESCAPED ALONE TO TELL THEE.'

Job.

THE DRAMA'S DONE. *Why then here does anyone step forth?*
– Because one did survive the wreck.

It so chanced, that after the Parsee's disappearance, I was he whom the Fates ordained to take the place of Ahab's bowsman, when that bowsman assumed the vacant post; the same, who, when on the last day the three men were tossed from out the rocking boat, was dropped astern. So, floating on the margin of the ensuing scene, and in full sight of it, when the half-spent suction of the sunk ship reached me, I was then, but slowly, drawn towards the closing vortex. When I reached it, it had subsided to a creamy pool. Round and round, then, and ever contracting towards the button-like black bubble at the axis of that slowly wheeling circle, like another Ixion I did revolve. Till, gaining that vital centre, the black bubble upward burst; and now, liberated by reason of its cunning spring, and, owing to its great buoyancy, rising with great force, the coffin life-buoy shot lengthwise from the sea, fell over, and floated by my side. Buoyed up by that coffin, for almost one whole day and night, I floated on a soft and dirge-like main. The unharming sharks, they glided by as if with padlocks on their mouths; the savage sea-hawks sailed with sheathed beaks. On the second day, a sail drew near, nearer, and picked me up at last. It was the devious-cruising Rachel, that in her retracing search after her missing children, only found another orphan.

FINIS

Leabharlanna Fhine Gall

About this Compact Edition

Moby-Dick was first published in 1851. This abridged edition retains the main narrative line which follows the obsessively driven Captain Ahab's attempts to hunt down and kill the White Whale, Moby-Dick. The cast of supporting characters, from the mate Starbuck to the strikingly individualized native harpooneer, Queequeg, feature strongly in this ill-fated voyage, but lengthy descriptions of whaling history and of whales, some philosophical observations, a number of other digressions and reflections are cut in the interest of the ongoing graphic narrative. Melville's individual style – this edition uses only his language – poetic, symbolic, factual – is there in its vivid particularity. It is full of compassion, humanity, sometimes spiritual overtones and wisdom about the nature of human life.